A CAUTIOUS MAN

Miriam A. Walker

ORIGINAL WRITING

ISBNs
Parent: 978-1-908817-87-7
ePub: 978-1-909007-02-4
Mobi: 978-1-909007-03-1

A CIP catalogue for this book is available from the National Library.

Published by Original Writing Ltd., Dublin, 2012.

Printed by Clondalkin Group, Glasnevin, Dublin 11

For Colin

CHAPTER 1

In the late afternoon one gloomy Thursday, Moss Mortimer felt an aura of victory in the air around him as he made his way through the throng that moved along Westmoreland Street, the aching grind of rush hour traffic accompanying the striding figures, as if urging them on towards a vital deadline. The idea of having to lay bare his plans before his sister Louise and his mother Clare impinged on his elation and so he dismissed it to the back of his thoughts for later attention then made a skilful break from the crowds, his expression softening as he opened the familiar door to the main entrance lobby of Bewley's Café where he felt instantly becalmed. This moment of arrival always caused him to pause and take stock of the world he had just accessed, with intention. Here he could shake off the intensity of city life and go through an interlude so agreeable it resulted in self-renewal, energising him for his return to the great outside.

A slight shadow accompanied him as he made his entrance, unsettling echoes of a news item he heard that morning on his bedside clock radio, the tone of the reader distinctly urgent, almost scolding. Unpleasant as the abounding rumours had been for several months, at least the finality of the announcement would dispel those speculations – the legendary café was to be closed down although no date had been set for the ominous day. He made himself a vow to savour every visit to the condemned edifice of soothing ambience and store the memories away in his heart then took his place in the queue for coffee, opposite the retail and bakery section. Instead of his usual frugal muffin, he carefully selected a chocolate éclair and a blueberry muffin from the softly lit display counter and placed the plates on a dark brown wooden tray. He felt justifiably reckless for this was the evening of a dawning new life although he needed time to consider how best to break such news to Clare and Louise later on and to brace himself for their reactions and the umbrage Louise would undoubtedly take. After paying for his treats at the till, he made his way through the labyrinthine spacious rooms with their vaulted ceilings and chandeliers and banquettes that flanked the walls, the centre floor space crowded with tables and chairs – most of them occupied - and arrived in the far side, the Fleet Street room, his eyes gleaming with pleasure as they scanned the vast stained-glass mullioned windows that dominated the wall. Their tiny coloured panes cast a pleasing mellow glow onto the bentwood chairs, enriching the deep red fabric of the banquettes and enhancing the gleam of marble topped tables many of which were laden with the cosy accessories of late afternoon teatime. It soothed him – the gentle vibration of conversations, the unobtrusive bustle, the sight of people reading newspapers or absorbed in a book, or in thought, or going meditatively blank from life's concerns and myriad stresses. On his previous visit, on Monday, he had recognized a department manager from a rival bank sitting rigidly on the edge of the sofa seat below the windows, his elbows perched on the table as he stirred his coffee noisily. He had seemed out of place, not because of his grey pinstriped suit and pale, dated tie, but by the display of hard indignation in his eyes as they projected a round, accusing stare, as if perceiving an incompetent world and his important, even superior, place in it - a futile affectation in such relaxing surroundings, Moss knew, and not without a shard of pity.

Settling himself contentedly in his favourite banquette, he felt comforted and reassured by its depth, sighing with relief at his good fortune in finding the seat unoccupied. He then set about enjoying his coffee ritual and opened a sachet of brown sugar, poured it in a circle over the creamy froth, watched it dissolve slowly before stirring it then took his first exquisite sip followed by a bite of his muffin. Fortified, he covertly surveyed the occupants of the other tables in the great room to see if he recognised any of them. The woman with the fox hair was there, in the banquette to the left of the fireplace where a reddened coal fire gave out a generous heat on that chilly early April day. She glanced up and gave him a brief, salutary smile. He smiled back, raising his coffee cup slightly in greeting and watched her return to her reading. This was the extent of their terms of familiarity so far, by silent mutual agreement. The strands of her lustrous red hair touched the collar of the short black jacket she wore, the lapel adorned with a silver brooch, a slender multicoloured silk scarf at her throat contrasting with a snowy blouse. He liked to watch her, surreptitiously, for she always appeared elegant, poised. Her eyes were usually focussed, if not transfixed, on a paperback book or a small notebook and she slowly sipped her coffee, wrapping the short, slightly chubby fingers – absent of rings – of her left hand around the cup each time as if drawing in its energy. She rarely looked up whenever a customer arrived in search of a seat but, like himself, seemed contented with her own company. On a few occasions over the years, they were obliged to share a table, even a banquette where they would sit side by side, each skilfully constructing an invisible barrier in the narrow space between them to avoid any physical contact that might be misunderstood, an action also perpetrated to defend private space, a territorial exercise. Their conversation, what little of it there was, was polite, lightly restrained, her speech betraying a studied attention to diction as though camouflaging an accent that might not inspire approval. They had limited their sporadic discussions to the mundane, or seemingly mundane, such as the length of the queue for the time of day, or a casual reference to the books they were reading, or planning to read, skimming the surface of life, of the personal, hiding the other sides, wearing the masks. The exchange of names had not taken place, although he privately named her Vixen and, due to that unspoken rule, was not intended, although the remarkable news of the café's impending closure threatened to expose such self-inflicted rules as overprotective. Nevertheless, their silent code of caution clinging onto anonymity for as long as possible protected them from crossing the line into familiarity in such a public yet hallowed place. To Moss, with his penchant for privacy, the café was, paradoxically, a space where he could retreat from the world. He regarded it as a refuge from smug conservatives, those of the blinkered minds who claimed their world to be the real one but who were terrified of suspending it for a second in case their lives might spiral out of control. Their prized respectability depended on the fervent engagement in the kind of busyness that discouraged self-reflection, recoiling at any evidence of independent thought. Being caught out relaxing in the café and considering a philosophical imperative would be repulsive, almost perilous and must be strictly avoided in case a change of mind might threaten their perceptions and cause them the distress of knee-jerk reactions.

Vixen, he knew, was averse to sitting on a bentwood chair. He had noticed her habit of moving over to a banquette the moment it was vacated, sometimes even before the occupants had fully disembarked. But she did it with dignity for both parties and suitable expressions of gratitude then claimed her place, unaffected by the detritus on the table. This she would shove neatly to one side and reassemble herself. He knew that she would even prefer to share a banquette, as she had done with him on those rare occasions, and kept a polite low profile in the presence of those wrapped up carefully in their own aura. He once noticed a couple of tourists ask if they could sit at her table, his sharp ears tuned in to the brief discourse. Vixen had smiled in agreeable acquiescence but mercifully did not engage in the conventional, *ville provencialle* 'Where-are-you-from?' ritual at the sound of a different accent but maintained an admirable focus on her book.

Moss watched her pick up a pen and jot something down in her tiny notebook, a word or two, a reminder of some sort, or it could merely be a shopping list. With a gentle shrug, he abandoned such observations and speculations and enjoyed his coffee and a read of a rumpled Irish Times that someone had abandoned on the table adjacent to his, glancing up occasionally to admire his surroundings. Vixen got up to leave, suddenly and with purpose, as was her habit. He felt vaguely disappointed, the congenial atmosphere dimming slightly after she had gone.

Absences seemed to be the theme of this particular Thursday. He frowned at the idea of the café being missing from his life. According to the news bulletin, the other café - Bewley's of Grafton Street - was also in danger of closure. He alternated his visits between the two places depending on his humour, or whom he was meeting although he was filled with affection for Westmoreland Street. For over twenty years he had enjoyed these ritualistic visits to the café, treasuring the fact that his institutionalised colleagues rarely ventured into such an atmospheric and cosmopolitan place, his expression brightening at the fact that he was about to experience their absence forever. That morning he had astonished them by handing in his resignation letter after twenty-three years with the bank – an item for the grapevine that was pounced on with blatant glee: '*You*, Moss! *You* of *all* people!' – for he had ignored management's previous offers to oust the mature, permanently established workers when the banking landscape began to change. In fact he had become resigned to such forces of change chipping away at standards, at people's sense of themselves, intrigued by how easily some of his colleagues had succumbed to an insidious severity that had infiltrated the organisation, compounded by a malaise that seemed to have evolved long before the economic boom that began around the mid-nineties. And just when it seemed that technical resources had won out over human ones, they too contracted viruses that put them out of action temporarily. Rescued by growing cynicism, and by the excitement and optimism he felt at the start of the new millennium, his decision was not a sudden one, he knew: it had begun as a gradual desire, even an ache, for change in his life, in his existence, manifesting as a strange craving for uncertainty after so many years of orderly routine. Yet he enjoyed the day to day work in the arrears department where he had achieved the rank of supervisor and remained there for over ten years, not wishing to climb any further up the unsteady rungs of the promotion ladder. Increasingly he had felt the need to break away from the rules, many of them self-imposed, to uproot the safety net of secure employment and find out if he was capable of surviving the disruption. He also hoped to discover a more satisfying world or perhaps a less dull world where goodwill was not confined to Christmas; a world populated with people that were not ridden with hidden agendas, people who thought for themselves – who were, in fact, themselves.

He took a sip of coffee, looked up and noticed Professor Tobias Ferguson in his all-season black wool overcoat make his painful way to a table beneath the window on the other side of the room, miraculously landing his cup and saucer without spilling a drop then settled himself in a dignified posture in his chair, defying the onset of arthritis that plagued his bones. With his usual discreet, magician-like ease, Tobias extracted from the depths of his coat pockets a number of books which he laid out neatly, like specimens, upon the table, followed by a bar of chocolate which he broke into squares and assembled them in neat pile on a paper napkin then turned the foil wrapper into a tiny ball with his pale, surprisingly slender fingers. Moss noticed the way he looked at his books, handling them with great care, rarely reading them for any length of time, almost as if by opening them fully, some overwhelming energy might be unleashed. His mane of longish grey hair, grey-white brows and intelligent, intuitive eyes imbued Moss with an obscure sense of reassurance, as if in the presence of a saint or a scholar recently promoted to sainthood.

Returning his attention to his newspaper, he quickly lost his concentration as he began to reflect on the decision he had made the previous summer, when, in the quiet of his room in the family home in Clontarf, he had secretly plotted the formula for his future onto sheets of white paper with a calculator at his side. He had winced at the diminishing figures, his face flushed with excitement at the prospect of such liberation although he knew that it was not unusual to leave a job in such a favourable economic climate, in fact it had almost become the norm what with people upgrading their skills, migrating to a new employer, the younger men and women bravely adventuring off for a year out, far away from the island. With an approving nod at the set of figures on his final sheet of paper, he had decided that he, too, would take his year off. And now, glancing around the café, he knew that the time had arrived, that he was at last ready to relinquish the money and routine that his job had given him. Against all of the sensible ideology of security, he was poised to plunge cautiously into the exhilarating pool of risk.

CHAPTER 2

Moss checked the time on the screen of his mobile phone - it was almost six o'clock. The café was now packed, the atmosphere even more companionable with the changing light of evening. He doodled leisurely on his newspaper opened at the Letters page, absently drawing tiny Celtic circles with a blue ball point pen, then looping them together. At that precise moment, another ritual was taking place. His sister Louise was in the self-service restaurant of a department store on Grafton Street, accompanied by her friend Susan King. As usual she inspected the food on display with her customary suspicion, mentally prodding it to make sure it was cooked through, unconvinced by the bubbling evidence, the aromatic steam and ended up choosing vegetable soup and salad sandwiches. She then looked longingly at the array of desserts and slices of cake but opted for biscuits sealed from outside influences by plastic wrapping. Susan, in front of her in the small but sedate queue, selected her meal decisively, found a suitable table for them, then ate heartily, making her way through a generous portion of lasagne with chips and garnished with salad. Afterwards she consumed a dessert of tiramisu and sat back, replenished, sipping luxuriously on her cup of strong black coffee, her brown eyes emanating satisfaction. The rest of the evening would follow an established format - they would go for a browse of the department stores and boutiques in Grafton Street, Louise armed with her usual thrift, rarely buying anything, her credit card pristine in its tiny enclosure within her well concealed wallet. As if to compensate, Susan would relish quietly but purposefully in various purchases with her own, easily accessed card. They would part around eight o'clock, Susan walking slowly in the direction of St. Stephen's Green, her shopping bags clasped against her briefcase, while Louise would head off at a brisk pace in the opposite direction, to College Green then along Westmoreland Street and on across

O'Connell Bridge towards the north side of the city, the Liffey flowing murkily underneath. She would make her way to her bus stop in Lower Abbey Street, satisfied yet again with her evening out for it was one that she fervently looked forward to, even depended on, her social life being a sparsely populated and uneventful one. Of course she was aware of the element of convenience: that the meal out coincided with Susan's rendezvous with her married lover later on that evening, the mystery man who arrived in Dublin on the last Thursday of each month, although Louise knew that his name was John. Yet such a fixed pattern indicated the stability, such as it was, of the clandestine affair. And the arrangement suited Louise who had quite literally bumped into Susan on Grafton Street one Thursday evening a couple of years ago on her way home from work, Susan explaining that she had 'time to kill' and was meeting someone later on, suggesting that Louise join her for a bite to eat. Louise had agreed instantly and followed her friend gratefully, thrilled at having been rescued from another evening wandering alone around the brightly lit stores, as she had done for years when she would give herself a break from her usual routine of dashing home straight after work. On such solitary Thursday evenings, when the city was alive with late night shoppers, she had often yearned to go into a café, but dared not enter one alone, not even the hospitable Bewley's, her eyes squinting resentfully at the sight of so many confident young women, especially women her own age, seated at window tables in the burgeoning cafes, or at a continental-style pavement table under an umbrella or canvas canopy in summertime, sipping wine or a cappuccino and talking into their mobile phones. After her fill of the shops, Louise would drift off home, to the substantial home-cooked dinner which her mother would leave in the oven for her, the table neatly set.

Louise had known Susan since their secondary schooldays, their friendship sealed when she was invited out to the King's house in Sutton, a rambling detached bungalow with a long front garden that faced the sea. She had eventually become a willing recruit to help prepare sandwiches for the summer tea parties that Denise King gave so graciously, usually in the secluded back garden or the conservatory which was filled with an assortment of tropical plants and wicker furniture. Susan's brothers Mark and Niall were dressed up mockingly as waiters, fetching and carrying, balancing trays, affecting outstanding good manners, Louise blushing madly at their innocent flirting. Once released from school, everything changed, Louise squirming at the contrast in their Leaving Certificate results – there was no question that she would join Susan in UCD, no united scramble for the number 10 bus in O'Connell Street. Louise obediently gravitated to the local vocational college to complete a computer course, resigned to her destiny as an office worker, her brother Moss already graduated from UCD and established in one of the large banking institutions. But to her amazement, Susan dropped out of college in her second year, abandoning her arts degree for work in London where she went to live with Mark and Niall who had already settled there and had offered her their spare room in Notting Hill. Subsequent reports in the form of an unbroken exchange of Christmas cards proved this to be a successful move for her, corroborated by the occasional chance meeting with Denise King on the bus home from town, although her reports were somewhat vague: 'Ah, she's grand,' Denise would say with a gleaming smile. 'Not a bother.'

Then, almost fifteen years later, Louise was again astonished to get a telephone call from Susan inviting her out to the family home. Yes indeed, she had returned to live in Dublin permanently, what with the tiger economy and plenty of work opportunities although Dad wanted her to take over the bookshop, paving the way for his looming retirement era.   Louise had felt comfortable, even excited as she drove along the Coast Road to the familiar house in Sutton, retrieving idyllic images from the tea party days, her usual reticence in abeyance as the destination was such a familiar one. The reunion had gone well; Susan had shown her around the spacious extension annexed to the main house where she was now living. It had been built for her grandfather Charlie who had lived out his retirement years there in total contentment, Susan had said, until he was taken by cancer. 'Did he die here?' Louise had asked warily. 'Oh, no. In the hospice. But peacefully, ever so peacefully.' Afterwards, Susan led her to the conservatory where an appetising afternoon tea had been laid out for them, explaining that her mother was visiting a friend in the Mater Hospital and her father Liam was off playing golf – 'Dad is addicted to it!' Over their tea, they had exchanged compliments about each other's appearance and how little each had changed although at one point Louise exclaimed: 'You sound so *posh*!' followed by a giggle as she tried to mask the scorn in her voice, the tone implying that Susan's accent was fake or contrived. During subsequent meetings Louise also succeeded in preventing any talk of London, her sudden light chuckles interrupting Susan whenever she said 'When I was in London...' A change of subject was effected, Susan's eyes giving a succession of rapid blinks at the implication that such references to her life there were mere indulgences, irrelevant reminiscences, as if they had to be cancelled out: 'You're not in London *now*, you know!' But Susan, armed with the mastery of polite reserve sculpted from her years away, adapted and kept her London experience and other adventures to herself in order to fit back in to such company. Louise was after all a familiar face; most of their school friends had either emigrated and those who had remained in Ireland seemed inaccessible, leading settled, even entrenched lives populated with spouses, children, colleagues, in-laws. And, as time went on, she appreciated certain qualities in Louise - she was not prone to giddy references to male conquests or hangovers and, more recently, could be trusted with the knowledge of her affair with John, resulting in her feeling consoled by her lack of interest, her sober detachment in such matters. Louise in turn found Susan a sympathetic ear for her earnest house hunt, a hunt that had been put on hold for years when prices in the late nineties stunned her into inactivity, for they had increased three-fold or more. Louise would recount her dismay at not having made her purchase sooner, describing the many houses she had almost bought. A year later, when they met in their usual Thursday venue, Susan had examined a number of estate agents' brochures that Louise had brought along to show her, illustrated with photographs of houses she planned to view at the weekend, her cheeks flushed with longing. 'Actually, I'm off on Saturday – I could go along with you, if you like,' Susan had suggested as she handed them back. 'Just for moral support'.

This was such a success that it became another new arrangement, although one that was subject to spontaneity, short notice, usually by a phone call on Saturday mornings every few weeks or so. Louise would set off to Sutton to collect Susan around two o'clock, and they would spend the afternoon wandering around the houses on Louise's list, discussing them in the car en route to Susan's gate where Louise would drop her off. Her yearning to be invited in for tea was long abandoned for Susan always seemed to have something on on Saturday evenings, her lack of elaboration giving the impression of an active, even vibrant social life.

Just as Susan took another sip of her coffee, two women claimed the table next to them, their noisy arrival interrupting her dreamy anticipation of her meeting later on. Still sated by her meal, she felt her usual surge of benevolence as she watched Louise nibbling daintily at one of her biscuits then taking a delicate sip from her tea cup.

'So,' she said languidly, 'I'm free on Saturday if you're planning to look at anything.'

'Oh yes, please!' responded Louise, instantly animated. 'There are a couple of houses in Drumcondra I'd like to look at. And one in Glasnevin. Yes, expensive I know, but definitely worth a look.'

'Great. Call over at the usual time then.' Susan had never openly questioned the fact that such viewings had not yet yielded a result, not even an offer despite her gentle encouragement to overlook petty flaws in what seemed an ideal property, or a property in an ideal location, but she stoically continued her support for she found such afternoons entertaining, sharing with Louise the thrill of seeing the inside of other people's houses.

She glanced at her wristwatch, rummaged in her briefcase and took out a tiny makeup bag, applied a fresh coat of lipstick, then removed the bobble that secured her long brown hair, the sequence of such routine acts signalling the time for their browse.

CHAPTER 3

Moss finished reading the Letters then folded the paper absently as he considered what lay ahead of him on return to the family home; Louise would have returned from her meeting with Susan, the mundane evening recounted to Clare and illustrated by details such as what she ate or almost ate, how she decided against the fish: 'It looked nice,' in case a bone got stuck in her throat followed by choking to near death. 'You have to be so careful of fish bones', she would say earnestly, 'so I had no choice but to have the vegetable soup and a sandwich and some of Susan's chips'. Swallowing the last of his coffee, he began to mentally rehearse the imparting of his news, although he felt a slight gnawing in the pit of his stomach at the thought of their reactions.

He was jolted out of his contemplations by the arrival of Stephen Devereux, a long term café acquaintance, who greeted him with his usual world-weary grin as he sat down heavily on the bentwood chair opposite him, shaking his head gently to settle his long, lank black hair. His Spartan tray was laden with a tall glass of hot chocolate, a pink and white marshmallow floating on top of the froth which emanated wisps of steam and alongside it a solitary spoon. Moss knew little about Stephen nor did he wish to know although he guessed his age to be late thirties, perhaps the same age as Louise who had just turned thirty-nine. He was not in the habit of intruding into personal territory such as occupation and place of abode but valued Stephen's opinions on wider issues such as social change, politics and even philosophy, views so well informed and passionate that he discounted him from the corporate world, his casual but fashionable attire defying the suit. He always lugged a worn, scarred leather briefcase around with him, bulging with papers and books and which he tucked underneath the table, propping it against his ankle as though it were part of his being. Feeling pleased by the prospect of stimulating conversation, Moss decided to stay a while longer and made his way to the serving area to treat himself to fried eggs and chips, Stephen promising to guard his seat and coat for him, as was their custom. Delaying his return home in such an agreeable manner, he enjoyed his meal as the night closed in, the two men speculating about the fate of the two cafes.

'Of course, there will be resistance,' said Stephen. 'Dubliners won't let Bewley's go without a struggle.'

'Still...it won't be enough to hold back the force of astronomical rents,' responded Moss. 'Grafton Street will never be the same again.'

Stephen chuckled in amusement. 'I doubt if it'll come to that, Moss,' he said, draining his glass. 'In fact I'd say the Mezzanine will be retained as a café, at the very least'.

'Let's hope so,' sighed Moss who loved to sit at one of the window tables where he could look down at the continuous movement of colour, of people, along the busy street.

'And then of course there's the lunchtime theatre,' went on Stephen. 'That'll have to stay. Like I said, there *will* be resistance. Let the struggle begin!'

Moss swallowed the dregs of his final coffee then made his goodbyes, Stephen laughing at his exaggerated pained expression. He then set off along Westmoreland Street towards College Green, pausing to admire Trinity College and the pale golden hands of the blue-faced clock while he stood waiting for the traffic lights to change. Continuing his journey along Grafton Street, he cast an affectionate glance tinged with sadness as he passed the three storey building with the name Bewley's Oriental Cafés Ltd above the main entrance. He wondered what would become of it if it did close down or become a modern, bland, functional eatery. Thinking about the Harry Clarke stained glass windows in his favourite part of the café at the back, he felt fearful that they would be removed or sold on, put out of sight to make way for a new type of customer, one that would fail to notice such things, such consoling beauty, oblivious to the glare of fluorescent lights that would surely replace the amber shaded lamps suspended from the high ceiling.

He made a right turn into Chatham Street and entered Neary's pub where he eased himself onto a seat in the ground floor snug and ordered a celebratory scotch and soda. The partially curtained windows and absence of a blaring television screen or sound system enhanced the calm of the cherished atmosphere. As he sipped his drink, he felt an enormous relief encompass him. Within a month he would leave the bank behind to fend for itself, knowing that, apart from the obligatory courtesies extended to departing colleagues on their final day, his exit would barely be noticed.

Just before eight o'clock he took a taxi home from the rank at St. Stephen's Green, arriving a few moments after Louise who had taken the bus, her aversion to taxis based on a perception that it was an extravagance as well as the wide open risk of being kidnapped. 'You can't be too careful,' she would say. As usual Clare put the kettle on for tea as soon as Louise got home. He was not included in this ritual, but neither was he excluded, for he would usually head straight up to his room, occupy the bathroom for a shower and come down at the appropriate moment timed from years of discreet attention to their habits. This time he braced himself, knowing that they would be taken by surprise, shocked even, although he figured that his decision would not adversely affect their routine-obsessed lives.

Feeling refreshed by his shower, he put on dark khaki chinos, a pair of trainers and a protective black sweatshirt, combed his damp fair hair then went downstairs to the kitchen where Clare and Louise were seated at the light brown formica table, an ascetically barren but durable item which he regarded with hidden distaste. Steam rose from their brown mugs of tea; a few biscuits were huddled on a small plate, the teapot covered with an insipid green cotton cosy. Around them the kitchen gleamed antiseptically, the counter tops pristine, all utensils in their precise places, under tight control. Moss blinked under the bright wattage of the overhead light. Louse was delivering her usual monologue, what she bought or almost bought, practically identical to the last one he had heard, Clare listening abstractedly. Preferring strong tea, he set about making himself a small pot, placing his favourite china cup and saucer on the table, Louise's mockery of his genteel tastes abandoned long ago. Sitting down opposite Louise and taking a sip of his tea, he said his customary 'Ah, that's nice, very nice.' When all the details of her evening were exhausted, he said he had some news.

'I'm leaving the bank. I handed in my resignation letter this morning. And I'm moving over to Sandymount. The largest flat is vacant now. The Lombardi's have left – gone back to Venice. Georgio got his Ph.D from Trinity.' He took another sip of tea and waited, feeling slightly disconcerted by the bleak reserve of their facial expressions although Clare's was softened by surprise. It was a while before either of them would speak. Louise's blue-grey eyes contained in them the dark glint of suspicion of the world at large, not cynical but not without guile, the fair hair framing her oval face maintained in a short, functional style, similar to Clare's although hers was not as tightly cut. Clare did not look her sixty-eight years; her eyes were clearer and cleverer than her daughter's and contained within them the shrewd knowing of a woman who had accepted divorce pragmatically, albeit a knowing that was trailed by a vague lethargy, as if her reserves of sympathy had been exhausted and never reclaimed.

As Moss sat there in that expectant silence, an incident over a year ago, in the wintertime, suddenly sprang to his mind. When he had taken to his bed for a whole week, struck down by the sudden onset of influenza, he was surprised and saddened by his mother's brusque manner as he witnessed, through the misery of the symptoms, the flurry of tissues, how this event had inconvenienced her, that her routine had been interrupted in a very tiresome way. Although protected by vaccination, she had pointedly made herself scarce whenever he had shuffled into the kitchen in his bulky dressing gown to make himself some tea and toast. Louise, who contracted a different, less virulent virus, had soldiered on, choosing to see life in terms of battle, joining the ranks of aggrieved workers who traded on the martyrdom of such efforts. One evening when he had felt too weak to get out of bed, he asked Louise to get him a cup of tea and she had surprised him by bringing up a tray with his favourite cup and saucer along with slices of buttered toast and marmalade. He remembered how deeply grateful he had felt by such an uncharacteristic show of tenderness, one that had somehow leaked out in this relatively minor act of kindness. During his recovery, the genesis of the idea of moving out of the house had occurred to him with such force, such clarity, that he had given a spontaneous laugh, although in his heart, he knew that it had been lurking there for a long time.

'Imagine giving up all that security,' said Louise finally, adopting her high, tragic voice.

'You'll be unemployed now,' stated Clare in her usual neutral tone.

'Ah well; you see I won't actually be unemployed. I won't be available for work,' explained Moss. 'I'm taking the year off, a nice long break, and then I'll find something else.' He paused. 'Just a year,' he repeated.

They seemed to struggle with the concept of time off as some of the masks disintegrated from their faces, exposing baffled expressions, furrowed brows, pursed lips and a glint of what could develop into contained fury once the information was truly understood and assimilated.

'I thought you liked your job,' said Clare.

Oh - I do! In fact I enjoy it; the work's very challenging,' he said, 'but I've decided that twenty-three years in the same place is enough. Well, enough for me anyway. It's time for a change'.

'But think of all the rent you'll lose by moving into the flat!' exclaimed Louise, Clare nodding in agreement. But Moss merely shrugged.

'So...when are you going then?' asked Clare.

'I'll be out of here in a month's time,' he replied. 'Then I'll be living rent free in my own home!' He gave a sudden hollow chuckle at the sound of his voice unwittingly uttering the last few words for it sounded gleeful. It was another reminder that that he was a landlord – a term he knew his mother found disagreeable; she preferred to say he 'set' his house, like a rat or mouse trap. The word home also seemed to make Clare wince slightly as she surveyed him, as if seeking clues for his decision. There was a clue – his hair; it was not cut in the usual style but had grown into a more careless shape. As if reading her thoughts he absently ran his fingers through the fine thin strands then took a few more sips of his tea. Louise had become quiet, her eyes downcast, unsure how his departure would affect her, clearly puzzled that he would want to leave the comfort of the family home and move into a flat.

'Does Dad know about all this?' she said sharply.

'Actually, I'm just about to send him an email,' he lied, glad of an excuse to leave the table and go up to his room where he was free to suspend his poker face until his next appearance, exhaling a deep sigh when he got there, thankful that he had released his news at last and which Clare and Louise were still digesting with their tea and rationed whole grain biscuits. Four weeks to go, he thought as he surveyed his room, eyeing his comfortable bed and familiar furnishings, reassured by its clutter, admitting to himself that living in the family home for so long into adulthood was almost entirely out of convenience and self-interest. When his father David had decided to relocate to Singapore twenty years ago, a gratifying business opportunity releasing him from the frenzied world of the stockbroker, Clare had simply refused to go with him. She detested travel. Places outside Ireland, even Dublin, did not interest her. His sense of duty to stay on and play the role of protector to her was misplaced, he knew now, for she had never asked for such protection, had given no visible signs of distress after David had left, even when the divorce eventually came through. Neither he nor Louise had taken their father up on his offer - and this was still open - to treat them to a couple of weeks in Raffles Hotel, flights included. They were home birds, he realised, clinging tenaciously to the nest in its quiet location on Lime Tree Road. A flicker of amusement crossed his mind at Clare and Louise's predictable lack of well-wishing, of celebration at the choices he had made. Looking around his room with a sudden twist of focus, he was filled with an urgent need to begin packing, the lingering bleakness of their faces still haunting the air.

CHAPTER 4

Time to email Kevin, he decided as he sat down at his cramped desk by the window, the glow of a streetlamp visible through a gap in the beige curtains that he had drawn carelessly earlier on. He switched on his computer, his expression brightening at the knowledge that for once he had news to report, that he had at last suspended caution and had taken action although such action would seem tame to such a risk taker, a man of accomplishment. He considered telephoning him, but remembered the time difference with New York: Kevin would most likely be out somewhere in the West Village having an early dinner with his wife Masami and their daughter Kim, joined perhaps by mutual friends or colleagues, Kim yawning in boredom at their discussions on the latest publications in social research. Kevin's life was widely populated and cosmopolitan, he knew, ruefully aware of his own entrenchment in a routine job with few friends beyond the homogenous corporate net, his degree in English and interest in philosophy superfluous to the work in hand. He also realised that such homogeneity had been intercepted, even rescued by the new era of immigration to Ireland, importing the multiculturalism that Kevin had longed for when they were students in UCD. He recalled his popularity even then, a regard enhanced by his vociferousness at meetings of the Students' Union while he, 'the Moss man', took on the role of spoilsport, biding his time quietly in the background, armed with essential facts, details that had been overlooked and which he would point out unexpectedly, just before the meeting would conclude, his cautious voice penetrating the restless silence: 'Well... actually...there *is* just one thing...' and Kevin would buy him a pint later on 'for saving my skin again Moss!'

As he watched the screen spring to life then listened to the eerie connection tones to the internet, his expression mellowed as he remembered those college days when they used to visit one another's homes although he had gravitated far more frequently to the O'Brien's Edwardian terraced house in the charming suburban village of Sandymount, in Glass Street close to Sandymount Green. Kevin's father John was a journalist of repute and would issue opinions furnished with acerbic witticisms; there was also the attraction to Maria's Italian cooking, her regular provision of lasagne - 'Garfield's favourite food, Moss!' And he tried to hide his attraction to Lucy, Kevin's youngest sibling, by then seventeen and who was constantly in demand, fending off admirers, treating him as another brother, another role he had acquiesced to, using it as practise for maintaining a check on his expression, and his behaviour.

Over in Clontarf, Kevin had quickly become a source of intrigue to Clare and Louise, with his tall, lean physique and mane of shiny black hair and dark eyes, the mood instantly lifting with his presence, his lack of inhibition – he would greet Clare with a kiss on her cheek - and wry sense of humour a novelty to them both. Louise, by then a quiet, reticent teenager, sometimes reacted to his visits as invasions and would eventually vacate the living room with a look of disgust whenever Kevin and Moss would clutch one another in a fit of mock hysterical laughter during the course of their banter, or when they would return from the gate of Bram Stoker's former house on Marino Crescent, pretending to be Count Dracula, their robust chuckles a sound so alien it seemed to be breaking an embargo. Clare would try in vain to appease her daughter's outbursts and ended up smiling weakly at the two men, providing them with snacks in relative silence, small talk too superfluous to bother with. On the rare occasion that David was at home during such visits, he would grin charmingly at their raucous humour as if it was routine in the world that he inhabited, and eventually encouraged Moss to join Kevin on a rail trip around Europe during the summer of his final year, as a treat for completing his exams. 'Travel broadens the mind,' David would declare without a trace of mockery. Moss remembered Louise's bemused expression as she watched him load up a backpack for the journey and when he sat at the kitchen table looking up trains in the international timetable.

'Now let's see: Amsterdam to Stockholm,' he would say in a casual tone, or 'The Trans-Siberian Express sounds quite interesting' or 'Maybe we'll head up to the Arctic Circle to see the midnight sun - that is of course if it's not raining', evoking one of her grimaces - 'You are *so* weird Moss; just as weird as weirdo Kevin'. He had wondered why his continental itinerary seemed so inferior to her, that it did not measure up to their father's pinstriped business trips, trips that led to his permanent move to Singapore. But he and Kevin were embarking on an adventure at that time, he knew, taking a different kind of risk, one that demonstrated the development of treacherously independent minds '...in a culture of stifling conservatism and conformity' as Kevin used to say in a tone of exaggerated gravity. The adventure had ended in Cambridge, in the home of Andrew Mortimer – David's twin brother – where they holidayed for the month of August, a stretch of time that Moss remembered as idyllic, for it contained everything that had appealed to his developing character: the informal atmosphere of his tolerant uncle's sprawling, cosy old house stashed with antiques and ancient furniture, the university colleges close by, his first brief but intensely romantic love affair beginning unsteadily with a kiss in a punt on the Cam. Arriving back in Ireland, tanned and elated, he had been struck by the frosty acknowledgement of his return, Louise indifferent to his enthusiastic accounts of their trip, her mouth curling dismissively although she liked the souvenirs he gave her - a tiny Eiffel tower and a framed Delft tile. And so he had discontinued his reports, disappointed and a little confounded as he stowed away the photographs of Paris, Amsterdam, Helsinki and other cities and landscapes and the people they had met on trains and in youth hostels, as if hiding the evidence. Clare's disinterest had been genuine, although she was visibly relieved to see him home safely, her slight frown betraying her fear of travel, of such vast distances covered, of the dangers they must surely have escaped. But Moss was eventually reassured by David's intent perusal of the photos and the news from Cambridge, the two men united in world affairs for a number of hours at the kitchen table one evening, and in the company of a bottle of Burgundy.

But such unity came to an end when both David and Kevin left Ireland in the same year, David to Singapore and Kevin, by then equipped with a doctorate in sociology, joining the ranks of emigrants fleeing to better prospects, as his brothers Peter and Tony had done in that era of high unemployment. Lucy had married and was living in Dun Laoghaire with her husband Austin, a baffling choice Moss thought now with a fraction of indignation, what with his corpulent shape and squinting eyes. His infatuation was over, he knew, but the traces of it had dissolved into lingering images of inaccessible beauty. And the sudden death of Maria O'Brien at fifty eight, from cancer, had left another, more distressing trace.

With a sigh, he picked up a book lying in the pile on his desk, a page marked at random by a postcard from Kevin when he was teaching in Kyoto for six months. 'Oh look - another postcard from your eccentric friend – still gallivanting around the world,' Louise would say mockingly whenever such cards arrived, cards that he would seize with delight, keen to track Kevin's progress. He examined the photograph on the dust jacket, approving the transformation from college bohemian to hair that was short and sleek, accentuating his clean-shaven aquiline features, his gleaming white teeth bearing up well as testament to the skills of his New York dentist, the brief summary concluding with the words: Dr O'Brien lives in New York with his wife and daughter. After all that gallivanting he got married and settled down, Moss mused. How old was he then? Thirty-two, and Masami only twenty-five, he remembered. She was wealthy, he had found out during a visit to New York after Kim was born, responding to his appointment as godfather, albeit one of several, Kevin eager to nurture his ties with Ireland and Italy where Peter had settled. They lived in a low rise building, their apartment on the fourth floor a wedding gift from Masami's parents. He remembered how he had cradled Kim in his arms on a sofa in their book-lined living room, her dark eyes gazing up at his, her tiny hand clutching his little finger. The perfection of the human being in its infancy, the mystery of her whereabouts before conception, had filled him with awe in that intense but fleeting moment, an awe that extended to Manhattan which both terrified and enthralled him. The guesthouse – a nineteenth century townhouse - that Kevin had booked him into was another surprise and where he rejoiced in the unexpected Parisian feel about his spacious room. During dinner at the O'Brien's the next evening after an exhausting day exploring the city with Kevin as guide, he suspected he had disgraced himself by admitting to his English ancestry to Angelina, the intense young woman in a bright green dress who was seated opposite him - 'Well, actually, my father was born in Cambridge...I was named after his Morris Minor, you know, his favourite car.' As Angelina was leaving, a little earlier than expected by his hosts, he had overheard her say to Masami in the hall from his vantage point in the kitchen where he had gone to fetch more beer at Kevin's request:

'But you *said* he was Irish!'

'He *is*, Angelina, he *is*.'

'But he doesn't *sound* Irish to me.'

But Masami had continued her unflinching graciousness despite his failure to conform to stereotype and when he had left New York, he felt somehow chastened by the combination of erudition and magnanimity that had prevailed during his four day visit, compounded by his secret, profound relief at being reunited with the horizontal world of Dublin, his ears still buzzing with the energy of Manhattan and the fact that Kevin had paid for his room. He did not return to New York but kept in regular contact, opened a post office account for Kim, mere pocket money, he knew, her birthdays acknowledged by a card, and a phone call. He smiled at the memory of the time she had played her violin for him when she was seven, imagining Kevin's indulgent expression as he held the phone in his hand, its function as microphone transmitting her nurtured talent across the Atlantic.

He put the book aside; it was one of a series of Kevin's published works, resulting in regular visits to Dublin to speak at conferences, contribute his opinions on radio programmes, give an occasional lecture in his resounding voice with its smooth, decisive tone. He would stay with his father in Sandymount and meet up with Moss for a tour of their favourite haunts, Moss amused by his nostalgia for Dublin, especially when he treated him to dinner at the Library Club – 'Gawd...this place...awesome!' Kevin would say whenever they entered the premises, filling the air with wisecracks as Moss showed the place off before leading him triumphantly to the dining room. The Club was now closed for renovations but a welcome vision of its interior manifested itself in his mind although he hoped that the atmosphere would not be affected by the changes.

He logged onto his email address then trawled through the listing of messages that he hoarded in his inbox. He reopened the one Kevin had sent him in response to his plea for advice during September the year before. He read the encouraging words again, along with recommended reading, Kevin's droll tone filtering through the words on the screen: Go for it Moss man; we've only got one shot at this life then we're six foot under. And talk to Valerie. She'll give you a straight answer. You know the Dutch. PS - Give her my love. He had followed his advice, sheepishly remonstrating with himself for such an obvious choice, for not having thought of conferring with someone whose friendship he valued so highly. As he clicked the email closed, he considered Oscar Wilde's words discounting the possibility of friendship between men and women: *There is passion, enmity, worship, love, but no friendship.* He still aspired to the idea that it was possible, perhaps even preferable, to sustain an amicable and fulfilling friendship with a woman or a certain kind of woman as long as they did not succumb to animal instincts, perhaps even strengthen their characters by the very resistance of such succumbing. This, he knew, would invite a sneer of derision from members of a populace that was anchored in superficiality and so he kept it to himself, even from Kevin whom he knew had become smitten with Valerie when he was an unexpected guest in her home, fate leading him there as if for that specific purpose and to introduce an unexpected alliance in Moss's life. Hard to believe that was barely three years ago, he thought, remembering the reunion with Kevin at the gates of Trinity College where Kevin had issued his routine adage to his cheerful greetings, clapping him dramatically on the back as they made their way towards Grafton Street: 'Well, here I am Moss, back in Grudge Country!' Moss's smirk was still in place as they claimed their bar stools in the snug in Neary's where he enjoyed Kevin's next ritual - a first swig from his pint glass of Guinness. 'Hm...hmmm...nectar....Turning to Moss, Kevin then said: 'So...guess where I'm staying this time, Moss man.'

'With your old man, the wily scribe.'

'Ah...no no, my corporate friend. No!' he had chuckled, lapsing into a Dublin accent.'The old fox has just fecked off to Tuscany for six months with Noeleen Harris, his new partner – she moved in with him in January. They've rented out the gaff to friends of hers. And of course staying with Lucy's out of the question,' adding cryptically 'after the last time.'

'Well then: obviously you're booked into the Merrion.'

'Ah ha now!' he had given a hollow laugh. 'Maybe next time, you merchant banker you – we'll have a few scoops there of course. Anyway the good news is that Noeleen has very kindly put me up in a private guesthouse in Sandymount, in Seagull Gardens, not far from your investment pad. It's owned by Valerie de Vries, a friend of hers from Amsterdam. It's truly amazing - very grand, olde worlde – your kind of place actually. *And,*' he paused to give a playful grin, '*we* are invited to dinner there tomorrow evening.'

'Excellent,' Moss had said signalling the barman to refill their glasses.

'Valerie,' Kevin had continued, 'is older than us by a few years – mid-forties I guess. Now here's the romantic bit: she never married but she has a son – a love child, she said! - called Johann. Met his father – a cargo pilot by the name of Niels - at a party when she was twenty one. She was working in the UvA library on the Singel at the time - you remember that incident on the Singel when we were over there, Moss? Well anyhow when Niels's sister Josie found out that she was pregnant, she called around to her flat on the Browersgracht and - surprise surprise,' he had raised his hand for emphasis – 'invited her to move into their house on the Herengracht, an even more salubrious address.'

'Course that wouldn't have happened over here,' Moss had remarked, intrigued by Kevin's ability to extract so much information so quickly, within twenty four hours in fact, details he would have left to fate, to a gradual leakage.

'No chance,' he had agreed. 'Well, at least they stopped turfing them into Magdalene laundries a long time ago – or is it that long? Of course there's still plenty of gobshite hypocrites who go to mass every Sunday and spend the rest of their time indulging in a little pious judging and shunning. Ahh! Our squalid, grubby little secrets lying in wait underneath the carpet - don't get me started on that one, Moss man. Where was I? Oh yeah - they came over to Ireland a few years ago because of Johann's job at the NCC and Val's work on translations. Novels, from Dutch to English.' He paused for another sip of beer. 'Talented guy is young Johann. Play's the piano really well. Niels seems to look after them from a distance; he's retired from flying and lives in Paris now, married to someone else. It's all a bit complicated in a charming, tolerant sort way...Josie never married and she basically raised Johann, from what I can gather.'

And so Moss had been briefed. He had taken a half day's leave the next day to meet Kevin, his lecture delivered that morning – 'Hey - I'm still alive, no scars!', their established nostalgia tour beginning with lunch in Bewley's Café in Grafton Street, then a lazy stroll along the busy street towards College Green, the city bathed in a gentle October light. They had stopped to watch a group of young musicians from the School of Music perform Pachelbel's Canon, then went down to Trinity College where Moss was rewarded by the sight of a marmalade cat grooming itself on the cobblestones in front of the Rubrics as he and Kevin strolled by the Old Library. Their afternoon had ended in the Merrion Hotel's cocktail bar, Kevin gleefully clapping his hands together at the prospect of 'a quick scoop before dinner!'

They had arrived in Seagull Gardens by taxi around six o'clock, Moss impressed by the location of the detached double fronted Georgian house set in behind a low stone wall with black railings and a small lawn garden. The black front door had swung open to reveal a tall young man attired in jeans and a long dark jumper, a mass of sand coloured shoulder length hair framing a handsome face. 'Johann de Vries,' he had said to Moss, shaking his hand firmly as he stepped into the spacious hall with black and white floor tiles. His attention was immediately drawn to a large, handsomely framed photograph of Koningen Beatrix that was prominently placed alongside a couple of Vermeer reproductions. He had taken an instant liking to Valerie when she emerged from the adjacent reception room; it was not just the way she had looked him in the eye – level, sincere - as they shook hands firmly, but her appearance which he found so appealing, her light brown hair carelessly long, a healthy sheen to her freckled complexion, her navy blue eyes shadowed with grey, a burgundy colour applied to her lips. Beautiful house, he had said admiringly as he discerned a shapely figure underneath her layers of dark, casual clothes.

'Yes it is,' she had agreed waving him into the drawing room, 'but we can't take full credit for it. We inherited the bulk of the furniture and wall hangings from the previous owner - a businessman who's now back in Amsterdam. We've actually changed very little - just the piano and a few odds and ends.' Moss's eyes had gleamed at the sight of the baby grand adjacent to the vast window, the heavy blond velvet curtains still wide open on to the night. Two cream sofas and matching arm chairs furnished with colourful throws and cushions were arranged symmetrically over a large blue rug before the white marble surround fireplace, its mantelpiece adorned with a collection of statues and oriental ornaments, an oil painting of a bluebell wood with dappled sunlight above it. The dining room was a complete contrast with its heritage green walls and darker furnishings, the other guests Henry, Sara and Nino joining them at the oval table to enjoy the meal of chilli con carne in an atmosphere of dignified conviviality, Moss deducing that the guests were in fact wealthy lodgers. While he had noticed Kevin cast appreciative glances at Valerie, he became seduced by the house as he tended to lavish his affection on buildings, architecture, furniture, rugs, objects d'art, keeping it in cautious reserve for people. He had left around ten o'clock that night, marvelling at the expansive generosity, the aura of contentment that the house exuded. He had also gleaned more information about Valerie through a number of eager questions from Sara, clearly a newcomer, a dinner table conversation he replayed in his mind en route home in the taxi Johann had ordered for him.

'Is it true that your father is a butler, Valerie?'

'Oh yes! But he's not English, my mother Diane was English. My father Erik's from Rotterdam. Used to work as a tram driver. Mum died when she was only thirty-six. I was still in school then of course. We were all devastated – naturally. Poor Dad was mournful for years and years - I couldn't wait to go and live in Amsterdam, but he didn't approve of it. I went anyway. Around five years later his luck changed suddenly: he moved to England to work in the home of a very wealthy industrialist.'

'Whose name you're not at liberty to reveal,' Kevin had cocked an eyebrow.

'Oh yes, it's top secret,' Johann had grinned.

'I wouldn't mind being a butler,' Moss had found himself saying.

'Yeah...*yeah*! I think you'd be good at that Moss man. With your poker face alone, you'd qualify for the job.'

'Why thank you, Doctor O'Brien.'

After Kevin's return to New York, Moss continued to visit the de Vries's either by invitation or by suggestion - books were borrowed and returned, usually on Saturdays when he carried out the maintenance chores in his own house in Dawn View. Sometimes he would settle against a cushion on the cream sofa listening to Johann practise, or sip coffee with Valerie at their large pinewood kitchen table. He applied his private rule of never overstaying his welcome, spacing his visits out with tracts of time, resulting in a sense of occasion whenever he stepped over the threshold, the front door opening wide in that magnanimous gesture of theirs. Sometimes he liked to think that he was entering another country, a peaceful territory in another golden age.

He typed the email at last and sent it to Kevin, promising himself that he would contact his father the following night, disconnected from the internet then began a game of solitaire. Soon he would be living close to Valerie and felt determined to repay her hospitality once he was settled into his own place. Valerie was in fact the ideal friend, he thought, or at least this had been the case so far. She had given him similar advice to that of Kevin over a coffee in Neary's – 'Oh definitely - go for it Moss. Be adventurous! And Sandymount is a great place to live...we love it. And we'll get to see you more often, hopefully.' Strange, he mused, the encouragement, the kindness, of friends. As he moved the cards around the screen, he felt a renewed sense of purpose, a curious feeling of optimism sweep over him, even though he lost the game.

CHAPTER 5

During the month of April Moss spent his spare time packing and moving some of his possessions gradually, covertly, to the vacant flat in Sandymount, in the evenings and at the weekends. He tried not to attract Clare's attention, but could tell she was taking note with a resigned eye resulting in him feeling more and more like a lodger sneaking off before the agreed departure date. His days at the bank, now numbered, were markedly less cautious, for he was beset by mixed sensations that manifested as a rite of passage, a breaking out, a ripping up of the rules, disturbing the established hierarchy, causing him to feel slightly light-headed, a mild but not unpleasant tension lurking deep within his gut. Dedicating over two decades of his life to the same employer, in the same building – a majestic light-filled structure with vast windows, marble columns, wide gleaming corridors and a first-rate canteen – could have institutionalised him. But his interests, modest as they were, protected him from yielding to what he regarded as the slavery of personal time deprivation or diminished identity, the fate of a number of his colleagues. He had at the very least succeeded in constructing and conducting a life apart from the institution; an undemanding, pleasant bachelor life, he frequently thought, and that it was largely uneventful did not diminish his contentment.

Moss was twenty-eight when David provided him and Louise with share portfolios, the divorce finalised, David well settled in Singapore. Hiding his delight at what felt like a private lottery winning, Moss had moved swiftly into action, taking the advice from his uncle James O'Neill - his mother's elder brother - to invest in property. 'Bricks and mortar Moss, bricks and mortar: that's the way to go,' James would urge him in his soft yet commanding voice over a drink in the Shelbourne bar, wearing his usual dark suit and striped tie, one of his slightly rumpled raincoats folded on the stool next to him, his astute grey eyes gleaming knowledgeably in a round, pink face, his brows so fair they were almost invisible, his soft, receding hair trimmed to collar length. As a child, Moss called him the Key man because of the assortment of keys he kept on his person, ones that gave him access to the houses and flats he owned around the city, having followed his other maxim: location, location, location.

He was instantly drawn to Sandymount where Kevin grew up, intimately familiar with its coastal location on the other side of Dublin Bay. He and Kevin had often gone for walks along the strand with its long promenade and Martello Tower, such walks enhanced whenever Lucy joined them. He also cherished its proximity to the city centre just a few stops away by the *Dart* commuter train and by the number 3 bus. It was a journey he made with Kevin countless times, when they would embark at the stop in the village, adjacent to the Green, the bus progressing through Irishtown, Ringsend, along traffic-congested Pearse Street, passing the hallowed landmark of Trinity College, then depositing them at the bus stop located conveniently close to Bewley's Café in Westmoreland Street. The recession was coming to a conclusion although at the time, Moss could not discern any notable signs of its ending, apart from subtle changes such as the trickle of established staff members leaving to take up jobs elsewhere, the rumours of their being head-hunted scoffed at by those still entrenched in the job-for-life-at-all-costs ethos. Rather than prevaricate, he was prepared to pay the high mortgage interest rates that prevailed at the time to secure number 11 Dawn View which was located in a cul de sac of houses of varying architectural designs and accessed by a labyrinthine maze of streets in the heart of Sandymount. The owner was living in Canada and wanted a quick sale, and although the tenants had vacated, the house still bore the stigma of being divided into flats, putting the price in Moss's favour. James had accompanied him to the second viewing and silently examined the interior, accessing the attic with surprising agility, torch in hand. He had then scrutinised the exterior walls, the roof, the chimney stacks, the long, overgrown garden, and, turning to Moss had simply said: 'Take it.'

Moss became the owner of what he considered a property of substance and charm; the double fronted Victorian-style structure built in the early nineteen hundreds had been converted in the sixties into four flats: a studio, two singles and one double. The immense front door with its half moon fan light opened onto a spacious hall with ornate tiles. The flat that was to become his new home was situated on the right hand side of the hall, a brass number 3 gleaming upon the door. It was twice the size of the two single flats - numbers 1 and 2 on the opposite side - with a fine sitting room, a dining room, a large bright kitchen with French doors opening onto the garden, a narrow staircase leading to the bathroom and two bedrooms above. Annexed to the rear of the house was an extension containing a long utility room and, situated above it was Flat 4, accessed by the original hall staircase with storage cupboards and shelves on the narrow landing. In the course of the redecoration work after he had taken possession, Moss had discovered, behind a panel disguised as a shelf unit, an upstairs landing still in its original state, as if spared from further conversion. An ancient carpet covered dusty floorboards that were in perfect condition on inspection, as were the original bedroom doors which were camouflaged by brickwork, plasterboard and wallpaper over on the other side. No wonder it's such a quiet house, Moss had thought. He kept that secret space in mind for it could, at some future time, be reopened, should he ever wish to return the entire house to its original layout. There was now a small table in front of the secret door for the use of the tenant. The utility room below housed a sink, washing machine, cupboards, shelves, gardening tools, tins of paint, old rugs, small furniture items awaiting repairs or a coat of paint or varnish. There was a tiny lavatory partitioned off it, Moss suspecting that, in greedier hands, the room would have been used as another rental space. He approved of the previous owner's regard for his tenants' requirements and the way the two single flats had been converted for maximum privacy, being mirror images of each other. They were totally self-contained, equipped with a small narrow kitchen at ground level, a living room with fireplace and furnished with sofa, table, chairs, bookshelves, a wooden partition at the entrance door creating the effect of a tiny vestibule complete with coat hooks. A carpeted staircase led up to a tiny landing, to the bathroom and then the bedroom where there was a double bed, armchair, wardrobe and other useful items that Moss had selected at auction rooms and second hand furniture stores, for much of the original furniture was worn out and had to be disposed of.

The house became a destination factored into his Saturday morning routine and where he maintained the common areas and the garden which was sheltered at the rear, a row of Leyland trees forming a natural boundary with the adjoining property and reinforced with chain link fencing. Although the owners had constructed a wall long ago as added protection, Moss could still stand on a stack of blocks while cutting the hedge and peer into their long garden, spying on the large greenhouse, a game played out occasionally on the tennis court, and, at certain times, two blond Labradors chasing one another round and round the lawn, exchanging affable barks, a tabby cat watching them from its perch on top of the trellis. A six foot wall divided the adjacent properties, those of numbers 10 and 12 and both flanked by trees, shrubs and hedging. Moss loved to sit on the wooden bench by the ivy covered wall where the sturdy branches of the oak tree next door created a private canopy, a pleasing space to relax in, protecting him from the glare of the sun or the chill in the sea breeze, a breeze that was rarely absent. He kept a low profile for the benefit of his tenants, using the utility room as his base, performing his chores quietly, mopping the hall tiles, running a carpet sweeper over the rug, dusting the table, watering the plants, wiping down the yellow front door and a host of other minor tasks until it was time to go to the village pub for lunch.

Now his visits to Dawn View were far more frequent as he quietly brought his possessions through the door of Flat 3. Surveying his rooms and then gazing at the back garden from his new bedroom window, he began to envisage numerous improvements to be made, projects to be embarked upon and so he began by sketching up a plan, citing the painting of the sitting room as a priority, for this was the room he intended using the most.

CHAPTER 6

Clare began to wander cautiously around the house while Louise and Moss were at work, her routine jolted out of complacency by her son's impending departure. She wondered what had brought on such recklessness, struck by the realisation that he had far more in common with his father than she had thought, although this did not distress her too much, apart from a vague disappointment, as if slightly affronted. Out of habit, she went into her bedroom and surveyed the contents of her wardrobe, her fingers lightly touching the fabric of an ancient evening dress that she could not part with, one that she had worn when playing hostess to David's clients and friends at dinner parties until these events had been phased out, their life as a married couple eventually ending when David went to live in Singapore. But he had tried his best to make her life as comfortable as possible, she acknowledged, with his usual magnanimity, transferring the house into her name, seeing to it that she was financially secure for her lifetime, and giving Moss and Louise what she regarded as their inheritance well in advance of any demise on his part.

Her lifestyle became far more restricted after the divorce was finalized, as if the official document contained a clause that she should keep an even lower profile, adding to her usual wariness. There had been no acrimony, no other woman at the time although she still felt resigned to the possibility of a change in this regard. But, despite her comfortable life, her decision to stay in Ireland, to let him go freely to his new life, had had other consequences. The shift in status had brought about unpalatable and at times puzzling changes to her relationships, friendships which had been forged during their marriage and were comprised of business acquaintances of David's, certain relatives and friends preferred for the significance of their occupations and earning potential, the merits of good character overlooked as though money and status would guarantee permanent harmony and social compatibility. Most of these people had dropped her, the wives instantly alert to Clare's new rank as an unattached female, perceiving their husbands to be endangered. She was by then ageing beautifully into her late forties and so territories had to be protected; the wives with the intact marriages - thrilled with the opportunity to indulge in speculative gossip - had consigned her to that dubious place for divorcees, the separated, the single (but not the bachelor), a lingering doubt cast over her suitability as though a pedigree was suddenly discovered to be flawed. They had closed ranks and she was discarded, silently voted out of the club. Clare had never questioned the sincerity of those relationships, that they might have been founded on tenuous and transient motives and that their very maintenance consumed so much time and energy that others had to be excluded. She subsequently suffered acute disappointment at the demise of a social life, a life in which such friends and acquaintances had regarded her as a somebody but in truth she was somebody's wife. The message had eventually reached her and been understood. Instead of battling for her place in society she had retreated, scorched by the evidence before her, that couples are accorded the kind of acceptability and respectability that triumphs over the divorced, the un-partnered. Yet David had somehow retained his status, she knew, in fact it had even been enhanced in their fickle eyes, their last sighting of him looking distinguished with his lengthening silver-white hair brushed back from a smooth forehead, lines evading it, his amused, wolfish smile arousing in them a remote possibility as they overlooked the crinkle of reserve around his sharp eyes.

Clare possessed an intimate knowledge of her financial affairs, studying her statements and documentation with the focus of someone reading an absorbing novel. Yet she was frugal, or had become frugal after David's departure. She continued to enjoy her weekly visit to the hairstylist in the salon located in the midst of a friendly row of retail outlets down on the Clontarf Road, glad of the cup of coffee that Celia gave her just the way she liked it - steaming hot, one sugar, a small amount of milk - and the treat of a chocolate biscuit, feeling a surge of gratefulness for the attention as it dissipated her sense of invisibility. The stylists smiled and expressed interest in herself and also Louise whose hair they were familiar with, Clare always reminding them how busy she was and 'of course Morris, my son, you know, who's with the bank.' She enjoyed hearing their little snippets of harmless gossip and chat although she had no contributions of her own to make. But she was a good listener and in her capacity of such role reversal became the recipient of confidences, which added to the enjoyment of seeing the reflection of her sculpted hair in the large mirror. She was aware of the advantages of keeping up a well groomed, fashionable appearance – *you never know who you might meet, especially in town* – and a special effort had to be made to maintain dignity. In this she succeeded, always looking impeccable in the stylish clothes chosen from her downsized wardrobe, resulting in an impression of quiet, gracious elegance. The black dress she now surveyed in the wardrobe still seemed beautiful to her, perhaps back in fashion, the fabric woven with golden threads that complemented the colour of her hair. How they used to admire it, she thought wonderingly, then remembered that they had discarded her. Closing the wardrobe door firmly, she realised that she no longer missed them, although for a very long time she had yearned for the telephone to ring, hankering after the news, being in the know, belonging to a social group even if it was constructed on falsity.

But she was not entirely bereft of friends. Jean Fitzgerald and Anne Leonard had remained loyal and consistent with their attention, almost as if nothing had happened, including her in their amicable little social routines, such as lunch or coffee in their homes, or in hotels, or the occasional concert or shopping spree in town. Jean lived in Sutton, her house overlooking the beach and accessible by bus along the Coast Road, although Clare usually got a lift with Anne depending on the weather. Anne lived on Pinewalk Avenue, a mere two streets away, Clare making the pleasant tree-lined stroll to a house where the change of scene was a striking contrast to her own home and which both fascinated and appalled her. The Leonard's house was in a constant state of untidiness with its scatter rugs, its fringes tangled, on polished wooden floors; music stands were poised somewhat lopsidedly in the sitting room, piles of worn sheet music were stacked upon sideboards and alongside a photograph gallery of beaming family members on top of the bulky upright piano in the corner. The connecting door was perpetually opened onto the bright dining room with its large oval table constantly set for a meal or displaying the detritus of one just completed; a gangly, leafy plant, cherished for its lemony scent, commanded the centre and was allowed to grow unsupervised, Anne in the habit of rubbing a leaf between her thumb and forefinger, sniffing it and exclaiming 'Ah, that's gorgeous, try it Clare! Isn't it divine?!'

Of course this was the territory of musicians, Clare reasoned, in awe of Alex Leonard's success as a violinist, an occupation she had difficulty in connecting a salary to, for it fell into the area of leisure pursuit in her mind. Their sons, both married, were also musicians: Raymond had mastered the piano and Brian the cello and all three had travelled worldwide with 'The Orchestra!' many times. The contentment that Anne exuded, and her gracious manner, always put Clare at ease, their home a zone free of striving for she was not expected to give an account of herself and was complimented on her appearance. And there was always a gentle emphasis on enjoyment - Clare, have a glass! Go on! Another cup of tea! Treat yourself! – resulting in an ambience of sunny relaxation and, while glad to return to her own comparatively sterile home, she always looked forward to the next visit, convinced that it somehow contributed to her wellbeing.

Clare's sister Elaine Lynch was less accessible over in the southside suburb of Donnybrook, the division by the Liffey river an advantage for Clare who did not relish being in close proximity to someone who was on constant duty, resulting in visits that felt more like trials. Once Elaine was safely married, Clare had witnessed her evolve into the archetypal queen bee, assuming a bustling manner to assert her busyness and buzzing with the need to impose her will on anyone within her orbit, especially onto her own adult offspring and their children, exhibiting blatant dismay that their preferences contrasted so vividly with her own. Her status as a secondary school teacher, even after her early retirement, and membership of a number of worthy committees served her as a form of calling card, of credentials, her husband Leo's identity neatly wrapped up in his career as a civil servant or former civil servant now that he too was retired. Their three offspring – Joan, Frances and Pauline - had transformed over time from babies into more teachers, worker bees. Elaine promoted a glossy image of them all as exceptionally successful people with busy social lives, is if striving to create carbon copies of herself, until Pauline suddenly opted out and became a disappointment by leaving the school to stay at home and look after her two boys, Elaine failing the recognise the value in it, dismissing her daughter's claims of feeling stressed out - 'Stress is it! But sure didn't I have three of you and I still worked fulltime. Stress my foot!'

There was no room for failure in Elaine's queendom, or what might be perceived as failure and Pauline's name was markedly absent from the newsy updates on the telephone or whenever Clare visited her or, more rarely, was visited not long after becoming a divorcee. Elaine would then enter the Clontarf hall in her bustling manner, as if on a mission, unable to halt the pursing of her lips, the downward moue of her mouth, indicating malcontent at her sister's lifestyle. Leaning forward in her chair in the living room, her hands joined in a way that implied that Clare had been up to no good, was caught out and needed guidance, she would urge her to 'Do something, keep busy!' She suggested that she go to evening classes, or take up painting, do voluntary work – anything to meet 'new people', as if there was also a deadline about such action. But something in Clare had closed down and while she listened to her sister's savvy advice, she didn't take it and settled instead to devoting her time to the house and cooking nutritious meals for Louise and Moss and engaging in other harmless routines.

Elaine wished she could affix a name to Clare's inertia, her chronic inactivity. Anxiety, even depression, would have been convenient in that such conditions would have given her a label, one that would emphasise her own glowing health, even exalt her to a plateau from which she could constantly lavish her with advice. But no such ailments were ever confirmed, to her hidden chagrin. 'Poor Clare...' she would say wistfully to family members and friends, unable to fathom her sedate, sedentary life. If there had been financial restrictions there would be suitable signs of a struggle. But Clare was wealthy yet did not seem to spend her money on anything other than minor upkeep of the house although when it came to clothes she could not fault her for they were of the finest quality and in a style that was constantly up to date, almost as if she possessed a keen knowledge of the fashion industry, information that kept her in pace with the high street catwalk. In spite of her apparent semi-reclusion, Elaine could see that Clare was somehow worldly, as if – dare she admit it – her sister was occupied, involved, perhaps on her way to a meeting or some other destination. Clare never lost the will to look good, she realised in an honest moment, remembering how her daughters practically fawned over her, their keen eyes identifying the designers of her clothes. And that Chanel suit of hers and the matching perfume said it all, she would think somewhat dolefully.

On the surface Elaine found Clare to be a good listener even to mild family woes but she would frequently feel vexed after their conversations, at her lack of reciprocation for Clare would try to neutralise emotions, to whitewash, living, it seemed, by a different currency, a neutral one, one that did not trade in gossip or small talk.

'I'd like to shake her sometimes,' she would grumble to Leo.

'Ah, Clare's okay,' he would say, 'she's just the quiet type. Always was. Hardly going to change now.'

'Well she should make an effort, Leo. She never goes anywhere. Neither does Louise. How can *anyone* live like that?' She had felt particularly aggrieved that they had never taken up her offer to use their apartment in Seville.

'Well: we don't like the heat,' Clare had said.

'But go in the spring,' Elaine had urged. 'Or the autumn.'

'Well...you know Louise; she won't like the food,' Clare had responded, making the invitation sound like a tedious work assignment and not a holiday that was being offered. 'They're strange,' she would say to Leo. 'Even Morris only goes to Wexford for his holidays now,' adding dismissively, 'to his little mobile home'.

'Ah well, they like the quiet life,' he murmured, remembering how he would shift uneasily in his seat as the aircraft bearing them to Spain took off and the discomfort in his ears when it made its descent, an ache that would last for hours afterwards. 'Nothing wrong with that at all.'

'Oh but it's so *boring*!' she would retort. 'How can they *stand* it?! Aah - *why* she didn't go to Singapore with David is beyond me.'

What puzzled her most of all was a life or way of life that was contented with so little attention, the opposite to her own well-maintained popularity, confirmed by a crowded social diary, tracking everyone's moves, satisfying her appetite of being in the know, trading in nuggets of gossip, presiding over meetings where such trading occurred in the aftermath, the minute book closed over, barely hiding the fact that her social life masqueraded under the guise of voluntary altruism. Out of desperation, she had resorted to making lewd remarks with the intention of encouraging Clare to find herself another man for to remain in a manless state was also perceived by her as weak, rendering her incomplete.

'Do you miss David?' she used to demand of her in the immediate years after he left, intending to shock her into reaction. She was never rewarded with the required complicity but instead Clare's tiny smile, the one that she could never understand. The smile seemed to imply that once she had married David, there was no further need to be impressed; all had been achieved.

'Those days are over,' Clare would say with firm conviction, as if she knew that by looking for a new relationship, a replacement husband, she would be found out to be foolish.

And because of her non-confessional state she did not divulge a particular incident to Elaine, one that involved a man, for she knew how thrilled Elaine would have been to hear the details preferably in a sequence, like episodes of a soap opera. And so Elaine remained ignorant of her sister's hard lesson, the brush with the consequences of trying to do the decent thing. Being decent, on that unfortunate occasion, was misinterpreted. The incident – an isolated predator experience for Clare – took place several years after David's departure. Out the blue one of his acquaintances had called to the house on the plausible pretext of getting his new address to resume some business contact with him. She vaguely recollected him from those far off sociable days. At first Martin had seemed impressive with his charming, confident smile and dark business suit, his Mercedes parked ostentatiously in front of the gate and blocking it. After her innocent, hospitable offer of a coffee or a drink – 'Just the one!' - he had begun to call in regularly, although it was during the daytime, in the late afternoon, she attributing this to his flexible work hours. Martin eventually revealed that he, too, was divorced but was sharing a house in Sutton with a nurse for years, five years in fact.

'The house is up for sale now,' he had told her one afternoon as he helped himself to another cup of coffee from the rarely used cafetiere and snatched a couple of biscuits from the plate, giving his backside a wriggle in the armchair to settle himself more comfortably.

'Sutton? Oh well: you'll make a killing then,' Clare had said, using one of David's phrases.

'Well actually *I* won't,' he had given a bark of a laugh. 'The house belongs to Martha. We're going our separate ways now.' After a slight hesitation, he had added in a more intimate tone of voice: 'As a matter of fact I'm on the lookout for a similar arrangement.'

She had then become aware that he was eyeing not just her, but her possessions, her rooms, for he would follow her into the kitchen and back, his eyes roaming around as if taking an inventory. This blatant intention had sent a shard of ice to her heart but she remained polite, aimed a few more casual questions to gather more information and became convinced of his sinister motive. Now it made sense to her why he had said each visit: 'It must be lonely for you...'. She determined to extricate herself from this man for she had just noticed his shoes were unpolished and he had not shaved that morning. And why was the nurse – Martha - selling the house? she wondered. She had managed to get him to leave without giving any response, as if she hadn't heard, taking refuge in her announcement that she had to get the dinner for her daughter and son who would be home from work shortly. As he was leaving, his charming grin had begun to seem decidedly sleazy.

Moss got home before Louise that evening, sniffing the air appreciatively – 'Hmm...cottage pie...scrumptious!' - and found her peering intently through the net curtains in the sitting room, her hand to her throat, toying absently with her beads, almost driven to a conviction that Martin was lurking out there somewhere, in his car, his luggage in the boot, ready to move in.

'Are you expecting someone?' he had asked her. At the sight of his concerned expression, she had crumpled and told him what had happened.

'He said he would call in tomorrow to discuss it – give me time to think about it. I just didn't know what to say, I was so shocked.'

Moss had taken the following afternoon off work. They waited until Martin arrived, Moss indignant at the way he rang the doorbell twice, putting undue pressure on it. He snatched the front door open, grimly amused by the double take in Martin's eyes as he stepped out onto the front porch step.

'Ah, hi. I've come to see Clare,' Martin had said amiably.

'She's out,' Moss had lied. 'I understand you're looking to rent a place. We've no vacant rooms here,' and began to walk down the path towards the gate, Martin automatically retreating. Without another word he got into his car and Moss watched him drive off, memorising the registration number which he jotted down as soon as he got back into the hall, satisfying his appetite for details, for evidence, just in case. Clare's relief was heartfelt.

'I feel such a fool,' she had said with a weak smile.

'*He's* the fool,' he had grinned, then added in a dramatic tone 'The brazen cheek of him anyway! C'mon, I'll get us a glass of sherry.'

That night Moss had dispatched an email to his father outlining the incident resulting in a lengthy phone call from him the next evening, one that had put Clare at ease, and made her cheeks pink, and the tiny smile playing about her lips.

CHAPTER 7

Clare felt irresistibly drawn to Moss's room several times during those April weeks and not without an obscure sense of trespass. By the Monday morning of his last week at the bank she was struck by the change in the atmosphere of the room: most of the plastic bags containing his belongings had disappeared; a few items of clothing were slung carelessly over the back of a chair, the paintings and framed prints of the Dutch masters had been removed from the walls leaving pale ghostly shapes in their wake. These were now assembled against the wall by the door, awaiting their relocation, most of them wrapped in newspaper, a couple with fabric and secured with string. Two cardboard boxes containing the last of his precious books lay stranded on the carpeted floor. She glanced down at their spines, the titles and authors obscure to her, puzzled by the Garfield cartoon books amid tomes of philosophical content and David's worn copy of the Book of Common Prayer, a relic from his Cambridge origins. Inspecting her absent son's life in this manner was like trying to size up a stranger and the results were inconclusive. His radio alarm clock with its glowing red digits was still in place on the bedside locker, but she knew it was just a matter of time before he would be gone away forever.

For a woman who yearned more for gratefulness than love, Clare was now in a predicament. In the years when David was at the height of his career as a stockbroker, both of them intent on the limelight of social scene success, she would indulge in the need to know that someone was grateful to her, under a compliment. After the bestowing of a dinner party, a lunch, the delivery of a gift for some special occasion, she had developed the habit of being on the alert for the telephone to ring with some recipient gushing effusively – 'Thank you *very* much Clare, *so* kind of you…'. But it was not kindness that motivated her but rather a keen desire to keep up the pace, to score well in her social milieu.

A sudden noise in the street jolted her out of her thoughts and she went to stand by the window veiled in white net curtains of a plain pattern, but could see nothing unusual. The garden below was filled with a stock of shrubs and lavender bushes with a neatly-trimmed hedge between the neighbouring gardens. Louise's red car gleamed conspicuously in the driveway, the gates closed over. Apart from the morning and evening hum of rush hour traffic, Lime Tree Road was otherwise quiet. She felt safe in her settled world but a frown fastened itself to her consciousness as her thoughts turned to the future and what it would be like without Moss, his altered room feeling somehow unwelcome. His burgeoning independence seemed thief-like, robbing her of his duty to be thankful to her for providing a comfortable home and nourishing meals although twice a week at least he would avail of the bank's canteen on certain days in accordance with the menu: 'They do a great chicken curry on Tuesdays!' he would declare, or 'Lasagne tomorrow,' rubbing his hands together gleefully. His breakfast hardly counted as it rarely deviated from a cup of tea and a slice of toast before he set off to the bus stop at least half an hour before Louise. After being conveyed into the city centre he would go to Bewley's Café on Westmoreland Street for a more substantial meal: 'Smoked rashers on toast – there is a heaven!' and a read of the newspaper, arriving at his desk just before nine. It dawned on her that he was in fact hardly ever at home during daytime hours, often going to his Library Club for dinner. But he was usually home on Sundays for the lunch hour meal of roast lamb or beef, his enjoyment evidenced by a hearty appetite and his usual 'Delicious mum...the best!', mimicking David's accent. There were also his frequent weekends away in Wexford. The sight of salmon steaks in the fridge on Friday evenings was the signal that Moss was off to his mobile home in Curlew Cove. The fridge light would reveal two pink cutlets on a white square dish covered over with cling film, and, stacked on an adjacent plate, a packet of smoked rashers, a carton of large, free range eggs, the glint of the gold wrapping on half a pound of butter contrasting with her easy maintenance margarine spread in its small plastic tub. Another sign was the foreign presence of a paper bag emblazoned with an unfamiliar baker's name containing croissants and a baguette which he would deposit next to the toaster upon the kitchen counter top. His departure time was unpredictable - sometimes he left late on Friday evening to avoid the worst of the traffic or the weather, otherwise he would rise before six o'clock on Saturday morning, leaving no trace of the buttered croissant smeared with strawberry jam and consumed with a mug of coffee, then set off with his hoard of luxuries, returning late on Sunday night. Clare gave a sigh of acknowledgement as she realised that he was now justified in withdrawing his monthly contribution to the household expenses, a sum she referred to as his keep, seeing her role of hotelier providing bed space for a set price slipping away. Now Moss owed her nothing, no bed space, no meals, no utility bills. She wondered how he would cope with his expenses over in Dawn View and realized that he would most likely manage very well despite that fact that he would be out of a job although this needled her and added to the freight within. We could rent out his room, she supposed, something Elaine would encourage, take in a foreign student, vaguely remembering reading somewhere about a shortage of accommodation for students. Then she instantly dismissed the idea for Louise would not like having a stranger under their roof, as was demonstrated long ago by her visible agitation when Sarah Mortimer, her much younger cousin – Andrew's daughter - from Cambridge, came over to Dublin for a brief visit. Such incidents were dealt a quick emotional burial, as if nothing had happened, although Clare would avert her eyes from Moss's quizzical look whenever he tried to encourage an airing of such matters. It occurred to her that she should have made the effort to visit Sarah more often since her surprise move over to Ireland with her husband Gerald - when was it? only five years ago. After all, Sarah's mother died when Sarah was only seven, Andrew grief stricken for years, according to David. But she's done very well for herself, she thought, her conscience slightly salved by the memory of a visit she had once made to them, responding to an invitation to lunch in Dalkey, in their house which they had renovated into a beautiful home with an art gallery attached to it. The visit was a complete success as Moss had accompanied her, admitting to herself that he could always be relied upon to do the right thing in such circumstances. And there was that daytime visit from Sarah one sunny summer's day when she was 'just passing by!'

To distract herself, she wandered into Louise's room to the rear of the house and looked approvingly at the tidiness of it. Her daughter's gratefulness was accounted for by her never having rebelled, by conforming, without question, to the status quo although she forgave her for failing to call her brother by his proper name Morris. Her diligent attention to her room, appreciative consumption of regular meals and her predictable habits pleased her: she would fill the kettle at exactly eight o'clock in the evenings when their favourite television soap opera came to another suspenseful end. Clare tried as usual to block from her mind the suspicion – already alluded to by Moss – that her daughter's effective weekend housework was a skilful ploy to avoid going out and socializing, in fact to be so physically occupied that she could give the impression of leading a busy and productive life, which she did in many respects but the quest for a satisfying or contented life or attitude to life was absent. Clare, ever protective, shut out her son's verdict and opted to witness Louise's life trundle along unexamined and change or the threat of change was regarded with fearful suspicion and dealt the defensive hand of stubborn resistance.

With the departure of Moss and Louise to their respective work destinations on weekday mornings, Clare would bask in the security of their employed states. She regarded workplaces as cocoons for this had been her own happy experience of the office she had worked in as a secretary with a firm of accountants until she married David. And so she assumed that they were safe, even protected from the world by being occupied in established institutions, as if a job guaranteed exemption from risk or danger. She had been mystified by Moss's decision to become a trade union representative during his seventh year as a bank official, cringing when she read a report in the evening newspaper quoting his warning of an impending strike, one that did not materialise, further reports confirming a settlement of the dispute after lengthy negotiations. Even more puzzling to her was his subsequent promotion to the rank of supervisor some years later, for had he not rocked the boat that people often referred to, caused some sort of embarrassing fuss? A sudden shiver sent her off downstairs to make her customary cup of coffee and relieve the chill on her skin caused by the disruptive evidence of Moss's new life. She wondered how to impart such news to relatives and friends in such a way that she would save face, the shame of having a son no longer traditionally employed beginning to sink in. Those vital words 'Out working' held within them messages of the utmost importance to her. It also kept them out of the house all day long which pleased her enormously for she relished in having the place to herself, her adult offspring functioning partly as security guards returning for night duty, Moss diligently checking the windows and doors, then setting the alarm against the dangers of the dark hours before retiring to his bed before midnight.

As she sipped her coffee at the kitchen table, and bit into a chocolate biscuit, feeling slightly guilty at such covert indulgence, such illicit pleasure, Clare's sense of respectability was yet again called into question: her son was defecting from the security of employment *and* from the family home. She would have to pay a price, she reasoned, although she was unsure how this would manifest itself. She dismissed the sound investment he had made, overlooking the prestigious locality that was Sandymount with its celebrated postal address of Dublin 4, the same as Donnybrook. She remembered her sole visit there, when Moss had declared the house ready again for habitation. Her brother James had persuaded her to accompany them to take a look around before the tenants moved in and she went along, amused by how animated James became at the prospect of looking at a property, a gleeful smile playing about his lips. While James and Moss had enthused about the charm of the house, the design, the repairs, the period features, the new décor, the furniture, the hidden landing, all she could recall with clarity, apart from the chilly air of the unoccupied rooms, was the colour of the front door: a bold and objectionable bright yellow. Her own door was mahogany – Why did he not follow my example? She gave a deep sigh: now he has chosen to live among his tenants, strangers, strange people. At nineteen years of age she had moved straight from the family home in the midlands town of Mullingar to the respectability of James's red brick terraced house in Drumcondra which she shared with him during her secretarial days and until marriage to David facilitated the seamless transfer over to the house he had bought for them in Clontarf. She regarded inhabitants of flats as transient, homeless types with shady backgrounds, incapable of cooking a decent meal, most likely drawing the dole. The economic boom had not altered such notions, fixed in her mind in a more secretive, emotionally clandestine era. Another sigh escaped from her mouth and she broke her routine by making more coffee and extracting another chocolate biscuit from the tin. Her mood lifted slightly as she drained her extra cup and savoured the sweetness of the chocolate, for it felt like an act of defiance. Instead of spending the rest of the morning doing mundane chores, she set off to the conservatory for a read of her library book.

CHAPTER 8

Cosseted by the house and the quiet established neighbourhood, Clare gave little thought to how Louise spent her workdays although she was given a detailed, earnestly delivered bulletin over the carefully prepared evening meal, but in a format that did not reach her, and about people that were meaningless to her, people that she was unlikely ever to encounter. In her eyes Louise had won the ultimate possession: not a husband but a job, permanent and secure, in a substantial insurance firm in the city centre. She interpreted her daughter's reports as acceptance, even graduation, into such an important and busy world, a world she imagined was filled with nice, efficient people, her mind blocking out any items on the report that signalled problems. Once she heard the front door close with its familiar clunk each morning, she had no further interest in Louise's work destination - an extensive open plan office with battleship grey partitions, a sea of serious, mainly female faces focussed glassily upon computer screens. The frenzied clicking of keyboards added to the background hum of printers, copiers, fax machines, the trill of extension phones, the odour of ink, data and personal conflicts tingeing the air with something unpleasant as though mutiny was being held at bay. Each working morning Louise would claim her desk which was located below a tiny window in a corner partition shared with her colleagues Cara Doyle, Eileen Shaw and Dorothy Green, the fluorescent lights bearing down unflatteringly upon them from the low ceiling. There was a canteen on the floor above, but at the coffee and lunch breaks, Louise, Eileen and Cara would move their chairs obediently over to Dorothy's desk, automatically gravitating to her patch, silently capitulating to her domineering nature. Between sips of coffee or tea and the nibbling of biscuits guarded in a tin by Cara, the dissection of the latest soap opera episode would take place followed by a session of tittle-tattle, their mouths relieving themselves of scathing criticisms and speculations, usually about other colleagues, the managers a favourite target of their collective ire.

Long assimilated into such a mindset with its strict codes of behaviour, Louise still suffered from pangs of conscience and bouts of confusion for she had been subject to certain errors of judgment over the years, potentially lethal ones such as confiding her financial health in her colleagues and her intention of buying a house of her own. 'It's well for some,' was the response, uttered almost in unison, their expressions hard. They had made no further comment about it, changing the subject with brutal transparency whenever she mentioned her house hunt, or tried to show them a brochure of one she had viewed, and so she learned to censor any other positive news reports. She would exit the drab building around half past five, emerging into the fresh air at the end of the day, squinting at the natural light, feeling dismayed whenever it rained, delivering a scowl at mild or calm weather, indifferent to the vista of a golden sunset as she made her way to her bus stop through the crowded city streets. Her eyes were habitually downcast for she felt a disquieting emptiness when the working day was over, the liberation into free time overtaken by the furrowing of her brow as she intently contemplated the next day's tasks. She felt a shadow of gloom cloak her on Fridays as the day signalled the demise of a regulated routine, presenting a blank space of time to be urgently filled with some other activity. Wary of alcohol and social interaction, she did not share the collective sigh of relief that marked the end of the working week and avoided the ranks of those urgently seeking inebriation. She would detach herself from the customary Friday exodus as her colleagues were disgorged from the office building, some of them fleeing to the pub as if running for cover, while she hurried off to her bus stop. She compromised by substituting office work with housework which began in earnest early Saturday morning with a fervent devotion to restoring perfect order to her bedroom so that it managed to look unoccupied, like a spare room or impersonal guest room. She would put everything away into drawers and fitted wardrobes, dust the sparse decorative items and return them to their shelf in perfect symmetry. She kept the window ledge bare, the view of the garden through the net curtain revealing a lawn, a variety of shrubs and rose bushes growing around the perimeter walls and a pear tree at the back, the rotary clothes line a displeasing blight on the miniature green landscape. Clare, in an effort to camouflage her own redundant role had secured the task of supervising the washing machine with her daughter's weekly work load circling inside, the wool cycle long ago dismissed with doubtful expressions, instructions carefully scrutinised, resulting in all woollen items being washed heroically by hand in the kitchen sink. Moss's laundry would be next, the items pegged neatly onto the side of the line allocated to his clothes as if to lessen the danger of them wandering into his sister's territory by a careless flick of breeze. With these tasks out of the way Clare would turn the dial to a rinse cycle just to console herself that the machine was cleansed of any residual grime. He was in the habit of strolling down to the clothesline to carefully wipe the lenses of his glasses with the leg of his cotton boxer shorts, or the tail of a white cotton shirt. He would then hold the glasses up to the light, return them to his face with an imperceptible nod of approval, as if to confirm a better result than that produced by the bland grey chamois that usually nestled inside a new spectacle case. 'Why can't he use a tissue like everyone else?' Louise would wonder aloud to Clare as she watched, with clenched jaw, from the kitchen window. The navy overalls he wore for maintenance jobs in his Sandymount house had long ago been banned and Moss, ever ready to find alternatives, washed them in the machine in the utility room there and hung them on a clothes horse in the greenhouse to dry.

Clare sometimes went out on Saturday afternoons, to visit Anne or Jean, returning in time for the weekly treat of sausages, fried eggs and chips that Louise prepared at half past five. Her Saturday evenings were usually taken care of by the ritual of Mass at half past seven which she attended with her mother, both having more or less shaken off years of guilt about the convenience of having Sunday mornings free of the obligation.

But often they gave it a miss, adapting to the new secular world, as Moss had done long ago, Louise then spending the remainder of the evening in front of the television or studying the estate agents' brochures if she had viewed houses in the afternoon. The occasional invitation to tea at Elaine's came through and Clare, as if responding to being served with a writ, would set off in the car around five, her expression condemned, knowing that Louise's claim of being tired or having a headache was an excuse to avoid the endless accounts of her cousins' lives, her aunt's triumphant emphasis on their achievements, their great careers, their exceptional children. She felt mildly guilty at leaving her alone to prepare her solitary meal on such occasions but knew that she was sensible about such matters and especially about security, her safety assured by the alarm and the locked doors.

Moss tended to make himself scarce on Saturdays having long ago discerned Louise's twisted pleasure in spoiling his lie in with her noisy household tasks. But he too had established routines to follow, although he was unpredictable in the evenings: sometimes he would stay in his room reading or watching his television, or he would head off to one of the local pubs or into town somewhere and was inconsistent in his time of return, and sparse with details, although he was usually back before midnight. Sometimes he would bring back a single of chips wrapped in creamy paper and consume them with buttered bread and a pot of tea at the kitchen table. Seduced by the tantalising scent, Louise would abandon her television screen and join him for a cup of tea, Moss immediately offering to share the chips, saying in his affable manner: 'Go on sis, take a few...' but she usually refused out of a fear of indigestion, trying to hide her irritation at his ability to eat so late at night.

With the business of Saturday behind her, Louise would give in to a traditional quiet Sunday, as if oblivious to the secularised spending spree taking place in the outlets now open seven days a week. After the substantial lunch, she would spend the afternoon reading the Sunday newspaper supplements then watch a film while Clare would go for a snooze in her room or in her favourite conservatory chair. Occasionally they would both go for a walk around four o'clock, returning before five, their cheeks glowing from the sea air. But it was a day Louise disliked, a punctuation mark that stabbed into her routine-driven lifestyle. From tea-time onwards, she was consumed with a combination of relief and restlessness as she ironed her work blouses in her bedroom, arranging them on individual hangers, ensuring that they faced the same direction, tilted slightly to the left, one for each weekday. With her shoes polished, tights and underwear assembled in the drawer, each day's clothing accounted for, she would spend the evening in front of the television again, her concentration impaired, her mind already in the office as she anticipated the work week ahead. She would take to bed early only to wake up almost hourly to check the time on the digital clock and to ensure that the illuminated alarm dot was still in evidence. On Monday mornings she would awake around five, vaguely assured that everything was back to normal in her world, a mild tension in her head signalling the headache that would probably follow later on, the painkillers already installed in her handbag.

Clare, oblivious to such concerns in the other bedroom, would prop herself up on the pillows, on the right hand side by the window, in the vacant space where David used to lie, as if keeping it warm for his return and would read for while, absorbed in the hectic lives of men and women whose fates were guaranteed a good outcome in the end. She enjoyed such nights for in the morning, her own routine would resume. Louise would bring her a cup of tea at half past seven; she would remain in bed until she knew that they had both exited the house, Louise the last to leave, then she would get up, wash, dress and go down to the kitchen, the detritus of their breakfast a welcome sight to her, giving her a task to accomplish in the wake of Louise's weekend cleansing of the house. Her day would progress benignly but routinely, with the planning and preparations of meals for the week, the live radio phone-in show after her frugal lunch linking her to the troubled, burdened world that seemed to lurk ominously beyond her mahogany front door.

Chapter 9

As he stood back to admire the coat of paint he had rolled onto the sitting room walls, the sash windows open to full capacity, Moss realized how fortunate he was with his current tenants. In fact all of the people who had been drawn to the house since he began letting the flats were carefully vetted by an agent that specialised in securing quiet accommodation for discerning tenants. The most memorable was Veronique Ash, the first occupant of Flat 2 with its garden aspect. A woman of means, she had devoted her time to research in various libraries and had published a book and numerous papers on her subject. He remembered her as an intensely private person, answering the door to him reluctantly, creating a no-entry barrier with her presence, a pair of small pale blue eyes in a thin pale face framed by wisps of light brown hair pushing him back. On rare occasions essential maintenance had to be negotiated with the art of diplomacy on his part in order to gain access to the flat where he was kept under her gaze, conscious of her wary body posture yet intrigued by the brief yet insightful glimpse into her scholarly life. The pleasant clutter of her papers, books and possessions gave an impression of peaceful contentment that was clearly perceived at risk in the presence of a landlord. His reassuring manner over the years had made little impact on such reticence and when, after seven years, she had revealed in her whispering manner that she was leaving to return to Australia, he had felt disappointed, not because she was marrying – a surprise as there had been no sign of a male presence or the reassuring effect of one – but that he was losing such a reliable tenant. He had immediately written out her deposit cheque and given it to her without bothering to inspect the flat, waived the amount outstanding on her electricity bill and wished her well, still failing to elicit a smile from her pallid lips. On the day following her departure he had braced himself before entering the flat to assess the wear and tear, apprehensively unlocking the door with one of the keys she had left in an envelope on the hall table for him, formally addressed to Mr M. Mortimer, the potent absence of a note like a spectre as he swung the door wide open, holding his breath. To his utter astonishment she had left it immaculate. He had wandered slowly through the rooms, sensing the chill hollowness that descends on unoccupied premises, taking in the sight of a sturdy blue bowl in the centre of the living room table, neatly folded tea towels on the kitchen counter top, a new bar of lavender soap in the white ceramic dish on the draining board. Trancelike, he had ascended the narrow stairs and discovered another fresh bar of soap in the sweet-smelling bathroom, a clean yellow and white striped bath towel hanging on the rail. The bedroom had revealed folded covers stacked neatly at the bottom of the bed stripped of its sheets and a couple of new pillows were perched against the dark wooden headboard. He had squeezed them, as if making sure they were real, intrigued by Veronique's unexpected gesture and feeling momentarily ashamed by his presumption that the detritus of so many years would have been left behind for him to clean up. He had then prepared the flat for the next occupant: he had the chimney swept, applied a fresh coat of paint to the walls, ceilings, doors and skirting boards, rearranged some of the furniture and completed the work by laying down a new rug in the living room.

Within a month Madeline Stewart, dispatched to Dawn View by the agent, had arrived on the doorstep claiming to be seeking mouse-quiet accommodation, explaining that she often worked night shifts as a nurse in a home for the elderly that was located nearby - a five minute stroll, Moss had figured, familiar with its location. She had assured him that the only noise she produced would come from her sewing machine as she liked to make clothes of her own design in her spare time. He had liked her immediately, not merely for her long chestnut hair and slightly glamorous air but that she turned out to be far more approachable than Veronique, responding swiftly to a knock on her door which she would open widely, decisively. It had seemed a magnanimous act after years of witnessing the figure peering out through a cautious chink. With Madeline, or Maddie as she preferred to be called, there was no second guessing. Her confidence seemed almost overwhelming compared to that of her scholarly predecessor, along with her hospitable offer of tea when he was in the house doing his Saturday morning chores.

Such a welcome contrasted sharply with that of Donal Walshe, who lived in the adjacent flat. It usually took several firm knocks on the door of Flat 1 to secure a reaction and when it did open, hesitantly, it would reveal a tall stout man with thin, receding black hair, a pale complexion despite his outdoor occupation, a small mouth with lips that withheld words, or rationed them out: 'Yes.' 'OK.' 'Fine.' 'Bye.' His expression was guarded, as if he was expecting a visit from intruders that had been held at bay, an expression which prevailed the time when Moss had arrived within a day in response to a complaint that his electric cooker was not working. Accompanied by Finn, his dependable handyman who lived on the Strand Road, he was admitted to the flat and Finn set to work in the kitchen, Donal hovering in the background, looking uneasy, as if fearful that the appliance would be confiscated and yet prepared to make a show of indignation if it was. With the job swiftly completed they had retreated, Moss affably reminding him as usual to call him if there were any further problems. 'OK.' Donal had said. 'Fine.' The delivery of those two slender words seemed to betray an imperative that the sentiment behind a routine thank you had be to hidden away, as if mannerly utterances might imply weakness, give a wrong impression, Moss smirking at the look on Finn's face as the door closed abruptly behind them.

Yet with his landlord safely out of the way, his frying pan back on the cooker, his fillet steak sizzling appetizingly, Donal had felt twinges of pleasure but tried to suppress them for he was reluctant to admit to himself how much he liked his flat, had in fact become deeply attached to it. He had endured a challenging rite of passage to get to it after he left his provincial home town, never to return, the town etched in his memory as a place where the heat of the sun had failed to reach the secretive hearts of its more sombre inhabitants including those of his family of origin, a clan who abhorred the concept of encouragement and success.

He had turned twenty one when he made his getaway and arrived in Dublin city, staying in a basic but charming lodging house in Glasnevin where he could avail of regular meals and where the friendly proprietor seemed immune to his taciturn manner. He eventually got work as a bus driver which he found satisfying but when he set about looking for a flat, he found himself entering a surreal and curious world. His search led him into a variety of dwellings, the worst being what he privately regarded as the suicide flats which were installed in spacious Georgian and Victorian houses where the interiors had been carved up into box-like units to contain human beings. During the viewing of a bedsit, he had spotted a lidless matchbox filled with rat poison positioned in the corner of the tiny attic room and had drawn the landlord's attention to the tiny box by pointing to it and eliciting the comment as he gestured the room size with his large hands: 'Not big enough for a rat. OK for a mouse, maybe.' The landlord had merely shrugged, his sense of humour long ago vanished, weary of the transience of tenants, blind to the frayed dingy carpet which the vermin would traverse unseen, but not necessarily unheard, in the dark nocturnal hours.

When he moved into a larger bedsit in a house with a view of an attractive Georgian streetscape, Donal saw how rat-like human beings could be when packed close together, scurrying around industriously and mating indiscriminately. A variety of sounds filtered in from the neighbouring flats at all times, many of them unidentifiable. Lying in his worn, narrow bed he would listen to the rhythmic creaking of the mattress in the room above and the moans of its occupants, oblivious to the audience tuned in to their private antics as he leered murkily in the gloom below them. He decided that Sartre had a point, that hell truly was other people. He endured six months of such a place during which time he was plagued with incentives to leave: he could forgive the shabbiness of the peeling décor and sagging chairs in the fine old room that began its own existence in another era but not the meagre partitioned walls, the other tenants who seemed afraid to sleep at night, who cowered in front of their television sets or clattered about their rooms, self-absorbed, aching with loneliness yet terrified to make contact with their neighbours unless exceptional circumstances drew them out such as the incident in one of the basement flats.

'He committed suicide,' announced the young, waiflike creature who lived in the room across the hallway, opposite his own, her door wide open to reveal another dingy interior. 'He was only twenty three' she had added. He noticed her door was usually open, or ajar. She had seemed at home in that environment although he felt repelled by her overly alert eyes. After that incident he became desperate to leave and eventually found a suburban townhouse to share with another man of similar age, a good move he knew. He settled at last into his work and living in reasonable contentment for a number of years until that house was put up for sale and he was on the hunt again, although the owner had given him three months notice. By that time he had changed jobs, joining a new landscaping firm that had secured lucrative contracts for the grounds and gardens of apartment and commercial buildings in localities close to the city centre, a portent of the tiger economy. Remembering with revulsion the bedsit experience, his quest to find a quiet house had become paramount, even obsessive as he began his search, wondering if such places existed. He considered buying a place of his own, calculating his mortgage options, but such a choice did not guarantee peace as he learned the night he had spent with a transient girlfriend. Shauna lived in a newly built apartment block in the city centre where a sign marked Luxury Apartments was erected inside the main gates. Sleeping with Shauna in his arms long after their return from the pub, both sedated from alcohol and lovemaking, he awoke suddenly, altered to noises, hearing thuds and muffled voices close by. Suspecting a break-in, he snuck out of bed and crept into the living room still illuminated by occasional lamps, then padded cautiously down the hall to check the entrance door where he paused, momentarily puzzled. All seemed to be in order. Then the pulse of pop music at night club intensity filtered through from somewhere and it slowly dawned on him that the sounds were coming from the neighbouring apartments, including the hollow staccato clatter of female heels across the bare wooden flooring above. He returned to bed, noting the small hour of three thirty, but slept badly, the counting of sheep replaced by calculations of Shauna's mortgage payments for such a poorly constructed home and inconsiderate neighbours. Over breakfast she had made a weak pretence of not having noticed the noise intrusion before, her eyes averted as she splashed milk onto her cereal.

'Well, I'm used to it y'know? I mean people have to live somewhere. That's *life* Donal,' she had snapped, irritated at being found out.

'No,' he had said in his measured way. '*That's* mediocrity.'

The sympathy of Barry Keane, his new boss, had been roused when he saw him scouring the papers for a flat during his lunch breaks. Barry took a night's sleep for granted in the semi-detached structure in which he lived with his wife and two children and where sounds from the amiable neighbours were those of routine family life. One of his contacts came up with Moss's agent and within a matter of days, Donal set off after work with an appointment to view Flat 1, 11 Dawn View in Sandymount, an area he had overlooked, feeling apprehensive as he made his way along the quiet street. Four doorbells on the grid surprised him for the house seemed large enough for twice that amount but he reckoned that this was because he was safely out of rat renting territory. When the yellow door opened to reveal Moss Mortimer he had presumed him to be a decorator by trade as he was attired in paint-spattered navy bib and brace overalls, in a style not unlike his own. He entered the hall where newspapers and sheets were spread out on some of the tiles to accommodate a large can of paint, trays for rollers and brushes, a step ladder arranged for access to the wall around the front door and fanlight, the other walls already covered in a soothing rose-white. When Moss showed him round the flat he tried to hide his astonishment at its size, its comfort and quality, his characteristic presumption of the hidden agenda convincing him that there was a mistake, a catch somewhere, a drawback lying in wait for him, the reasonable rent and a seemingly reasonable landlord evoking suspicion in him. Moss showed him the utility room which contained a washing machine – 'Oh yeh, it's grand... works fine.' Then he saw the long garden to the rear where he spied a patch ideal for growing vegetables, visualising raspberry canes, sugar peas, lettuces, and maybe coriander and parsley in the greenhouse. He accepted the flat with concealed optimism, agreeing to pay the deposit and sign the lease the next day when he would receive the keys. He was in by the weekend, pausing to register astonishment at the envelope on the hall table with his name printed clearly on it in blue ink. He opened it suspiciously and extracted a green rent book, his deposit and first month's rent neatly written in. He settled quickly into a new routine, sleeping deeply at last, sinking into sheets over a clean mattress like a man who had returned from a long and arduous journey, for it was the quietest, most charming house that he had ever lived in.

But now, almost five consistently quiet years on, Donal noticed that Moss's car was parked in the driveway with increasing regularity but this, he reasoned, meant preparations for the next tenants, a sighting of Moss in his overalls and the odour of fresh paint a sure sign. After all, the Lombardis had gone back to Italy, having said effusive goodbyes to him – 'Ciao Donal! Ciao! - even though he had studiously avoided them, as he did Maddie next door. Apart from his routine morning exit for work, he would go on the alert for the sound of her door closing whenever he wished to go out. And when it did, he would stand at the living room window, listening attentively as she left the house and shutting the front door in her discreet but decisive way. He would then watch her make her brisk walk towards the gate, then wait a moment or two before making his own exit, such strategies leaving him safe to keep himself to himself. He discounted Karl Weissman, not merely for the annex Ph.D after his name on some of his postal items, but that he seemed to use his flat only occasionally, making a rare but jovial appearance, the stairs creaking dramatically from the sudden impact of his footsteps. It seemed to Donal that the world Karl returned from was a satisfying, even amusing place, Flat 4 functioning as some sort of pit stop before moving on again. Well for him, being able to afford a flat he hardly ever stays in, he would think disconsolately, gritting his teeth. *Well for some...*

CHAPTER 10

With his departure date looming, Moss became intensely occupied at work putting his files and desk in order, his intrigued and well-wishing close colleagues and fellow union representatives treating him to lunch or a drink after work. His boss Adrian Connolly, confided that he, too, would soon be going, hanging on until his fifty-fifth birthday, hinting at an agreement that would set him free to pursue other opportunities. Moss already felt mildly nostalgic for his office, a spacious elegant room on the first floor where tall Georgian windows let in natural light much of the time to the background hum of city centre traffic. The desk he was about to forfeit was adjacent to a pure white marble fireplace with an effective electric mock flame fire that cheered him especially on overcast days when the light beyond the windows gave off an unnatural but atmospheric hue that helped him concentrate on his work.

His replacement – for his job was not yet automated or farmed out to a company that would handle the increasing number of defaulters – was Thomas Murphy, a short, thin man of thirty who was introduced to him on the Monday of his final week, for the handover, 'Ah now, call me Tom!' and to lay claim to the desk by the Friday. As he appraised him, Moss was surprised by his demeanour for it was a striking contrast to that of the modernised, well-groomed, image-conscious confident new millennium breed of young men, noting his scuffed light brown shoes untouched by polish, a stingy oiliness about the infrequently washed dull brown hair. Adept at computing, Tom's sleazy telephone manner implied a dire, uncompromising outcome for customers, his expression relishing the power he would soon have to influence the repossession of houses. As he briefed him on the procedures and tasks, Moss was ruefully aware that both he and Adrian were members of a near extinct species, the gentlemen bankers of mythology. Yet his relief at abandoning ship was immense as Friday loomed even closer – the disillusioned ranks among his colleagues would neither sink nor swim but would cling onto the meagre driftwood that kept them afloat, never to be certain if they would reach a safe harbour, moving precariously into a future that no longer concerned him for he was becoming a former employee. And he knew that any good news that filtered back about such a species was absorbed with a particular kind of discomfort by some of the workers, those hapless members of the organization's cliques of moody men and women whom he regarded as begrudgers, or envy mongers - a term he had heard Kevin use. He did not willingly seek out their company over the years unless it was on union business but would gatecrash one of their tables in the packed canteen occasionally. He had observed the way they relieved their pain by a combination of overt and covert scoffing and sneering or, alternatively, feigned indifference, depending on the offensive news item. He remembered the time when he witnessed visual evidence of how success struck them with a terrible blow. One morning in the crowded canteen, while he was seated at their table, Jack Shannon - a misfit, celebratory type - joined them, squeezing into the spare chair next to Moss and, after taking a gulp from his tea cup, unwittingly produced a copy of a newly published adventure novel for teenagers written by Frank Doyle, a former loans clerk, along with a photocopied newspaper review. Jack had handed both items around in a jubilant manner, as if providing evidence of life beyond the office. Feeling pleased for Frank, gone at least two years by then, Moss had watched the begrudgers' reaction as he sipped his coffee and bit into his buttered fruit scone: a predictable round of shrugs of apparent boredom, lips pursed in an effort to indicate irrelevance as the book was quickly passed around, unopened, as if it might singe their fingers. They expressed their disappointment by withholding approval, affecting disinterest as their narrowed eyes scanned the text on the photocopied page for negative words, hungry for a bad review, one of them emitting a belittling 'Ah sure what would he know? He doesn't even have kids!' to the grim agreement of the others.

Moss wondered why they had made the choice to inhabit such a fragile, murky world where their hunger after failure or perceived failure in others was a constant force, gnawing greedily at their minds. They would regard his departure as a failure of sorts, he knew. He had resigned. They would approve of the word resignation; it implied defeat, a significant loss, or a loss of face, the glamour of transferring like the head-hunted to another place of employment satisfyingly absent. In fact Patrick O'Grady had remarked 'Retiring are we, Moss?' as he passed him, leering, in the corridor one morning, although he was somewhat taken aback by Mareid Moore's acidly smug 'Mid-life crisis Moss?' as he exited the building at lunchtime that same day. He had read somewhere long ago that other workplaces were similarly populated, even overpopulated, and so to withstand such influence, he had squirreled away his soul for safekeeping over the years, determined to avoid becoming such a demoralised and fragmented being. Yet he was still a customer of the bank and would continue to be one, he reflected now, although he had redeemed his mortgage, quietly, without reference, six months ago. A week ago at the canteen table, a colleague asked him how he would continue paying it '…without a job to go to!'

'I don't have a mortgage,' Moss deadpanned. 'I redeemed it ages ago,' eliciting a disappointed 'Jaysus, Moss; you're one dark feckin' horse, aren't ye?'

His last day of employment began as a seasonal end of April day that progressed with sudden sprinklings of rain, blasts of radiant sunshine that were obliterated by moody grey clouds. By late afternoon, the day settled into a calm phase, as though the weather had exhausted itself. Around ten o'clock that evening, Moss stepped out onto St. Stephen's Green, the celebrations over for him, glowing with delight after the treat to dinner in the Shelbourne by Sam, Adrian, Monica, Jenny and Tom, a large scotch snugly inside him and another left behind on the table as evidence of the slow pace of his intake, his reluctance to push his limit. He had slid the glass over to Tom with his best wishes just before he left. Feeling touched by their goodwill, he walked along the pavement towards the taxi rank, lugging his briefcase happily, then stopped briefly to pat his jacket and trousers for phone, wallet, keys, listen once again to the crackle of the envelopes containing a cheque, his P45, a book token, then opened his briefcase to take another peek at the fluffy Garfield Jenny had given him. He lined up for a taxi and within minutes was conveyed to Sandymount for it was unthinkable that he would go to Clontarf.

CHAPTER 11

M oss awoke, gave a delighted stretch as he checked the time on his new clock radio, the late hour confirming a good lie-in then reached out his hand to turn it on. The cobalt hue of his peaceful bedroom was immediately filled with the sound of angry voices dramatizing a family living out their lives in the misery of caustic snipes and spiteful arguments splattered with expletives. He continued listening for a while, impressed by the sound effects – fists contacting table tops followed by a violent door slamming leading the characters to a change of scene, the pub, where more spitting anger ensued, the play achieving a convincing picture of malcontent. With a smirk, he pressed the off button, got out of bed, shrugged himself into his dressing gown and set off downstairs, the kitchen pleasantly warm from the overnight storage heating. While waiting for the kettle to boil, he surveyed the range of cups and mugs clustered upon a shelf on the white dresser and chose a scarlet china mug painted with a horoscope motif in black. He dropped an extra tea bag into a yellow teapot, its bulging centre patterned with a row of navy blue pigs as he savoured the colourful diversity after years of the clinical arrangement over at his mother's house where bland was the predominant colour of choice.

As he drank his tea at the white table, he began to write up a list of friends and contacts for notification of his change of address and phone number, placing Valerie de Vries at the top. Then, with a contented yawn, he made his favourite breakfast of scrambled eggs on toast, another pot of tea, more slices of toast to smear with butter and marmalade, and, his appetite sated, went upstairs for a shower. During a careful shave afterwards, he paused to inspect his reflection in the bathroom mirror. A pair of cautious brown eyes regarded him, the solemn expression the result, he presumed, from years of arranging a poker face. He bared his teeth in a manic grin as if getting into training for smiling, smoothed his angular chin with his fingertips, gave his reflection a parting wink and went off to get dressed in casuals and his favourite pair of trainers.

He roamed around the flat for a while, side stepping the unpacked boxes and bags, mentally consigning the contents to their new destinations and visualising the furniture items he intended bringing in and the pieces he would dispose of. He felt the urge to begin more painting, a task he found soothing and appraised the sitting room walls which he had already completed, pleased with the effect of the sea and chrome greens. But this was a Saturday, the first one in May, and he wanted the feel of a weekend off, even though an entire year off spread out before him and he decided to leave the bulk of the unpacking until Monday when he would collect the rest of his belongings in Clontarf where his car was still parked outside his mother's house.

In the spare bedroom, at the front of the house, he found a picture left behind by the Lombardis - a large framed print of a black cat with intense green eyes in a relaxed pose as it lounged amid a cluster of poppy flowers. He removed it, brought it down to the kitchen where he hung it in the place where a calendar had been. He then sat down at the table to admire it, his mind drifting back to the precise moment in time when he felt inspired to move into the flat, that fine summer evening the year before when he had called into Dawn View for one of his routine checks and to carry out a few minor chores. He had strolled around the garden in the balmy air, stopping to gaze appreciatively at the house outlined against a clear sky traced with gold from a glowing sunset, his eyes drawn down to the yellow lamp in the Lombardis kitchen and which emanated another uplifting glow. As he was monitoring the healthy progress of Donal's trays of parsley, dill and coriander in the greenhouse, Georgio had appeared at the door and greeted him warmly, asking him if he had time for a cup of coffee. Moss gave his usual response - 'Ah yes please, Georgio, that'd be very nice', and followed him down the path, amused by the young man's confident swagger in his jeans and leather sandals. He had sat at the kitchen table, feeling the usual wave of pleasure at being invited into the home of such congenial and hospitable company, to be around such joie de vivre. Maria had poured the coffee and placed a box of chocolates in the centre of the table, her long black hair draped over bare shoulders, a necklace of delicate coloured beads reaching the cleft in her breasts, their shape outlined under the flimsy lilac dress that she wore and revealing long, tanned legs, her feet bare. 'Grazie,' he had smiled, raising his cup, listening intently to the sound of their impeccable, pleasantly accented English as they told him about life in Venice where they planned to return in early March the following year. As he sipped his coffee and enjoyed the smooth texture of the dark chocolate in his mouth, he glanced at the garden from time to time. The realization came to him like a filtering, unstoppable dawn, that this was in fact his own house, that he could move into the flat after they had gone, the flat that they were clearly so much at home in. He had kept this idea to himself for the simplicity of it had come to him as a pleasant shock, energising him in a way that raised his hopes as the ideal solution to effecting the kind of change of lifestyle he had been hankering after. He could have moved into his cottage in Wexford, he knew, abandon city life - and this was till an option - but it was the appealing locality that was Sandymount as well as the character and atmosphere of his house that had captivated him that evening and so the following day he had begun to plan.

Now the Lombardis were back in Venice, their safe return confirmed by email. In his reply he promised to forward any residual post to them and thanked Georgio once again for presenting him with his long black leather jacket, one that he had openly coveted – 'Great jacket Georgio...*very* nice!'- to the Italian man's amusement and which now fitted him like a second, almost protective skin, a portent of a favourable transit to his new life. He transferred his gaze from the picture of the cat to the change of address list that he had placed against a vase on the dresser then got up to make himself a cup of coffee, as if marking the anniversary of that significant evening with Maria and Georgio. He enjoyed the sensation that he was now on a long holiday yet he determined that he would not lapse into a creature of complacency and sloth or a recluse like Vincent Flannery who lived in the house opposite. Vincent had abandoned the outside world after the death by suicide of his youngest bother who had passed away in a house in London, a place where he had lived a seemingly charmed life until some private tragedy triggered the drug overdose clinically devised to strike himself out, a letter explaining it all although there was no guarantee that it would ever be understood. Vincent's next door neighbour Orla Brennan had long ago delivered this information to Moss, informing him in her hushed manner as they strolled back from the supermarket at Sandymount Green one Saturday morning, that Vincent ventured out usually under cover of darkness, or in the early morning hours when he went for a stroll through the quieter streets and along the sea front. His sister Lily made regular appearances, parking her car in the driveway, extracting a number of bags from the boot and taking them round to the rear entrance. 'She doesn't stay long,' Orla had told him, 'but at least he's eating well.' The vigilance of such a neighbour should never be underestimated, he mused as he poured milk into his coffee and stirred it slowly. A light smile formed on his mouth as he remembered Orla's report for it also contained her own good deeds: she put Vincent's refuse bin out and wheeled it back to the side passage after collection; she also telephoned him occasionally and the news was overall positive, Moss detecting a very slight disappointment in her tone. It occurred to him that being a recluse had certain advantages: almost total privacy, solitude, self-exemption from the efforts of presenting oneself to the world, although such seclusion would, surely, require admirable endurance in the long term. He had already devised a secret spot beside the front bedroom window to spy on his house, intending to call over at some stage, maybe drop in a note to offer support in an emergency, if required. But Orla had already established such a role, he realized, and, not wishing to invite disharmony by stepping on her toes, he let the idea slip away for the time being.

That afternoon he made a brief trip into town, to Grafton Street, to seek inspiration for new casual clothes, admiring a pair of black leather runners he saw on display behind a spotless windowpane. Scanning the crowds in the bright sunlight, Kevin's seasonal comment 'Ah: no tights! It must be May!' echoed in his mind, for May seemed to mark the time when women discarded their tights - or stockings, he thought with pleasure - to expose bare skin to air that now officially belonged to the summer season. In recent years he noticed how the power of this custom had been diluted by the arrival of fashionable trouser suits and other flexible garments and accessories. But the stalwarts of convention – Why change now? - were unlikely to admit to the discomfort of goose pimples even when breezes tinged with arctic air whipped their shins, despite the fake tan. Perhaps such women found consolation in the lengthening of the days, he thought, imagining their reasoning: the clocks went forward *ages* ago, so it *must* be summertime! Yet the sun did not, could not, at that latitude, deliver the longed-for heat, giving rise to daily analyses and injured but harmless commentary about the weather. During his reconnaissance of the department stores for his own uncomplicated wardrobe he made no purchase but planned to return next week, in the daytime, satisfied at the choices available to him.

By evening time, he settled himself in a chair by the hearth, the fridge and cupboards replenished after a trip to the supermarket, a bottle of beer glistening before him on the low coffee table, his stomach digesting the Singapore fried noodles which he had eaten in the restaurant near the Green around seven o'clock. He perused the newspaper for a while, then cast it aside and idly leafed through a fashion magazine Maria had left behind on the dresser, his eyes drawn to the cleavage and slender, flawless legs of the perfect models. Still hungry for print, he rummaged in a box in the hall and extracted a Nero Wolfe novel and became absorbed in its pages until he was eventually overcome by a wave of fatigue, his eyes dry, his beer bottle empty. He placed the fireguard firmly before the smouldering briquettes, glad of the warmth for in May there was still a distinct chill in the air, especially in the evenings. He contemplated having an early night and made a final cup of tea which he drank at the kitchen table. Afterwards he drew the curtains on the evening twilight and, yawning hugely, set off for the luxury of bed and another read of his book to the sound of soothing jazz playing in the background, the radio dial now changed to Eternity FM, the local community station that broadcast a variety of innovative and entertaining programmes. He eventually put the book aside, lazily turned off the bedside lamp, pressed the off button on the radio and drifted leisurely into slumber.

CHAPTER 12

onal knew that Flat 3 was occupied. There was the occasional odour of cooking, and as he approached the yellow front door upon his return from the pub around eleven, he noticed a sliver of mellow light in the narrow chink in the sitting room curtains. The large gilt framed mirror had disappeared, the one he had seen propped against the wall in the hall before he set off for work that morning to face a busy day supervising his crew as they planted up trees and shrubs in the grounds of a new apartment complex. But it was the sight of Moss's aged Volvo in the driveway that convinced him that his landlord had moved in, by stealth, no doubt gloating at his reflection in the mirror. He retreated into a reverie of doubt-infested thoughts and hidden agenda conspiracies, assuming that Moss had installed himself to upgrade the flats, beginning with the largest. Then he would increase the rent – a sum that would banish him – or else he would sell up and make a fortune. During his coffee break the following day, he reacquainted himself with the flats to let section in the previous evening's newspaper, grunting in dismay at the current rental rates. Barry pointed out, in an effort to reassure him, that Moss sounded like a reasonable fellow and, if anything, he was undercharging.

'Why don't you just ask him straight out what his plans are?' he asked him. But Donal shrugged in response for he could not admit to the discomfort this would cause him, even though it would provide him with instant knowledge. His speculations suddenly ended on Friday evening after his colleague Declan Brady dropped him off at the Green after work. As he wearily made the turn into Dawn View, his steak and mushrooms a pleasing weight in the plastic supermarket bag, his heart plummeted when the saw the Auction sign in the front garden, erected prominently near the gate. The sudden jolt of confusion he felt when he approached number 11 gave way to a relief so profound he felt immobilised, although no change in his

75

expression took place as he realized that the sign emerged from the corner of the garden next door. When he opened the front door, he heard voices and saw Maddie and Moss conversing amicably by the hall table.

'Hello Donal,' Maddie greeted him politely. She was dressed glamorously in a sleek black dress and glossy black high heeled shoes. 'The ESB bills are in' she said flicking her envelope resignedly. 'Actually we were just speculating how much next door will fetch at auction.'

'It'll be outrageous, whatever it goes for,' said Moss.

'So…you're not tempted to sell then?' Maddie asked him pointedly. 'Cash in on the property boom?' she added with an arched brow.

'Ah no. No chance of that,' he replied. 'I love this house. Anyway, it's my pension.' He handed Donal a number of envelopes. 'There you go. Today's post.'

'Thanks.' Donal tucked them under his left armpit, inserted his key into the lock of his flat then turned round stiffly: 'Are you living here for good now?' he blurted out, relief having suspended his reserve and at being spared another upheaval. Before Moss could respond, Maddie exclaimed: 'Oh yes! Isn't it marvellous? If we need any work done we have our landlord right here at our beck and call!' And with a cheerful smile she returned to her flat in a perfume trail, the pulse of her telephone ringing breaking up the conversation as they all retreated into their respective worlds. As soon as his door was closed firmly, the key turned in the lock, Donal allowed himself a can of beer and a thin smile to celebrate the news, then set off for his shower, and afterwards relished his steak and mushroom dinner. By midnight, the smile had long faded into a mild scowl. Well for him, he thought, living rent-free in his own house. In the biggest flat. *It's my pension*', he mimicked scathingly as he got ready for bed. *Well for him…*

CHAPTER 13

The days glided by to a new rhythm as Moss unwound from the tensions which are woven into the body and mind by routine and compounded by the duties and responsibilities of employment. It was a process that left him feeling exhausted, as if coming down with a virus, resulting in him stretching out on the sofa for an afternoon snooze and succumbing to a succession of early nights. The tension that seeped out of his mind and limbs was replaced by an emergent delight at the new expanse of time in his days, and the thrill of being free to direct such time replaced the initial guilt he had felt at such liberty. He began to enjoy the luxury of not having to get up at a particular time, or be obliged to go out to a somewhere wearing a suit all day long. But during that unwinding phase he experienced a worrying pattern of disruptive, unsettled nights when he would awake suddenly, alert and slightly startled, at twenty to seven, the time his alarm had been set for workdays. He would slump back onto the pillows with exhausted relief, hugging the duvet, descending into vivid dreams of being back at the office where he puzzled over reams of printouts of mortgage arrears, or typed in his computer password repeatedly, the screen denying him access. In one of the dreams two emaciated men in oversized dark suits pounced on piles of unfamiliar files scattered over his usually tidy desk and said in a menacing tone: 'Aha Mortimer! Where are the keys? We want those *keys*', while shaking bundles of large cash notes at him, the currency obscure, until he awoke, feeling mildly panic-stricken. He then got up and headed down to the kitchen in search of tea so that he could relax in the knowledge that he was safe, that he had redeemed his own mortgages. He plucked the key ring off the dresser hook, a much smaller version of his uncle James' bundle, fingering the keys carefully as if making sure they were all accounted for. It's just an anxiety dream, he told himself as he replaced them, putting it all down to stress or the offloading

of stress, intrigued at how rapidly, even instantaneously, he
was transported from those vivid images in sleep to the alert,
conscious state.

Routine quickly found its way back into his life. In the
mornings, after breakfasting in his sunny kitchen, he made his
way down to the sea front for a stroll along the promenade
around ten o'clock. Stopping at the Martello Tower, he admired
the view of the skyline of Dublin Bay, from Howth to Dun
Laoghaire, soothed by the familiar sight of the ESB's twin
chimneys spiking the air, his eyes scanning the vast expanse
of sand and distant strip of dark blue sea, then upwards to
admire the shapes of the clouds. When he reached the end of
the promenade he retraced his steps, passing briskly by the dog
walkers and returned homewards, calling into the newsagents
at the Green en route, then back to the welcome yellow hue of
his kitchen where he made a mug of coffee and settled down for
a read of the newspaper in the wicker chair. He had salvaged
it from a skip outside a house on Ailesbury Road one dusky
summer evening many years ago. The chair was a constant
reminder of the kindness of strangers; as he was hauling it out
of the skip to inspect it, a car had pulled into the driveway, the
owner leaping out and approaching him exuberantly.

'Ah: a skip scavenger!' the silver haired man had said, his
white teeth flashing in a wide grin of amusement at Moss's
expression. 'I've always wanted to meet one in the flesh.'

'Well...it is a nice chair,' Moss had responded with his
characteristic reverence for items of furniture, the chair now
positioned on the pavement. 'Shame to throw it away.'

The man had laughed heartily and offered him another wicker
chair – 'It's a bit more tatty'; a garden bench – 'Needs a lick of
paint'; an occasional table and a wooden coat stand, and had
them all delivered to his house in a van the following evening.
Later on that summer Moss had painted the best chair white to
match the kitchen table and dresser, its shelves now cluttered
with his own additions, many from auction lots such as the
white china tea set with golden rims, a set of delft plates, and

an enormous green vase decorated with hand painted orchids. On the main shelf, adjacent to a bundle of magazines, lay a stack of tea towels faded by constant use and time, in checker, stripe and floral patterns, matured by innumerable excursions in the washing machine, journeys to the clothes line, out in all weathers, flapping in gentle breezes, battered by winds, bathed almost rigid by the sun during rare heat waves and now neatly folded again, on standby for another turn at essential but mundane tasks.

As he sipped his morning coffee he entered a mild reverie as he diverted his attention from the newspaper print to the expanse of garden beyond the French windows, the greenhouse door opened onto an inviting scene of foliage, the side of the other Ailesbury chair visible amid empty pots clustered on the flagstone floor. He felt increasingly fortunate as the days began to blend into one another, as if he were destined to drown in obscurity, or navigate his way through a welcome fog of uncertainty, dithering between worlds, states that were punctuated by actual sensation such as the hot, milky coffee passing his lips or the texture of buttered toast in his mouth as he watched the branches of the trees swaying gently in a green mobile patchwork of shining leaves, the sudden appearance of a robin landing on the bird table filling him with delight.

The welcome idyll was interrupted one evening by a call from Louise who expressed dramatic concern for his wellbeing, saying there was some post for him, then adding, in a surprisingly haughty tone: 'We haven't heard from you for *ages* – you could be *dead* for all we know.' He decided to pay them a visit the following evening, a Wednesday, timing his arrival to coincide with the rolling of the credits on the soap opera which they were watching, still absorbed, while he hijacked Louise's task by putting the kettle on for the customary tea. He was aware of being back on a territory that vibrated with an inexplicable tension, struck by the tinge of frost in the atmosphere adding to the usual cool temperature. They turned on the central heating only as a last resort, allowing the familiar chill of the house to triumph over their comfort, while they seemed to find cold comfort in the virtue of saving money, or, more significantly to them, not spending it. As usual, when in their presence, he found himself suppressing the well of good cheer within and became serious, cautious, as if laughter was off limits and only permitted while watching television. He automatically arranged his poker face and went along with their small talk over tea, careful to give an impression of being intensely occupied with work in his house.

'These old houses…always something to be done, you know,' he said convincingly. He noticed Clare give a slight smile when he took a second slice of Bakewell tart from the plate. 'Mmm… Scrumptious…' Before he left, he offered to put the bin out, failing to humour Louise by his mock helpful hints on how best to cope with her new task.

'Easy: just tilt it – it's got wheels – see?' he said, pushing it down the path. 'I have my own bins to take out,' he added, seeing her glowering at him as he positioned it outside the front gate. 'You'll manage.'

As he drove off to the southside, he felt appeased by the silent offering from Clare as he was leaving – a large slice of the tart and a quantity of scones wrapped in aluminium foil and which now lay in a plastic bag on the passenger seat. Feelings of having left them stranded began to creep into his mind but he resisted them, for choices had been made: he had chosen to act and would face the consequences, he reasoned. Louise, by the choice of inaction, would have to deal with hers.

CHAPTER 14

Asense of unease descended upon Louise during the last week of May as she contemplated her impending routine week off, for her colleagues knew that she had no plans. They made an issue of it, eliciting predictable remarks such as 'Pity you're not going anywhere'...'It's not like you can't afford it'...'Don't you get bored?'... 'The weather forecast doesn't look great' and so on. She rewarded them with a mute blush and worked stoically on, recognizing the futility of competing with their great sun holidays in Spain or the Canaries. These they would furnish with photographic evidence and smugly delivered reports about delays at busy airports and such late nights - 'We didn't get to bed till five a.m...!' Then they would reminisce about their hangovers as if these, too, were compulsory and part of the package deal. Such hellish images, such strenuous effort and inconvenience convinced Louise that she was not missing out, but had in fact secured herself a good deal by staying at home.

En route to her usual meeting with Susan on Thursday evening she stopped outside Brown Thomas's windows to gaze longingly at three mannequins poised on the other side of the glass, admiring their stylish trouser suits with short fitted jackets, the cuffs of pretty blouses protruding from the sleeves, a pastel silk scarf draped around each of their slender necks, her eyes drawn to the footwear – those comfortable ankle boots that Cara sometimes wore and a pair of black trainers that were not ugly or too bulky. Over her meal with Susan she gave the trouser suits a casual mention, hiding her sudden yearning for one. But Susan was focussed on appetite, quietly applauding the curried chicken with basmati rice although she brightened when Louise gave her an update on Moss before taking a bite of her ham and tomato sandwich.

'Hmm…yes, big change for him. It all sounds so exciting,' remarked Susan approvingly, 'especially moving over to Dublin 4. Fair play to him.'

'I can't understand why everyone thinks it's so great,' responded Louise as she stirred her tea noisily. 'I mean, he's unemployed now you know.'

'Well, not necessarily,' Susan said in her considering way, tilting her face thoughtfully. 'Not if he's taking a year off. A cousin of mine took a sabbatical recently - gone off to visit some of the largest observatories in the world.' Mistaking Louise's frown for concern she added hastily: 'Anyway, I wouldn't worry about Moss - he's a landlord: that should keep him busy! But if he ever feels like getting back into the rat race there are plenty of jobs around.' She beamed one of her tolerant smiles as she turned her attention to her dessert of fresh fruit salad, her forehead smooth and free from worry lines. She also reflected on Moss, on his solitary browsing in the shop, his elegant hands examining a cover or his fingers delicately turning pages, treating the books as treasures, to be replaced with a fraction of reluctance upon the shelf.

'Actually Moss is a regular customer of the shop,' she told Louise. 'Buys several books a month from us.'

'I know, he's a real bookworm,' said Louise mournfully, as if divulging a character flaw. 'Oh well, he won't be able to afford so many of them now, will he?'

'Of course he will!' chuckled Susan. 'Well, I'm off to get another cup of coffee…more tea?'

'No, thanks.'

'Oh, by the way, I have some news,' said Susan when she returned with her steaming cup. 'Not terribly exciting really. I'm starting a summer course soon – it's in art history in Trinity. I missed out on it last year so I'm determined to go for it now. It's on Monday and Thursday evenings, six thirty till nine, so we'll have to postpone our meals here I'm afraid, until October at least. And John will be away most of the summer anyway. But if you need me to look at houses on Saturdays, just give me a ring, okay?'

As Louise set off home that evening, she felt mildly displaced by the suspension of their Thursday meetings, mystified that Susan would want to waste her summer evenings in a classroom. The following day she worked at a frenetic pace in preparation for her week's absence. 'Have a nice rest,' was Dorothy's parting shot as they exited the office that Friday evening, her teeth bared in a twisted moue of sour amusement.

Clare had long ago abandoned her attempts at encouraging Louise to go off somewhere for a break, a change of scene, and simply adapted to her presence in the house during the daytime. She also turned the week to her own advantage, seeing it as an opportunity for a change of routine for herself where Louise functioned as a companion to accompany her into town where they would have lunch in a hotel or one of the department store restaurants and drink coffee in one of the myriad cafes. Such excursions enlivened Clare who would visibly brighten up in these establishments and would want to linger, Louise slightly edgy, always making a prompt exit, the lunch or coffee a mere punctuation mark in her day. Clare also took delight in breaking their habit of minimalist shopping and on the Monday morning of Louise's holiday, she persuaded her to buy some new clothes, the casual stroll through Brown Thomas's no coincidence. It yielded several purchases, Louise eyeing the extra bags warily as they were conveyed home by taxi, wishing that they contained the trouser suit she had admired but dared not buy after seeing Clare's doubtful expression, already resenting the calf length skirt and blouse which she had bought instead.

The following day, the heat of early summer sunlight drew her out to the back garden, to the little suntrap patio where she was joined by Clare bearing a tea tray to the tiny round wooden table, both of them giving in to a bout of relaxation. Rejuvenated by the solar energy, Louise decided to do a little day time house hunting and began in earnest by arranging a number of viewings with estate agents. And ten o'clock the next morning, they set off together in the car, Louise navigating with her usual competence, her expression filled with anticipation.

Such viewings gave her access to the homes of strangers, satisfying her inquisitiveness and fulfilling a voyeuristic need as the agent escorted her through the rooms, rooms that she mentally tidied up and could take possession of if she made the decision. When faced with the bright colours of a child's room with its contingent of fluffy toys and miniature trucks and figurines battling out wars in other parts of the universe, she stalled, finding it hard to imagine how it could be emptied of such life, such chaos. Yet she was fascinated by these homes especially the minimalist townhouse she entered on Thursday morning with Clare at her side, its surgical cleanliness arousing in her an energy that bordered on excitement, for this was how she would live, she imagined, as she explored the rooms carefully, almost holding her breath - in pristine comfort but without the male presence.

'It belongs to a businessman...he's trading up,' confided the agent. She had no intention of buying it; it was beyond her price range, but viewing it had reassured her that she was getting close to her target, to finding the perfect place. And this seemed likely to her later on that afternoon as they made their way on foot to view an apartment nearby, in Clontarf. Armed with a glossy brochure and following its directions, they passed the familiar string of shops then turned into a tree lined avenue off which a three storey block had grown around a courtyard with parking spaces and a communal garden. At first they were seduced by the newness of the building, by the blast of light when the agent opened the apartment door after they ascended a stark concrete stairs to the first floor corridor - a dingy uncarpeted stretch punctuated by a row of doors furnished with numbers, handles, locks and peepholes. This contrast from shadow to light and habitation confused them both as they roamed uncertainly from room to room, enthralled by the freshly painted magnolia walls awaiting pictures and mirrors, the timber floors poised for rugs and furnishings, the gleaming white bathroom awaiting towels, Louise gazing longingly at the view of mature oak trees from the large double-glazed windows. Despite the agent's reassurance that the lighting in the corridors would be completed within days, the walls painted and the stairs put to rights, Clare caught Louise's eye and they made a sudden, swift departure, fleeing from the hushed anonymity of people living side by claustrophobic side. A nearby door had been opened then slammed shut abruptly, as if the occupant had changed his or her mind on hearing their voices, the pace of their steps accelerating as they exited the building's main entrance, the scent of burnt food trailing behind them as they stood for a moment on the steps where they drew in gulps of fresh air as if recovering from pursuit by some invisible force. Back home, Louise's disappointment was palpable, Clare witnessing her study the brochure with its attractive illustrations, and mournfully saying: 'But it *looked* so nice, Mum,' her hopes dashed yet again. After their subdued evening meal Louise suddenly remembered Susan's offer and telephoned her to see if she was free on Saturday to accompany her to a number of viewings, including a couple on the southside, in Ringsend, her search now expanded, more flexible. 'Delighted,' was Susan's positive response. 'See you two o'clock as usual then.'

Overnight the weather changed to a brooding, indecisive phase. Louise remained indoors watching a film, her property hunt now on hold until Saturday, although she felt restless, yearning for some other distraction, for somewhere to go for she constantly turned her mind to work and began to long for her return to routine, to the fixed predictability of days that would consume her energy. The idea of paying Moss a surprise visit suddenly occurred to her, an idea so simple she exclaimed out loud: 'Now *why* didn't I think of that before!' Satisfied at having a legitimate destination in mind, she consulted her map and plotted her route via Ringsend to Dawn View in Sandymount, areas that she tended to bypass whenever she went for one of her aimless drives. She set off around eight o'clock that evening, the light sombre under vast pale clouds tinged with grey, and arrived in Dawn View, parking a few doors up from number 11. She hesitated outside the open wrought iron gates, taken aback by the lushness of the trees in the gardens then squinted at the door number for the house appeared unexpectedly elegant and impressive, its bulk dwarfing the family home. The gravel front garden was bordered by bushes and clumps of fuschia and intercepted by a flagstone path. She recognised Moss's Volvo parked next to another mud spattered car. A light rain began to fall and she hastened up the path to the yellow front door then stopped to examine the grid of doorbells on the left side, noting the selection of initials: MM, DW, MS, KW. She eagerly pressed the bell marked MM, anticipating her entry into the interior, imagining a grand tour of the house followed by a mug of tea, regretting that she had not thought to bring a cake or a packet of biscuits. But there was no response. She tried rapping the lion knocker, the peephole eyeing her. After pressing the bell marked DW twice, the door opened to reveal a dark haired man attired in a white t-shirt and grey combat trousers. He regarded her with a suspicious look. She was about to step into the hall but the way he moved forward stalled her, his bulky frame blocking her access.

'I'm here to see Mr Mortimer,' she said.

'He's out,' stated Donal in his curt fashion. 'No idea when he'll be back.'

'But his car is there!' she exclaimed, waving a hand at the evidence.

'Could be in town.'

Her emphatic 'But I'm his sister!' was met with a stonewall shrug.

'I'll leave a note to say you called,' and he shut the heavy door dismissively, Louise wincing at the sound of the firm clunk. She drove back to Clontarf feeling enraged by the unexpected reception.

'The *cheek* of that man,' she fumed as she recounted the incident to her mother on her return, her ire mounting as her forefinger snapped the digits of Moss's new number into the phone. At the sound of his reassuring recorded voice requesting that a message be left after the tone she snapped the phone back onto its cradle. It was beginning to dawn on them that Moss was no longer available, his whereabouts uncertain, although he was traceable for he telephoned them later on that evening after noticing four calls from the Clontarf number on his screen, a detail he withheld.

'Is everything okay...any problems?' he asked guardedly.

'No,' replied Louise in her tragic voice, 'no problem except that horrible tenant of yours. He wouldn't even let me in the door. It's my week off and I just wanted to see your flat.' She paused, then added accusingly: 'You're never in, are you?'

Glad that he had given that impression, Moss began to dissuade her, choosing a convincing item from his armoury of excuses.

'Well, you have to understand that my tenants are *very* security conscious,' he told her smoothly. 'You have to be these days. Anyway I was in town for a bite to eat in Bewley's. I'm still redecorating the flat and I got some new paint,' he lied. 'The smell of it would give you a terrible headache. It doesn't affect me at all. And the place is still a mess,' he said, adding another untruth. 'Still trying to sort it all out since the last tenants. These old houses are a lot of work,' he clichéd. 'Never ending.'

With her enthusiasm waning, the image of that cosy visit disintegrating in her mind, she conceded that the paint fumes would indeed give her a headache and the communication ended, Moss realising that he had had a lucky escape. He had simply gone for a stroll along the promenade after his return from Bewley's in the company of Stephen Devereux with his routine hot chocolate and floating marshmallows. With the rain imminent, he had walked as far as the Martello Tower then went home at a brisker pace and found Donal's note on the hall table. He immediately knocked on his door and thanked him, reassuring him that he had indeed done the right thing. The rule still applied; no one was allowed entry unless by prior arrangement. Donal found himself punching the air with vindication when he was gone, deriving immense satisfaction in the knowledge that Moss, too, was avoiding members of his family, a grim smile curling his lips as he recalled his landlord's wary expression at the mention of his sister.

After the phone call, Louise's sullen voice still echoing in his mind, Moss opened a bottle of beer, poured it slowly into his favourite glass and took it to the sitting room where he placed it on the coffee table, on a coaster depicting a Parisian scene. He settled himself in the deep sofa, blowing out a sigh, admonishing himself for such an unchristian attitude - blocking my own sister from visiting me, he thought. But this he put down to the futility of guilt and tried to shake it off. As the beer delivered its mellowing effect, he recalled her response or lack of response to kindness or kindly gestures, to past efforts to include her, to encourage her. Whenever he would express concern over one of her severe headaches she would resist, behaving as if not entitled to rest or take refuge in her bed for an hour or so, as if giving way to healing indicated weakness and that taking to bed implied defeat. She chose to suffer on until it was time to effect a ritual, always in the presence of either himself or Clare, of taking soluble painkillers which she would unwrap, drop them into a mug of warm water and watch them dissolve, then sip the liquid very slowly, shoulders hunched, cupping the mug with both hands. How did such martyrdom evolve? he wondered. Perhaps she feels exempt from receiving or expressing kindness, the lack of sympathy for herself mildly worrying. It also saddened him, for he felt inadequate to coping well with it, realizing that evasion was his usual way of coping. A sudden recollection from his teen years sprang to his mind: his mother's ambitious glazed smile, the excluding one she had used to dismiss Louise to her bedroom during the dinner parties on the pretext that she was too young although she was encouraged to help with the preparations. He was aware of how differently he had been regarded, invited into the dining room to be shown off, the indulgent female eyes roving over him, their smiles registering that it was some sort of treat, disapproval of his then long hair suspended for the occasion. He could see how Louise had been overprotected, in fact David had said so to Clare many times. Yet for all his prolonged absences he had treated them well, he knew, very well indeed, his generosity faultless. Yet perhaps his absence, or sequence of absences, had taken their toll in some obscure way on Louise, although David often telephoned her, their conversations always delivering a smile to her habitually glum face, David laughingly tolerant at her fastidiousness whenever they had dined in hotel restaurants. 'She's just shy,' Clare would say, as if this was of little consequence, a passing phase. That the phase had not yet ended caused a wave of sympathy to overcome Moss, yet somehow he could not gather up enough concern now to invite her over to Sandymount: she had after all never shown any interest in his house before. And he felt convinced that once she got in the door, conflict and unpleasantness would eventually follow, knowing that her sudden interest in visiting him was calculating, self-serving and not out of any notable affection for him.

'Cheers!' he said aloud as if surrounded by a group of reassuring friends, drained his glass then exhaled a satisfied belch into the air.

CHAPTER 15

By the Wednesday of the following week, Louise furrowed her brow on her way to work, impervious to the radiance of the warm sunny June day. Her pace quickened as she entered the office building for there was an element of excitement around the upheaval that had taken place in her week's absence, what with manager Gerry Dunne being transferred to another department, sidelined out of sight it seemed, his replacement the tall, fair haired Andrzej Januszczak, his name raising brows and commentary: 'Well - *he's* definitely not Irish, is he?!', Louise and Cara following Dorothy's example by calling him Andy Whatshisface behind his back. There was also the surprise resignation of assistant manager Chris O'Donnell who was migrating to another company in spite of her bland, neutral style, her defeatist mantras: 'We'll just have to muddle through,' or a meek 'Ah well - that's life', mantras that Louise had promptly added to her own repertoire. And Eileen was out on sick leave with a chest infection for a week at least, Louise's lip curling contemptuously, for she regarded any malady that excused going to work with suspicion, the sufferer expected back in a state of sniffling discomfort or with a contrite, careworn expression. Feeling smug at having arrived moments before Cara and Dorothy, their usual mechanical greeting replaced by 'Any news?', she joined them in a bout of speculations before establishing herself at her desk, the vague dread of change that trailed her lifting as soon as she gave herself over to her work, submerging herself in the extra papers and files in her in-tray, and in the data to be typed into the screen for hours and hours. But around ten o'clock the sudden trill of her extension phone interrupted her concentration and she answered with her usual evasive 'Hello'. Susan's pleasant voice took her by surprise, tinged as it was with an urgent tone.

'Sorry to ring so early Louise. Do you remember the house we saw on Saturday – the one in Ringsend?'

'We saw four houses on Saturday,' Louise snapped unintentionally, stunned by the unexpected call. 'I can't remember them all offhand.'

'The one in Ringsend,' Susan repeated. 'Number 8 Willowhaven Close. Edwardian with car parking in front and a little garden with rose bushes behind?'

'Oh. Yes. I remember it now. A bit old fashioned. Why do you want to know?'

'Well: do you want to buy it?'

'Buy it?' she echoed in astonishment. 'No, I don't want to buy it. I preferred the one in Fairview, the Emmet Lane one, but it's overpriced.'

'Right...so you've no intention of putting in an offer then, on Willowhaven Close?'

'No, I just said so. Why do you ask?'

'Well, I'm thinking of buying it,' sighed Susan with a relieved chuckle.

Louise tightened her grip on the phone. 'But you weren't looking for a house,' she hissed, lowering her voice for fear her colleagues would overhear her. 'You've never mentioned it before.'

'I know I know. I wasn't actually *looking*, but I fell in love with that house,' she explained. 'It just happened. I've had a talk with Mam and Dad about financing. I can afford it now. Remember I mentioned that Grandad left me something? Well I've decided to use the money...no point in holding onto it. Anyway I'm off to see the house again this morning. I'll let you know.' She paused. 'You're sure you're okay with this Louise?'

'Yes of course,' she responded automatically.

'Great! Wish me luck then!'

Unnoticed by her colleagues typing away industriously, Louise replaced the receiver carefully, her expression stricken, as if she was the recipient of bad news, such as a morbid medical test result. As the day progressed a numbness crept over her, for this unexpected outcome of a routine house hunt manifested itself as menacing, an intrusion that threatened to alter her life in some way. The work day at last dispensed with, she was relieved to get home before half past six only to discover her mother in a state of elation: Susan had phoned her around five to relay the message that her offer on the house had been accepted.

'Good for her,' enthused Clare, although she did not seem too surprised by such news.

'I was up to my eyes when she rang me this morning,' said Louise stiffly as she took her seat at the kitchen table. 'I don't know why she bothered really.'

'But it was a nice thing to do,' said Clare. 'She wanted to give you the chance of buying it yourself - *if* you had wanted it. *Very* nice of her actually,' she emphasised firmly as she put the dinner plates down on the placemats.

'Well, lucky for her she can afford it,' said Louise lifting up her knife.

'So could you, you know. If you really wanted to,' said Claire. 'That house in Emmet Lane sounds just right...and it's not far from here. Maybe you should take another look at it.' Louise fell silent at her brisk, concluding tone, mechanically consuming her dinner of neatly mashed peas, creamed potatoes and moist roast chicken slices with gravy, trying to disguise the invasion of feelings of shock, assault even, that had infiltrated her and resulted in muscle tension and a chill that would not dissipate even with the pale green cardigan she had pulled on as soon as she got home.

After dinner, she went about her chores, keeping an eye on the time for her appointment with the soap opera, overwhelmed by a sense of being hoodwinked. Her forehead beginning to throb, she went up to her bedroom and quickly checked the estate agent's brochure that she had filed away in a folder on Saturday. She re-examined it, scrutinising the colour photograph. She remembered that the house was situated in a quiet street with cherry trees in some of the gardens and that it felt hollow, emptied of its life and furniture, although Susan, with her love of old houses, had said her usual: 'Ooh, lovely fireplace!' She compared it with the redbrick in Emmet Lane, in Fairview, that they had viewed on the way back to Sutton: it now seemed far more practical, surrounded by every desirable amenity as well as being just a few bus stops from Clontarf, possibly even within walking distance of Lime Tree Road. But she had found the interior repugnant with its cluttered pokey rooms. Large abstract paintings dominated the red walls in the sitting room where the polished wooden floorboards were partly obscured by a couple of patterned scatter rugs. The detritus of a recent coffee break was visible on the bulky low table before the cast iron fireplace, its mantelpiece congested with ornaments and, nearby, a tall bookcase heaved with untidily placed books, while she stood there yearning desperately for order, for neutral. Susan, she now remembered, had exclaimed that it was 'Gorgeous...very atmospheric,' and began to wonder why she had chosen Ringsend, for Emmet Lane would also have been far more convenient for her, being on the same bus route as Sutton. She transferred her gaze back to the photograph of Willowhaven Close: while it had made no impression on her at the time, the house suddenly loomed before her as beautiful, the curved wooden gates to the narrow driveway closed over, a separate gate opening onto the tiny garden.

With a sigh, she put the brochure aside and absently flicked through the file. A picture caught her eye. It was a first floor duplex apartment in Monkstown, one that she had viewed several years ago, just as the economy was picking up. Uncle James had telephoned her from London urging her to buy it, making arrangements for her to see it before it went on the market. It had belonged to the aunt of a business acquaintance of his and was an executor's sale. Moss was in Wexford for the week and was not due back until Sunday and so Clare had accompanied her to Monkstown, both of them enthusing about the location as Louise parked the car, for it overlooked the seafront with a view of the harbour in Dun Laoghaire nearby and was set in behind security gates with its own front door accessed by stone steps flanked by silver railings. She could barely remember the face of the tall, slender man who had allowed them access, but she had been impressed by the unrestricted view of the sea from the living room and front bedroom windows although she could hear the shriek of gulls filtering through them, a sound she did not like. But it was the first time she had felt the raw desire, the gripping prospect of owning a property, of being in control of a territory, as well as setting up home and being in command of her independence. A quick mental calculation had informed her she could afford it by selling a large portion of her shares, delve into her savings account and maintain a small mortgage and still have money in the bank. As they had looked carefully around, Clare cautiously approving it, Louise was rendered almost mute, unable to find fault, overlooking petty flaws such as a crack in two of the tiles above the bathroom sink. She had told the shadowy Mr. Lawrence that she was very interested... and would be in touch. Her mind racing, her pulse quickening, she had spent the rest of the week thinking it all over, drawing diagrams from memory at the kitchen table, Clare urging her to put in an offer first, her enthusiasm also alerted, seeing it as a fine place to visit even though it was on the southside. But Louise had procrastinated because of the one proviso: it was to be sold fully furnished. She wanted the thrill of choosing her own.

'My God!' Moss had exclaimed on hearing about their adventure over tea upon his return on Sunday. 'You turned down an apartment - a duplex in Monkstown for that price', he had paused for a second. 'Monkstown,' he had repeated, incredulously. 'On the seafront,' he added, aghast. 'The views...' he had sighed. 'And the furniture is probably worth a small fortune. I would have shifted it for you, no problem. I have contacts.'

'But Mr. Lawrence doesn't know yet. You could come over with me to take a look at it tomorrow evening,' she had said in a reasonable tone, regarding him quizzically.

Moss had exhaled a prolonged sigh. 'It will have been *sold* by now. Property prices are going up and executor sales like these always go fast, instantly even, snapped up.' And he snapped his fingers dramatically in emphasis. 'James was doing you a favour, Louise. You're supposed to make a decision straight away.'

She had discovered that he was right when she made the discreet telephone call from her desk the following morning,

Mr Lawrence's potent, quietly delivered words ringing in her burning ears.

'Yes, yes indeed, Miss Mortimer – it's sold. You didn't get back to me, I took it you weren't interested. The price is considerably lower than the market value. I thought you were aware of all this.'

After the call, a searing disappointment had set in as she realised her error of judgment, one that led to months, even years, of regret. She could have lived with the furniture which, on reflection, was not unattractive, remembering how Moss had groaned when they had described the sofas and armchairs.

'That's chintz,' he had said sadly. 'I love chintz. Pity I wasn't there with you. A real pity. You should have phoned me on the mobile or left a message for me at Strand House. I could have sorted it all out,' he had sighed again, finishing his tea. 'On the seafront,' he had repeated dismally, leaving the room to go off and unpack. 'Monkstown,' they had heard him hiss as he treaded heavily up the stairs.

As she filed the brochure away, she noted that the price was a fraction of what it would now fetch on the open market. She suddenly caught a glimpse of insight, of how she had opted for the strict greyness of her mother's house, as if she had written herself out of the script of a fulfilling, independent life, and was again overwhelmed by regret. She had opened a door and seen an ideal interior, perhaps an ideal life, only to have obstructed her own access. Now, within the space of a few days, Susan had taken that risk and was about to become a homeowner, Louise cringing with bitter regret at having made that phone call, Susan's routine but obliging 'Delighted!' echoing in her mind. The numbness began to thaw and was replaced by a slow dawning rage culminating in a raw energy that seemed to assault her whole being but she internalised it instinctively, snapped the folder shut and, with her head throbbing, set off to the kitchen to take her painkillers. She watched television for a while but, her concentration ruined, she went off for her bath and then to bed, hoping that the feeling would go away.

Chapter 16

Moss savoured his newfound lifestyle where time seemed to have become altered, more flexible, divided into various zones that could be accessed or infiltrated on a whim. In the city centre he would mingle illicitly with the zealous workers as he made his way into bookstores, into the inner sanctum of Bewley's Cafes or Neary's pub, his pleasure blending with the practicalities of grocery shopping, cooking, the laundry, and a variety of other mundane chores, his morning walk adding to the patchwork of benign activities. Somehow there was no time left over to make a visit to Clontarf although this he intended doing - any day now, he would tell himself, aware of the shallowness of his intention.

Just as he got home from his walk one Tuesday morning, newspaper in hand, the telephone rang. It was Valerie de Vries, inviting him to dinner on Thursday: 'Come over early for tea at four, and we'll eat at six thirty,' the times appointed leaving no room for the ambiguity and second guessing of customary late arrival. 'Meant to ask you over sooner but we're not long back from Amsterdam, on Bloomsday actually – Elias was in his element of course. Anyway Josie's much better now.'

He smiled as he contemplated the agreeable invitation and that Josie, to whom they were devoted, was much the better for their visit. He suspected that the distinguished Elias Schultz was her favourite guest of the three that were currently in residence, Elias now well into his second year, hosting meetings twice a month in the drawing room for his literary friends and their earnest discussions and for whom Valerie provided coffee, snacks and glasses of port.

A hazy drizzle shadowed Thursday morning, Moss frowning slightly at such a poor start to the solstice, but by lunchtime felt reassured by the forecaster at Eternity FM as she announced 'A clearance to brighter weather.' And, almost on cue, the clouds parted to reveal a welcome patch of blue, the sunlight shyly reappearing and dispelling the dampness. By two o'clock he was in the city centre attending to his finances, beginning with a sedate Building Society then on to his bank branch located in an historic building that he admired, feeling at ease within its institutional solidity, its potent hum of finance as he exchanged a few amicable words with a teller he had known for years. Then he strolled up to Aungier Street to investigate the furniture outlets, spotted a tall, narrow Chinese chest of drawers that he figured would look well in the dining room. After a brief discussion with the vendor about the price, he paid a deposit, promising to collect it early Saturday morning. Glancing at his mobile phone, he decided he had time to hit the books and set off to Nemesis for an extended browse, Susan's absence vaguely disappointing, and he eventually left without purchase. Returning to Grafton Street, he bought a selection of éclairs and cherry buns in Bewley's bakery then made his way to the bus stop, gently swinging the plastic bag containing the maroon cake boxes tied with string.

After a lengthy wait, he boarded the number 3 bus which emerged from the metallic haze of traffic, claimed a seat near the front and sat back to enjoy the drama of passengers alighting and boarding at each stop along the familiar route, the city centre receding. As the bus nosed its way along Sandymount Road, he noticed a sleek black cat poised like a sculpture behind the first floor window of a Georgian house and figured it was a lucky sign: while the cat had not crossed his path, he had been chauffeured past its oblivious gaze, a focus reserved for its homecoming owner and the prospect of a filled stomach, he assumed. As the bus halted outside the supermarket at Sandymount Green, he watched a woman laden with a cluster of bulging plastic bags embark, her eyes suspicious and resentful, squinting in the manner of one who harbours a secret wound, her mouth pursed to a tight pucker. He did not take it seriously, for it was transient, he knew, a familiar expression symptomatic of the late arrival of the bus.

He got off at the second stop on the Strand Road, for he was in good time for his meeting with the de Vrieses, a prospect filling him with such pleasure that a slight warmth began to emanate from his cheeks. He intentionally took the long picturesque route through the beloved streets as if feeding an architectural habit, glancing furtively at the houses, taking note of their bulk, their red bricks and picture windows, stealing glimpses of interiors, catching sight of the back of a sofa in a bay window and feasting his eyes on interesting front doors with gleaming knockers, handles and letterboxes. The sea air felt cool against his face, the journey culminating in his arrival at the great black Victorian door in Seagull Gardens at two minutes to four, where he hesitated before pressing the doorbell to give himself time to admire the building's façade.

Valerie welcomed him in with three firm cheek kisses, the bag received with exclamations of appreciation as he was ushered into the drawing room where he was surprised to find both Elias and Michele there, welcoming him warmly. 'Ming, our new arrival, is away in Connemara for a week,' explained Valerie as he sat down on the spacious sofa opposite the window, a robust cushion supporting his back. 'He was inspired by Johann, needless to say. Ah...here's Johann now.' And the front door opened again and Johann entered, accompanied by his friend Shane Turner who placed his violin case on the floor behind the piano, both men similarly attired in dark illustrated t-shirts and jeans. After another round of handshakes, they all assembled themselves in the chairs and sofas to enjoy the tea that Valerie poured from a large ceramic teapot into teacups with a floral design, Michelle passing them around with care. The coffee table was laid with a large square plate filled with shortbread biscuits and the éclairs and cherry buns, a jug of milk, a bowl of sugar cubes, a tiny blue dish containing slices of lemon, another with butter. Elias and Moss helped themselves to the buns; Johann and Shane each devoured an éclair, their cheeks bulging. Michelle declined one saying she was watching her figure. Shane gave a flick of his raven black hair and told her that she wasn't the only one watching it, Johann nodding in mirthful agreement.

Apart from the O'Briens, Moss had never known a more relaxing household; all occupants gave the impression of being on a perpetual holiday or an extended weekend off. The house itself seemed to be enveloped by an aura of contentment, as if breathing an air independent of outside influences and where flexible working hours were the norm, that tea at four in the afternoon was a subversive activity, or even a rebellion against the frenzied busyness of the booming economy raging outside. As usual Moss was mesmerized by Valerie's ease at sharing her home with so many people although she was well paid for the full board service that she provided, he reasoned. But he could tell that she enjoyed being hospitable, and that the wellbeing of her guests concerned her, evidenced by the attentive way she listened, her steady eye contact not in the least bit disconcerting as she absorbed comments and opinions, happy to facilitate lively discussions. Like his favourite café acquaintances she did not indulge in overtly personal questions, those casual but intrusive ones regarding occupation or lack of one, as if entitled to know. He found it refreshing to find himself in a milieu that valued character over economic or social standing, that for Valerie and indeed her cosmopolitan residents there was clearly more to life than brandishing a career status. Through Kevin's influence, he had become aware of the angst of status in others, or signs of that angst, such as forming an opinion of new acquaintances by quickly ferreting out their occupation, where they lived, where they were from, such interrogations designed to pigeonhole them, strap them safely into a convenient stereotype, one with appealing limitations, the hunger to diminish and undermine never too far away.

They had aperitifs around a quarter to six, then the group adjourned to the dining room where Moss took his place at the oval table enhanced by a number of nightlight candles flickering in red glass bowls, emitting his usual 'Scrumptious!' from time to time as he consumed 'Valerie's legendary chilli con carne..!' and sipped happily on a glass of cold beer, joining his companions in a toast to Valerie for such a delicious meal. By the time they returned to the drawing room for coffee and reclaimed their seats, he felt mellow, his appetite for food and eloquent, witty conversation utterly satisfied. The atmosphere of the room was now altered by a shift in the mid-summer evening light. Johann switched on the occasional lamps and Elias set a match to the church candles on the mantelpiece then resumed his place in the straight back chair that he preferred. Moss noted the elegance of his posture, his dignified profile, the well tended moustache above lips that pursed in judicious consideration, the strands of his light brown hair flecked with grey combed back and curling out at the nape of his neck, the cut of his clothes signalling wealth. Yet he's chosen to live here, mused Moss, no doubt for the kind of company and ambience that would be lacking in an apartment block or, to a lesser extent, a hotel. It was also convenient to Trinity College where he was immersed in postdoctoral research. He turned his attention to Michelle whom he admired covertly – she was sitting on the other sofa, next to Shane, her bare legs crossed sideways, a cream linen skirt draped over her knees, her straight brown hair reaching her shoulders, a pair of mischievous green eyes encouraging laughter. A free spirit, he figured, impressed by the fact that she had left her father's prosperous business enterprise in Marseilles behind and was now devoted to the study of Celtic illustrations and mythology. A well-heeled free spirit, he revised, returning her smile.

He was taken by surprise when Johann handed glasses of port around and Valerie presented him with a large gift-wrapped package, the group raising their glasses and exclaiming in unison 'To your new home, Moss! To your new life!' Elias added, in his gentle Canadian accent 'And welcome to Sandymount.'

'Thank you all very much,' smiled Moss. 'Cheers everyone!' After a swig of port, he unwrapped the gift ceremoniously and produced a pair of ornate brass candlesticks with three branches looping from the centre. 'Perfect for my sitting room mantelpiece,' he said delightedly. 'Thanks a million.'

'Okay...and now for some music,' said Elias. 'How about it, maestros?'

Johann gave a mock swagger as he made his way over to the piano to a round of applause, Shane plucking his violin from its case. With a dramatic drawing of the bow across its strings, he deftly tuned it to a piano note, then, the banter dying away, the tiny audience fell silent as the music began: Bach suite No. 1 in G, Moss closing his eyes meditatively as the sounds filled the conscious heart of the room.

He left around ten o'clock after making his farewells and delivering kisses to the cheeks of Michelle and Valerie then strolled the short distance in the still twilight air towards Dawn View. He stopped en route to buy milk and a sliced pan in the brightly lit convenience store adjacent to the Green, his eyes blinking rapidly from the effect but he felt rejuvenated, ready for action, as if he had stumbled back into the country after a short break. Back in his sitting room, a dark but aesthetic space that cloaked him with tranquil seclusion, he opened the bulky plastic bag and pulled out the candlesticks. He placed one at each end of the mantelpiece and stood back to examine the effect then adjusted their position to complement their reflections in the mirror. As he inserted the ivory coloured candles that Valerie had thought to include he caught sight of his own reflection and was startled by the tenderness in his expression. Later on, over a cup of tea at the kitchen table, he examined the gift wrapped in olive-green paper that Elias had given him, stunned by his thoughtfulness. It was a hardcover book containing two Nero Wolfe mysteries.

After his tea, he went out to the garden and inhaled the June night air, marvelling at the day: even Donal had given him an audible greeting as he passed him at the front door earlier on. Looking up at the clear sky he noticed a few summer stars shimmering, their light blending with the benevolence, the generosity of spirit that had trailed him that long, leisurely solstice day, in fact ever since the day he moved over to Sandymount.

CHAPTER 17

During the final days of June Moss got up earlier than usual in response to the munificent morning light, intrigued by the way it changed the atmosphere of the day, hour by mysterious hour, as it filtered into the interior of his flat and illuminated the spaces filled with his beloved possessions. One morning, a Tuesday, he busied himself with the laundry, his sheets and duvet cover dwarfing Maddie's huddle of colourful underwear, each scant item pegged neatly onto the line. By lunchtime he was at the kitchen table looking appreciatively at the new clothes horse which he had erected on the flagstones outside the French doors, his towels and pillow cases draped upon the thin white bars. As he bit hungrily into a slice of brown soda bread with smoked salmon, the telephone rang.

'Are you on for a drink in Neary's this evening?' Sam Hunter asked him. 'Unless you have some other pressing engagement of course.'

'Nah, nothing urgent,' he mumbled through a full mouth. 'I'll be there.'

'Excellent. See you six o'clock then.'

He spent the afternoon tidying up the utility room, filling up two refuse bags with junk but managed to salvage a wool tapestry of roses in a blue bowl which he dusted off in the garden, cleaned the frame and placed it on the dining room sideboard then sat at the table to admire it over a pot of tea. Afterwards, he showered, put on a clean black cotton shirt and denim jeans, tied the laces securely on a pair of favourite leather shoes. On impulse, he grabbed his leather jacket and set off to the bus stop on Sandymount Road where he stood in the intense sunshine of late afternoon, the lenses of his glasses darkened by the dazzle. The number 3 arrived like a benevolent and forgiving god, rescuing the waiting flock from its anonymous limbo state and he claimed the first vacant seat he saw along the aisle, his companion a teenage girl who was staring fixedly into the distance beyond the dusty windowpane, her mouth busy chewing gum, creating snappy bubbles from time to time. He disembarked at Pearse Street train station and snuck in through the pedestrian entrance at the rear of Trinity College then made his way through the grounds, keeping an eye out for the corpulent tabby cat usually seen lazing in the vicinity of the Berkeley Library, but there was no sign of him today. He strolled out through the Nassau Street exit and, with a characteristic bracing of his shoulders, set off towards the top of Grafton Street, made the right turn into Chatham Street and entered Neary's pub. Sam was waiting for him at the bar in the ground floor snug with the agreeable view of the gas lamps down the main bar counter. Sam's suit jacket was suspended from a nearby coat hook, a pint of Guinness before him. He grinned a welcome, his recently cut blond hair framing a round face with shrewd blue eyes, his white shirt still spotless after a corporate day. He ordered a beer for Moss and briefed him on life that had continued at the bank without him. But somehow it sounded like an unfamiliar world as the barman placed the beer on a circular mat before him, Sam having little of significance to relate, Moss listening keenly all the same as he watched a group of actors from the Gaiety filter in through the rear entrance and claim the corner sofa in the main bar. His attention increased when Sam told him that he had some news - a baby was on the way after years of trying. Moss tilted his head slightly to relieve himself of an amused smirk at the metaphor which usually conjured up appealing images for him, imagining how enthralling the act of lovemaking must be if the creation of a new person was the imperative. It has to be premium sex, he thought, to immerse yourself in countless, exhilarating romps then to get the baby. And another. But replicating another human being had never appealed to him, he knew, a truth revealed to him after he had fallen in love at the age of twenty-five, his smirk fading as he was suddenly plunged into the past.

It began at a book launch in Waterstones where he was sitting in a chair in the back row, utterly conscious of the attractive girl next to him, his eyes flickering sideways to look at the slit in her calf-length red skirt while the author read an extract to the seemingly rapt audience. But he had not heard a word, tuned in as he was to a new, stunning vibration. He did not have to ask her to adjourn to the pub for a drink afterwards - it simply happened, the two of them setting off hypnotically together to Davy Byrnes. Once there, in a seat near the window, he was able to focus on her name – Aisling – and the soft, dark brown hair hanging limply over her shoulders and framing a sallow face, her forlorn brown eyes fixing him with a tenderness that melted him. They quickly became lovers, absorbed in an affair for over a year, a liaison that was sustained by a discreet but intense physical passion. This was suddenly snatched away when Aisling became pregnant, both of them thrown into a state of astonishment at the reality of a child, or prospect of a child, betrayed by the elaborate precautions taken to prevent such an outcome. Moss spent days and edgy nights ruminating on an uncertain future, concluding the terrible insight at the time: that he was inadequate, or felt inadequate, could not cope with her giving birth to a being that he was not yet ready to welcome into the world.

Within a few weeks of heightened tension, Aisling quietly announced that she had had a miscarriage - an early one, as she called it. They were sitting side by side on the dark green sofa with its meagre cushions in her tiny flat on Pembroke Road, sipping camomile tea, the ironic glint of a teddy bear's eyes catching his from an ancient armchair in the corner. When he failed to mask his deep relief at the convenience of such an event, in that instant the relationship also died, Aisling having read his reaction. Infuriated by this revelation about his character despite his concerned phone calls, his marriage proposal only the week before in the Front Square in Trinity College, the cobblestones hesitating under the soles of their shoes, the blue-faced clock marking the moment from its great height above the archway, she withdrew, taking refuge in silence, or the silent treatment.

Refusing to answer the door or the telephone, she eventually sent him a note on a piece of lined paper torn roughly out of a notebook, implying anger, impetuousness, to say there was no point in seeing him anymore. The impact of such rejection resulted in his retreat from intimate friendships for a long time, and he submerged himself in his work, determined to resist a further risk of love. He also found meagre solace in music, attending concerts regularly, the poignant beauty of piano notes, violin and cello strings tugging upon his sadness and gradually appeasing it.

Time, endowed with the reputation of healer, moved sluggishly alongside him for over a year when his eyes would search out Aisling in the throng in Grafton Street, hoping for a chance encounter, dwelling in a twilight world of loss and yearning until he reached a turning point when he conjured up the nerve to telephone her parents' home number. He learned, through the friendly, pragmatic voice of her father, that she had emigrated to Canada where she was teaching and, from what he could discern, was enjoying life with a young mechanic. Feeling physically shaken after the call, his fingers trembling, he was rewarded by a profound relief as he gave himself permission to consider other women. His sexual self that had been suppressed to mere urges, or solitary episodes, resumed with intermittent but not unexciting affairs with women who recognized the advantages of transient intimacy, were even intent on it, reassuring him that the necessary precautions were guaranteed.

He was now astonished by the way Sam's news of the baby had instantly resurrected such vivid memories of long ago, but no longer feeling burdened by them, he turned to congratulate him with a genuine smile, shook his hand firmly and they both took a deep draught from their glasses to mark the news.

'By the way, how's the Doctrine of the Mean going?' Sam asked him as he gave a significant nod towards his empty glass.

'Slowly,' replied Moss motioning the barman to refill them. 'I'm slipping up already, although it's early days yet. Aristotle wouldn't approve. I've been on a spending spree: splurging on furniture and stuff for the flat and investing in some casual gear for my leisurely life.'

'Like this jacket?' he remarked quizzically, stroking the soft black leather astride a spare stool.

'Nah, my tenant gave it to me before he left for Venice. A parting gift.'

'Nice of him. So…all in all, a temporary lapse then,' said Sam and they both chuckled at the idea that, in this instance, there was progress in regress.

They promised to meet up again after Sam's summer holiday in Norway with Tessa and their six year old daughter Anita who, he reported, was very excited at the prospect of a new sibling. As Moss made his way home on the number 7 bus, he felt relieved to be going back to an empty flat, at ease with his bachelor state and the fact that he had at least made one marriage proposal although he had never mentioned this to Clare or Louise. As far as he knew, Louise had shown little interest in marriage, in finding a husband, or being found, although there had been a trickle of boyfriends over the years, not that such things were discussed, at least not in his presence. He recalled the time she had rushed to Clare shouting gleefully: 'Oooh Mum!…Moss is crying…I saw him *crying!*' during his morose grief at the loss of Aisling, then Clare entering the kitchen briskly, demanding that he pull himself together. 'You'll have to stop this crying business, Morris,' she had said crossly. 'You'll meet someone else,' then adding automatically 'There are plenty of other fish in the sea.' That incident had as usual been exaggerated by Louise, he knew: while waiting for the kettle to boil, he had simply removed his glasses to wipe a solitary tear from his left eye. But their collective dismissal of grief, their abhorrence of the natural function of the tear ducts, resulted in him firmly clamping his jaw shut and assuming a poker face as he acknowledged to himself the futility of defence or explanations.

He disembarked on the Merrion Road and strolled up Sandymount Avenue, passing the Dart station en route to the village, conscious of how far away it now seemed from Clontarf, that Sandymount was virtually another country, one that he had claimed and felt at home and at ease in, as if he had passed over a border that harboured dangers, even if such dangers were simply thoughts and ideas and memories. He felt a sudden surge of gratitude towards his father for giving him the money to effect such an exodus. Judging by his correspondence and occasional phone calls, David's own exodus to Singapore was a total success - he seemed to be living an independent, reinvented life of delight, of fun, enthusing about his part-time teaching for the Ministry of Education, Raffles Hotel the epicentre of his contented social life.

When he got home, he satisfied his hunger by preparing a cold supper of tuna with mayonnaise, mixed lettuce leaves and cherry tomatoes which he consumed at the dining room table, pleased by the sight of the red roses in the rescued tapestry. Later that night, after a coffee and a brief scrutiny of Vincent's inert house from his usual vantage point, he went off to his bedroom, and, sinking into the clean bed linen, propped himself up on his pillows and read into the small hours.

CHAPTER 18

It was the last day of June, the brink of the traditional holiday season, Moss's morning stroll cancelled by the sight of raindrops trickling down the French windows, rain that was forecast to continue for the day. He sat at the kitchen table sipping a late morning coffee and sifted through the post, seizing a home interiors magazine that he subscribed to. Ripping off the plastic wrapping he went through it page by glossy page, his attention quickly drawn to a feature on apartment living. The photographs yielded an impression of vacant premises with gleaming chrome, steel and glass, the light in the spacious, scrupulously tidy rooms insipid, the angular furniture blending with pale walls adorned with abstract paintings or prints resulting in a portrait of display and storage rather than a home or a 'living space' as the article said. He wondered where the occupants were, assuming they felt compelled to stow themselves away somewhere leaving no trace of digestion, personality, interests, sleep or other nocturnal activities. But he was gratified to find another feature on an Edwardian mansion in an English rural setting, with a photograph of two golden Labradors lying upon the entrance hall tiles, the other images revealing rooms cluttered with antiques and gilt-framed ancestral portraits. Of course, this was an idyll, he knew, yet the articles inspired in him an appreciation of his own surroundings as he put the magazine aside. After depositing his empty cup on top of the unwashed breakfast dishes in the sink, he drifted into the dining room to admire its crimson walls and the Chinese chest of drawers that he had positioned below a large framed print of Vermeer's *De Keukenmeid*, gazing at it with ardour for a moment or two by the light from the plain chandelier suspended from the ceiling rose and which he had fitted with low wattage pearl bulbs to reduce the glare. He then cast an admiring glance at the mahogany sideboard now covered with books and a considerable stash of quality bric-a-brac which he had acquired over the years, along with an assembly of assorted glasses and liquor bottles poised for convenient access.

He decided to light a small fire of briquettes in the sitting room grate to abate the slight chill in the air then set off to the kitchen to prepare his midday meal of a grilled salmon steak with mashed potatoes and garden peas and which he ate at the dining room table set with his best china and cutlery and a crystal goblet filled with beer from a can. He finished off his feast with a ripened pear then took a cafetiere of coffee into the sitting room where he switched on a couple of lamps with red and ochre shades. The warm glow cancelled out the greyness induced by the rain descending heavily beyond the tall sash windows framed by ivory velvet curtains, the writing desk underneath piled with books and papers, the cordless telephone nestling incongruously upon its charging stand.

He then sank into the Chesterfield sofa, absently stroking the plum moquette upholstery with his fingertips, the coffee table before him flanked by two wing armchairs covered in faded chintz and which were turned towards the hearth like companions. He felt satisfied with the muted ambience of the room, or dim religious gloom as his father would have called it, for it was gratifyingly similar to Andrew Mortimer's drawing room over in Cambridge. He imagined him sitting in a relaxed pose in one of the armchairs, gin and tonic in hand, the Persian rug stretching out majestically under his feet despite its faded, worn state, most of the threadbare patches and stains obscured by the furniture. As if rewarding himself for his efforts he opened the box of Belgian chocolates which he had brought in on the tray and sank his teeth into one, his eyes narrowing with pleasure at the texture. Topping up his coffee cup and selecting another chocolate, he read for the rest of the afternoon until the eerie sound of the telephone ringing snapped him away from the print. Recognizing the Clontarf number, he hesitated then allowed it to ring out, pretending he wasn't in. He added a couple of briquettes to the fire in response to a mild shiver and turned to look longingly at the framed print of Rembrandt's Nightwatch on the opposite wall as if seeking reassurance, his eyes drawn to the red sash across Captain Banning Cocq's costume and to the little girl flooded with ghostly light, then resumed his place on the sofa. As he watched the silent flames, he reflected on the stark lack of atmospheric comfort over in his mother's house, a fine fifties terrace in a plain, unremarkable design. But the interior was a reflection of someone else's mindset, he thought, for it now seemed stagnant; little had changed in over twenty years, although he was unsure if this was a result of his father's absence. Clare and Louise would fail to appreciate his cluttered rooms, he knew, his untidiness or lack of neatness anathema to Louise's need to keep her surroundings sanitised, in symmetric order.

'How can you live with all this stuff, this junk?' she used to say whenever she would stop to take a peek at his room, a place automatically off limits for her as a result of his hoarding. 'Quite easily,' he would respond in his English accent. He wondered what had become of his old room – it was unlikely they had embarked on any alterations yet, remembering their mild distress the time the new hall table arrived to accommodate the telephone and its directories. Then there was the fuss over placing the Japanese ornament – a gift from Kevin – on the sitting room mantelpiece, the hearth below inhabited by a faded dried flower arrangement in a copper vase all year round except at Christmastime when a fire was permitted.

Such memories, prompted by the unanswered telephone call, evoked a sudden stab of unease at the idea of either Louise or Clare entering what was now his sanctuary, his haven and then laying claim to it, resulting in an uncomfortable tightening in his gut. His mind entered siege mode, inventing strategies that would protect him from such a fate: after all, Louise had already attempted to get in but, thanks to Donal's vigilance, had not succeeded. Yet Clare had never shown any interest in visiting Sandymount, her lack of curiosity a bonus, almost a gift to him. She was predictable and, like Louise, was attached to the house and her routines, but Louise, he realised now, was prone to compulsiveness and would be far more erratic were it not for her inhibitions, her timidity. He puzzled over their world: they had so much money to spare for beautiful things; Clare could afford the very best if she wished to transform the house. But they were not acquisitive yet they, too, pored over home interiors magazines, Louise avidly watching house-hunting programmes on the television, enthralled by the ones specializing in the vigorous transformation of derelict houses into fashionable homes. But she hasn't followed through to a sale for herself, he thought, still hoarding her money, although she changed her car every three or four years and took it for occasional solitary spins usually around the northside coastline, to familiar places such as Sutton, Howth, Portmarnock, Malahide, as well as navigating the city centre streets after rush hour or at weekends, cruising along with admirable competence, the doors locked, her suspicious eyes ever watchful.

Feeling the need for a drink, he set off to the kitchen for a beer, uttering a heartfelt expletive as he realized he had drunk the last can at lunchtime. He opened the French doors for a few moments to let in the fresh, damp air: the rain had stopped but the sky was laden with dull sluggish clouds. On a sudden impulse, he shrugged on a light jacket, put the fireguard in place then set off to the village pub for a beer, absorbing a reassuring energy from the men seated alongside him at the bar, their silence punctuated by harmless political and sports commentary every now and then, his siege worries slowly disintegrating as he finished his second glass of beer. He bought a bag of chips on the way home and consumed them in the kitchen with a pot of tea, watching a Hitchcock film from the easy chair. Around midnight, he headed up to his bedroom, closed the curtains over on the lingering twilight and read until he was overcome by the irresistible urge to sleep. Switching off the lamp, he settled back onto the pillows - a cautious but contented man.

CHAPTER 19

Clare began to feel apprehensive about the deterioration in Louise's demeanour which had become magnified without the backdrop of Moss's discreet comings and goings. She would now arrive home from work sighing, disgruntled, a scowl stealing the fine features from her face, her mouth tightening and releasing words of disappointment mainly at changes in the office, a place that had remained so predictable, so reliable, for so long. It seemed to Clare that these changes were largely benign, many of a technical nature of which she had little comprehension, a flurry of resignations resulting in Louise having to work late occasionally. She found the news of the new manager with the European name intriguing but hardly a cause for concern, merely evidence of the multiculturalism she was hearing so much about on the radio especially the live phone-in show she loved, some of the callers responding to the new prosperity by claiming that the country was 'awash with money' but had yet to reach their part of the island, their comments sometimes prefixed with a 'Well now, don't get me wrong, I mean I'm not racist, but....' She began to watch Louise more attentively now as she devoured her dinner, mentally pencilling in her eyebrows and lips to enhance their colour and shape and wishing she would apply a nice tinted foundation to relieve the pallor that had invaded her face. A wave of relief overcame her, along with a mental sigh, whenever she heard the clunk of the front door in the mornings as Louise set off for work leaving her free to go down for breakfast, bringing with her the teacup that Louise had placed loyally upon the bedside locker earlier on.

A recent visit with the doctor near the end of June reassured Clare that she was in excellent general health. She had relinquished her pride by admitting to increasing bouts of insomnia, exacerbated by her daughter's behaviour which she presented as family worries, and now took a mild sedative at night after a lifetime of suffering. The novelty of a full, uninterrupted night's sleep seemed to melt away the brittleness of her days and this she treasured, feeling deeply grateful to her doctor, amused by his kindly pragmatism: 'At your age Clare? No point in feeling guilty about such things'. Within a few days of exquisite sleep, the pills hidden in a spare makeup bag in a drawer in her dressing table, a new energy began to grow and accumulate within her and she dared to fantasise about ways of being free of her daughter's unhappy influence. This house hunt has gone on far too long, she thought over breakfast on a Monday morning in early July, frowning as she considered Louise's intensive treatment of the previous Saturday - it was like having an invisible bear in the house. And her summer holiday leave was due soon, she remembered, around mid-July, for two whole weeks... With a sigh, she got up to wash up her breakfast things and by the time she had finished, she determined not to trail around looking at properties with her this time.

Around eleven o'clock, her usual slightly hesitant stroll to the newsagents was more strident, purposeful, and after buying a magazine, a sliced pan and a carton of cream for a strawberry mousse she planned to make later on, she was pleased at being joined for the journey home by Hilda Grace, her next door neighbour. Hilda complimented her on her lovely summer dress and linen jacket and told her the two grandchildren were coming to stay until the end of the month then they would all head off to Kerry for August, Clare expressing her delight for she loved the sound of the children's voices during the summer holidays, although her smile faded slightly as she remembered Louise's dismay at such sounds. By the time she was back in the conservatory drinking her solitary coffee and nibbling on a digestive biscuit, her magazine poised for reading, she felt restless, knowing that she would have to take some form of independent action. And so she devised a new routine beginning the next morning when she took a bus into town after rush hour, proffering her free travel pass tentatively. Once safely inside Clearys in O'Connell Street, her apprehension evaporated and she began to enjoy her adventure, as if she had found a new occupation, taking her coffee break in the café there, her pleasant browse in the familiar department store resulting in a number of spontaneous purchases. She returned home by bus around half past twelve, a group of paper carrier bags nestling on the vacant seat beside her.

When Louise narrated another distressing report that evening, Clare tuned out, already plotting her next day's outing. By Saturday morning, her routine well established, she gave her the slip by setting off to the bus stop a little earlier this time, around half past nine, having made careful preparations, dressing in best clothes and wearing discreet but effective makeup and her favourite comfortable but stylish shoes, for she planned to expand her excursion by going to the southside, and walk around the shops in the Grafton Street area then treat herself to a cappuccino in one of the new cafes. She would take a taxi home, when her wristwatch hands would indicate a time when it was safe to return, that the domestic frenzy would be over and her daughter would be watching television.

As she strolled in her careful but elegant manner along Grafton Street after an intensive browse of Brown Thomas's, marvelling at her newfound stamina and at how pleasant Dublin seemed on a Saturday morning, the weather sunny and mild, the throng looking prosperous and carefree, she felt her elbow being gripped from behind. Automatically clutching her handbag, she swung quickly round only to see the familiar face of Moss smiling in that slightly mischievous way of his while apologizing profusely for having given her such a fright. When he kissed her on the cheek she felt startled, as if wakened out of a trance. Her surroundings came into sharper focus – perhaps the real world that people spoke of, but of this she could not be sure. He introduced her to his companion with the long voluminous hair: 'This is Valerie,' he said and the two women shook hands, smiling and exchanging pleasantries. They invited her for a coffee in Bewley's, its entrance a few yards away, the scent of roasted coffee beans wafting by them, but she said no, she had just had one in a little café on Nassau Street. 'How about lunch in Neary's, then?' suggested Moss. 'They do a lovely fresh salmon sandwich there.' But again she found herself saying 'No, Morris, thank you, I'd better get home; Louise is on her own.'

They accompanied her up to the rank at St. Stephen's Green where Moss saw her safely into a taxi and they waved her off home to Clontarf where she narrated her adventure to Louise who feigned disinterest, making a show of indifference to pleasing details about how well Moss was looking and 'his girlfriend – well, I think she's a girlfriend – seemed very nice.' As Clare hastily assembled ham and cheese sandwiches for their lunch and sliced the Madeira cake she had bought on impulse in the Kylemore bakery, she was struck by the dramatic contrast between Louise and the serene Valerie with her unfamiliar accent, her unusual clothes and make up, as if following a private but accepted code for her age - 'She wore a dress over her jeans!' Admonishing herself for turning down the invitations, she remembered Valerie's sincere look of disappointment: 'Another time we hope.' *We...* I could have had a glass of sherry or wine, she thought while gazing intently out of the kitchen window as if seeing a landscape strewn with possibilities beyond the clear pane.

That afternoon, while resting in her conservatory chair, she reflected on the encounter, dramatic despite its brevity. She was struck by a sudden awareness of her son as an utterly separate, almost alien entity, but also of a tenderness in him that she had somehow overlooked; his genteel manners, his manliness, and that dimpled smile of his – reassuring, kindly. How had it all come about? How come he seemed so contented, so much at ease with himself? Investigating her conscience about how this had been achieved without her influence and intervention was immediately rejected although she knew that she could not take the credit for such radiance. Memories of his boyhood began to emerge but these were unremarkable, and she quickly dismissed the idea that motherhood, too, had been uneventful for her. A host of other thoughts rose up like prompts, clues and shadowed her through to her walk back from Mass with Louise that evening and leaving an imprint, a puzzle frown on her forehead as she prepared for bed after they watched a

.film, a psychological thriller that she had seen before, realising guiltily what little impact Moss's absence had had on her so far although she missed his presence in the house at night time. But she had adapted well and trusted the burglar alarm, the code and spare house keys safe with Anne for emergencies and Moss still had his for contingencies.

As soon as she got into bed, the pillows firm against her back, she carefully swallowed her white pill with filtered water and tried to read her library book but felt a little distracted although not uncomfortable. Her innocent morning excursion had after all produced valuable results - she had met Valerie. Will he marry her...? She had also purchased a cream cotton polo neck top and had seen a jacket she liked in a new boutique. And it was time to update her cosmetics, she decided, try a new lipstick colour and a different foundation shade, already looking forward keenly to her next outing on Monday, or Tuesday at the latest. With the pill taking its pleasant effect, she closed the book gently, placed it on the bedside locker, stretched out her arm and turned off the light.

CHAPTER 20

'Continuing warm and humid with patchy drizzle and a clearance will follow from the West later on this evening,' promised the forecaster at Eternity FM while Moss munched rice crispies with slices of banana, the French windows opened onto the garden. He yearned for a great heat wave, a scorcher, as he buttered a slice of toast, indulging in a ritual fantasy about Mediterranean climate conditions manifesting in Ireland for several months without interruption. Pouring tea into the scarlet mug, he opened his diary to revise the summer bookings for his cottage as a cancellation had arrived by email, leaving the latter ten days of July free. A sensation of delight stole over him as he considered using the cottage himself, satisfy his need for a change of scene, a holiday atmosphere, instead of waiting until September when he went there for his routine two week break. Ten days is a bit short, he thought, drumming his pen absently. After breakfast he busied himself with the washing up and the laundry, his t-shirts, jeans, boxer shorts and socks engulfed by white suds in the machine, then he set off to the supermarket in the humid air, thinking of the waves breaking on the beach at Curlew Cove. As soon as he got home and deposited the newspaper and bag of groceries on the kitchen table, he decided to telephone Strand House, a guesthouse he had discovered in his late twenties and where he stayed in many times. The familiar voice of its proprietor, Judith Mulcahy, greeted him warmly.

'Moss! How are you? And how is your new place? Are you settling in well?'

'Excellent thanks, Judith. Have it all sorted now. I'll tell you all about it when I see you. I've had a cancellation and I'll be down for a week or so, till the end of July, then the Bretts will arrive for August as usual. Now my current guests are leaving on the twenty-first but I was thinking of coming down sooner - could you fit me in for a few days before they go?'

'Certainly Moss, of course we can - why not treat yourself! I'll check the book...yes, I have the eighteenth or nineteenth available, if that suits?'

'The eighteenth please, three nights full board.'

'That's fine Moss, look forward to seeing you then.'

Closing his diary and putting his pen down triumphantly, he put the kettle on for another pot of tea to celebrate not just his holiday plans but his lack of caution in making so spontaneous a decision. He intended telling Clare about his plans but hesitated as he eyed the phone warily; Louise had left a message in his voicemail a couple of days ago, her tone unusually harsh and sarcastic: 'Just ringing to let you know we're still alive...' followed by a clattering sound as she hung up abruptly, Moss then deleting the other five unanswered calls from her number on the display screen. As he drank his tea he decided to defer the call until after dinner.

'Ooooh it's you!' exclaimed Louise. 'We're so privileged to get a call from *you*...' When she learned he was going to Wexford, her voice instantly assumed a saccharine tone as she offered to look after his flat while he was away. 'I'll be off for two weeks anyway so I've plenty of time,' she said earnestly, Moss's expression sceptical as he regarded her offer as another opportunity to secure a destination, a place she could use for a change of scene for herself without making any effort. A very convenient option, he thought, his eyes narrowing at the idea of her snooping around his rooms and trying to befriend his tenants. No longer caring if his concerns were irrational or selfish, he immediately discouraged her by using his stockpile of evasive tactics.

'I've someone else doing that,' he told her. 'It's all arranged, organised, no problem.'

'But you could give me a spare key in case of an emergency,' she persisted, seeing her plans dissolve again.

'There's no need,' he said smoothly. 'Like I said, I have someone who takes care of all that sort of thing. I've been doing it for years now. It's routine stuff. All part of being a landlord.'

Feeling slightly unsettled after the call, he went out to the garden to retrieve his clothes from the line, a wave of guilt coursing through him until he remembered the display of indifference Louise would affect whenever he returned from Wexford after one of his peaceful weekends there. Words of welcome or even enquiry would be absent except when it had been raining, when she would then express a keen interest.

'Raining? Nah, not where I was,' he would respond cheerfully. 'It was grand. It's not called the sunny south east for nothing, you know.'

'Oh but the forecast was for rain in all areas,' she would say sharply. 'It lashed here the whole weekend.'

His temper rising, he would feed her the biting words in an even, casual tone: 'Ah well, I had a great time. There's plenty to do down there anyway, whatever the weather.'

Her barely concealed preference that his weekends had been spoilt or diminished in any way still irked him, compounded by her reaction when he first bought the mobile home all those years ago, on his second visit to Strand House. As soon as he got back to Clontarf he had told Clare and Louise, in a buoyant manner, that he had bought a mobile home from the Mulcahys, on their site close to the beach.

'But sure you've only just bought a house!' Louise had exclaimed, adding: 'A mobile home...that's just a sort of caravan, isn't it? Is it very small?' He was also mystified when some of his colleagues had made similar remarks. By the time he had traded up and bought a renovated cottage from the Mulcahys around five years later, his decision to withhold the news was easy, although not effortless as he tried to conceal his elation while establishing the deception that he still went to the mobile home. After returning to the kitchen with his slightly damp clothes nestling in the laundry basket, he gave a weak smile at the realization that this deception was well into its seventh successful year although he had once let it slip to Louise that he was off to the cottage for the weekend.

'Cottage,' she had repeated. 'What cottage?'

'Eh no, the mobile, I said mobile.'

'No you didn't, you said cottage.'

'Did I?' he had chuckled. 'Ah well, I always visit a friend there – an artist chap who rents a cottage for the summer.'

'Oh.'

CHAPTER 21

A sense of foreboding overcame Louise as she made her way home from work on Friday, wondering how she would fill the lengthy two week stretch of time that lay ahead of her. Over her dinner, she found herself complaining about Moss, telling Clare plaintively: 'I just don't know what's got into Moss. He won't even give me a key to his flat while he's away. I mean I was only trying to be helpful,' she paused to stab a chip with her fork. 'He just doesn't trust his own family, does he?'

Clare, who was watching her daughter's sullen expression, replied with unexpected severity: 'Well you should have found a place of your own by now - then you'd be independent like your brother. *And* Susan. I bumped into Denise King in town the other day. She told me she'll be in her house by September.'

Louise flinched at the news and the tone of her voice for it hit her with the acid sound of truth and fell quiet, eating the rest of her meal in the awkward silence that followed. Taking refuge in her bedroom afterwards, the door resolutely closed, she fumed in the corner chair, the shrieks of the Grace's grandchildren playing in the garden adding to her irritation. She leapt up and impulsively snatched her keys off the dressing table and set off to Ringsend to take a covert look at Susan's house from the seclusion of her car. Close to the front gate was the estate agent's board, the sight of the words Sale Agreed slanting across it filling her with a sudden, bleak dismay, relieved by the knowledge that she would not have to face Susan and witness her triumph, that the postponement of their Thursday evenings was now an advantage. Taking a detour home to steady her nerves she drove around the city centre streets, making a loop around St. Stephen's Green over and over again until she finally went back to Clontarf. After she parked the car and closed the gate over, she became acutely aware, as if for the first time, that this was not her own home, it was her mother's house. And when she inserted the key into the front door lock, she felt trapped, incomplete, despite the security she felt behind it, the phantom image of the Sale Agreed sign lingering in her mind.

After a restless night, she was shocked the next morning to see the digits on her bedside clock reveal that she had had an unprecedented lie in and, feeling vaguely embarrassed, prepared herself then went down to the kitchen where Clare was finishing her coffee, a magazine opened in front of her, the table set for Louise who set about making the toast and clicking the kettle on. Closing her magazine neatly, Clare announced that she was going to do a clear out, 'a major de-cluttering' she said, the idea gleaned from a recently viewed television programme and backed up by the magazine article. 'You should do the same Louise,' she said as she headed for the door.

Still feeling disorientated at the late morning hour, Louise ate her breakfast hastily then began to tidy up the kitchen, already planning to immerse herself in various chores. Hearing muffled thuds in her mother's bedroom, she hurried upstairs to investigate and was stunned by the sight of Clare engaged in intense activity, the contents of her wardrobe sprawled over the bed, most of the items still on their hangers, the chest of drawers looking ransacked, a pile of shoes lying in a heap on the floor next to a large cardboard box.

'There are three piles,' Clare explained. 'Keep, give to charity shop and throw away. You have to be ruthless,' she emphasised as she opened a black refuse bag enthusiastically and shaped it for filling up. Louise backed out of the room and set off truculently to face her own wardrobe. But as soon as she opened the doors she froze at the idea of giving away any of her clothes, her lips parting in disdain. The same sensation occurred when she opened the chest of drawers, her eyes drawn nostalgically to a pale pink lambs wool jumper she had bought with her first pay cheque. She then studied her collection of shoes and thought it repugnant that someone, some stranger, would want to wear them.

'How are you getting on?' Clare's voice interrupted her thoughts as she entered the room, briskly stripping a bag from the roll and placing it on Louise's bed.

'Imagine wearing someone else's clothes,' Louise said scornfully. 'And why would anyone buy someone else's shoes let alone wear them?'

'Why not? They might be expensive ones and worn just a few times. Anne gets some lovely things down at Barnardos.' Clare paused to smooth back a lock of her hair. 'You'll never sell them,' she told her, surveying the tired, dated items that Louise was spreading out on the cream coverlet. 'We can take them down there on Monday, then you can treat yourself to something new,' she said encouragingly.

'But I got some new stuff in May - in Brown Thomas's, remember?'

'Then all the more reason for getting rid of your old clothes. If you were moving house, would you really want to take all this with you?'

Louise felt wounded by what felt like another stinging remark uttered in Clare's new tone, as if she had finally lost patience with her fruitless search for it was now clear that she would not be accompanying her to any viewings this time although she had lost her incentive to go house hunting since her last visit to Ringsend. For years she had convinced herself that she was doing her mother a favour by staying in the family home, as Moss had done, both responding to a need to protect her. But it now began to dawn on her that such protection was not required. Clare's energy and strength astonished her as she watched her haul a bulging black bag down the stairs with ease; she seemed far more durable and resilient than she had ever anticipated, settling in for a lengthy elderly age with no sign so far of the presumed decline and its attendant illnesses. And in the event of her eventual demise, the house would not be hers, Louise knew. It would have to be sold so that Moss would get his share - as if he hasn't got enough already, she thought darkly.

She parted reluctantly with a beige jumper and a skirt, its waistband now too loose, put them in a carrier bag and stowed the rest of her clothes away then slunk down to the kitchen to make herself a mug of coffee without telling Clare. The unexpected de-cluttering exercise was bringing to light her fear of upheaval, the sheer effort that packing to move house would involve. And there were so many risks, she thought as she opened the biscuit tin, the internal list of what-ifs that she conveyed in her mind springing to life: what if her new neighbours were hardened criminals, or hosts of rowdy, endless parties, or one of those male loners, the silent, sinister type, a potential serial killer? Within the solidity of the Clontarf house no unusual sounds filtered through the party walls with the Grace's: Pete and Hilda were elderly but vigorous, walking the promenade daily with Rambo, their King Charles spaniel, and visited regularly by two loyal sons and a daughter whose children's exuberance filled the house and garden in July until the silence of August would descend after their departure to Kerry. Clare called in to them occasionally, and always at Christmas, bringing a bottle of port with her and returning, an hour or so later, with a box of chocolate biscuits in an ornate tin, her cheeks flushed from the glass of mulled wine. Every summer, the whiskered Pete would ring their doorbell to hand in a bag of tomatoes from his greenhouse, or roses from the garden, Louise usually leaving such neighbourly gestures to Moss to handle. A side entrance protected them from sounds from the neighbours on the other side although that house had been put though a vigorous overhaul when the Campbell's moved in only three years ago. But once they had settled down, Louise carefully studied their routines and was satisfied with their predictability, with the sensible rhythm of their daily lives.

But in Clare, predictability had been transformed to spontaneity, Louise dumbfounded by this transition, by her frequent comings and goings, her own former role as companion now apparently redundant.

'I'm off to lunch with Anne,' Clare announced on Monday, although this was not unusual. But on Tuesday morning: 'I'm meeting Jean and Brenda today - we're going to the Concert

Hall for the lunchtime recital and then we're having afternoon tea at the Merrion. With champagne!'

As Clare exited the house Louise took note of her determined pace, the folds of her calf-length floral summer dress swinging under a snug cream cotton jacket, her handbag slung tightly across her left shoulder, her manicured fingers adjusting her silk scarf. 'Afternoon tea at the Merrion,' Louise mimicked later on as she tugged sheets from the washing machine into a grey plastic laundry basket, scowling at such audacious expenditure on pleasure, her mother by now submerged in the city centre. '*With champagne...*'

Chapter 22

After much ruminating about asking Valerie to water his plants while he was away, Moss decided to put his trust in Maddie who agreed without hesitation. He felt no sense of invasion at the idea of her entering his space in his absence, reassured by the knowledge that his contact numbers were tucked safely behind her fridge magnet, the spare key to his flat handed over and lying discreetly in a tiny bowl on her display unit with its books and sewing paraphernalia. On the eighteenth, the morning news bulletin ended with a favourable weather forecast and after an early lunch he put his luggage in the car and set off for the N11, passing the familiar suburbs. Then, at a certain point along the road, he saw the Sugarloaf mountain and its lesser twin emerge from the vast green landscape, the blue sky patterned with bulky white clouds. He could feel the weight of the city drift off his shoulders and opened the windows instinctively as if releasing a host of urban ghosts. And the car felt cleaner, lighter as he drove along steadily through the Glen of the Downs, on and on towards the southeast coast with his favourite U2 cd keeping him company until he signalled for the exit for Curlew Cove. Within minutes he arrived at the opened white iron gates, drove carefully along the familiar curved driveway flanked by chestnut trees and parked outside the Georgian manor house. When he got out of the car, he hesitated as usual as if steadying himself from the impact of the resounding silence, the air intensely fragrant. He gazed fervently at the façade of the magnificent building before him, knowing that it was not a functional bed and breakfast establishment where guests were expected to be up at a predictable hour, consume a traditional breakfast then make themselves scarce for a day of intense activity, set off to a golf course or go horse riding or hill walking or visit various tourist attractions, then return in the late afternoon to freshen up before going out again to dinner somewhere. At Strand House, he knew, you took up residence.

He entered the spacious front hall through the vast open door and stood still, inhaling the aromatic trace of wood smoke and beeswax, feeling an overwhelming sense of being grounded, of being completely at home in the world. He was about to read the compliments in the guestbook on the hall table when Judith Mulcahy emerged from an adjacent room, her long auburn hair tied back in a loose braid, her competent, kindly face exuding contentment, a state that was derived from the legions of visitors who had lived in her home, he presumed, even if only for one night. They exchanged warm greetings, Judith telling him that he was in luck, they too had had a cancellation and he could have Room 4 for a change. He followed her elegant progress up to the guest quarters accessed by a crimson carpeted staircase then along a wide landing, the floorboards under their tread whispering creaks and arrived at a heavy panelled door at the front of the house. She pushed it wide open and gave a gracious wave to usher him through, Moss exhaling an audible gasp of delight at the sight of the four poster bed and bulky antique furnishings and dark wood panelling, a collection of paintings and watercolours of seascapes and horses adorning the walls. Beyond the large window he could see fields bordered by hedgerows and, over the tops of the trees, the glint of the sea.

'Dinner's at seven as usual,' Judith said, smiling broadly at his reaction and handing him his key. 'How about some tea, Moss? Come on down to the kitchen when you're ready.'

After unpacking and using the en suite bathroom with its worn but spotless navy blue towels, he went down to the brightly painted kitchen where Judith motioned him to a wicker sofa opposite a pink range that emanated a soothing warmth. A tea tray was laid out invitingly upon the coffee table and he feasted on a hot fruit scone, the butter melting into it as he spread it with home-made strawberry jam and a layer of freshly whipped cream. Judith sat down in an adjacent red armchair draped with a multicoloured crocheted throw and she poured out strong tea for them both into sky blue mugs, the conversation easy and convivial, both united in the language of property and the auction rooms where she sourced most of her furniture. She also gave him an enthusiastic update on the family and the farm which was managed by her husband Alan and their son Keith, both men off on another building renovation nearby. Their eldest daughter Lucinda who lived in Australia, in Perth, had had another baby – 'George: not a name I'd have chosen myself, but there you are!' Marie, the youngest at twenty-two, had moved to Dublin and had got herself a job with an estate agent - 'The property market's gone bananas altogether, Moss, hasn't it?!' Keith's son Ricky was still in the local primary school and was 'totally soccer mad!' The guesthouse was busy enough - 'A lot of French this year,' but she was blessed to have Caroline as her housekeeper and her niece Debbie was a great help with the dinners. Other names were mentioned, credited with their invaluable assistance, Moss losing track, fascinated by her ability to surround herself with such a reliable, productive team, relieved that Caroline still had the time to arrange the cleaning of his cottage in between bookings.

Later on, feeling refreshed after a long soak in the bathtub and a change of clothes, he went for a stroll around the grounds then returned to the spacious sitting room where a number of other guests were helping themselves to aperitifs from the display of bottles on an ancient sideboard. He poured himself a sherry, raising his glass in a polite gesture then sank into an armchair by the wood-burning stove, a number of logs glowing inside. The young couple reclining on the adjacent sofa greeted him with wan smiles, their faces still pale from jetlag, attributing their condition to their exhausting journey from New Zealand. At a few minutes past seven, they were summoned for dinner, his stomach aching from the scent of roast lamb as he followed the guests and Debbie along the dimly lit hall into a room of elegant formality where they assembled themselves around a long, gleaming candle-lit table. He seated himself comfortably in a high back chair next to an American gentleman who introduced himself as Dwight. A

French couple gave an amusing account of their week touring the West, furnished with anecdotes of cultural differences and price comparisons. Two glamorous elderly women who had missed the aperitifs made a dramatic entrance, claiming the chairs opposite Moss, declaring their nationalities by the first course as if presenting credentials, listing the countries they had visited so far on their monumental itinerary, while Moss felt fleetingly like an impostor, a gatecrasher, when he admitted his Dublin origins, even though they all smiled approvingly, even indulgently at him.

Sated by the food and two glasses of claret, he returned to the sitting room to sip his coffee and searched out a book from one of the shelves, then reclaimed his chair, enjoying the peaceful room, the vanished guests equipped with information about the local pubs and traditional music venues. Someone had replenished the stove with another log and turned on the occasional lamps. He closed his eyes for a moment, convinced that Strand House was ideal for holidaymakers in search of a quiet that had become elusive in the places where they existed from day to day. Something, some element, perhaps the atmosphere itself, seemed to protect the house from the attention of hard-nosed corporate drudges who were more at home in large impersonal hotels, unfazed by the fussy encampment of a wedding party as long as there was access to bars and bedroom mini-bars, feeling obliged to work at pleasure, fun a form of enforcement.

The next morning he felt utterly at ease when he awoke from a dreamless sleep. As he was shaving, he realized that the tensions of his former corporate lifestyle had been shed like a reptilian skin over the previous months. He breakfasted on cornflakes with strawberries, then scrambled eggs, grilled bacon and tomatoes, a rack of toast and a pot of tea, joining in the exchange of greetings and analysis of the quality of the night's sleep, the New Zealanders transformed, the previous night's pallor replaced by a healthier, somewhat amorous flush as they discussed their plans for the day. Around eleven he made his way down to the beach along the narrow road that served as rear access to the estate, and took the turn into a wide sandy lane where he stopped for a nostalgic look at his former mobile home. It was still owned by his successor Ian Ross, released from his occupation in the city to paint seascapes and churches for the summer. After breakfast Judith told him that Ian was off sketching in Wexford Town for the day and would see him in the Harbour Bar that evening. No doubt the entire village knows I'm here, he thought as he appraised the height of the eucalyptus tree near the gate and which he used to watch from the lounge window. The other mobile homes, seven in all, were situated in the adjacent plots bordered by trees and hedges, with private access through wooden gates. A car with an English registration was parked in a narrow space in one of the gardens, a motorbike next door, the mobile's opened windows releasing the tinny, companionable sound of a radio programme. He resumed his walk until he arrived on the beach through a gap in the dunes. Its sparse population was clustered into tiny groups, some of them protected from the mild breeze by colourful wind breakers. He walked along the shoreline to the village of Curlew Cove, admiring its terraced houses and the boats in the harbour overlooked by the pub, its name - Harbour Bar - in faded blue lettering with gold surround. After a leisurely stroll along the main village street he entered the Sea View Hotel where he found himself a seat in the lounge. He ordered a coffee, assuming that the tall, poised, blonde young waitress was one of the new migrants, perhaps Latvian, or Lithuanian. He read the Irish Times for a while, finished his coffee then went for a walk around the harbour, resisting the urge to take a look at his cottage in Falcon Lane, just a few streets away and returned to the guesthouse, retracing his steps along the beach, casting appreciative glances at the line of detached wooden houses perched along the tops of the dunes. Most of them seemed occupied, their windows open, the towels and swimwear swaying on the clothes lines evidence of carefree holiday life. The sound of a child crying somewhere suddenly pierced the air. Down by the water's edge, he saw a man wade into the sea with a little boy then they plunged into the waves and began to swim.

Passing by the mobile home again, he remembered the time Louise and Clare had made a visit to it - perhaps out of desperation, he thought now - for it was during an exceptionally hot and prolonged summer. But the visit had been quite a success what with Louise going for a swim with him, the embargo on their collective caution lifted in honour of the perfect day. Clare watched them both anxiously from the beach towel, her expression betraying her illusion that Louise was delicate, despite the visual evidence of those strong legs that were somewhat hesitant under the workaday clothes and leisure wear and the shimmering body glowing with vitality as she dried herself vigorously with a large striped towel, blind to her hourglass figure. Back in the mobile Clare and Louise reverted to cautious reserve as they sat down on the narrow cushioned benches around the lounge table, their tour upon arrival confirming that the structure, although narrow, was much larger than expected, eliciting a surprised 'Oh - you have an oven here? And a fridge?!' when they were shown the kitchen. 'Yep, *and* a proper toilet too, of course, see?' And Moss opened the door onto a bathroom with a full size bath, then the main bedroom with a double bed, and next door, a tiny spare room with a narrow bed.

They surveyed his shelves filled with books and ornaments while he set the table and put down a plateful of ham and salad sandwiches, then jam, butter and a wicker basket filled with warm scones wrapped in a tea towel then ate their meal hungrily, Louise forgetting to be finicky as Moss poured the hot, dark liquid into mismatched teacups from a large silver teapot. He was surprised when Clare suddenly suggested that Louise should come down sometime for a break, would it not be nice? But Louise looked doubtful, her sunburnt face clouding slightly. 'Why not try it just for one night' he said. 'It won't cost you anything.' But he could see by her evasive frown that she found it too primitive, or perhaps unsafe. Undeterred, he had then suggested they treat themselves to a weekend at Strand House, enthusing about the rooms, the atmosphere and the international dining arrangement. But Louise shrugged another response or lack of response, stacking the cups and plates with a sudden hastiness for they were both beginning to show signs of the restlessness that precedes an urgency to go home, saying 'We must get back soon, it's a long drive,' while he lazily poured himself another cup of tea.

'Suit yourselves,' he said. They were gone by four o'clock and never returned.

Taking a deep breath, he banished such memories from his mind as he continued his stroll back to the guesthouse for it would soon be time for lunch of soup and sandwiches in the sun lounge, then a languid afternoon reading until it was time for tea and scones at four o'clock. After that, it was off for a walk on the beach and a swim before dinnertime. And there was the evening's entertainment to look forward to, for Dwight had agreed to join himself and Ian 'for a few scoops' in the pub, Moss assuring him that the musicians would arrive around nine thirty or so and that he was in for a great night.

CHAPTER 23

Moss finished his final breakfast at Strand House then returned to his room where he took his time packing his belongings. When he paid his bill in the kitchen, Judith reminded him to avail of dinner any evening '...for the usual charge' but to let her know by noon. He went the short distance to Curlew Cove village, driving carefully through the narrow streets until he reached Falcon Lane. He parked on the verge outside the front gate and got out to survey the cottage with its white walls and red front door and overlooking the walled gardens of a row of sizeable old houses, many of them popular bed and breakfasts. Dirk and Hugo Stein's jeep was parked in their new driveway next door, the brothers back again for another season of pigeon shooting when they would embark on their daily adventure early in the morning and return for dinner around six o'clock.

Carrying his bags to the front doorstep, he put the key in the lock, pushed the door open then went in, exulting in the reclamation of his property, his holiday home that Keith and Alan Mulcahy had renovated from a derelict state along with three other cottages. They had given him first option to buy number 4 contingent upon the return of the mobile home to them, Moss instantly seeing myriad advantages in having a warmer bricks and mortar structure in the village centre. The mobile contained a penetrating chill for much of the year, although it was quickly warmed up once inhabited.

He wandered around looking approvingly at the way Caroline had put it to rights earlier on that morning, her payment secured the night before, missing him by minutes perhaps, the departed guests probably in Dublin Airport by now and about to board a flight to Brussels. He opened the lounge window to let in the fresh salt air, the raucous shriek of gulls resonating in the harbour, and admired the unobstructed view of the familiar curved coastline with its patches of rocks and dunes.

In the small kitchen with its rose coloured walls, he filled the
kettle, switched it on and made a pot of tea, cut a slice of tea
brack then settled himself on the crimson sofa in the lounge
where he opened a bag filled with books. Spreading them out
upon the pinewood coffee table, he arranged them in an orderly
pattern, intent on concentration, like an addict preparing a fix,
his expression contemplative as he carefully considered which
one he would read first.

He quickly fell into a routine – after breakfast he would go
for a walk along the beach towards the rocks at the headland,
wearing trainers, a long, loose fitting t-shirt and a pair of
Bermuda shorts patterned with vivid colours that Kevin had
given him long ago as a souvenir. Joggers often joined him,
slowing down their pace to exchange greetings then jog doggedly
on with a friendly parting wave, intent on health, vitality as he
lagged behind, making his own pace, at ease with his aversion
to exercise and lack of ambition to strive or be seen to strive,
regarding sport the domain of another species. He preferred
to submit his senses to the maritime landscape, a contrast to
Sandymount Strand where the vibration of traffic persisted in
the background and the tide retreated to a great distance leaving
water trails and pools in the rippled sand. In Curlew Cove he
could tune in to different, more dramatic vibrations – the waves
breaking on the sand, the determined force of gravity, the deep
silence during the small night hours when he entered a state of
stillness, forgetting to sleep until sleep engulfed him.

At lunchtime he would go to the Harbour Bar, usually laying
claim to a window seat, the barman already pouring his beer.
'The usual is it, Moss?' 'Yes, thanks, Ronan!' He would sip
his drink for a while, then, his appetite whetted, would order a
bowl of seafood chowder with slices of brown bread and butter,
enjoying the sound of tourists chatting away, although he rarely
made any effort to converse apart from a few pleasantries with
Ronan, or one of the girls who took his order or cleared tables
inconspicuously. One time he was joined by Breda Nolan, a
former neighbour from the Mulcahy site, down from Dublin for

the summer, her visiting friends in tow, animating the air with their voices, lamenting Dublin's traffic gridlocks and apartment block constructions and property prices – 'Scandalous!... Ridiculous!', Breda teasing him routinely about his love life: 'On your own again Moss? Have you not met the woman of your dreams yet?'

'Nah, well I did,' he replied, 'but she went off with someone else,' just to humour her.

One afternoon he began to reflect on moving permanently to the cottage while he was lazing on a deckchair in his secluded back garden, shrouded by the pungent aroma of sun lotion, a baseball cap shielding his eyes. While it seemed tempting, and was still open for serious consideration at some future time, he knew that such a move would change his social landscape in Curlew Cove, that it would be futile to try to befriend the locals, welcoming as they were to him as the regular holidaymaker, the city slicker. But he would be informed or reminded, in subtle ways, that he was an outsider, as Ian had explained to him one evening in the Harbour Bar, his tone confidential. A permanent move would cause the tribal reserve characteristic of provincial towns and villages to seep up to the surface, his altered status as a fulltime resident never to be fully endorsed. While no one would be so uncouth as to tell him to his face to feck off back to where he belonged, unless of course there was drink taken, the menacing sentiment would always be there like an elephant lumbering awkwardly alongside him. Moss promised Ian he would bear this in mind although he doubted his own incentive to actively seek out new friends or acquaintances if he did make the move for he would stay in Dublin regularly, he thought, reclaim the studio flat as his base there once Karl had moved on. At Strand House he noticed that such clannishness was absent, or obsolete, perhaps as a result of long term exposure to the cosmopolitan hoards of seasoned outsiders who holidayed there, for the welcome was genuine, never contrived, and was extended to him far beyond his status as an occasional visitor. Judith sometimes arranged bookings for his cottage and Keith attended to any repairs, such matters dealt with in an obliging yet pragmatic manner. His expression softened as he thought of his visit later on that evening, his dinner reservation secured, looking forward to taking his place at the candle lit table and the companionship of the guests and the dishes Judith would produce from her pink range. He enjoyed the slight frisson of being unpartnered in such situations. But as he lay there in the balmy heat, entranced by the splendour of the quiet afternoon, the blissful peace that had grown within him since his arrival in Curlew Cove gave birth to a generosity of spirit, and out of this generosity evolved a desire to share it. But with whom? The answer was logical, he mused, wondering if Valerie would enjoy a break from those translations, imagining her in her little office, dictionaries to hand, her computer screen glowing, flicking her pen as she struggled over a word – *vriendschap; onzekerheid....* His eyes were drawn to the window of the main bedroom in the eaves with its pale slanted walls - Valerie could stay there and I'll take the spare room below, he thought doubtfully, no longer so keen to preserve their platonic status, allowing himself to feel open to alternatives.

When he got back from his swim around half past five, he gathered up the courage to telephone Valerie and was greeted by the soft, trance-inducing voice of Elias: 'Ah... Moss...How are you doing? They've gone to Amsterdam for a week or so. To be with Josie...' He recovered quickly from the disappointment as he got ready for dinner, feeling sympathy for Josie whose photograph he had seen on a sideboard in their drawing room, next to the one of Niels, her round, smiling face framed by short, curly reddish hair, a pair of bright eyes behind blue-framed glasses giving an impression of vitality despite her battle with multiple sclerosis. Yet Valerie's journeys to Amsterdam were not entirely for her benefit, he had discovered the time he gave Shane and his violin a lift into Merrion Square. 'Any excuse to go back to Amsterdam,' Shane had told him, chuckling. 'There's actually no need for them to go dashing off that often...Josie gets first rate care. Valerie just likes to hang out with her old friends from the UvA, and Johann gets the train to Paris to meet his father for a few days,' Moss smiling inwardly at such information, effortlessly acquired.

Energised by the food and conviviality at Strand House, he made his solitary way back to the village via the beach, the summer light enhancing its colour and shape as he strolled along the smooth sand, dodging the tide as it swirled towards his shoes. He paused to watch a radiant sunset render the water pink and silver. Another perfect or almost perfect day ended in the Harbour Bar, in the company of Ian and a group of Swedish tourists staying in the Sea View Hotel, a music session underway, Moss tapping his right foot to the beat of the bodhran as he sipped his drink. He decided to slink home before closing time, amused at the sight of Ian talking conspiratorially with the woman next to him. As he was squeezing past a couple near the door, he overheard the woman whisper quizzically to her partner, her accent American: 'Why is no one dancing?' When he arrived at the turn into Falcon lane, a group of youths materialised from the shadows, cigarette ends glowing.

'How're yiz lads,' he said pleasantly and they parted silently. He heard a hesitant, reluctant 'Okay...' as he continued along the lane, pleased to see the Stein's jeep and the lights on in their cottage, the two brothers now likely to be pitting their wits against one another in a game of chess. After locking the doors, he made himself a pot of tea and a couple of slices of toast, then settled down on his sofa, drawn back to the book he was reading and the world portrayed in it, unobtrusively enjoying a very late night.

CHAPTER 24

It was a hot sunny day, the sky cloudless, yet Louise found herself at a loose end as she walked briskly from her car to the shopping mall entrance, the structure functioning as an alternative to the city centre where she deplored the unwelcome pressure of the street crowds and the prolific beckoning cafes that she dared not enter alone. It was a Monday afternoon, the second week of her holiday, and Clare had gone out to lunch again, exhibiting yet another independent streak by taking on the weekly shop on Friday mornings now. Louise felt deprived of a task they had always done together on Friday evenings when she would make her meticulous way through the familiar aisles and check the prices against their list, ever vigilant for a discount or a bargain. She passed an agreeable hour browsing in the department stores and speciality shops, splashing out on a lilac t-shirt and some underwear then drifted into the supermarket, wandering aimlessly around its aisles without a list, rashly buying sausages, ice cream and the coffee Clare liked, then making a hasty exit through the express checkout, the mall having suddenly lost its appeal. Back home, the random items stored away, the ice cream safely in the freezer compartment of the neatly stocked fridge, she tried to relax in the garden over tea and a slice of the carrot cake she had bought in a bakery, responding to an urgent need for a treat, for the injection of sugar, of intense sweetness.

Clare got home in time to prepare a chicken salad with bread rolls, insisting they eat their meal in the conservatory for a change. Afterwards, while sipping coffee, the heat and the sight of the cloudless sky triggered a longing in Louise to get away somewhere and absorb the sun in a different place in the hope that it would ease away the persistent inner chill that had invaded her. Around half past eight she decided to take the car for a spin around the environs of south Dublin, driving as far as Dalkey where Sarah lived, slowing down as she passed her house. She had visited her once before, reluctantly, not long after she had bought the car, capitulating to Moss's suggestion of going over to Dalkey and drop in on Sarah and Gerald, check out their art gallery. Their welcome had been warm, even indulgent, as if they were famous, Sarah explaining that Gerald was away in London for a few days. After tea and biscuits, they were shown the gallery, Moss captivated by Sarah's paintings and Gerald's sculptures, Louise's eyes narrowing at the glowing abundance of her cousin's lifestyle and roving critically over her bohemian attire, her hair an artificial red and tied up carelessly with a sequined bobble and decorated with glittering clips. Another visit would be out of the question now and so she drove on to Dun Laoghaire then back through Monkstown where she felt the usual pang of regret mingling with curiosity as she pulled into the parking lot of the apartment she could now be living in, had she not been so timorous. Ruefully admiring the building's architectural splendour, she sighed enviously at the sight of the open windows of the duplex and the owner's access to the stunning, unobstructed sea views. She continued her coastal drive until she reached the Strand Road in Sandymount then found herself heading for Dawn View again, the yellow door unresponsive, Moss's Volvo missing from the driveway. Back in her car she gave the steering wheel a sudden rap as she exclaimed aloud: 'Of course, I forgot! He's gone to Wexford!' Then, satisfied with this explanation, she set off home.

Another uneventful, acutely boring day passed by and on Thursday afternoon she began to despair at her own inertia. While she was half-heartedly watching a film after a spell of sunbathing in the garden, the idea of going to Curlew Cove and paying Moss a surprise visit suddenly came to her, selective memory retrieving pleasant images of the light-filled lounge of his mobile home, the beach lying in wait behind the dunes, the fall of the waves resounding upon the pale sand. She thought longingly of plunging into the water and going for a long swim. But she did not relish the prospect of going there alone, grimacing at the idea of contacting Susan and so she began to search her mind for an alternative companion, a social alibi, and discovered a glimmer of hope in its recesses.

A few weeks ago she had seen Robert White emerge from his car outside the church to usher his mother into the passenger seat - an unusual sighting as Linda usually attended Sunday mass. The sky had been overcast that Saturday evening, the threat of rain imminent. As Robert was getting back into the car he had paused then called to Louise over his shoulder: 'Give us a bell sometime,' accompanied by a wink and a prompt departure after a dramatic revving of the engine and a trail of exhaust fumes. After giving a reflex wave, she had fallen silent as she walked the short distance home with Clare, for Robert had seemed altered, more convincing than her last sighting of him, two years ago at least. She now felt a tinge of regret as she considered the long gap in communication with a man with whom she had been so intimate, a blush rising to her cheeks as memories of their weekend in Connemara sprung to mind, Robert having secured a discount hotel deal. That intimacy had resulted in a nightlong preoccupation with her feelings or lack of feelings in the darkness of the comfortable but bland, standardised hotel room, sounds from the corridor and the car park below filtering through distractingly. Robert had snored beside her, oblivious to her wakeful state and her astonishment at how unaffected she had felt by the vigorous encounter for it ended just as she was beginning to relax even to the point of enjoyment as he collapsed away from her and, after a gentle grunt of satisfaction, slept almost instantly. She had turned away and curled up protectively on her side, wondering why she still felt unqualified, unaltered as the first sign of dawn filtered through a chink in the heavy drapes and she drifted into a few hours of treasured unconsciousness.

Another night of broken sleep in that uncertain bed and Robert's covert thrusting attentions combined with the long drive back to Dublin had taken their toll and resulted in her giving Moss and Clare a litany of complaints about the hotel, the food, the noise, the traffic on the way home – 'It was animal!' Yet she had continued to meet Robert sporadically; he was after all from a respectable family in Pinewalk Grove, off the street where the Leonards lived, and where they had met one another at the funeral of a neighbour. She had been drawn to his sombre, almost sepulchral temperament, Robert making the first traditional move by eventually asking her out to dinner. At the time she harboured a vague aspiration to marry, or become a married woman, although she felt uneasy about motherhood, seeing it as the job of other, more capable, brave women, women that were not filled with trepidation by the gestation and delivery of babies. Not unlike Moss, it was to the security of a structure in the form of property, a potential home that appealed to her, convinced that it would deliver far greater fulfilment.

And such a home had come within her reach just months after their Connemara weekend when Robert bought a penthouse apartment in one of the new city centre blocks. He had shown it off to her one Saturday afternoon, her eager footsteps echoing in the unfurnished rooms, her enthusiasm activated by its convenient location, so close to her office. Her hopes of moving in with him were dashed when she found out that his neighbour had found him lying unconscious outside his front door late one evening, only a month after he had moved in, the key still clutched in his right hand. Such dramatic news had been delivered by Anne Leonard who called in on her way home after her visit to the Whites, Clare and Louise listening raptly on the sofa. For the first time in his life Robert had gone out on regular binges until the night of his collapse. The next day he had returned shakily to the family home, his independence abruptly terminated. The doctor had confirmed mild depression and Robert – 'poor fellow' – was now on medication. '*And* he left his *job*,' Anne had said breathlessly, pausing to take a sip of tea, Louise visibly recoiling in dismay at the idea that he would relinquish a career in his father's firm. 'Oh well, I'm sure he'll be fine - given time – and of course you can always go over and cheer him up Louise!' But Louise had retreated, abhorred at the idea of visiting Robert now that she had been furnished with the facts, so reliably reported by Anne. She had instinctively abandoned him, commitment looming as a chore, seeing depression as an inconvenient illness unlike a physical impairment such as a broken or damaged limb – then she would have visited him in hospital, bring him grapes, chocolates, treats, a get well card which would be propped conspicuously on his bedside locker. Yet despite her avoidance, she listened avidly to the occasional vague report on his progress from Clare, gleaned from Anne or other sources, eventually discovering that although his nerves had been badly affected, they had not broken down. One time she had snapped at Clare for nagging her to at least telephone him - 'Well...he can always phone me if he wants to...I mean, he knows I'm busy at work all day.' But she did eventually send him a card, behaving evasively around the telephone for weeks afterwards, for the call that never came.

Shaking off such memories, she impatiently grabbed the remote to turn the television off then went into the kitchen to prepare a bowl of ice cream and strawberries and took the snack into the conservatory where she could see the azure sky beyond the opened windows. She considered her recent surprise encounter with Robert outside the church – fleeting as it was. For a man banished to obscurity, he looked unexpectedly well and composed, his physical stature somehow more viable and durable than before, his black hair sleekly cut, his smile slightly suggestive. *Give us a bell sometime...* On impulse, she abandoned her snack, strode into the hall, seized the telephone directory, looked up his number hastily then telephoned him. His mother answered in her usual kindly tone: 'Ah...hello Louise! Lovely to hear from you. He's in the garden...just one moment now, I'll go and get him.' There was an agonizing, hollow interval while she waited, feeling tempted to hang up, her heart racing. But as soon as she heard his voice it was as if nothing had happened, as if resuming a conversation held only days ago. He agreed to accompany her to Curlew Cove the following day.

'Why not?' he said decisively. 'No time like the present.'

Catapulted into a frenzy of activity, her companionless state solved, Louise spent the rest of the day making meticulous preparations, and, after a restless night, was relieved to get up at seven the next morning, the sunlight already strong in the cloudless sky. Wearing the lilac t-shirt under a short sleeved white blouse and jeans, her feet bare in a pair of white sandals, she was ready for action only to feel deflated over breakfast, displeased that Robert did not wish to go out any earlier than eleven. Clare was planning to go into town with Anne on one of their flagrant shopping sprees and was somewhat vague about her return, as if keeping her options open although she seemed pleased that Louise had what promised to be an exciting day ahead, encouraging her to enjoy herself as she surveyed her tense face and the way she glanced constantly at the clock on the kitchen wall.

The longed-for departure time arrived. She put a bag with her pale blue bathing suit and a towel onto the back seat of the car then returned to the house to snatch an apple and a banana from the fruit bowl. She drove off to Pinewalk Grove and pulled up on the kerb outside the gate, the blue Victorian door in full view, filled with the sudden dread of a last minute change of plan. But Robert appeared, secured the door behind him then sauntered along the path. He closed the gate over and eased himself into the passenger seat with a grin and the welcome aura of musky after shave. They set off on their journey, Louise emitting a silent sigh of satisfaction.

CHAPTER 25

As they headed down the Clontarf Road, Louise was taken by surprise when Robert suggested they treat themselves to lunch in a hotel in Wicklow. 'Sure we have all day,' he said in a reasonable tone after he had given her directions, Louise trying not to scowl as she began to see the day receding into a vault of wasted time. As they made their way out of the city, she stole curious glances at him at traffic lights, at his casual ease in a black polo shirt, beige combat trousers and dark trainers, his pale blue eyes obscured by a pair of snugly fitting sunglasses. By the time they reached the Glen of the Downs he unwrapped two chocolate snack bars without offering to share them, snapping them decisively then flicking the wrappers out the open window as she tried to suppress a glare while he munched softly in the seat beside her. She was able to take a better look at him when they sat together on a spacious blue velveteen sofa in the hotel's lounge, a place he seemed at home in and well known for he was greeted with a cheerful smile by the receptionist when they entered the foyer - 'Good afternoon Mr. White!'

His former lacklustre skin was transformed, his face gleaming and smooth from his morning shave, her appraisal confirming that the slender gaunt man she had known from the past had been replaced by a far more solid, comfortable looking being. She was not unimpressed as she sipped her still mineral water, in fact she was amazed by the metamorphosis as she scanned his face, searching for signs of the depression that had caused her to flee, trying to come to terms with such a positive image, realizing that the caricature she had formed in her mind of a deflated, downbeat, hangdog man in solitary confinement was now out of date, if not entirely obsolete.

Robert ordered a second glass of sherry for himself, clearly delighted to be there, his eyes ranging over the menu, his phone bleeping occasionally, chuckling to himself as he read a message on the screen. 'Hah,' he said each time with a knowing smile.

He did not reveal the identity of the senders but he did transmit the air of someone involved, occupied, possibly in demand. They both looked up automatically as a small party arrived for aperitifs and settled themselves in the cluster of chairs by one of the tall, wide windows overlooking the gardens. It was a quiet, peaceful place close to forest and mountain walks but Louise longed for the beach, seeing the lunch as a tedious interruption to her own plans, her day lagging behind schedule. In the elegant restaurant with its plush chairs Robert placed a couple of pills beside his wine glass: 'My vitamins,' he said with a sly grin and a wink then gave in to his appetite as he consumed a starter of smoked salmon, followed by rack of Wicklow lamb with roast potatoes and steamed vegetables.

'Excellent,' he would murmur from time to time, taking a generous sip of the red house wine. 'Hm...first rate..!'

Louise picked at her plate, unaccustomed to such hearty lunchtime nourishment. By the time her dessert of strawberries and cream arrived she looked distractedly at the view beyond the windows, aware of time deviously slipping by and, with a resigned sigh, changed her mind about going to Curlew Cove, for Robert had ordered an Irish coffee and a pot of tea to be delivered to the lounge then asked the waiter for the bill. When it was brought to him, she watched him examine it, turn it over, produce a pen from a trouser pocket then scribble out figures and told her how much her share was to the cent.

'One main course, one dessert, one mineral water and one tea,' he announced indicating the total sum with a spotless forefinger.

As if hypnotised, she extracted her wallet from a zipped compartment in her bag, followed by her coin purse and quietly handed over the cash which he counted carefully, stowed it away in his pocket then paid the bill with his credit card. Later on, when they were seated in blue armchairs in the lounge now filled with a consoling, muted light, the tea and coffee already laid out on a polished low table furnished with a vase of freshly cut roses and copies of Country Life magazines, she felt unsettled about the transaction. An archaic notion that he should have or could have paid for the meal, given her a treat, even waived the price of the mineral water or tea as a gesture, was reluctantly dismissed by her for this was the currency, or aspired currency, of their previous relationship. If he pays, she reasoned to herself, then I'll owe him something.

'You're looking well,' she told him, the mild compliment masquerading as an invitation to explain why. Taking a sip of his coffee laced generously with whiskey – 'Heaven!' – and skilfully dabbing cream off his lips with a white linen napkin, he gave a contented shrug and a simple 'Thanks'.

'Are you going to go back to your apartment then?'

'Ah no. Apartment living doesn't suit me,' he replied, adjusting his posture to settle himself comfortably in his chair, 'specially in the city centre. Too hyper for me. I have the place rented out to a Danish fellow now and it's appreciating as we speak. Great investment!' he winked.

'But you left your job,' she reminded him, vigorously stirring the tea which he had poured out for her, the spoon resounding off the interior of the white cup.

'Well…yeah…but that was a good while ago.' He took another sip of coffee, his eyes focussed thoughtfully on the windowpanes behind her. 'Ah well, I needed the break. No regrets there! Dad was fine with it, to his credit. Sure I'm grand now,' he smiled at her. 'Keeping busy!' As if to corroborate this, his phone bleeped an incoming call and he excused himself as he went off to the foyer to respond to it.

'Would you care to take a walk around the gardens?' he asked her when he returned.

'Might as well,' she replied resignedly.

After draining his glass and absently giving it an affectionate pat with his fingertips, he led the way out to the hotel's extensive gardens where they went for a stroll in the intense afternoon heat, Louise's stiff gait creating a gulf between them, although she admired the rose garden where she inhaled the scents appreciatively. Then, in the late afternoon, they returned to Dublin in relative silence. When she parked outside his gate he leaned over to place a light kiss on her cheek – 'That was great

Louise...we must do it again sometime!' And then he was gone, the door clunking firmly behind him, the trail of his after shave and another evocative scent still lingering in her car.

She returned to an empty house, struck by the hollow absence of her mother, the note on the kitchen table saying she had gone to Anne's and that the sandwiches were in the fridge. There was evidence of her shopping spree, a reward perhaps for the de-cluttering episode, she thought, surveying a number of carrier bags huddled on a kitchen chair, as if deposited there in haste. Returning her redundant beach bag to the bedroom, she stowed the contents away, took the apple and banana down to the tea tray which she brought out to the patio table with a mug of tea. She reflected on the way the day had enfolded and how Robert's will had taken her over with such ease. Was it that male company – even that of a miser – was better than none? And I forgot to ask him what he does now, she thought, peeling the banana slowly, still mystified by the change in his demeanour, realising that he had not offered such information, had skilfully avoided so doing. Yet he was able to take a day off at short notice, she mused, convinced that he had some form of occupation. But their time together had not been entirely wasted for they had discussed the property market at length, Robert listening sympathetically as she updated him on her own quest, omitting Susan's victory. He had little advice to offer, simply echoing Moss's encouragement to buy as there seemed to be no sign of house prices coming down, and, since she had access to a considerable down payment, why not go for it? Sitting alone in the shade of early evening, she gave into the disappointment of being deprived of her swim and seeing her brother. Moss would have treated me to that meal, she realized. What was it he used to say about Robert...? Oh yes... Is he still beating the moths out of his wallet? She blushed now as she understood the question and the dimpled smirk that accompanied it. By eight o'clock the sound of her mother's safe return drew her back into the house where she set about getting the supper, trying to hide her rising anger at being cheated out of an entire day as she gave Clare a synopsis of it over their sandwiches and tea, Clare's complexion radiant after the spell in Anne's back garden.

'Oh well, never mind,' Clare said. 'We can always go to Malahide or Portmarnock tomorrow if you like. If the weather's fine,' she added doubtfully. 'Anne said there's a change on the way. Still...at least you had a nice day out with Robert.'

Louise gave a reflex start at the sudden shrill ringing of the telephone, her mother moving swiftly into the hall to answer it.

'That was Morris,' she announced when she returned, another pink glow illuminating her cheeks. 'He's leaving Wexford tomorrow. Those English people are coming back again to rent the mobile for the rest of the summer.'

CHAPTER 26

Moss looked appraisingly at his cache of strawberries on the kitchen table: he had bought five punnets from Keith before breakfast that morning when he was making his rounds in the jeep with Ricky. He began packing them into a shallow cardboard box, reflecting on the phone call to Clare moments before, intrigued by the change in her voice, her usual vague, slightly dithering tone almost vanished, her vocal chords imbued with a lively timbre, saying how delighted Louise would be when he said he would call round with some strawberries tomorrow evening - 'She loves strawberries.' His mouth twisted cynically at the idea of his sister expressing such delight, the smirk changing to an uncertain grin as he contemplated Clare's news that Louise had intended paying him a surprise visit with Robert White that morning but had got delayed; by the time they had finished lunch it was too late to go to Curlew Cove, she had told him, a wave of relief racing over him. He imagined the confusion had she actually arrived at the mobile home. Ian was a bit cagey about answering the door to unexpected visitors; he preferred to meet up in pubs and cafes or by arrangement, Moss conceding that if he had responded, assuming he had been there on such a beautiful day, then the cat would be out of the bag as far as the cottage was concerned.

He shrugged on a black cotton jacket and set off for a walk on the beach to discourage himself from dwelling on the consequences of Louise's discovery of his deviousness, his duplicity. As he walked along the sand in the still air, the waves lapping gently against the shore as if suspending their power, he thought about his last day in Curlew Cove. It had begun with vibrant sunshine, the sky cloudless when he went for a late morning swim in one of the deserted rock pools beyond the headland. On his way back along the water's edge, the beach was quickly filling up with families, couples, groups, youths, the mood one of encampment, dishevelment, exhilaration, albeit vaguely cacophonous. The shrieks of children swimming or playing at the waters edge mingled with the pulse of the waves and the sudden cries of rage when he saw the ramparts of a little girl's freshly constructed sandcastle being stamped on by a couple of boys around eight years old, their faces flushed and eyes gleaming zealously as they made their agile escape towards the shelter of the dunes. Lunch in the busy Harbour Bar had also been slightly discordant as he squeezed himself into the only available seat between Breda Nolan and one of her ebullient friends, capitulating good humouredly to their boisterous joie de vivre. After a satisfying meal he had left them in even higher spirits having treated them to a farewell round of Irish Coffees. He returned to Falcon Lane to prepare for his guests, throwing himself into his tasks, cleaning the windows, mowing the grass, a phone call from Caroline confirming that her sister Audrey would give the place a final going over in the morning. He was fond of the Bretts and liked to be there to welcome them, and, their comfort in mind, had put briquettes into the copper scuttle with its clawed feet and a packet of firelighters and matches in the kitchen cupboard. August was a tricky month; autumn, or autumnal weather, could strike any minute, the back to school radio ads a reminder of the elusiveness, the brevity of the summer season.

By the time he reached the rocks, he saw clouds gathering on the horizon and, with a sigh of regret at the idea of packing, made his way back along the sand, the lights in the village already twinkling, the beach deserted apart from a man walking two dogs and an elderly couple ambling close together, hand in hand. After an early breakfast the next morning he stood at the opened front door to watch the steady descent of rain, the foliage and rooftops glistening: he had sensed it the night before, a damp scent in the air heralding the break-up of the unusually long dry spell. The heavy clouds now cast their gloom over the beach and turned the water silver and grey, the waves tinged with an ethereal green hue as they splashed upon the darkened sand, yet he spotted one of the joggers making drenched but steady progress towards the headland. As he was assembling his luggage at the front door he saw Audrey make her way hastily up the path, her nimble fingers gripping a canvas bag.

'Not a great day for your guests, is it Moss?' she commiserated with him. In the lounge he paid her the usual sum of cash which she tucked deftly into a protruding breast pocket in her denim shirt, then said he would make himself scarce for a while to give her a chance to get the work done. 'No bother, Moss, no bother at all,' she said. 'I'll have this place sorted for you long before they arrive.'

He put the luggage in the car boot, the strawberries on the back seat and drove down to the Sea View Hotel for a coffee and a danish and a read of the paper. When he got back, he marvelled at the results of Audrey's efforts, yet despite its pristine cleanliness, the place felt wiped of his happy occupation and had taken on an air of vacancy, abandonment, as if affronted by his departure. But the atmosphere lifted the moment Julian and Emma Brett arrived a half hour later, Moss welcoming them warmly as he ushered them in, reassuring them that the rain was just a temporary setback, that he had spent almost two weeks there himself.

'This'll clear off; the forecast is actually very good,' he told them displaying his tanned arms, 'it'll be sunny again tomorrow.'

'No worries mate,' smiled the bearded Julian as he clapped him on the shoulder. 'We don't come here for the sunshine, now do we?!' Emma also gave a broad smile, her shoulder length, white hair accentuating her dark medium-like eyes. After ensuring they had everything they needed including his contact numbers as well Keith's for emergencies, he made his farewells then drove up to Strand House where he handed Caroline a bag of his surplus novels for herself and Judith. 'She's off shopping,' she said with her gentle smile. Leaving her with his best regards for them all he returned to his car and paused at the door to cast an affectionate parting gaze over the manor house, drawing sustenance from its splendour, the ginger cat watching him blithely from the shelter of the front doorstep. After wiping the raindrops off his glasses with a tissue, he drove out through the gates and headed for the wet road to Dublin.

By the time he got back to Sandymount, the rain had cleared away to a reveal a muggy, sunny haze. When he was reunited with his flat he could see with renewed clarity the results of his efforts as he roamed lovingly around each room, opening the windows to let in the warm air which was accompanied by a gust of laughter from the garden - Karl had returned, as he did every summer. From the bedroom window he could see him sitting at the new patio table beyond the bench, the umbrella patterned with green and white stripes arranged at a lop-sided angle. His visitor was a man with a head of thick blond hair and a cherubic face, beaming in the way Karl did, he noted - perhaps a brother, possibly a twin. In the front bedroom he peered at Vincent's house, hoping to see some movement, some sign of life, but it looked back defiantly, unchanged. He had yet to see his sister Lily arrive with the shopping but figured that Orla was keeping more efficient track of such comings and goings. He returned to the kitchen to sift through the post which Maddie had left in an orderly pile on the dresser, amused that life had gone on inexorably in his absence, depositing bills through the letterbox. As he read a postcard from Kevin, Masami and Kim on holiday in New Zealand he got up hastily to respond to a knock at the door. He welcomed Maddie in, her skin wafting of sun lotion as she passed by him in a sleeveless pink cotton dress, one of her own creations, he supposed admiringly.

'You look great Moss!' she exclaimed. 'Look like you're just back from the Bahamas!'

Over mugs of tea at the kitchen table she returned his key and he presented her with a decorative paper bag containing a cluster of tiny coloured soap bars arranged in a white ceramic shell-shaped bowl which he bought in a craft shop near the harbour.

'Just a little something for taking care of the plants,' he said, 'and some strawberries.'

'Oh...gorgeous! Thank you very much...and this is lovely,' she said, examining the gift. 'Really nice.'

'So - anything strange while I was away?'

'No, Moss, nothing strange thank heavens, not here anyway. Well, Karl's brother's over from Berlin for a few weeks.' She sipped her tea, her expression clouding slightly. 'Actually last week two of our residents died within a day of each other - both almost ninety. Oh well: death never takes a holiday,' she said pragmatically and bit into a strawberry. 'Mmm!...anyway I'd better get going soon, lots to do...I'm on night duty this weekend.'

The sight of his empty fridge turned his mind to practicalities and he headed off to the supermarket in a daze of pleasure as he realized that he was still on holidays, his tread almost weightless as it sunk in that there was no workplace to return to on Monday, no leaden routine looming ahead to puncture his time. After his food supplies were replenished, he treated himself to a Chinese takeaway of Singapore fried noodles which he ate in the dining room, exhaling a prolonged spicy belch into the silence afterwards. After checking his emails at the desk in the front bedroom, he got ready for Clontarf and drove over around half past seven with the window open, the mellow air ruffling his strands of lengthening hair. When the mahogany door swung open, he greeted Clare with a kiss on her cheek then made his way to the kitchen where he placed a paper carrier bag on the counter top - 'There we are...all the way from Curlew Cove!'

'Thank you Morris,' she said taking out the two punnets. 'These look lovely and ripe.' As she clicked on the kettle she surveyed him, saying: 'You look like you've had a good holiday... good colour, it suits you.'

'I did indeed...I was very lucky with the weather,' he agreed, noting that her face had become more prone to spontaneous smiles, in fact there was no trace of the pique he expected after he had left home in May. On the contrary, she looked rested, almost contented in a glamorous yet plain cream linen dress, her skin glowing healthily from the summer air, her hair a new style. He had just sat down in his usual chair at the table when Louise strolled in from the conservatory.

'Hi sis. How're things?'

'Oh, you're back,' she responded, sitting down opposite him, Moss smirking inwardly as she engaged in her usual contrived nonchalance by withholding words of welcome, of commenting favourably on his appearance, as if passing him a compliment would injure her.

'Yeah, I'm feeling great actually, great holiday...best ever in fact,' he said evenly, adding quickly 'in the mobile. The Bretts are there 'til September; no point in going there now. So: what's new? How's young Robert then? Is he still beating the moths out of his wallet?'

Louise threw him a withering glance as Clare passed around glass bowls of strawberries dusted with sugar and a generous topping of whipped cream, gave the teapot a stir and poured out the tea. 'Hmm...scrumptious! Fanks Mum,' he said exaggeratedly, raising his spoon dramatically, a gleeful grin stealing through his poker face. As they ate the strawberries, he realized his attempt at levity had failed to reach Louise, might even have irritated her, and wondered at her sulky preoccupation considering she had had two weeks holiday leave, culminating in her day with Robert although her brief narration of the day was laden with dissatisfaction. Reverting to evasive mode, he told them he planned to begin painting the upper floor of his flat, beginning Monday, intending to give an impression of a busy time ahead, realizing instantly that it sounded weak, insubstantial.

'Oh well, you've plenty of time to do it,' said Louise testily. 'I'll be back at work on Monday; some of us lead busy lives you know...earning a living.'

He let the remark hang in the air, Clare adopting her usual bemused expression as she began to gather the empty bowls and spoons, moving them to the sink, Louise abruptly declaring she had a film to watch. And so he left quietly, feeling slightly burdened by the now familiar feeling of having failed them somehow as he eased the car out onto the Clontarf Road.

'Choices...choices...' he murmured to himself and decided that he would have to acquire a far more convincing time alibi than his harmlessly obsessive house painting. As he headed for the city centre, keen to see civic and commercial buildings and rows of Georgian houses, he recalled Eternity FM's regular plea for volunteers to join its community-spirited team, in fact he had toyed with the idea of ringing the number as far back as early June, the radio station located somewhere in Sandymount, he knew. As he drove along Baggot Street he gave his shoulders a wriggle. I'll give them a bell, he told himself, maybe next week. Might be worth a try.

CHAPTER 27

Louise's eager return to the office was clouded by her dread of Dorothy's usual sneers - 'Just stayed at home did you? Didn't go anywhere? Oh well, at least you had a nice rest...' But this time she had news of her day with Robert, an item she planned to narrate to her advantage, hinting at the certain prospect of future meetings, his words – *we must do it again sometime* – still reverberating in her mind. As she walked briskly through the familiar basement terrain, she could see Cara and Dorothy in intense whispered discussion at Cara's desk, both women ignoring her as she reclaimed her workspace although she felt heartened by the volume of papers in her in-tray, the disorderly sight confirming a backlog, a state she thrived on. She picked up a helpful note that Eileen had left for her, frowning at the idea of her being on a two week holiday break after her week's sick leave of absence in June.

'Cara resigned on Friday,' Dorothy eventually told her through tightened lips as she handed her a bundle of papers. 'Leaving us in a month's time.'

'No more commuting,' grinned Cara as she swivelled round in her chair when Dorothy was well out of earshot a number of partitions away and talking earnestly to Joanne Devlin who was rumoured to be in line for promotion to Chris O'Donnell's position as assistant manager. 'I've got a part-time job in a legal firm only a five minute walk from our house. I'll have the dinner on the table at six thirty. Declan's over the moon, needless to say. Anyway, as soon as I leave here, I'm going to get rat-arsed. Then we're off to Bulgaria for a week with my sister and her husband, and *then* a week back in Cork with Mum and Dad. I'll be a new person by the time I start the job!'

Stunned into speechlessness by such planning, such premeditation, Louise slid back into her work, forgetting her report about Robert. As the day wore on she became engulfed by the tense, awkward vibration that emanated from Dorothy who made a show of ignoring Cara. Louise emulated her tactical freeze-out, as if hypnotised, treating Cara's resignation as an act of disloyalty, of dereliction, resulting in Cara going to the canteen at break times for the first time, her expression resolute, the biscuit tin and tea bag supply and coffee jar placed conspicuously on Eileen's vacant desk. But she found that she could not keep up the momentum, the shards of inner ice thawing by Wednesday as she realized that she would miss the familiar presence of her defecting colleague. Dorothy's expression was livid, her usually sharp, dark eyes clouded, and had taken to working intently through her coffee breaks and becoming engrossed in a magazine at lunchtime, resuming her work a half hour earlier than usual, the shattered routine putting Louise even more on edge as she sipped a solitary tea at her own desk.

On Friday morning, just as Cara and Louise were exchanging glances of surprise by Dorothy's absence, they saw the tall figure of Joanne in a black trouser suit make her officious way to their corner where she stopped to tell them, in her gratingly cheerful, forthright manner, that Dorothy had phoned in sick. 'A sore throat - should be back on Monday.'

They assimilated the information without comment, their expressions smug as they set about their tasks, neither admitting to the distinct levity in the atmosphere that day. When Dorothy returned on Monday morning she said she felt grand although Louise noticed that her shoulders were hunched as she sat stiffly in her desk chair, her eyes squinting wearily at the screen. This is hardly the result of Cara's resignation, she mused as she made a routine visit to the Ladies room where the truth was revealed by the two women touching up their makeup in the large mirror, assuming that she knew.

'A bit dodgy at her age,' said one of them thoughtfully, the other nodding resignedly.

Dorothy was pregnant, unexpectedly; a new person was being generated and would emerge into the world in a matter of months. Back at her desk, Louise wondered if her weekend ailment had been a cover for a visit to England for discreet disposal of the problem, for it was clearly an unhappy event.

But Dorothy's frequent exits from her workstation to the Ladies informed her that the trip had not occurred and, to her own horror, acutely regretted even thinking such a thing.

'Wonder why she hasn't told us herself,' Cara said after lunch that day, her fingertips padding over her keyboard, the news gleaned from confidential sources in the canteen. On Thursday morning she told Dorothy she was taking the following day off to use up her holiday leave.

'But we're up to our eyes,' Dorothy snapped, her eyes blazing, Cara merely shrugging indifferently and reminding her that Eileen would be back on Monday.

The next day the office was cloyingly stuffy as the air conditioning had broken down overnight, Louise adding to the fraught atmosphere by refusing to get Dorothy a packet of crisps and a bar of chocolate from the nearby convenience store at lunchtime.

'Oh but I'm not going out in that – it's lashing rain!' she told her, Dorothy's expression flattening as she realized that Louise was not as biddable as Cara who, at the raising of a brow in her direction, used to hurry off to the water cooler to fetch her a mug of water or put on the kettle which they kept on top of a filing cabinet.

'Don't worry...I'll get it myself,' she said grimly and went off to the shop while Louise set her desk with her usual lunch items. She knew that Dorothy would not dare ask Helen who was eating sandwiches at her tidy desk on the other side of their partition, not after the frosty unwelcome Dorothy had given her when she returned to work in February, after the permissible maternity leave, regretting her own complicity in it and the cold level look in Helen's eyes at her attempts at friendliness ever since. She bit into a slice of home made brown bread and aimed her fork into her salad container, mulling over the throbbing silence surrounding what was usually regarded as welcome news, worthy of congratulatory remarks, concerned enquiries, delighted smiles, the photograph of an ultrasound passed around for admiration. But none of this had happened, at least not so far, the inkling of Dorothy's unpopularity beginning to formulate in her mind as an uncomfortable albeit liberating fact. Their friendship, such as it was, was narrowly restricted to office hours and confined to their work clique, a clique that was now imploding. There was no other contact with her, no chummy outings to a café at lunchtime or to the pub on Friday evenings; they simply joined the mass disgorgement at the end of each day, each making a hasty exit through the security doors and heading for transport home. She wondered how Dorothy would cope with her commute as time went on and weight would be gained. The office was at least a ten minute walk to the train station followed by a half hour journey standing in the aisle of a packed carriage – one of her bones of contention - and then another walk to her house. And she had a son, she knew, Fergus, who was still in secondary school or would be returning to school after the holidays. As Louise was flicking longingly through her desk calendar to work out her maternity leave, Dorothy returned clutching a paper bag, droplets of rain gleaming on her lank black hair. She snatched up the phone for the second time that day to find out when the air conditioning would be fixed. With a silent sigh, Louise pretended not to notice and, not unlike Helen, obeyed her instinct to retreat. She also released her territorial grip on her work by accepting Joanne's offer to assist with the backlog, resignedly handing over a bulky file after lunch. She then focussed on her tasks, her screen glowing before her, ever relieved by the energy it consumed from her.

'What a day! Hectic!' she declared upon her return to Clontarf that evening while Clare mashed the potatoes into a smooth texture, noting an unexpected note of triumph in her daughter's voice.

'*What a day..!*'

CHAPTER 28

After two weeks of cautious vacillation, Moss rang Eternity FM and was impressed by the prompt response, the friendly female voice inviting him to the station the following morning at eleven o'clock. Just like that, he thought in amazement, no waiting about; he had expected to be put on hold, put on a waiting list and under a compliment. Maybe they're desperate for volunteers, what with the booming economy and talk of full employment, he speculated as he set off the following morning via Sandymount Green, casting his usual admiring glance at the height of the horse chestnut trees inside the railings of the triangular park. He found the station's inconspicuous entrance leading into a small courtyard and, on the dot of eleven, opened a black door onto a tiny lobby where he was welcomed by the receptionist, a slender androgynous young woman with short dark hair, her black eyeliner dramatically slanted.

'Graham will be here any minute,' she told him as she led him down a narrow corridor with bright yellow walls.

'Who's Graham?' he asked.

'Graham Moore - the station manager,' she replied, opening a red door and waving him into a small meeting room, its walls an azure blue. Moss was again surprised to see three others assembled around a table and who nodded, murmuring polite greetings. By the time he had joined them, a man strolled in with casual ease, the atmosphere instantly brightening. He introduced himself - 'Graham' - and shook hands firmly with each of them, Moss appraising him curiously. He was around fifty and attired in black denim jeans, a black t-shirt underneath a dark brown leather jacket, his long grey hair tinged with silver strands, his tanned face giving in easily to lingering smiles. Exuding an air of exuberance, of bonhomie, he lounged against a filing cabinet and asked the group members to introduce themselves and share their aspirations for a career in radio broadcasting to groans of mock embarrassment.

'David Reynard,' intoned the dark haired man who wore a smart pinstriped suit, his voice deep and modulated, the pleasing aura of quality cologne around him. 'I'd be interested in doing a phone-in show.'

'Ahm...we don't actually *do* those, I'm afraid. At least not at the present time. Any other ideas?' asked Graham encouragingly.

'Well...a current affairs programme then,' said David raising his right hand in the polite, conciliatory gesture of a civilised boardroom. 'Nothing heavy, with a little music thrown in,' he added, negotiating his way.

'Very good,' responded Graham with an approving nod.

'Martin Walker,' said the skinny, denim-clad young man in the chair next to David. 'I'm sports mad,' he offered. 'Anything to do with sports...anything at all.'

'Fine.' Graham raised his brows enquiringly.

'Ruby Molloy,' announced the girl with a halo of scraggy blonde hair, Moss watching her short chubby fingers absently move a tiny silver crucifix back and forth on its chain, her open, cheerful face and smiling, confident voice awakening the well of mirth in his being. 'Well actually I'd like to do interviews, y'know? - vox pops, and maybe that drama that goes out on Thursday evenings.'

'Excellent!' smiled Graham. 'A very popular programme, always short of voices.' He then fixed his blue eyes on Moss.

'Moss Mortimer,' he said tentatively. 'Em...announcements, ads, the weather...that sort of thing.'

'Very good,' chuckled Graham, rubbing his palms together, 'a rare, *not* so popular choice. Well - you're all *ad*mirably suitable and so we're going to throw you in at the deep end. Starting next week. Learn on the job as it were, but don't worry! There will be plenty of training to a high standard even though we operate on a shoestring budget. Our sound operators Jason and Lorraine will also guide you along. Okay,' he straightened himself up and indicated the door, 'meanwhile I'm going to take you all on a little tour of the place…see what you're letting yourselves in for!'

They followed him to a small, dimly lit control room where they crowded in behind a man seated at the mixing desk, his auburn hair partly obscured by a pair of headphones, his left hand raised briefly in greeting. 'Jason,' Graham lowered his voice dramatically as he indicated him then went on to explain the functions of the desk and sound equipment, while an animated discussion about the merits of third level education was taking place between two women beyond the glass window. The tour group proceeded to the editing studio – 'For Ruby's vox pops!' - then along a passage to another, larger studio, where they learned about the play and variety of programmes that were either recorded or broadcast live.

'And finally…our little canteen,' Graham said gleefully as he escorted them through a purple door into a room with white walls and furnished with a couple of very worn dark brown leather sofas, several chairs and a number of small tables. Maria had forsaken her reception desk and was standing at a counter top pouring coffee from a glass jug into Styrofoam cups as the group assembled themselves appreciatively in the sofas, eyeing the plate of biscuits perched invitingly upon the low pinewood table. They thanked her as she placed the tray of coffees, a carton of milk and plastic spoons before them, David passing a cup to Ruby murmuring 'Ladies first.'

'Right, well I have to head off now,' said Graham. 'Maria here will get you to fill out application forms and arrange your training schedules. By the way, any questions?'

'Well, there is just one thing - why are the doors painted different colours?' Moss asked him.

Graham gave a broad grin: 'A painting spree by a group of transition year students from last year. *And* they produced a fantastic programme too! Okay - enjoy your coffee.' And he excused himself with a parting wave, his grin lingering in the room.

'Now this coffee is super, Maria,' deadpanned David. 'Absolutely first-rate.'

The room was filled with a bout of prolonged laughter as they released nervous tension into the air.

As the group exited the courtyard into the street, David quickly stepping into the passenger seat of a waiting Merc, Moss felt obscurely disappointed to see Ruby walking ahead of him with Martin Walker until she suddenly turned round and called out to him – 'See you on Tuesday Moss,' their eyes locking for a few beaming seconds. Feeling the need for fresh air he headed off towards the promenade and made his way to the strand through a gap in the rocks so that he could feel at one with the vast expanse of sand and sky, nimbly crossing pools and rivulets left behind by the tide. In the distance, he spied a couple of sea anglers digging for bait, a black dog prancing around them, chasing and retrieving a stick. He returned to the village pub and ordered a glass of beer and lunched on roast beef, mashed potatoes and cabbage then returned home to spend the afternoon in the garden, the sky now cloudless. After changing into a white t-shirt and a pair of shorts, he looked forward to the rest of his day to unfold with no further plans or calls on his time and fell into a trance of lazy pleasure as he relaxed on the bench in the shade of the vast umbrella, pleased that such a minor investment from a sale in the garden centre was getting so much use. He surveyed Donal's allotment which was protected by a wire mesh fence secured at regular intervals by tall bamboo stakes; it was now laden with mangetouts, the raspberry canes towering over them at over six feet tall, the lush green foliage spattered with bulging fruits like rubies, and beneath them clusters of cherry tomatoes were ripening. A white butterfly flittered off into the garden next door; bees made their systematic way around the fruits; the fragrance of sweet pea clung pleasantly in the air, their delicate petals forming a pastel mosaic as they traversed the trellis adjacent to the greenhouse. He watched the neighbour's tabby cat patrol its routine way past the trellis and head for the shade of a lavender bush where he burrowed a space for himself, grooming his face casually with a languid paw then curled up his lithe body for a snooze.

Listening to the gentle rustle of leaves from the surrounding trees, the grass cool beneath his bare feet, Moss felt tempted to pluck a few raspberries but figured that Donal would know they were missing, as if he had them all counted, certain that a sample would never be offered. Yet he acknowledged that the plot was a wild and pleasing curved shape with no sign of the intensity of its creator whose taciturn expression distorted a handsome face and a mouth that seemed to nurse grievances. Maddie, surfacing from her sleep after a night's work lay down on her lounger, a jug of iced lemonade on the ground beside her. Moss covertly admired her ample figure in a pair of tiny red shorts and scant white top, her hands busy applying lotion to her smooth pale skin from time to time, then collapsing back on her seat, rendered mute by the heat. Around half past four he stealthily plucked a handful of raspberries and consumed them in the secrecy of his kitchen before venturing out again with a pot of tea and a couple of slices of fruit cake.

'You should cut back those sweet pea,' Donal advised him an hour later as he gathered mangetouts, tomatoes and raspberries for his evening meal – 'more flowers will grow.'

'Thanks Donal,' said Moss appreciatively, pleased at the idea of him parting with unsolicited free advice. He went to search out a scissors in a kitchen drawer. Maddie, still stretched out on her lounger, declined the bundle that he cut, saying she found the scent too pervasive indoors. No point in giving them to Valerie, he knew, for her garden was ablaze with flowers. He found a blue glass vase on the dining room sideboard, filled it with water, placed the delicate stems inside and positioned it on the bathroom window ledge.

After a light supper that evening, he sat at the kitchen table perusing the anaemic print of the radio training schedule and programme list copied from a machine in need of a fresh supply of ink and realised how structured and populated his life would become over the following months. He went off to search a bureau drawer for his diary to begin a new phase of the year, a phase he would not divulge to Louise just yet, for he needed to gather his thoughts. Her remark about time - that he had plenty of it - was true, he knew, but her surly delivery of it revealed a chronic restriction within her own world, a world where the imperative was to fill time with constant activity however mundane so that by sunset you could sit back and say to yourself: I filled my day. He had heard her often say after her day at the office 'I was so busy I just didn't have time to think!', this aversion to thinking or thinking for oneself being the objective, he supposed, although suspension of thought did have certain benefits whereas reflecting would pose risks, revelations, the terror of self-insight. He thought of her in one of her typical, unsettling poses, wearing her yellow rubber gloves and clutching a colourful cleaning cloth, her eyes seeking out more clean surfaces to wipe. She'd have a field day here, he thought, unfazed by the pile of dishes in the sink, the untidy clutter on the counter tops, reminding himself to mop the floor in the morning. Resuming his place at the table, he opened his diary at next week's pages, satisfied that he now had a convincing time alibi for both Clare and Louise although he knew it would not impress them. Nevertheless, it would account for his unavailability and establish an acceptable whereabouts for him. And so, with a determined sigh, he picked up a pen and began his new phase.

CHAPTER 29

With his newspaper tucked under his left armpit, Moss exited the radio station in a state of elation and headed for the pub to treat himself to lunch for having made his first live broadcast of the midday weather forecast after rehearsing it several times from a sheet of yellow copy paper: 'and continuing mild and breezy with sunny spells and scattered showers...' In fact each time he entered the lobby of Eternity FM and signed his name in the book on the reception desk, he felt a surge of merriment, of possibility, having discovered in the course of his training that ideas were regarded as valuable currency, that he was in a place where punctuality was not perceived as an irritating personality quirk or character flaw but was an essential requirement - 'Twenty seconds...' He also felt uplifted by the frequent, universal sound of laughter that emanated from the studios especially when the weekly play was being rehearsed, the banter in the canteen littered with wisecracks and witticisms, gusts of hilarity finding their way spontaneously and uncontrollably through his poker face until his cheeks and ribs ached with mirth.

Replete from a meal of stir fried chicken and a glass of beer, he leaned back against his favourite window seat and opened the newspaper's property supplement to read an article that had caught his attention, the writer opining about extortionate house prices and the plight of young people trying to get onto the property ladder, a term that conveyed an image of scrambling intensity, as if these people were destined to consume houses step by exhausting step, beginning with the starter home - a simplistic phrase, he thought. It implied something childish, makeshift, inferior, that such a home would eventually be discarded, perhaps even dismantled if the starter home had not already imploded and there was no choice but to move upwards, on to the next invisible rung, to the second more qualified house, commuting from mortgaged space to workplace in a state of constant transit, breakfast ingested in the car en route to minders where children were deposited then reclaimed twelve hours later. The portrayal of home, or the concept of home, was that of a lost entity, not even considered in the equation except as an investment, a compulsory one. It no longer seemed to be the place where the heart was, merely functioning as a pit stop before resuming work, the home for a lifetime long out of date. So this is living, he thought ruefully, folding the paper in distaste and getting up to leave; this is a nation basking in the crass limelight of self-conscious economic prosperity.

On his way home he saw Orla Brennan struggling with her shopping bags outside the supermarket entrance, a smile breaking out on her narrow face when he offered to carry the heaviest one. They set off together towards Dawn View, Orla immediately launching into one of her favourite topics of conversation – Vincent - but her latest report, delivered in the hushed tone of the pious, did not match the information he had seen on Vincent's website where his collection of erudite essays were available to the world at large and with no trace of the victim that Orla seemed to regard him as.

'Poor Vincent,' she said as they strolled along the pavement, nodding her head sympathetically, her eyelids lowered humbly. She then told Moss the news that 'some foreigner' had bought the Maguire's house at number 12, next door to his own. But he feigned surprise, withholding the fact that it had been withdrawn before the auction and sold to a man who emigrated to Australia in his early twenties and was ready to return to live in the same locality he grew up in. Judging by the beaming John Maguire who had called in to him one evening – a sighting Orla had somehow missed - the arrangement was highly satisfactory, the agreed sum divulged to him in confidence over a whiskey and soda, the way now clear for John and his petite wife Nora to buy an apartment in Paris and be close to their son and grandchildren there. As they turned the corner into Dawn View, Moss maintained a neutral expression of polite forbearance, accepting Orla's need to be seen to be in the know although he could not resist asking her, with a mischievous twinkle in his eyes, if she had visited Vincent's website recently. Clawing the air in a defeatist manner with her right hand, she yawned open her mouth and released a dismissive giggle - 'You mean the internet? Ah now Moss, I'm far too old to learn about that! And sure anyway I don't even have a computer!' But they have them in the library, he thought, surprised that she would consider herself old at barely sixty.

After retrieving a pair of jeans, socks, several t-shirts and boxer shorts from the clothesline, he decided to go into town, the property article having triggered a hunger for the companionship of substantial architecture, the mere sight of Trinity College's front façade fulfilling such a need in him. Passing by Nemesis bookshop he was unable to resist a browse and opened the ornate door, saluting Susan who was busy with a customer, a frisson of pleasure passing over him at the sight of the book spines upon the stacked shelves. While he was engrossed in the psychological thrillers section, Susan came over to greet him warmly - 'Long time no see!' – and saying that they would soon be neighbours – 'Well...almost.'

'Neighbours? How so?'

'I bought a house in Ringsend. Didn't Louise tell you?'

'Ringsend? Jesus no, she never mentioned it,' he replied, his expression utterly mystified. 'When did this happen?'

'Oh, back in June – Louise asked me to go along with her to some viewings and *I* ended up buying a house instead!'

'Well congratulations!' he gave a wide smile and shook her hand gently. 'Another defection to the southside - to leafy D4 no less. What'll people think?'

She grinned. 'I'm really excited about it. Mam and Dad are going to help me move in next week and I'm renting out one of the rooms to a Filipina nurse to help with the mortgage. So...how's Louise then? I haven't heard from her since June although I spoke to your mum to tell her my offer was accepted,' she said heading for the till where she inserted his chosen book into a paper bag. 'She sounded delighted. But then again I've been out of touch lately, had such a busy summer, what with here and an art history course I'm doing in Trinity.'

'Well...Louise's the same as ever, I suppose,' he replied vaguely, noting the hint of concern in her tone and the presence of another customer hovering patiently behind him and cradling a number of books in his large hands. 'Thanks,' he said taking the bag and his change. 'Mum seems to be keeping well, doesn't seem to miss me at all. To be honest Susan, I'm hardly ever over there now. Busy with my own place. Of course I should have left years ago,' he added with a sheepish grin and headed for the door, wishing her the best of luck moving southside. As he made his way to the bus stop on Merrion Square, he felt amused by the aptness of meeting a new property owner so soon after the article he had read that lunchtime although he puzzled over the omission of such good news from Clare and Louise, figuring that in Louise's case, it had been deliberately withheld, his mouth curling resignedly. Yet as soon as he got home around five o'clock, curiosity impelled him to pick up the phone and ring Clare but just as he had pressed the first digit, he changed his mind - she would be getting the dinner ready now and he had after all washed his hands of Louise's house hunt long ago, ever since the Monkstown fiasco. Let sleeping dogs lie, he decided.

After a light meal of a poached egg on toast and a pot of tea, he ironed his clothes in a leisurely manner, keeping an eye on a television documentary about parallel universes or the possibility of such places. Afterwards, he was drawn into the garden where he inhaled the fragrance of woodbine, the light pleasantly subdued after the blaze of the day's sunshine. He closed the greenhouse windows then ambled to the end of the garden in the dusky air and peered into the neighbouring garden to watch the Labradors chase one another around the freshly mown lawn. When he closed the patio umbrella, he noticed a pink cardigan which Maddie abandoned on the bench when summoned by her doorbell earlier on that evening. Glancing up at her window, he could sense the presence of her regular visitor, a man, in the bedroom, the window open slightly, the curtains quivering suggestively. He gazed lovingly at his house for a while, at the red bricks, the roof tiles and the chimney stacks, the flat illumined from within by his assorted lamps, as if part of him was still inside. He regarded the structure with a sense of permanence, the one and only, complemented by a small but comfortable holiday home in Wexford, perhaps qualifying him to climb the next rung of the mythological, media-invented ladder. Yet he did not envy those young people taking regular flights to visit their apartments in Bulgaria or Spain, but he thought them brave, for they would experience the romance of travel, the drama of airports - an excitement he failed to engender - and embrace the heat of southern places. He no longer craved such intense heat but he did yearn for blue skies, even those of wintertime. He felt at home in Ireland, his temperament suited to its general mildness of air and the city centre places that he loved so much, all located within a radius of a few kilometres. And less than an hour and a half drive away lay his cottage further down the eastern coast and in an area now categorised as commuter territory by estate agents. Even Curlew Cove was showing signs of development, for, during his July holiday, Keith had told him that he sold off a small piece of land where several houses would be built within a year.

He gathered up the cardigan, folded it and returned to the house where he placed it carefully on the hall table then decided to spy on Vincent's house for a while, mesmerised by its blank appearance, as if it was hesitating. Orla had assured him that Vincent confined his outings to the very early morning hours but he did not have the heart to tell her about the time he had spotted Vincent strolling along the strand late one evening, his balding head covered by a dark woollen hat. Moss had watched him stop to converse with a woman, a familiar; they had continued walking together, the sway of their bodies implying closeness, linked by a potent intimacy although he could not discern from his vantage point on the promenade near the Martello tower if they were holding hands. Over the salty air, he had distinctly heard Vincent exhale a gust of knowing laughter from his bearded mouth and, satisfied that all was well, or far better than expected, he had made his own solitary way home.

He gave the house a final scrutiny, wondering if Vincent ever watched him from behind his slightly shabby net curtains. Orla said that he spent most of his time in the extension at the back. Perhaps she's watching now, he mused, plotting her next good deed. He drew the curtains then set off for a vigorous shower, washing the day's dust and pollen from his skin, put on a clean t-shirt and boxers. He got into bed, the new novel on standby on the bedside locker, his expression contented as he curled up by the light of his blue-shaded lamp and the prospect of entering a thrilling albeit fictitious world.

CHAPTER 30

Moss's lengthy browse in a city centre music outlet was far more rigorous than usual for Graham had asked him to prepare a programme for broadcast beginning in October, for thirteen weeks: 'One hour, easy listening,' he had grinned optimistically from the worn chair behind his cluttered office desk. 'An opportunity to put your voice and training to good use!' Moss left the busy store with a number of discs he felt would evoke relaxation and consolation and headed off to Bewley's on Westmoreland Street shortly after five o'clock, the September air stirring in him a mild regret at the fading season. As he approached the café's entrance he noticed a familiar figure as he walked against the throng, the rush hour traffic grinding by as usual. He raised a hand in greeting as he recognized his former colleague Phil Doyle who stopped to look down into his face with bloodshot, sunken eyes, an aura of dishevelment about him, his tie knotted carelessly, his suit jacket slung limply over his broad left shoulder.

'Ah howya Moss, how's life?' he asked him with a weary sigh.

'Grand, not a bother, and yourself Phil?' he replied.

'Ah well, ye know yerself,' he said resignedly, adding 'Jaysus, the head...' accompanied by a wriggle as if expelling a sudden attack of shivers. Moss recognized the reflex - a sign of pride at his weekend hangover and the fashionable exhibition of it and he went along with the practised charade of looking impressed by his obvious display of discomfort from the binge. With contrived innocence he suggested that he join him for a coffee, giving a nod towards the café entrance, adding deviously:

'How about a good fry up Phil? Great for a hangover!'

But Phil modestly excused himself, saying that the solution was to go and have a few scoops. They waved farewell, Phil's expression confirming that his esteem was intact as a result of misinterpreting Moss's sympathetic response while Moss relieved his poker face of a mirthful grin as he entered Bewley's, picked up a tray and selected a blueberry muffin from the display.

'A pot of tea please,' he smiled at the girl at the urn counter.

'Tea bags or leaves?'

'Leaves, please.'

He set off for the corner banquette by the fireplace in the Fleet Street side where Stephen Devereux was absorbed in conversation with Professor Tobias and claimed the seat next to Stephen, nodding a greeting which they both reciprocated as they continued their discussion, Tobias's right hand gently chopping the air as he made a point. Moss settled in to examine the trak times on the discs he had purchased earlier on. By now, Phil would be sitting before a pint somewhere, he knew, and, his amusement beginning to fade, pondered his own resistance to drinking to the state of drunkenness. His best effort at a binge was limited to five slim jims with two malt whiskey chasers somewhere in between over a period of several hours although this was a rare occurrence as he found that alcohol whetted his appetite and resulted in an earnest search for food, usually for a substantial meal although he enjoyed a drink before lunch, especially before lunch since he had moved into the flat. He figured that he was being somewhat reckless by so doing, breaking the conformists' custom of drinking after traditional work hours and under the cover of darkness, usually as a group activity with its supply of witnesses who would trade vociferous, competitive accounts of their hangovers at the Monday morning coffee break. Experience informed him long ago that hangovers deprived him of time and energy and so he tailored his drinking to suit himself, aware that such behaviour failed to engender popularity with many of his colleagues, his choice of a frugal slim jim over a pint glass giving rise to gentle mockery. But over the years he had felt obliged to join such colleagues occasionally in their regular haunt near the bank – a themed pub with the atmosphere gutted out. He remembered the men, including Phil, seated on the hard bar stools, shoulders hunched self-consciously, studying the pints before them on the gleaming wooden counter. But once the third one was placed on the bar mat, they would summon up the courage to consider joining their female colleagues grouped together in a cackling pack in the lounge seats nearby and still attired in their office suits, a selection of bony, fleshy knees protruding unflatteringly from skirt hems, a collection of beer bottles assembled on the low table bearing testament to their drinkability. In those days he had found it useful to sit with the men at the bar and enjoy a social drink from time to time, his late arrival explained away as being off on an errand, seeing a man about a dog, his stomach secretly lined with a cheese burger and large fries after his detour to McDonald's. He would hunch his shoulders like the rest of them as gossip and information that was rarely divulged in the daylight of sobriety would eventually be relayed to him in the dull, slightly sleazy room with its low ceiling and dim lighting. When a shriek of hard laughter erupted from the girls, energized by the stabbing of an absent colleague's back, it was a sign that tongues were loosened and the ritual character assassination session had begun.

With a tiny sigh of relief he cast aside such memories and sipped his tea, looking up to admire the chandelier with its contingent of glowing lamps, comforted by the pleasant rumble of the philosophical debate going on beside him, the two men discussing Nietsche as if they expected him to arrive any minute. Moss imagined him strolling into the Fleet Street side, claim the empty chair beside the Professor and join in the conversation. As he munched on his muffin, the discs returned to their bag, he reckoned that his relationship with alcohol was balanced between that of the solitary and the convivial and arriving at the simple conclusion that he was a solitary drinker who made public appearances in Neary's, his locals in Sandymount and special appearances in the Library Club.

Yet at times his need for a lone, private drink was triggered by a vague angst that would seize him out of the blue. He would go into the dining room where his collection of bottles lay assembled on the sideboard, standing over it in intense concentration, probing his chin with his fingertips as he made his choice, his need for alcoholic comfort determined by the humour of the day. On this occasion, upon his return from Bewley's, he exhaled another sigh as he surveyed the familiar digits of the Clontarf phone on the tiny screen, seven this time but no message. He chose a Jameson with soda water, enjoying the ritual of selecting a particular glass from the cabinet, the robust hiss of the water as he twisted its yellow plastic cap, the meeting of gold with clear, then conveying the glass to the sitting room sofa where he relished his first sip. This was not a prelude to a binge but the simple recognition that his resources, the inner ones, were not up to scratch, and some outside influence was required to deliver comfort to him resulting in a subtle shift from insecurity and angst to moderate relaxation.

As the night closed around him, one of the new discs now playing in the background, its eloquent pace helping him transcend his concerns and, he hoped, those of his future listeners, he poured his final drink of the day and settled in to the company of his books. He hesitated for a moment, as if listening to them breathing quietly, like a group of kindly, lifelong friends, unobtrusive, durable, accessible, ever agreeable to share their knowledge, their secrets.

CHAPTER 31

A solitary auburn leaf, dry and brittle, lay stranded like a sign on the mat outside the front door when Moss returned from the radio station after taking a detour via the promenade where gusts of unseasonably cold air moved along the strand and white horses were visible on the distant waves. He gathered up the post in the hall and laid the items out neatly on the table for his tenants, taking his share to his kitchen table then, his stomach rumbling, switched on the oven and inserted a frozen pizza on the rack, disobeying the instructions, and prepared a salad. Reading through his bank statements and bills, he was jolted into a frenzy of calculations as he registered the impact of his reduced income although he felt appeased by a cheque from Judith Mulcahy to cover a weekend booking at the cottage for her overflow guests. Another payment would follow from the group from Estonia when they made their annual visit to Ireland in October for the Wexford Festival Opera in Wexford town. They usually took the cottage for four weeks, leaving around mid-November. He arranged an emergency review meeting with himself, putting on the agenda a return to employment in the future, not the immediate one but early the following year, keep on the alert for some suitable or appealing occupation coinciding with the anniversary of his departure from the bank. An intent perusal of the appointments section in the newspapers assured him that there were numerous choices available, and so many vacancies that immigrants were arriving daily to fill them, the days of emigration, of exodus, seemingly long over. Despite the economic boom humming around him, he began to devise more ways of curtailing his spending, jotting the ideas down on a notepad he kept on the dresser. He toyed with the idea of putting up the rental, get carried away on the surge of greed, but decided against it as he did not want to distress his long-term, peace-loving tenants or lose them altogether.

Just as he switched off the oven a text bleeped through on his mobile phone – it was from Sam. On 4 Neary's 6pm? He responded instantly - Yes c u then. As he was munching hungrily on a slice of pizza he re-read the welcome contents of a pale yellow envelope. The Library Club was to reopen after almost a year of refurbishment, putting an end to the rumours that it had been sold or bullied out of existence by avaricious developers, rumours fuelled by the sight of the crane-infested city going about the business of reinventing itself. The invitation card inviting him to a celebratory dinner was accompanied by the practical reminder of the new subscription rates, markedly increased, and he pushed the items aside for later consideration. By mid-afternoon the cutting breeze had subsided and the sunshine drew him into the garden where he presented his face to the heat of the sun, allowing it to sink into his cheeks, his brow, as he relaxed on the garden bench, his eyelids closed against the glare. He felt the need to drink in the sunlight, to absorb it before it was too late, lapsing into a state of awe at the clockwork turning of the earth on its axis, silent yet forceful, taken for granted, another equinox having drifted by unnoticed. Now that he was no longer confined to an office with its daytime office hours he decided he would make the most of the wintertime, and take advantage of the daylight hours, cheered by the prospect of packing a bag and going off to his heated cottage on any weekday. He intended going there in early October before his radio programme began and prepare for the arrival of the Festival guests, perhaps trawl the water's edge for driftwood and burn it in his little grate, or, if he found an attractive shape, keep it as an indoor sculpture or an ornament for the garden. As he sat on the sunny bench, mindful of his list of refuges, his equilibrium returned, his budgetary panic over, he knew that he would write out the cheque for the Club before the week was out.

The next morning he opened the French doors and watched the rain drip steadily down the panes of the greenhouse and drenching the open patio umbrella, the foliage gleaming with moisture. He retreated to the kitchen table and gave in to a bout of reflection that darkened his mood, a mood synchronised with the grey sky. With weary cynicism, he considered the frailties of the human body and mind, the weight of the body edging out the soul, the human species tricked by reproduction in its pursuit of pleasure - men enslaved by their genitals and impulses, women by their fertility, by the presence of a womb which they longed to have filled with a new life, or rejecting such an outcome. He got up to make a cafetiere of strong coffee, eyeing the new bottle of Jameson he had left on the dresser a week ago: a capful would be nice in the coffee, or maybe two, he thought, his mood lifting slightly. His wall clock with its reliable punctual face marked the time as half past eleven and, given the bleakness of the day, it might as well have been night time.

This morose episode was triggered by the news that Sam's baby had died prematurely, through miscarriage, the sparse but harrowing details imparted in the snug in Neary's the previous evening, both men in the humour for an extra drink and for Sam a space away from his colleagues where he could hide his torment and regain his composure, a chalky pallor evident beneath his tanned holiday skin. He winced again when Sam told him an unscheduled audit of his department had begun the day before, describing how some of his colleagues had been flung into a state of irrational, ill-concealed panic while the auditors performed their scrutinising tasks around them. The tension in the office, Sam had said with a grim smile, was like a repetitive depressing weather forecast: cloudy, with the threat of thunderstorms, and continuing unsettled against a backdrop of persistent soul-destroying rain.

As Moss sat meditatively at the kitchen table sipping his coffee laced soothingly with whiskey, he was gripped with heartfelt sympathy for his friend's plight as he considered the loss, the aching disappointment for Tessa, wondering how they would explain to Anita that her new sibling would not materialise. He scowled at the randomness of Nature in its dealings with propagation, its whimsical denial of those who fervently wanted children, their hearts overflowing with welcome and nurture, unlike the victim mongers who could not even withstand a compliment, quick to apportion blame to other influences such as the drink which they would credit with the power of speech – 'Ah sure it was the drink talkin'!' His ruminations were interrupted by the sound of the telephone ringing in the sitting room and he went off to check the number on the screen: Private. Not Louise this time, he thought pursing his lips and, leaving it unanswered, returned to his place at the kitchen table as if resuming a trance that had been interrupted, turning his thoughts to the complexities of relationships, the mystery of friendship. It seemed to him that the societal preference favoured casual, tenuous, public house acquaintanceship, the kind that could be dropped without offence, superficiality the preferred, more comfortable option.

He poured himself another coffee and added a capful of whiskey, realizing that he now felt capable of commitment, even yearned for it, but the kind of commitment that would lead to marriage or some sort of lifelong partnership had so far remained elusive. But he felt a surge of hope: he had after all sought out Valerie de Vries, drawn magnetically to the munificent household and the sheer sincerity of its members, feeling that with them he was on solid territory. Not that Valerie was always there, for he had learned that she had a private flat with its own front door at the back of the house, and where she could come and go via a narrow passage beyond the kitchen. He was shown into it once, the tiny office-sitting room where she did her translations and accounts, and where Mara, the young woman who did the housekeeping, wordlessly made them coffee in an adjacent kitchenette, her black hair tied back firmly. He was obscurely impressed by so simple an explanation for the high domestic standard of the main house, that Valerie had her own private life, that she was intensely occupied yet did not advertise it in any way, Louise's household chores and petulant dramatisation of her hectic days at the office rendered childish by comparison. Around Valerie and her cosmopolitan contingent, he felt permitted to be himself; relating to them was easy, natural, the shifty eye contact or avoidance tactics of those who were secretly afraid of or even threatened by friendship refreshingly absent. Yet he valued some of his café acquaintances for this precise limitation. Their ability to set an appropriate distance suited him, had taught him to do likewise, although Vixen carried it to extremes with her lofty smile and slightly vacant, bemused expression, adopted perhaps from a repertoire of facades. And there were distinct advantages to being aloof, reticent even, he mused, for he cherished the freedom of being able to present himself in a café full of strangers and fair-weather acquaintances although he did not discount their potential for kindness should it ever be required.

The clock marked lunchtime, and, in an effort to cast his broodings aside, he occupied himself by switching on a lamp to dispel the grey chill of the day, the room instantly coming to life again, and prepared a lunch of smoked salmon on slices of brown soda bread and garnished with diced cucumber. He spent the afternoon reading in the sitting room, in an armchair drawn close to the hearth were a fire burned in the grate, the dignified vibration of Bach violin partitas providing a background balm for his mind. By early evening the morose mood that had trailed him all day began to lift and he got up to extract a can of beer from the fridge, still deep in thought as he sought out a favourite pilsner glass from the cabinet, his eyes blinking in discomfort from such a prolonged reading session, from his craving for the printed word. He went up to the bathroom, soaked a facecloth in tepid water and pressed it gently against his eyelids and forehead, then, feeling refreshed, returned to the sitting room and took a gulp of beer. Moments later, he telephoned an order to the Chinese restaurant and set off to the Green to collect it, glad to be out in the air, the dampness easing away to a pleasing humid breeze. Tomorrow, he thought decisively, his pace resuming its usual vigour, I'll go to Wexford.

CHAPTER 32

The month of October began calmly, a blanket of serene, pale grey clouds covering the city for days without discharging rain or permitting sunlight through until it moved off, as if bored, revealing a clear, aqua-blue sky. Moss sighed with fulfilment as he watched the mellow light filter into his rooms. Autumn was his favourite season, and this time it delivered a sense of profound release after the intense light of summer, pleasurable as it had been; it seemed as if a clearance was taking place to make way for fresher air while the dust and pollen of that elusive season was being carried away on a decisive breeze. It was also the time of year when he felt his intellect sharpening alongside the air temperature as he strolled along the city centre streets, occasionally sidestepping a pool of vomit on the pavements with practised agility. In the grounds of Trinity College his mind was filled with longing to return to the ardent pursuit of learning, to be at one with the students who would soon be clutching bags of books and essays en route to lectures or libraries or the Buttery for a snack. Their pace was less strident than that of the office workers in their uniforms of corporate fashion, many accessorised by laptop briefcases, their young faces exuding self confidence and looking far less careworn than those who had endured the era before the economic boom.

By mid-month he felt infused with optimism for he had made his first live broadcast of Chilltime at eight o'clock on a Tuesday night, grateful for Jason's calm presence next to him as he was overseeing the sound operation in his jeans and black sweatshirt imprinted with the station's logo, his complexion pale and freckled, his blue eyes framed by auburn lashes. Ruby had also been there that night 'For moral support, Moss!' in the spare chair behind them in the cramped control room, her hands busy knitting a garment with pink wool. 'Ah no, it's not mine,' she had laughed in response to Moss's enquiring look while the first trak was playing. 'It's for my neighbour's baby girl'. As he set about gathering discs for the following Tuesday, the programme now seemed tame, unremarkable compared with the high jinks humour of the other presenters and their eclectic guests although he had not expected to find it so engaging, so much fun. And on the morning of the reopening of the Library Club, he was filled with so much joie de vivre that he got the bus to Clontarf and paid Clare and Louise a surprise visit. Clare seemed pleased to see him, relieved even, putting on the kettle for coffee then opening the bag of éclairs that he had got in Bewley's en route via the city centre. He told them about Chilltime, and how it necessitated him spending a lot of time in the radio station. Clare seemed disinterested, as if he had made a passing comment on the weather, Louise betraying an inbred deference to the wage earner by saying: 'But it's just voluntary, isn't it?' her mouth twisting disdainfully. 'Oh well, it'll give you something to do I suppose,' the jutting of her lower jaw giving her an aged look far beyond her thirty-nine years as she reached for an eclair. Undaunted, he told them about the invitation to dinner in the Club that evening, describing the facilities which he had missed so much, resulting in Louise giving a mock yawn: 'Oh! Oh my god, so *so* boring! You're *welcome* to your fuddyduddy airyfairy club then. I wouldn't be caught *dead* in such a place.' He gave a chuckle, still high on joviality, then, in a sudden flash of inspiration, mentioned how Susan had moved into her new house and was renting one of the rooms to a nurse from the Philippines to help with the mortgage. Clare become quite animated, saying she must go into town and get Susan a house-warming gift, Louise's glowering 'Any excuse to go off gallivanting around town,' automatically causing his smile to fade.

But his smile returned later on that evening when he approached the Club's building, the illuminated chandeliers discernable beyond the tall windows as he made his way up the shallow steps to the red Georgian door and entered the foyer where Marcus, the concierge, greeted him amiably. A champagne reception was being held in the bar, a place also cherished for its mid-afternoon tea and toast and a potent mulled wine at Christmastime. He joined the throng, wending his way down the narrow room and nodding at familiar faces and exchanging greetings with acquaintances. He looked approvingly at some of the newly upholstered chairs including his favourite wingback by the fireside, the coals now glowing red in the large grate. The green velvet sofas were still in place, the maroon carpet also covered by a variety of chairs and coffee tables, the walls flanked by bookcases and paintings. In his speech, the Chairman declared the Club a safe zone, likening it to a protected species for another century 'hopefully!', the assembled members giving a spontaneous round of applause, teeth gleaming in celebratory smiles. Champagne glass in hand, Moss then made an investigative tour of the premises, gratified that the overall aesthetic comfort still prevailed; some of the walls had been given a new coat of paint, the hall a muted gold, the dining room divided into violet and stone. He treaded up the wide staircase with its new royal blue carpet and entered the music room, its atmosphere enhanced by a subtle blue hue but was otherwise much the same with its bare polished floorboards, the Steinway grand piano situated in its usual place by the window, a couple of music stands poised at random for rehearsals or performances, an assortment of chairs lining the borders of the room. He peeked into the reading room, his heart soaring as he realised that his visits would no longer be limited to the occasional evening or weekend days of his previous life when he was a servant to office hours, that he could now enter its muted interior during the daytime, as early as ten o'clock when the Club opened.

When he returned to the dining room, he heard his name being called and made his way over to the Long Table where Stefan Katz had saved him a seat, his eyes gleaming with pleasure in being reunited with his fellow bibliophiles, in the company of such an agreeable congregation, some of them collectors, bookbinders, writers, and researchers. Tall white candles in gothic black marble holders flickered at intervals along the black cotton runner that covered the centre of the solid oak table. From his high back chair in front of the window he surveyed the stark, dimly lit room with its high ceilings, the other members and guests clustered into groups around the other tables; a magnificent Belgian tapestry dominated the wall opposite him, and two vast gilt framed portraits of the Club's founders adorned the adjacent walls, Moss intrigued by their watchful eyes even from that angle. As he tucked into his dinner, he was thankful for having renewed his membership, realising how much the Club suited his temperament, that it was a place of such benign activities it rendered the place and its inhabitants almost invisible although robust philosophical discussions were likely to break out at any time. He also found it a pleasing alternative to the pub in that it lacked urgent alcohol consumption, and television screens and sound systems were banned from the building apart from the basement kitchen, thereby disqualifying the Club from the buzz so fervently enamoured by members of the general populace. Louise would be aghast at having to dine here, he thought as he took a sip of red wine, imagining her squirming in discomfort by such an intimate gathering of strangers while automatically dealing them the title eccentric although he conceded more than a grain of truth in this. In fact right now, she was likely to be pressing the button on her TV remote control device springing the screen into action, or disappointing viewing inaction, and gratefully being spared the eccentricities of Stefan Katz. He was now circulating a leather-bound volume around the table, his fellow diners adopting a reverential interest, emitting murmurs of admiration as pages were carefully turned until it made its way back to him.

'Aah...no title on the cover' remarked Paul Frost, adding 'It's in German.'

'So it is,' said Stefan in a level tone, his well tailored black suit covering a lean stature, a pair of pale, slender hands extending from spotless shirt cuffs, a narrow black tie drooping over a pale yellow shirt. 'I got it in Vienna last week - a rare edition, unique in fact,' he added, replacing it carefully in his weathered black satchel briefcase, his expression exuding satisfaction. Paul then began to tease him about his recently published book, assuming the manner of mock interviewer.

'So, tell us Dr. Katz, is your novel autobiographical?

'No, well, not entirely, an element of it. Maybe.'

'It's based in Paris - you lived there, didn't you?

'I did, yes, but I also lived in Madrid and London. I happened to have a guide book of Paris. It was convenient.'

'The critics described your story as pedestrian, middle of the road.' Paul gave his shoulders a triumphant wriggle.

Amanda Stafford's thin voice suddenly penetrated the candlit, shadowy air from the other end of the table: 'The middle of the road is risky for pedestrians,' to a round of hollow chuckles.

'I propose a toast to Stefan's book,' said Moss decisively.

'Hear hear,' chimed the others and Paul began to pour out the port, his eyes shining playfully.

'So what are you working on now Stef?' asked Michael Purcell with interest.

'Another mystery. Gothic of course,' Stefan smiled fiendishly, his jagged white teeth gleaming from his badger moustache and beard, his grizzled black hair framing a ruddy face. They all raised their glasses:

'To the Club *and to* Stefan's next Gothic novel everyone', said Michael. 'Cheers!'

'Cheers!'

CHAPTER 33

On a mild Thursday evening in late October, Louise stopped outside a footwear outlet in Grafton Street on her way home from work and gazed at the shoes on display beyond its gleaming window. Suddenly she heard a familiar voice exclaim 'Hello Louise, haven't seen you for ages!' and she swung round to face Susan King, unable to stop herself from gawping at her appearance. Susan seemed to have undergone a reinvention, her hair a dark reddish hue and cut in a shorter style, the shiny strands hanging below the collar of a short, cream wool jacket with pink flecks - a dramatic contrast to the loose fitting navy of her pre-homeownership days. She took in the pink cashmere polo neck jumper adorned with a trio of coloured beads, the black denim jeans and the toes of burgundy leather boots. Then she noticed how Susan's face was glowing with an enhancement, not merely the superficial one achieved by the clever application of cosmetics, but something else, the unshakeable radiance of contentment, a stabbing frown stealing into her heart while she searched her artillery of verbal weaponry for a put-down to strike a blow to Susan's esteem.

'I hear you had to take in a foreigner to help with the mortgage', she blurted, her voice unintentionally high-pitched. The smile that accompanied Susan's greeting came to an abrupt halt then made a subtle transit to a cooler one as a flicker of understanding was being swiftly registered. She regarded the unpleasant curl of Louise's mouth and instantly censored the words she was about to issue: an invitation to tea on Saturday afternoon. Instead she drew Louise's attention to the bundle of shopping bags clasped in her left hand by raising them slightly: 'Just some things for the house,' she said somewhat lamely.

As people continued to jostle past them, an energy began to dislodge Susan from her position and to which she willingly succumbed, as if rescued, and she moved on up the street where she was absorbed by the crowds, her parting word an apologetic

'Bye', Louise's lips still arrested in a moue of displeasure. As Susan continued her dreamlike way along the street, a sudden feeling of weakness crept over her, and she put it down to the after-effect of seeing the sinister caste that had manifested in Louise's face and compounded by her tone of voice - brittle, angling for argument. A shiver ran through her and she made for Bewley's, hurrying through the main entrance as if claiming a safe haven. She felt quite drained by the encounter with its lingering vampiric effect but made a gradual recovery over a cup of steaming coffee with a sachet of white sugar stirred into it, aided by the relief that she had managed to stop herself from inviting Louise into her new home and by the strangers chatting alongside her, at ease with themselves and their surroundings. She wondered what on earth had happened to the seemingly innocuous person she had known since schooldays, the reliable friend she met on Thursdays for years and, apart from a few initial jibes, who had seemed so pleased by her return to Dublin. As she was pondering the way Moss had said *I'm hardly ever over there now...I should have left years ago* her phone gave a bleep, the message from John alerting her to his arrival at the hotel, the table already booked in the restaurant, her spirit instantly soaring as she memorised his room number and looked forward to the night ahead.

Louise meanwhile lost interest in the shoes she had been keeping under surveillance that week, daring herself each time she stood before the window to enter the shop and try them on. But her heart was no longer in it and she set off home, feeling piqued by the blithe evidence of Susan's purchasing power, the expensive change in her appearance, considering it an extravagance for someone who had a mortgage, as if life should deal out continuous harsh blows to the borrower. Susan, it seemed to her, was getting off far too lightly, just as Moss was, for every time she saw him, he, too, looked prosperous and contented instead of hanging his head in shame for leaving a secure job and doing nothing, not even making an effort to disguise such a state. 'My brother doesn't work anymore,' she had told her colleagues back in May as if referring to a toy whose batteries had run out, with no prospect of replacement ones. Such scornful thoughts kept her company all the way home, the bus making its heavy progress to Clontarf, the other passengers who had begun the day showered and alert, now somnolent, subdued, some of them reading or tuned into walkmans. Occasionally a phone would bleep in a message or a call, compounding her irritation...'I'm on the bus...going through Fairview now....' Her eyes were focussed glassily ahead, to the onset of the winter months and the long dark evenings, with only the glitzy festival of Christmas to punctuate the bleakness. As she was conveyed past houses of Victorian and Georgian design, her heart plummeted as she thought of Susan's front door and her access to a home of her own, under her control, the unexpected meeting with its unfinished, inconclusive conversation beginning to fill her with an obscure regret.

Clare was out when she got home. A shepherd's pie was in the oven and she turned the switch on immediately, the table already set neatly for her. As she waited for the pie to heat up, she wandered tensely into the living room seeking the remote control device and activating the screen, hungry for distraction from her daily round. She stared at the screen, at the flickering colours, at the drama of the lives of strangers. In a few hours, it would be time to go upstairs, to her childhood bedroom and the duty of sleep then make another uneasy transit into the next working day.

CHAPTER 34

As Halloween made its supernatural transit, Moss was filled with nostalgia for his boyhood vampire persona when he saw clusters of children move from house to house in their ghoulish disguises and clutching bags of miniature chocolate bars and lollipops. On his way to the radio station he heard a man's voice sternly issue a warning to the little group he was chaperoning from a house, an illumined pumpkin grinning crookedly from the front porch: 'Ok guys. Now: you see that pumpkin? It chases kids after nine p.m.' resulting in mock fearful shrieks filling the damp air as the children hastened through the open gates onto the safety of the pavement and laughing hysterically, their costume robes flying, one of the girls clutching her witch's hat.

Then November descended like a cloak, bringing a misty, murky haze to the dark evenings, viruses doing the rounds in workplaces already plotting Christmas and the predictable festivities that lightened the freight of mid-winter. Moss welcomed the early twilight, the clock adjusted back one hour to official wintertime. He switched on his various lamps around four o'clock, or earlier; two he kept on all day for effect, for atmospheric necessity, a pair fitted with low wattage bulbs ensuring a constant yellow glow from the kitchen, the elegant standard lamp in the dining room extending its peaceful rose hue into the sitting room and along the narrow hall. He kept the hearth well stocked with briquettes and lignite coal delivered by a local firm and, on days that teemed with rain, the air outside chokingly damp, he lit the fire early, before noon, enjoying the smoky fragrance, the steady heat, its visual appeal. He would read his books and magazines, the hours punctuated by cups of tea and a glass or two of beer or a whiskey and soda. Sometimes he lounged in the easy chair in the kitchen corner watching films or murder mysteries or late night thrillers, the curtains drawn protectively against the night.

As if responding to a homing signal one Thursday afternoon, he gravitated to Bewley's Café in Westmoreland Street where more coal fires glowed in the grates on the Fleet Street side, cancelling out the dreariness of the congested homebound traffic and the windswept pavements as a gale made its disruptive transit. It was still his favourite weekday, he realized as he settled himself in a banquette in the mellow sanctum of the café, enjoying the rustle of a paper bag containing a new novel in his pocket. He looked forward to a winter absent of commuting, basking in a state of appreciation of his workless state, the lack of striving or obligation to report to another entity suiting his temperament more than he had ever imagined. Yet he submitted himself willingly, even happily, to Eternity FM, he reminded himself, and to Graham, the sound engineers and administration staff, the novelty of such an agreeable and effective team adding to his usual surge of merriment on Tuesdays when he arrived to broadcast Chilltime, armed with his running order, notes and a collection of cds.

He was gratified to see Vixen in the banquette opposite him, absorbed in a book as usual, although she failed to catch his eye. He stirred brown sugar into his frothy coffee, the Irish Times on the marble table before him, folded neatly at the Letters page. Two young women made a boisterous arrival shortly after five o'clock and claimed the adjacent banquette opposite the fireplace with its glowing coals, dramatically stripping off their coats and scarves and piling them in the corner of the seat. It was otherwise very quiet, as happened at unpredictable times, the café itself becalmed as if taking a break from visitors. Moss began to eavesdrop on the women, feigning an absorbed scrutiny of the newspaper. They appeared to be close friends, or possibly sisters, yet he was intrigued by the competitive verbal battle taking place alongside him as they scored points against one another, batting comments and snipes back and forth like a table tennis match. He listened to a plethora of names being dropped, the emphasis on their occupations and determined assertions of how busy they were, the brunette trying to get the upper hand in the busyness stakes over her blonde companion by illustrating her vigorous social life, a life punctuated by ferocious hangovers that sounded to him like weekends of harrowing invalidism. The subject of their mortgages, about which they obsessed for a while, seemed to unite them, Moss smiling inwardly as he imagined their gasps of disdain, of censure, if he announced or worse, gloated that he did not have one, that he owned - outright - a house in Dublin 4, not to mention his Wexford property, modest as it was compared to the nouveau continental apartments he had read so much about.

Their battle was interrupted by the arrival of a mutual friend, to robust greetings: 'Oh *Hi*, Sharon! How are *you*?!' then immediately resumed after they joined ranks against her, as if possessing an inbuilt antenna for rivals, adopting a barely veiled air of superiority. This was provoked, it seemed to him as he unfolded the paper to access another page, because the friend, he covertly discerned from her cheerful greeting, had just finished lectures for the day. Trinity no doubt, he thought, eyeing her discreetly, a mature student perhaps, an aura of the campus about her attire, her hair not as immaculately coiffed as the other two who rattled out, almost in unison, the 'It's well for some!' reflex on hearing about Sharon's day, as if engaging in academia was a luxury, or time off to indulge in a leisure activity. Then they set about emphasising again how busy they were, listing their packed sardinesque schedules as if these contained an important message for Sharon, backed up by the bleeping of text messages and, for the brunette, a call ringing through and to which she responded with an exaggerated display of surprise. Did they not know that such stratagems caused friendship to be edged out, fended off, he thought and wondered what would become of them, of their need for control and to score points, to win pointless battles, resulting in minds coarsened by the incessant noise of competition and egotism. The strenuous effort to keep a step ahead of an imaginary posse, to be constantly winning, broke out in their slightly wild faces – a coldness to the eyes, an arrogant pouting of the mouth, compounded by a loosening of the manners, dignity and civility misplaced somewhere along their awkward paths.

As if to prove themselves, the two women began to make fussy preparations to leave and affect an important exit, uttering cries of astonishment: 'Oh my *gawd*; look at the time! Have to dash!' followed by a gushing: 'We *must* meet up another time, Sharon! Lunch or coffee, okay? Will be in touch!' This of course was phoney, not to be taken literally, he smirked knowingly, rustling his paper then finishing his coffee which had gone cold. It was just for form's sake, a meaningless remark, merely a vague nod of approval, instantly forgotten, utterly insincere. Meeting up for lunch or a coffee involved making an arrangement, consulting a diary perhaps or the organiser in a phone, one preferably stashed with appointments, maybe jot down a contact number, a new or mislaid old one, on a paper napkin or the back of an envelope, choose a place, date, time, venue: such work! Commitments were a weight and was it not best to keep things casual, shallow, vague, play it all by ear? Clearly student Sharon understood all of this for he saw her smile at them, wryly he suspected, waving them off with an almost absent gesture. She then immediately rummaged in her bag and extracted a couple of hard covered books, a sheaf of papers, a pen and a lined notepad, quickly forgetting the encounter it seemed and the worldly veneer of her hyperactive friends, their parting suggestion of little relevance, for no arrangement had been made. He tried to read the spines of her books, curious to know her subject but she had already opened them both, poured herself another cup of tea and bowed her head to her studies, her chin and cheek supported by her left hand, a lock of light brown hair partly obscuring her face; it was a posture he found inordinately attractive. With a slightly reluctant sigh, he withdrew his covert gaze and, folding his newspaper and laying it aside, released the paperback from its bag and placed it on the marble table. He picked it up to feel its weight, its texture and admired the cover for a while then glanced at his mobile phone: it was almost six o'clock. Valerie should be here any minute, he thought, rejoicing in their new routine, now into its third week, his eyes gleaming with anticipation as he kept watch for her arrival.

CHAPTER 35

'Johann's totally smitten with her,' Valerie was saying as they sat side by side enjoying their meal of bacon, fried egg, sausage and chips, a treat they consumed without obsessive dietary concerns and, of late, with added fervour, ever mindful of the café's impending closure, the dreaded extinction of such a dignified and atmospheric forum of public conviviality. 'And I've no problem whatsoever with her staying over so often, but I told him I draw the line at her moving in, so we'll just have to wait and see how it goes.'

Moss nodded in sympathy with her maternal concerns about Johann's new girlfriend although to him it seemed natural that Rachel was drawn to the ambience of Johann's hospitable home. As far as he knew, she lived in an apartment in one of the new blocks in Ringsend, sharing it with three other girls, an arrangement that sounded youthful, transient. After their meal, the banquette firm against his back, another frothy coffee on the table before him, he felt almost drugged with contentment, forgetting time, sensing that he was somehow safe within time itself, the sheen from Valerie's hair and her floral scent adding to the sensuous surroundings.

He was oblivious to the ritual taking place at that point in time, in the parallel world of his sister. Released from her basement office, Louise was making her way along Grafton Street on her usual route, delaying her return home by dawdling in the shops, as she did most Thursdays. She paused outside the window of Bewley's Café, inhaling the scent of freshly roasted coffee beans that perpetually filled the air, as if marking the location. She longed to go into the beckoning café, but her feet remained anchored to the ground, her reflection in the glass peering back cautiously, the idea of making her solitary way in and searching for a seat then claiming it filling her with trepidation and causing her pulse to accelerate, a reflex shiver running through her. On a few occasions she had gone as far as the front shop counter to buy a packet of coffee and some of the cakes that Clare liked. She wondered if Moss was in there now, knowing how devoted he was to the place, remembering him express his concern about the rumours of its closure. Of course he could be in the other Bewley's, she thought, the one down on Westmoreland Street.

An image of its interior sprang to her mind for she had been inside it once before, over a decade ago, the time she had met Moss and Kevin O'Brien by chance as they strolled along Westmoreland Street shortly after five one Friday evening. Kevin, true to his courteous and magnanimous nature, had invited her to join them, and mutely, she obeyed, feeling awestruck as she entered the cafe flanked by the two men. They had chosen a banquette table in the vast front room with its incongruous cherry tree, Louise astonished by the sight of so many strangers gathered together with casual ease around rows of tables and in the banquettes alongside the walls. When Kevin and Moss abandoned her to fetch tea and cakes, she had suddenly felt exposed, a sense of being watched although no one had made eye contact with her apart from the auburn haired woman in the adjacent seat as she moved her coat in an obliging manner to make way for her bag, flashing her a brief, impersonal smile then resuming her focus on an item of correspondence. While Louise longed for the return of Kevin and Moss, a figure loomed in front of her table. It was a tall young man, his left hand gripping the handle of a briefcase, his right one holding a tray. 'Is there anyone sitting there?' he had asked her with a slight nod at the vacant chairs, a lock of shiny black hair falling over his brow. 'No,' she had replied defensively, possessively, 'they're taken'. It was the kindly grin he had given her and a look that seemed to sweep over her that made her feel on the brink of falling in love as she watched him disappear through a wide entrance leading to another part of the café. This is how it happens, she had thought, or could happen, her skin tingling with an alien but not unpleasant sensation, enhanced by the return of Kevin and Moss with laden trays. Kevin ceremoniously passed her a cup and saucer, a white plate, the little cake with pink icing perched appetisingly on it, then a knife and a thin white paper napkin imprinted *Bewley's* EST. 1840. Moss filled their cups from a gleaming tea pot. After what seem an infinitesimal time to her, although it was only three quarters of an hour, Kevin and Moss then prepared to take their leave, heading off to some urgent appointment, Kevin saying he had a lot to pack into his week in Ireland, catch up with old friends, etcetera. She had got up to leave with them despite their urgings to stay and enjoy herself, to treat herself to another cake, fearing that she would have become immobilised in the snug red velour had she done so, unable to face the ordeal of making her way out alone.

Ambushed now by hunger, she cast the memory aside and retreated to a nearby fast food outlet where she found herself able to walk in with relative ease, state her order, secure a seat and consume her meal, feeling safe and anonymous in the functional layout, the bright lights, the durable surfaces, the atmosphere of transience, of quick dispatch of food, and the detachment of other customers. But her yearning to be over in Bewley's would not abate as she imagined herself being escorted inside by a man, one of those confident, self-assured types she had witnessed so many times going in or striding out, many alone but purposeful, like the young man in Westmoreland Street, his smile and lock of black hair still etched in her memory all those years.

A variety of feelings burdened her that evening, for it dawned on her how much she missed her brother, his irritating habits and little eccentricities fading away for now. After her meal, she returned to the café entrance but catching sight of a beggar woman's vigilant eyes single her out, quickly moved away and set off to browse in the department stores, looking at clothes, shoes and cosmetics. Passing by a boutique she was drawn in by the vibrant colours, seized by an impulse to liven up her wardrobe as she surveyed the myriad garments made of fragile fabrics she felt impractical for the season, then withdrew, horrified at the price tags. Once back on the chilly, windy street, she decided it was time to go home.

As she approached the end of Grafton Street she spotted the familiar figure of Susan in her black winter coat with the faux fur collar and a glimpse of her profile as she stood poised on the pavement edge opposite Trinity College, waiting for a break in the traffic. But to her annoyance a group of youths began to walk as one in front of her, blocking her view of Susan with their colourful rucksacks, the hems of their jeans scuffed by the pavement, the Italian language catching in her ears, her eyes instantly narrowing as she slowed down her pace. By the time they shuffled aside, Susan had reached the other side of the street, Louise watching her make a decisive right turn into the main entrance of the College then disappear, absorbed by the dark chasm of the tall archway door to the mystifying world of academia on the other side. She continued her journey via College Green towards the northside, abstractedly passing by Bewley's Café in Westmoreland Street then walking briskly across O'Connell Bridge. She reached the bus just before it pulled out, relieved to find a choice of vacant seats this time, the fleeting image of Susan accompanying her all the way home to Clontarf.

'Anne has a bad cold...taken to her bed with a hot toddy,' Clare said, responding to Louise's surprised expression at finding her at home. As they waited for the kettle to boil, Louise provided her mother with a censored report of her day, withholding her sighting of Susan. While they were sipping their tea, Clare tentatively handed her an invitation card that had arrived in the morning post. 'It's Sarah's art exhibition,' she said resignedly, watching her daughter examine it critically. But Louise gave a sudden gasp of awe, her mother rewarded by her emphatic avowal of their attendance, for a soap opera actress that she revered was to perform the official opening. Clare topped up her teacup and took a second biscuit from the plate, delighted with Louise's unexpected reaction and already wondering what she would wear.

CHAPTER 36

Moss propped the invitation card against the vase on the dresser, shook off his jacket, slung it on the back of a chair, pulled open the fridge door and seized a bottle of beer. He had left Dalkey around half past four after a preview of Sarah's work, his stomach filled with a variety of sandwiches trimmed of their crusts and a fruit scone and tea, then spent over an hour in traffic, a gridlock having formed along the Merrion Road, on the inbound lane. A crash, he had supposed, his fingers gently tapping a silent melody on the steering wheel, for surely this volume of traffic was not a regular occurrence. Yet he had often heard about such gridlocks on radio traffic bulletins and marvelled at the stamina of commuters.

He had promised Sarah he would do his best to persuade Clare to attend her exhibition, Sarah also aware of her reluctance to go to social venues alone without the loyal Anne or Jean by her side. As he poured beer into a crystal glass, he decided to apply gentle persuasion, knowing how Elaine's patronising, pushy manner riled her, although he was gratified to learn that she and Leo were in Seville and would not be back in time for the exhibition. The pang of sympathy he often felt for his mother grew stronger as he recalled Elaine's salacious interest in Clare's wellbeing after David relocated to Singapore, interest disguised as concern in her gushing phone calls - 'O hello Morris. And *how* is my poor sister?' she would say in her slightly hushed tone, a tone laden with false sympathy. He imagined her head cocked slightly to one side, the greeting accompanied by widened eyes even on the telephone, an expression cultivated to invite confidences and implying an assurance of being given the benefit of sound, know-best advice - 'Now, if *I* were *you*...' Whenever Elaine had paid them a visit he noticed how she tended to relate everything to herself; if Clare had an opinion, she had a superior one, her delivery suggesting that hers was the more solid, more reliable one with official and social connections to back it up.

And when Clare told her the news of his leaving the bank and moving to Sandymount he suspected she had rushed off in a tizzy of rapturous self-righteousness to bombard Leo with her verdict: 'Ah *hah!* Wait till you hear this! Morris Mortimer is retiring: at *forty-four!* Mid-life crisis of course! Moving out of the house! Going off to do a little navel gazing! Irresponsible... just like his father! Well well, I just knew it! Just goes to show you doesn't it?!' With a smirk, he drank deeply from his glass, then telephoned Clare and offered to be chauffeur.

'You'll be able to have a glass or two of wine if you like,' he said encouragingly.

'Louise is coming too,' she told him.

'Excellent. See you both on Thursday so.'

He collected them at the arranged time, both women hovering expectantly at the front door, Louise smoothing her black silk dress under her open winter coat, her hair sleekly styled, her face enhanced with make up, her lips a glistening red. It was a cold, clear night and, despite the sprawling urban light, stars were visible high up in the blurred-ink sky. Inside the car, an aura of mute anticipation enveloped the group of three as Moss drove along the Clontarf Road. From the front passenger seat, Clare cast little glances at his familiar profile, noting how his cheeks had filled out a little and emphasising the dimples that had charmed her as a boy although she winced inwardly at his hair, the long, thin strands now sparsely peppered with silver-grey, an elastic band securing the tiny pony tail that sprouted at the back of his head. And what would people think of that gangster leather jacket of his? Yet despite his unemployed state he exuded an air of prosperity and quiet confidence that she knew would go down well with the vigilant females attending the exhibition.

'How many years have you had this car now Morris?' she asked him absently as he navigated his way over the East Link bridge. 'It must be ten at least.'

'Well, I've just had it serviced. It's a grand car...in great shape. There's a good few years in her yet.'

By the time they arrived at the gallery, a steady stream of guests was making its sedate progress around the room, mostly manicured female hands equipped with the traditional exhibition props: a glass of red or white wine or mineral water. Gerald and Sarah welcomed them warmly with kisses and hugs, Clare smiling appraisingly at Sarah's low cut floral dress and the strands of her plum-coloured hair hanging loosely over her bare shoulders. Sarah guided Louise over to the actress who gave her a bright smile, shook her hand saying 'Lovely to meet you Louise,' then, with an apologetic raising of her brows, turned her attention to an elderly couple also eager to meet her. Relieved by so brief an exchange, Louise retreated gratefully to rejoin Clare and they began to admire the paintings mounted on the creamy walls. Moss had disappeared. People began to cluster into little groups. Clare suddenly recognised an acquaintance in one of them and was instantly absorbed into its hub to cries of: '*Clare*! How *are* you? Long time no *see!* You look *lovely!*' The room became so crowded that it was impossible to pass another without physical contact, not the mere brushing of garments but the necessity of using force with dramatic apologies lest a temper might flare. The high babble of voices increased in volume and intensity, the paintings no longer the focus of the many pairs of eyes that were flickering back and forth on the lookout for a familiar face, ever on the alert for someone worth knowing or being recognized by. At the sound of Gerald tapping a glass firmly, the babble ceased for the official opening, the actress assuming the role of speechmaker in her natural voice and accent beside a beaming Sarah, a number of cameras clicking and flashing nearby.

Afterwards, when the applause died down, Louise began to feel slightly uneasy by the sea of unfamiliar faces surrounding her on the hardwood floor. She claimed a spot that gave her a commanding view of a large oil painting of a vast living room with bookcases stretching from a polished wooden floor to a high ornate ceiling, a shaft of sunlight filtering through French windows and illuminating a rug and a writing desk piled with books. A tabby cat was snoozing on a blue cushion with golden tassels upon a faded pink chesterfield sofa; in the corner was a cabinet containing silver and glassware. Two armchairs were angled in front of the fireplace and above the mantelpiece was a gilt framed mirror; near the window was a round wooden table containing ornaments, a pile of magazines and an oriental vase filled with flowers. She leaned forward, squinting to get a closer look at the flowers – they were roses. She saw a tiny red circle stuck to the lower right hand corner of the frame indicating its eventual removal to someone else's home.

'Good, isn't it?' she heard a male voice say over her shoulder and swung round to see a man with thick, dark brown hair framing a round clean-shaven face, his blue eyes twinkling.

'Well, yes...I suppose it is,' she replied. 'But I wouldn't want a picture of someone else's place in *my* house.'

He gave a chuckle, revealing gleaming, uneven teeth. 'I'm Matthew,' he said. 'And what's your name?'

'Louise,' she replied, shaking his warm, strong hand uncertainly.

'So. Tell me about yourself Louise.'

Startled by such an unexpected question, by his intense interest, she looked around the room as if seeking clues for an answer then suddenly caught sight of Susan King who was staring fixedly at her from within a little group near the drinks table on the other side. Louise gave a cautious wave, a reflex gesture, unintended, instantly realizing it was too late to snatch it back. Susan began to detach herself from the group and, with a sinking feeling, Louise returned her attention to the painting, her pulse surging with angst as she wondered what to say when Susan made her way over. Matthew took a sip from his glass of white wine, his expression polite, awaiting her response patiently. When Louise stole an apprehensive glance over her shoulder, she saw that Susan had moved further away towards the exit and was talking to two women attired in richly coloured saris, then she left the room abruptly, disappearing through the door into the tiny hall. Louise's angst altered into acute embarrassment as she registered that Susan had deliberately, pointedly, avoided her.

'If you would like a decent glass of wine we could go somewhere else...quieter than here,' Matthew was saying. 'Oh hello Moss.'

To her intense relief, her brother had materialised in front of them and the two men shook hands with a familiarity that indicated long acquaintanceship. Moss introduced them to Valerie and then to Herbert, one of her Dutch friends from the Embassy, Louise mechanically offering her hand bereft of such physical gestures for so long, her throat dry and uncomfortable. Then Valerie and Herbert turned to the painting, crowding around her brother as if he was a tour guide, or an authority on art.

'Congratulations Moss,' said Valerie. 'It's stunning. It'll look great in your front room.'

'Well actually, I was thinking of the dining room,' he said, thoughtfully fingering his chin, 'although the light in there might be too dim. It's my Uncle Andrew's house in Cambridge,' he explained to Matthew and Herbert. 'Sarah grew up there. That's exactly how it looked when I stayed there over twenty years ago. My grandfather died in that very chair,' he pointed to the sturdy wingback to the left of the hearth. 'Reading Dickens - Martin Chuzzlewit in fact.'

'An excellent way to go,' remarked Herbert.

'Absolutely,' responded Moss.

'Such *detail*,' commented the softly spoken Matthew as he scrutinized the picture, Louise maintaining a reserved posture alongside him, unable to respond to Valerie's encouraging smiles, apart from saying she had never been to Cambridge, Matthew murmuring 'Never say never.' She felt numb and managed to endure the remainder of the evening with a glazed expression and fuzzy head, the actress long gone, the magic of the night punctured by Susan's abrupt disappearance and the eclipsing of the painting by Moss and his friends. She was glad to get home, Moss delivering them safely to the door and waiting in the car until she had reset the alarm. Clare was elated as she put the kettle on for tea, her cheeks pink, the evening a resounding success for her, a number of invitations to meet up in town secured but Louise felt drained by the memory of Susan's expression and her sudden hope that their friendship could have somehow been reconciled in the gallery.

After her cup of tea she got ready for bed, setting her clock for the working day ahead. As she replaced her silk dress on its hanger in the wardrobe, she remembered she had not responded to Matthew's words - *Tell me about yourself Louise.* He had drifted off somewhere, engulfed by the crowds while Valerie and Herbert chatted to her although she could not remember a word except that their accents were strange, almost American, gratefully accepting the glass of still mineral water Herbert brought her and which had helped to ease her constricted throat.

Lying back on her pillows, she felt exhausted but sleep evaded her, her mind filled with questions until, just before she fell into unconsciousness, she recalled seeing Matthew standing by the drinks table watching her intently, his expression solemn. Then he gave her a significant wave as she was leaving.

CHAPTER 37

Clare stood by the window in Moss's bedroom listening to the wind beating its invisible fists against the double-glazed panes. The weather made little impact on her temperament although she liked the winter as it complemented her reclusive lifestyle. She decided to give the room a vigorous cleaning, the end of November being the time of year when she gave the house a thorough going over before the Christmas season began in earnest. Feeling twinges of guilt about eliminating her son's lingering presence, she surveyed the pale blue walls now bare and forlorn. A number of books had been left behind and she stared at the neat stack of paperbacks on the bookcase shelf, some of them ragged, their former white pages now edged with a murky brown, a title she recognized catching her eye: Madame Bovary. She then opened the heavy wardrobe door and peered inside, the empty hangers rattling hollowly: there was a folded blanket on its floor, a pair of abandoned leather shoes hiding in the corner, yet there was still a faint trace of his musky scent.

The sudden ringing of the telephone cut into her thoughts and made her jump, her right hand automatically going to her throat as she hurried down to the hall to answer it. It was Kevin O'Brien inviting himself over for a cup of tea that evening.

'Would seven-thirty be okay?' he asked.

'Yes Kevin, that would be lovely,' she replied. 'See you then. Looking forward to it.'

Kevin always paid them a courtesy visit whenever he returned to Ireland, usually after he had dispensed with his lecture or other engagements that were rarely elaborated on, yet his call always took her by surprise. She immediately abandoned her previous task, a flush of anticipation having entered her cheeks. Last year he had surprised her with an account of his brief visit to Singapore, illustrated by a photograph of himself and David smiling into the camera from the Long Bar in Raffles Hotel, two jovial men of the world enjoying a beer together. The photo was now in a frame on her dressing table next to a cluster of photos, postcards and letters from David; from time to time she would pick it up and admire David's halo of snow white hair, her gaze a study of intense affection.

Louise exhaled a dramatic sigh of annoyance when she got home from work, not just from the vague discomfort she felt whenever anyone visited the family home but to conceal her keen interest in Kevin. After a hasty dinner and a shower, she hurried back to her room, frantically trying on various garments until she settled for a navy blue polo neck jumper and black trousers. Rummaging in a bottom drawer she found a royal blue silk scarf that Susan had given her for Christmas years ago and wound it loosely around her neck, surprised by its transforming effect. Half an hour later a waft of unseasonably mild, damp November air accompanied Kevin as he was being ushered into the tidy sitting room. He also carried with him a whiff of the wider world, his quality attire confirming yet again that it was a successful place, even desirable, where work could be found, money could be made, where people somehow survived the ordeal. Relieved of his coat which Louise had hung carefully on the banisters, after taking a longing inhalation of its scent, he settled his tall frame into the beige sofa, exuding his usual unwavering quiet confidence, his longish hair still a youthful shiny black. Louise's nose twitched at the sound of his American drawl as they made small talk for a while, Kevin delivering an update on his New York life still populated by his wife Masami and their daughter Kim, now twelve years old and devoted to music, to her violin practises and performances. John, his father, was in great form, good health, he told them – 'still scribbling away!' In fact he had lunch with John and Noeleen in Sandymount today and afterwards went to visit Moss in the radio station where a friend of his – 'Ruby, charming girl!' - had persuaded him to do an interview. Louise and Clare absorbed the information without comment, prompting Kevin to switch focus.

'So Louise, how's life with you?' he asked. 'Still in the same job then, in the insurance business?' the timbre of his voice setting her teeth on edge and her cheeks to redden. Recognizing her daughter's discomfort and finding the question somehow provocative, Clare jumped to her defence by emphasising how hard-working she was - '*And so busy*!', Kevin nodding sagely, his black brows raised as if expecting to hear of some new development. Louise then gave a dramatic account of her hectic office life, but when she narrated the story of her protracted but inconclusive house hunt, Clare was startled by the realisation that *still* meant lack of progress, stagnancy the outcome of her daughter's anchorage at home. She had the feeling they were being mocked yet not a trace of this was apparent in the Zen calm of Kevin's face.

After they brought in the supper trays, Clare felt consoled by the genuine pleasure that shone through his eyes as he buttered one of the warmed fruit scones she had baked that afternoon, watching him spread it with strawberry jam and spooning whipped cream on top. When he bit hungrily into it, his eyes narrowed with pleasure. Louise poured out the hot tea into floral china cups from the set that Moss loved.

'Thanks Louise...mmmm!....these are delicious Clare. And I sure could manage another one. Or two!' he chuckled.

Clare did not doubt the sincerity of his compliment and gave a smile as she recalled the student version of himself and Moss devouring the snacks she used to prepare for them in those days. After his final cup of tea, he got ready, with an air of slight reluctance, to leave.

The visit was a brief one, barely an hour, both women recovering from his light kiss on their cheeks, the dizzying effect of his presence and his lingering aftershave energizing them into action, to tidying up, repairing the broken routine for they had missed the nightly focus on the television screen, Louise lamenting the loss of an entire episode of the soap opera.

Around eleven, as she prepared for bed and the welcome company of the white pill and a library book, Clare reflected on how she had automatically turned down Kevin's invitation as she was making her goodbyes at the front door. He had asked both herself and Louise to dine with him and Moss in the Merrion Hotel the following evening. She was filled with a sudden yearning to be in a place of refinement, of grandeur, to be treated gallantly for she knew that both men could behave this way and would be, in such a context, utterly charming. She could almost taste the sherry or perhaps champagne, remembering with pleasure the daring champagne afternoon tea she had had in the Drawing Room with Anne and Jean one July afternoon, their shopping bags nestling against their comfortable chairs, then treating themselves to a taxi home afterwards. Her pleasure faded into annoyance with herself, with her habitual deference to Louise's moody sensibilities. She remembered her tense face that evening and how her presence had evolved into a cantankerous state in recent months, although she felt grateful that no unseemly bad manners had occurred during Kevin's visit. She would have refused his invitation and make up some excuse, she knew, for she lacked appreciation of beautiful hotels, would in fact be embarrassingly tactless, asking fatuous questions about the food, affecting confusion at the French language as she had done whenever David had taken them to hotel restaurants as a treat. Kevin's invitation rekindled memories of how David had literally wined and dined her during the heady days before their marriage, she besotted with him, his occupation, his English accent, high on the victory of having being chosen over others. Unwrapping the cellophane from the *eau de parfum* Kevin had given her, for he never arrived empty handed, she opened the box and extracted an ornate bottle, removed the silver lid and applied the fragrance to her wrists, inhaling it with pleasure. Of course it's not too late; I could call Morris in the morning and tell them I've changed my mind, she thought then returned the perfume to the bedside table, positioning it under the lamp on the other side of her glass of water.

Propped up comfortably on her pillows, she swallowed her pill and tried to concentrate on the printed page, to enter its fantasy world only to find it blurred by the reality of Kevin, his loyalty, his mannerly refinement and also that he evoked genuine pleasure, a worthy reminder to her of the romance of men. She also felt intrigued by his air of success and by another quality that enveloped him – what was it that Morris called it? Yes, of course: *the art of living.* Morris and his little phrases, she smiled, some of them gleaned from James. Kevin was the quintessential rule breaker, she knew, not unlike David, his very presence threatening destruction or imminent destruction of the status quo. Yet she did not feel threatened by this, or no longer felt threatened, her subconscious fear of the free spirit in abeyance as the pill began to take effect. Closing her book and placing it on the pillow beside her, she leaned over and switched off the lamp. But as she lay there in the darkened room, the nagging doubts in the wake of Kevin's visit drew her mind back to another reality, a predicament now, of Louise's tenacity to the family home. She blamed herself for influencing her in the early days of the house hunt before prices increased so dramatically, when they could pick and chose at leisure, both easily discouraged by petty flaws, almost as if they were seeking excuses not to commit to a purchase. But at least Louise has her job, she consoled herself, instantly reassured by that sacrosanct entity which guaranteed predictable routine for them both. And there was an additional glimmer of hope - Louise had recently begun to go out after her dinner to view houses that were only accessible during the evening hours although she was somewhat vague about the locations, saying that the car needed a spin anyway. Clare was surprised but pleased by her efforts and that she seemed confident enough to go alone, even eager to be unaccompanied. At last, feeling pleasantly drowsy, she snuggled into her pillows, consoled by the prospect of Louise buying a home of her own and then she would be free of her, although she was not yet sure how this freedom would manifest itself. With a gentle sigh, she gave in to the cherished abyss of sleep.

CHAPTER 38

Clare overslept the following morning, the cup of tea that Louise had deposited on her bedside table stone cold. Feeling discomfited by the incision into her routine, she quickly washed and dressed then went downstairs for breakfast, glancing continually at the clock as if doubting its timekeeping. She knew that she would not be going to the Merrion that evening, her dithering and oversleeping having gone against her, although her spirit lifted at the prospect of her appointment with the hair stylist at two o'clock and the sight of the property brochures Louise left behind on the kitchen table. As she sipped her tea she was surprised yet again by her acute longing for the day when she would hear her daughter packing, to the sound of the keys to her own front door.

She was oblivious to the fact that Louise's nocturnal journeys were clandestine missions to spy on Susan's house. Louise's new occupation had begun during the summer months while the legal paperwork was being carried out in the office of Susan's solicitor. She picked a night or weekend afternoon at random, driving over to Ringsend, parking in Willowhaven Close then pretending to consult a map, or a paperback book she had found abandoned in Moss's empty room, watching the vacant house for a few moments then driving away. The exercise gave her a thrill, especially after Susan had moved in, a thrill that was enhanced by the furtive darkness of the autumn evenings when she felt protected by the subdued street lighting.

Feeling gripped by restlessness in the wake of Kevin's visit, she made another impulsive visit to Ringsend the following Tuesday and found a convenient parking spot almost directly opposite the house. There were the usual signs that Susan had taken possession - her car was parked in the driveway, the gate closed over, although the little gate that led to the front porch was opened invitingly. She watched the house intently, feeling mesmerised by it, by the dim glow of the hall light discernible through the fanlight panel above the blue front door. To the left, the sitting room, heavy curtains were drawn but a chink revealed a cosy pinkish light. She contemplated getting out, marching up to the front door and ringing the bell to put an end to her voyeurism and reclaim their friendship, but felt immobilised by an alarming tingling in her stomach. A light flicked on in an upstairs room, probably the landing, or bathroom, she thought, for it cast a glow into the front bedroom, the curtains not yet drawn. She had yet to catch sight of either Susan or her lodger entering or exiting the house. On her previous visit she had seen Denise King park her car outside the gate and, with the familiarity of the regular visitor, stroll up to the front door and insert a key into the lock and let herself in, releasing a brief shaft of light. She stiffened at the sound of a gate clanging and saw a figure emerge from the shadows further along the street - it was a man walking two greyhounds. As the moments passed, Susan's house seemed to expand, to pulsate. The man with the dogs had vanished. Suddenly a white car, the distinctive Garda model with its familiar markings pulled into the street and made snail progress along the other side. Someone has noticed, she thought, panic stricken as she bent her head to her map, furtively watching the tail lights pass by to the top of the street. She heard the sound of a car door close firmly, her heart pounding as she waited for the authoritative knuckled rap on her window by a uniformed figure, wondering wildly what to say. But nothing happened. After a few agonizing moments, the car turned round and passed hers slowly in a huge white blur, so slowly it seemed to pause at her car, as if scanning it, then it exited the street. She waited a full ten minutes before turning on the engine and driving off, looking intently into her rear view mirror, her senses alerted for a siren, for flashing lights all the way home. She arrived in Clontarf without further incident, relieved that her mother was out, this time to dinner in Jean's house, and would not witness the after-effect that set in. As she shivered in the safety of her bedroom, she vowed to put an end to her spying, for how would she have explained her presence there, had she been caught, she wondered. It occurred to her how useful a mobile phone would have been for she could have faked a call, pretending to have lost directions. She recalled the purposeful way Moss used his, glancing at the tiny screen while holding a conversation with her and their mother, or speaking in a lowered tone of voice while on a call, his thumb racing over the keypad as he composed a message, a sight that had often evoked disdain, even rage within her. Still shivering, she went downstairs to the kitchen and made herself a mug of tea, her fingers trembling. She felt acutely aware of her solitary state, her mind bombarded by suspicious thoughts; perhaps a neighbour had phoned the guards and she was now being kept under surveillance, or had been for some time. A familiar sensation in her forehead registered the onset of a headache and she quickly took two painkillers in tablet form. She then went from room to room pulling the drawn curtains tightly together to obliterate any chinks. Longing for her mother's return, she watched television for a while with the volume low, as if expecting someone to ring the doorbell any minute. When the telephone resonated she jumped, knocking her empty mug over.

'Hello,' she said cautiously. There was silence.

'Hello,' she repeated, then heard the sound of someone hanging up. Probably a wrong number, she told herself, her heart racing again. It happened occasionally. She sat rigidly on the sofa in a hyper-vigilant state until she heard her mother's key in the front door lock around half past ten, the alarm alert beeping, then Clare tapping the code into the panel. They drank tea together in the over-bright kitchen, Clare telling her about the interesting guests at the dinner table. Jean's son Bernard was over from Copenhagen with his wife Roisin and their little boy, Anton – 'He speaks fluent English and Danish at only seven!' They were thinking of coming back to Ireland and avail of the booming economy, Clare describing their shock at being priced out of Sutton. They had a number of places in Raheny and Marino to look at tomorrow, although Roisin would consider somewhere closer to town, perhaps in the city centre itself. But Louise, her head now throbbing, tuned out from further details and excused herself, setting off to bed in a tense state. A restless night ensued but the pain subsided, caught in time by the tablets, and she sank back with relief upon her pillows, glancing occasionally at the digital clock to ensure the alarm's red dot was still there. It was a slow night, as if some force had altered the rhythm of time.

CHAPTER 39

Moss felt a familiar ache at the back of his throat signal the onset of the common cold and began treatment by suspending a spoonful of neat whiskey in his mouth for a moment then allowing it to trickle slowly down his tender throat, imagining the virus being decimated, or at the very least, being discouraged by such a force. He kept a low profile for two days, taking a couple of paracetamol tablets in the morning and evening, eating regular meals, drinking numerous cups of tea and a small quantity of hot toddies. He also gave into sleep, curling up in his bed or in front of the fire, under cover of the spare room duvet which he dragged down the narrow stairs and arranged it on the sofa. The box of tissues within easy reach was imprinted with the words Man Size and he wondered if members of the equality brigade found this vexing, those members who tended to pounce on the pettiest of issues, eager to find something to feed the seething umbrage within.

Outside, the early December air was filled with sunlight, the nights frosty and calm as the earth made its progress to the point of solstice. When his wellbeing returned he felt hungry for crowds, for streetscapes, and set off in the mid-afternoon to the city centre where he became absorbed into the shopping throng, glancing wonderingly at those who were still dressed for springtime, their necks, heads and hands bare, exposed to the elements, as if there was an unspoken code of resistance to the piercing seasonal air temperature, that conspicuous comfort was perhaps out of fashion for them. He was satisfied with the two recent acquisitions that he wore - a pair of comfortable black buckle boots and a long black wool overcoat which he had bought in November. The coat was a similar style to Professor Tobias's one, with deep pockets for his phone, a couple of Kitcats, a packet of chewing gum, a tube of throat lozenges and a wad of tissues, his wallet and keys secured tightly in the pockets of his jeans. He was also glad of his fur hat, a gift from Kevin on a visit to Moscow long before Russian-speaking immigrants had made Dublin their home or transient place of abode. He recalled with affection his student days when he and Kevin used to carry a copy of Pravda around as a pose, reading it conspicuously on campus or in pubs and cafes, both having mastered the Cyrillic alphabet as a subversive activity. The first time he wore the hat in public, on an icy wintry day, a coatless man of middle age and clad in a shabby navy suit stopped him on the pavement in O'Connell Street and, sniggering and shifty-eyed and striking a dramatic pose, pointed podgy fingers at his head, then exclaimed loudly: 'Ha ha! Are you a spy for the government, are ye? Ha ha!' his mouth stretched in a mocking grin. 'Which one?' Moss had responded stonily as he hurried on past him, the man cackling after him and shouting to passers by: 'Did ye hear that? Which government! Ha ha! Would ye look at him in that get up! Aah...feckin eejit...!'

He went into Neary's snug for a coffee, assimilating the atmosphere, sensing it permeate his clothes, his skin, nurturing him back into civic wellbeing. Afterwards, he strolled along Grafton Street, admiring the festive lights suspended from each side of the street with large red lanterns in the middle, then wandered in and out of shops in search of ideas for gifts for Louise and Clare and Valerie. Pleased with the choices available, he promised himself he would return in a couple of days time. He then felt drawn down to Clarendon Street, to St. Teresa's Church where he lit a candle by the statue of St. Anthony and sat down in a nearby pew and allowed the hollow silence to envelop him although this he interrupted to blow his nose discreetly. He felt meditative, filled with gratitude for the way his life was progressing, his mind drawn back to friendship again, and to Kevin's recent visit. Disappointed that Clare had turned down Kevin's dinner invitation, he made up for it by inviting him and Valerie to dinner in the Library Club two days before Kevin left for New York, bracing himself for a snowy, icy winter.

In the Club's dining room, they had listened raptly to Valerie's revelations, dramatically narrated, about Johann's sudden break-up with Rachel only days before. Elias, who had been laid up in bed with a cold, had gone downstairs to the kitchen to make tea and was surprised to hear voices in the drawing room. Despite his cold, he had detected the unfamiliar smell of cigarette smoke that lingered in the hall for he had assumed everyone was out. He had tiptoed along the passage to investigate: the door was ajar, and, peering through a crack, he had seen Rachel and her friend Anne-Marie squatting on the sofa, glasses of white wine in hand and two bottles on the table. Their conversation was filled with shrieks of laughter as he had heard Rachel boast about her plans after she and Johann were married the following spring. She had it all worked out, she told Anne-Marie: Valerie would have to move out of the apartment and they would rent it out; she would get rid of those lodgers and change the place around. The piano – 'that effing piano cluttering up so much space!' – would go back into Johann's room to free up space for parties instead. The sudden pauses in Rachel's damning list were filled by the sound of sniffling as Elias, still watching intently though the crack, witnessed them both sink to their knees, heads bent reverently to the coffee table where they snorted lines of cocaine through reddened nostrils. Elias had crept back to his room and awaited Valerie's return from town. Within hours, Johann had sat stone-faced at the table in Valerie's office as he listened to Elias's account of the incident. But Johann had wanted proof, to hatch a plan, trick Rachel into confessing her intentions while Valerie wanted a direct confrontation, get it all out in the open. The large fake For Sale sign – Elias's idea – had been erected beside the front gate in time for Rachel's arrival for dinner the following evening. But Rachel never made it to the dining room, Valerie had told them. As soon as she entered the hall, she installed herself in Johann's room where an intense discussion took place followed by a brusque exit out the front door as she hurried off - 'fleeing the scene so to speak.' Johann had been reluctant to furnish any details but the handshake he gave Elias confirmed the truth, that Elias had, in effect, saved him from making a terrible error of judgment. 'But do you know what upset Johann the most?' Valerie had asked them after taking a deep gulp from her wineglass. 'Trying to get rid of you I guess,' Kevin had said, 'and then getting her gold-digging mitts on a piece of prime real estate in leafy Dublin 4.'

'Not just that, Kevin – it was the piano, wanting it out of the way, shoving it into his room. She actually admitted that she hated the piano.'

He watched a woman light a candle on the other side of the church, below the statue of the Virgin Mary. He sighed deeply, silently, then finalised his visit by asking his mysterious creator for further guidance. Moments later he stepped across the narrow street into Bewley's for his evening meal and a read of a discarded magazine, barely glancing up at newcomers or his fellow patrons, contented to be alone. In the radio station later on that evening, he was conscious of his voice having taken on a huskier tone as he introduced Chilltime and the first trak. His running order contained a mixture of classical and tranquil new age sounds which he assumed were received by the small, anonymous audience whose members were suspended from the chaos of their routine lives and delivered into a mild, trance-like state for a while, perhaps shifting their focus away from their deepest concerns. The programme was repeated on Sunday evenings to complement the seventh day of rest or perceived rest, as Graham had said one morning in the office where he was revising the schedule, adding 'Rest from *shopping* that is!' with his glowing smile. Moss had tuned into the repeat programme the previous Sunday, smirking at the sound of his own voice and the fact that Ruby had been there, in the spare chair which she had positioned close to his, chatting amicably between traks, her knitting lying idle in her bag. But tonight he was alone, apart from Jason who arrived just as he was ending the broadcast with his customary well wishing, the signature tune fading into Christmassy jingles thanking sponsors. While Jason was busy setting up the next programme, Moss gathered up his belongings, hung up his headphones, retrieved his coat and hat from the wooden stand in a corner of the studio, then set off to the canteen. Sinking into the sofa, he watched the steam rise from his mug of tea, the low table patterned with the intertwined ring imprints of countless cups and mugs and strewn with newspapers, magazines. A local history programme was being re-broadcast when Jason sauntered in and settled himself on the opposite sofa then flourished the list he was compiling to cover the 'holiday season.'

'You can put me down for Christmas day,' Moss told him.

'That's great Moss,' he said approvingly and ticked his name off with a contented flourish. 'The Reynard's coming in on New Years eve,' he added. 'His chauffeur will drop him off as per usual'.

'Fair play to him,' said Moss, amazed but satisfied with his own impulsive decision to break a long-standing routine: it would corroborate his absence from the dinner table at his mother's house and spare him from inventing a white lie for the day.

'By the way, Graham asked me to remind everyone about the twenty-first,' said Jason. 'It's on the notice board,' he added noting Moss's blank expression.

'What's happening?'

'Invitation to the party in his house for all volunteers and staff. He gets someone in to oversee the station that evening. You can't miss it Moss,' he insisted, reading his slightly dismayed expression. 'His parties are great y'know. Well, it's really a dinner. We all sit around a massive table. Caterers do the grub. Presents under the tree. Starts on time and ends before midnight.'

'Before we all turn into pumpkins.'

'Exactly. Guarantee you'll enjoy it.'

'Well...it certainly sounds good, very civilised,' said Moss thoughtfully, his expression repaired. 'What kind of presents?' he added curiously, sipping his tea.

'Ah now! That'd be telling,' grinned Jason. 'Put it this way: Graham knows how to look after people' and, mimicking Graham perfectly, adding '*especially* our volunteers...'

On his way home Moss bought a single of chips and devoured them in the sitting room with a bottle of beer, the hearth bereft of its usual glowing embers. A solstice dinner at Graham's festive dining room table in the company of his new colleagues began to loom temptingly before him. He realised that for the first time in his working life he would escape the office party at the bank, a place that now seemed like a distant, almost inaccessible country. As far as he could recall, the party had rarely deviated from its usual Saturday night format: the shifty awkward reserve of his colleagues at the outset when they clustered themselves into departmental groups in the ground floor foyer which was transformed into a large bar. After a certain quantity of alcohol was ingested, they would be summoned to the decorated canteen where a traditional meal would be served, one that he always enjoyed. He was usually consigned to the directors' table, a colleague eventually explaining, after persistent questioning, that they could rely on him not to make a show of himself. Moss was amused that the only night in the year when not being a drunkard was in his favour, the disapproval of his relative abstemiousness lifted for the occasion. As the night would make its bedraggled way, female colleagues who had barely acknowledged him all year long would perform a sudden volte face as they engaged him in conversation, regarding him as if he were a new source of fascination, attraction, game for a laugh or a dare, invariably making a conspicuous play for him, vying with one another to lay claim to him. With well-practised politeness and good humour, he would extricate himself from their clinging arms, clutching hands, hungry eyes, lewd suggestions, some of them burdened with desperation, the elusive confidence of sobriety now fully asserted but slurred and hyper. Then there would follow the drama of his leaving early at two in the morning to strident cries of 'You're not leaving *now* Moss! Sure the party's only just beginning for feck's sake!' For you maybe, but not me, he would think, throwing them a fixed, charming grin, wishing them all a great time as he escaped with no explanation out the side exit, leaving the shrieking babble behind, greedily breathing in the welcome damp night air. He would then take a taxi home to Clontarf where he knew that Clare was wide awake, monitoring the sounds of his sober return. Then he would tiptoe up the stairs, pause on the landing -'Night mum' - and smile as she would utter her distinct but relieved 'Good night Morris' leaving him free to close his door and pour himself a scotch at his desk, carefully adding soda water to it. Cheers, he would whisper, raising his glass as usual, as if toasting a cherished but invisible companion.

But now he cherished the end of such tiptoeing and evasion as he made his leisurely preparations for a night's sleep in his own haven, indulging in a brief glance at Vincent's seemingly lifeless house before heading for his bed. He placed his glasses in their usual spot under the lamp and tried to read for a while but blinked rapidly, his eyes feeling dry. He turned off the lamp and, lying on his side in the darkness, his heart was filled with affection for Valerie and hope for Johann's recovery from his recent deception, seeing an image of a pretty, golden haired young woman running along the streets of Sandymount, fleeing from the red brick house she could not have, as he drifted into the chasm of sleep.

CHAPTER 40

Louise opened a box of Christmas cards and placed them on the kitchen table next to a folder of stamps and a pen, then retrieved a list from a bottom utensil drawer. She then settled herself on the hard chair to face her task, an absorbing prelude to the festive season when her generosity would be unleashed, her credit card allowed out for its annual airing when she would take advantage of her employer's seasonal perk: a half day off to go Christmas shopping. She looked forward to the long stretch of holidays between Christmas Eve and the early new year, reassured in that it applied to all employees, was legitimate, official, by order of management. The first card she selected depicted a cartoon Santa Claus being conveyed through the sky by his reindeer against a backdrop of a giant full moon shining upon snowy rooftops below. But she hesitated, her pen hovering over it as she felt a shadow envelop her, as if entering another zone of uncertainty, for her list now required certain amendments to reflect the changes that had taken place since the previous Christmas. She then began her task, writing the greetings routinely, including one to her father, until she faced a dilemma as she wondered whether to send Moss a card in the post or give it to him with his present during the familiar exchange on Christmas day. When she saw Susan's name, still written in under the old address, the new one etched in her mind from her sessions of covert surveillance which had come to their sudden, nerve-wracking halt barely a week ago, she froze, her pen poised mid-air. They usually exchanged cards and gifts on Christmas Eve or on one of the days after St. Stephen's day, unless the Kings migrated to London to be with Mark or Niall for the season. She put her pen down carefully, leaving the card to one side, along with her brother's one, to be dealt with another time for she had lost her concentration. Unsettling memories crowded her mind - the way Susan ignored her at the exhibition, the Garda car incident, Kevin's visit, and now the daily tension in the office compounded by the prospect of the Christmas party which was to take place the following Saturday.

It was an occasion she dreaded each year, the wrench from the shelter of her desk to the public arena of a prestigious hotel stunning her into nervous silence. Then there was the ordeal of the dining room where the seating arrangements were controlled and devised by a manager who tried to encourage social interaction by deliberately dismantling cliques, strategically placing name cards upon brilliant white table cloths. She cringed at the memory of last year's party when, flanked by Dorothy, Cara and Eileen, she had stood in the elegant hotel foyer where candles glowed and flickered upon a mantelpiece above a convincing fake log fire as they were served drinks. She had accepted a glass of white wine to deflect remarks against her usual sober mineral water, taking tiny sips and wincing at the acrid taste, her colleagues drinking quickly in an effort to repress the discomfort of the imminent separation to different tables. In the dining room, she had remained mouse-quiet as she found her place, trying to hide her dismay when she saw a couple of the returned emigrants claim their chairs at her table, bracing herself for the onslaught of their international travel anecdotes filled with names such as Shanghai, New York, Sydney, Moscow, Chicago – 'You've really gotta see Chicargo!' The exotic currency of banter and delighted laughter resounded as the meal was served by silent, efficient waiters and she had picked at her food while her audaciously confident dinner companions cleared their plates, exchanging reminiscences about meals they had consumed in those faraway cities. She also remembered how Frank, a dreaded senior manager, began to leer at her from across the table between puffs of his cigar, his face scarlet. He had complimented her on her dress and tapped his glass – 'C'mon Louise, drink up!' then, winking slyly at her, shouted 'Garcon! More vino here s'il vous plait!' She had faked a smile and took a sip of her wine, biding her time, certain that he would have limited, if any, recollection of the evening.

Her discomfort began to ease by the time coffee arrived, and, sneaking glances at her watch, realized it was close to the moment when she could leave discreetly. Around midnight she had stepped warily into the complementary taxi provided for the occasion and overseen by the security man who waved her off. As the car had sped off to Clontarf the tension returned as she sat rigidly in the back seat, vigilant in case the driver might make a sinister or fatal detour. Once safely delivered to her front gate, the driver had cheerfully called out 'Happy Christmas love!' The relief that the evening was dispatched at last had swept over her and she trudged upstairs to say goodnight to Clare, then headed for her bedroom, impatiently shrugging off her dress reeking of cigarette smoke and she tossed it into the laundry basket with a dismissive gesture, got undressed quickly, put on her nightdress and went to bed.

Dreading a repeat performance, Louise wondered what to wear on Saturday as it loomed even more threateningly now that Cara was gone. And Dorothy, whose hands would lie resignedly upon her protruding abdomen at break times, had already announced that she was 'giving the party a miss this time.' Louise began to brood about her office, about the instability that had come about since Cara's departure. The succession of temporary workers had unsettled her, some of them leaving within a week or two, the message that there was a new generation with a vast choice of jobs in the booming economy slowly dawning on her. She was relieved when Hazel accepted a short-term contract in early November, to take on Cara's job, her continuity a godsend in the light of the previous disruptive months. But there were no guarantees that she would stay, her manner brisk and impersonal as she went about her work in her navy trouser suit, her brown hair efficiently cut, her makeup minimal. And Eileen had broken the long established custom by accompanying Hazel to the canteen at break times, exhibiting a sudden independent streak, taking upon herself the task of helpful coach, showing the newcomer the ropes, leaving Louise with a lacklustre Dorothy to sip their tea in an edgy, awkward silence.

Time to make a mug of tea, she thought decisively as she shrugged off such concerns and returned the cards to their box until the following night. Clare was over in Anne's house for her usual Sunday evening visit and would by now be enjoying their traditional supper of sandwiches, cakes and tea. Just as the kettle clicked off the boil, the telephone rang. Louise hurried down the hall, plucked the receiver off its cradle warily, expecting another anonymous silence. To her relief she heard Moss's familiar voice.

'Hey sis, how are you?' he said in his mock English accent and told her he would not be able to make it over for dinner on Christmas day. 'We're broadcasting from ten in the morning,' he said, his tone apologetic. 'Have to do my bit...it's a fundraising thing, but I'll be over on Boxing Day, in the late afternoon.'

'You mean St. Stephen's day,' she nitpicked.

'Well...yeah. Incidentally, I think Valerie will be coming with me – you met her at Sarah's gallery. Anyway, I'll give you a ring Christmas week to confirm that. Have to go, have a few things to take care of now. Bye!' And he was gone before she had time to respond.

The next morning Louise made her way to the bus stop on the Clontarf Road where a north-east wind penetrated her camel coloured wool coat and swirled around her legs, her knee length skirt and beige tights offsetting a favourite pair of shoes. She was glad of the navy cashmere wool jumper which she had pulled on over her blouse, her boxy jacket hanging in a cloakroom at work, the last minute snatch of a silk scarf from a drawer falling short of expectation for warmth on such a cold day, the short strands of her fair hair tossed about briskly by gusts of icy air. As she watched with longing for the familiar shape of the bus to emerge at a turn along the busy road, her attention was drawn to a young woman she had never seen before standing next to her in the informal queue. She was wearing a calf length black suede coat buttoned up to the collar, the hem of a mauve skirt protruding over the tops of shapely black leather boots, a red woollen scarf wound around her neck, a matching wool hat pulled down over her ears. Strands of long, shiny brown hair were assembled over her shoulders as if for extra protection. Louise's lips curled ominously at the sight of the comfortable demeanour of the woman and when her mobile phone rang, she glared as she watched her fish it out of her bag with a mittened hand, her eavesdropping rendered fruitless as she spoke briefly to the caller in Polish. Within a minute or so, a car pulled in alongside the kerb, the back door opened and Louise watched her become absorbed into its interior, the car leaving a trail of rock music in its wake as it rejoined the steady flow of traffic, the driver honking his horn to thank the motorist who had slowed down to let him back in. By the time the bus arrived, she felt frozen, antagonistic, wishing she could have snatched the phone out of her hand, smash it into the pavement and demand that she speak English, fuming at the girl's effortless defection from the queue whose impassive members were now boarding and taking their places in the aisle, for all seats were occupied as usual.

When she arrived in the office just before nine o'clock, she discovered Lisa, one of the regular temps, seated at Cara's old desk, engrossed in a magazine.

'Oh - *you're* back!' she exclaimed in surprise. 'And where's Dorothy?'

'On maternity leave,' said Eileen who bustled in with Hazel, both clutching takeaway coffees and placing them carefully on the filing cabinet. '*God* it's *freezing* out, isn't it?! She went a few weeks early, to use up her holidays,' she said shaking off her coat, her smirk revealing that she had known about this all along. 'Lisa's with us until she gets back, thank goodness.' And she promptly moved her coffee to Dorothy's vacant desk.

'Yeah,' said Lisa, switching on her computer and shoving the magazine under her in tray, 'you're stuck with me now!' And with a toss of her highlighted blonde hair, she gave them a cheerful smile, her lips pink and glossy.

Louise tried to hide her fury at being excluded from the news of Dorothy's premature departure, her eyes squinting sourly into the screen. By morning break time Lisa, Hazel and Eileen left their desks swiftly and disappeared off to the canteen together leaving Louise to her solitary mug of tea. At lunchtime, after they deserted their desks again, Louise opened her plastic container of lettuce with chopped ham and cheese, slices of brown soda bread covered with low fat margarine spread and a piece of tea brack – another one of Clare's specialities - wrapped in foil, items that she assembled each evening and stowed in a bag in the fridge overnight. She felt slightly exposed eating alone but her ire subsided as it sunk in that Dorothy was gone, at least for a few months, that her absence already felt like a deliverance, and that some form of optimism might soon break out. With her lunch dispatched, she was unable to bear the sight of the mound of papers in her in-tray and returned to her work before her colleagues got back. She arrived home that evening feeling exhausted, the skin around her eyes tight and dry for she had somehow skipped her afternoon cup of tea.

'Someone rang looking for you,' Clare told her as she placed the plate of succulent roast lamb slices with creamed potatoes and diced carrots before her. 'A man called Matthew?'

'Matthew?' echoed her daughter, picking up her knife. 'I don't know any Matthew.'

'He said he met you at Sarah's exhibition.'

'Oh. Him.'

'Well...he said he'd call again another time. Anyway, I asked him for his number,' Clare passed her a piece of white note paper. 'Maybe you'll ring him Louise. He sounded very nice.'

An image of a pair of blue eyes in a kind face penetrated her consciousness as she took the piece of paper and left it lying on the table beside her dessert bowl, hearing the distant echo of his voice again: *Tell me about yourself Louise...*

After dinner she went into the hall and, hesitating in front of the telephone perched expectantly on its table, moodily inserted the piece of paper into the bulky directory, randomly, as if burying it, then set off to the living room to watch television for the rest of the evening.

Louise's dread of the Christmas party was in vain. By midweek she succumbed to a virus that began with a sore throat, transmitted, she figured, by one of her sneezing colleagues or fellow bus passengers, dismayed that the tablets and a night's sleep had not cured it, had, it seemed, made it worse, her limbs aching, her stamina depleted. She was so rarely struck down that she felt mortified at having to ring in sick to the office, her fingers trembling as she tapped in the unfamiliar digits.

'Never mind Louise,' said Joanne. 'It's going around - half the office is out with it. Anyway it's Thursday - you may as well stay off till Monday. And don't worry about the party. Just look after yourself now.'

After the call, Louise climbed the stairs wearily, her right hand on the banister rail, Joanne's consoling manner and such pragmatic forgiveness at variance with her long held belief that absence though illness meant weakness, disloyalty, being marked out for possible dismissal, still convinced that someone, somewhere was taking note. An entire day anchored to her bed felt utterly alien, a state compounded by the suspicion of having interrupted her mother's routine. And Clare's strange disdain for dressing gowns became obvious when she returned from the hair salon the next morning, frowning at the sight of Louise curled up on the sofa watching television in her fleece cocoon, a box of tissues by her side.

'Oh. You're up,' she said, her tone disapproving. 'You should get dressed if you're feeling better, or else go back to bed'.

Fuming at this dismissal, at the message that the garment should be confined solely for trips to the bathroom, Louise retreated to her pale bedroom where she lamented the fact that she did not have a home of her own, seeing with sudden but vivid clarity her lack of freedom, of autonomy. She determined to buy a place as soon as she recovered, a place where she could do what she wanted when she wanted how she wanted, although she felt appeased when her mother brought up a tray with a bowl of chicken soup and toast for her lunch. She spent the afternoon studying her property folder until, exhausted by calculations and the grip of the virus, fell into a deep, comforting sleep. She was immensely relieved when her vitality began to return on Saturday, and by Monday morning was glad to be setting off for work although she felt slightly dazed by the virulence, the sudden pounce of illness. Breaking her routine, she went into a pharmacy near her office and bought a vitamin supplement to safeguard herself from further attack for the idea of being off work again, or, most abhorrent of all, being out of work, filled her with dread.

Back at her desk around ten to nine, she felt diminished in the presence of Hazel and Lisa, both looking outrageously fit, in control.

'You still look a bit peaky,' commented Hazel in a concerned tone.

'*And* you missed a great party on Saturday,' added Lisa, Hazel nodding in agreement: 'Yeah, we both got rat-arsed on Saturday, didn't we Lisa? No idea how I got home. Or when!' she laughed.

'Must have been well before four a.m.' Lisa took a swig of her latte and a bite from her doughnut. 'You left long before me,' she told Hazel. 'I ended up having breakfast in a place in Dame Street at six a.m. A whole gang of us went. We had a huge fry up, it was great!'

They all looked up as Joanne leaned over the partition wall.

'Welcome back Louise: now it's Eileen's turn – she rang in sick just now,' Louise's lip tightening with satisfaction that she was not the only one. She plunged into her work, relieved by Lisa and Hazel's disappearance to the canteen at break times, at being spared further reminiscences of the party, and their very late night. After a nourishing lunch, she began to feel more like her old self and by five o'clock she left the office promptly, anxious to get home, the bus journey seeming longer than usual. As she walked the short distance from the bus stop to Lime Tree Road, she found the heaviness in her legs slow down her usual brisk pace, a dull headache beginning to form. But Clare blithely reassured her that it was just an after-effect of the virus as she served up her dinner, Louise consuming it with surprising gusto, swallowing her first vitamin pill with water after scrutinising the instructions.

'To be taken on a full stomach,' she declared.

After finishing her dessert of stewed apples and custard, Clare showed her the card from David which had arrived in the morning post, his warm, loving greetings to them written in fountain pen ink as usual. His gift of an elaborate bouquet of flowers would soon follow, she knew, delivered to the door during Christmas week. There were other cards, Louise searching through the small bundle for one from Susan. Perhaps tomorrow, she told herself as she read the greeting from Sarah and Gerald – *So lovely to see you at the exhibition!* Clare went off to answer the telephone and returned a few moments later, her cheeks glowing.

'That was Morris. He's delighted you're feeling better. Valerie is definitely coming with him on the twenty sixth - just for tea. They're going to some do in Howth at eight o'clock, he said.'

'Well isn't that nice for them,' said Louise coldly, pouring herself a cup of tea.

'Hmm....oh by the way, he said he was talking to Susan King today, in her shop,' she said. Then, heading for the sink, added absently 'She's spending Christmas in London - they're all off to her brother Niall's for a change.'

CHAPTER 41

On a sunny, frosty morning during Christmas week Clare raised her eyes heavenward at the sound of Elaine's telephone voice uttering the familiar words 'How *are* you', her usual throaty delivery now laden with the duty-bound inclusiveness of the looming festivities. Clare instantly regretted telling her that Moss wouldn't be there on Christmas day, for Elaine immediately assumed her brisk tone:

'So...it'll be just the two of you then, will it? Well now, we can't have you and Louise on your own on Christmas day, now can we? You'll come over to us of course. All the girls will be here. Hardly worth cooking just for two, now is it?'

Clare felt irked by the implication that quiet celebration was inadequate, that larger numbers amounted to superior quality. By the time she replaced the receiver having said she would get back to her, adopting one of Moss's phrases to play for time - 'I'll get back to you on that,' he would say to a tenant, or, 'Leave it with me,' – a mild temper began to rise within her. She felt bulldozed into conforming to a force, one that extended beyond her sister into a culture that played at happy families, its members snapping out a derisive 'For one?' or 'Just for yourself, is it?' as if solitary self-care was an indulgence, good nutrition an entitlement confined to members of the selective group arrangement.

Yet she recalled an incident long ago when she had arrived home from Sutton one Sunday evening and was surprised to find Moss back from Wexford so early, his car parked on the kerb outside. The scent of cooking had drawn her into the kitchen where she stopped to gape at the table and the plate he had just set upon the placemat: a grilled salmon steak, a knob of butter melting into the garden peas and sliced carrots, a mound of mashed potatoes over which he was grinding black pepper. It had struck her then as outrageously selfish that he could go to so much effort *just for himself.* He had immediately offered to share it, as was his nature, getting up to fetch a plate, mistaking her gaze for longing. She had quickly declined for she had already eaten in the accepted group style over at Jean's but felt stricken to the point of muteness by his self-containment, as if noticing it for the first time.

Now she dreaded the prospect of dining *en famille* at Elaine's whose daughters had probably been summoned with their husbands and teenage offspring in tow, as if returning to headquarters. There would, she knew, be the inevitable veiled barbs aimed by Elaine at herself and Louise to emphasise their unpartnered states, the absence of grandchildren magnified in such a setting, Louise's failed house hunt raised for gushing advice. Morris's defection to the southside would be a feather in their caps too, she thought somewhat wildly. She knew that the invitation had nothing to do with concern for their wellbeing, was in fact little more than an opportunity for Elaine to patronise her. With a rising sense of alarm, she also recalled that they dined very late, well after four o'clock, some of them no doubt hiding their inebriation well, or as well as could be expected. She rarely deviated from her own festive dinnertime of two o'clock. And there was the glass of sherry she enjoyed with Moss and Louise beforehand and the quiet meal that ensued, then the exchange of gifts, the day a success for all of them because of its absence of drama and expectation. Fingering her pearls and the collar of her blouse as she did when gripped by anxiety, she realized it was unthinkable to go to Elaine's and set about her chores to distract herself.

By lunchtime, when she turned on the hob to heat the vegetable soup she made the day before, her chicken salad sandwiches standing by on a plate on the counter top, she decided to pour herself a small sherry to help calm her nerves while she thought the matter through, searching her imagination for a white lie. Christmas is troublesome in so many ways, she thought with a sigh as she telephoned James to try and persuade him to change his visit to Christmas day, leaving a message to phone her. Then, feeling reassured by having taken action, she settled down to enjoy her lunch, the sherry having taken its soothing effect. The return call came through that evening when Louise was home from work and ensconced in the sofa watching television: James had made other arrangements for the twenty-fifth as he called it, without elaborating, but looked forward to seeing them on the twenty-sixth as usual.

Disappointed, she began to dither over Elaine's slightly cunning invitation but quickly acknowledged to herself how vital it was to be in her own home on Christmas day, to be spared any upheaval, her craving for peace paramount, peace that was now under threat by Louise whose increasingly brooding presence edged her almost to the point of obvious irritation. Yet after James's telephone call, Louise surprised her by taking control, declaring emphatically: 'I am *not* going over to Aunt Elaine's!' then snatching the phone off its cradle, tapping the digits in firmly, Clare listening with awe as she told her aunt pointedly that they were staying at home as James and Moss were coming over on Stephen's Day and they needed time to prepare. 'And Moss's girlfriend is coming too,' she added and said her goodbyes before Elaine had the chance to interrogate her for further details. Reeling from the implications of their rejection of Elaine's hospitality and not without the birth of a mild pleasure, Clare realized that her sister no longer had the upper hand. Not only would they escape her influence on Christmas Day, she had been made aware that they were not entirely friendless. She remembered how Elaine, either through stupidity or a vein of spite, constantly gave elaborate accounts of her own successes and social victories, their property in Donnybrook – 'Didn't we choose well!', – her numerous committee meetings, along with the dropping of conspicuous names and the divulging of intimate details about her high-status friends: 'Well now Clare, between ourselves and not of a *mention* of this to *anyone*, but...'

Her angst dissipating, Clare set off to the kitchen to make herself a spontaneous cup of tea – Louise had gone up to her room as if exhausted by the phone call - and began to look forward to Christmas, and to the visitors on St. Stephen's day, to the novelty of Moss bringing Valerie with him, a woman she felt possessed some quality that she liked - what was it... kindness?...tolerance? Whatever it was it presented no threat whatsoever, although her status as girlfriend, or partner, had yet to be established, she mused, and of course it would be a nice change for James, liven up the usual routine. As she waited for the kettle to boil, she pondered the obvious loathing Elaine harboured for their brother: 'Ah, that one, the black sheep,' she would say dismissively, her expression emanating the conviction that her own offspring were exempt from ever giving birth to such a species. A flicker of a smile crossed her mouth as she recalled Moss once saying to her: 'Ah well, Elaine - don't forget: James is an *asset-rich* black sheep, what with all those properties of his,' adding, in his measured way, 'to his credit,' giving rise to a change of subject. Yet each year, a calm aura would follow James into the Mortimer house after he was dropped off around three by his mysterious partner, a divorcee, who would then drive off to spend the day visiting her own relatives and friends. Around eleven, she would return to collect him, with no variation on this arrangement for years. Clare found his visits relaxing, comfortable, James always appreciative of the food and drink on constant supply. Conversation would be sparse, merely a listing of events or non events since they last met until Moss returned in time for supper having completed his own circuit of seasonal visits. Then the atmosphere would perk up: Moss and James would fill their glasses with beer and join Louise in a boisterous game of monopoly, Clare watching their game from the sidelines, coming and going from the kitchen and sitting room with drinks and food. James always brings such lovely gifts, so carefully selected, she thought now, sipping her tea luxuriously, remembering the way Louise would unwrap her package solemnly, fold the decorative paper neatly and put it aside then focus her attention on the revealed item, always an expensive surprise, treating them to one of her rare smiles, one filled with delight and warmth as she leaned over to kiss her uncle on the cheek.

Feeling a weight drift off her mind, she finished her tea. Christmas no longer seemed so troublesome and she determined to go into town the following day to seek out gifts for them all, including Elaine whom she planned to invite to Clontarf for a change, perhaps before new year's day, knowing she would be avid for information.

Over in Donnybrook, Elaine's ears resounded with Louise's rejection of her generous invitation and the list of visitors expected in Clontarf on St. Stephens day. She felt stung for it proved that they were still viable, still strong over on the other side – the less relevant side - of the river. She swept into the living room where Leo was lounging in his fireside armchair and launched her grievance with the familiar herald: 'You'd think they'd be grateful, Leo. After all, I was only trying to help...Anyway, they're not coming.'

'Ah well - never mind, pet, they can come another time,' he said reassuringly as he flicked through the latest issue of the Free Press to see if his history contribution was in, gave a satisfied grunt to see it in print, then emitted a sudden bark of hilarity:

'Ah ha! You should see this: there's a picture of young Mortimer right here. It's a feature on Eternity FM. Fair play to him for working on Christmas day all the same.'

'But he's just a volunteer - doesn't get paid, does he?' she said dismissively while taking a defensive peek at the evidence over his shoulder, obscurely irked that her husband validated it as work. She snapped her eyes away from the black and white image of a smiling Moss Mortimer lounging against a mixing desk, a pair of headphones around his neck; he was closely flanked by a young woman and a long haired man, all of them exuding the sort of beaming self assurance that raised the hackles of her soul.

'Brady's daughter works there, you know,' Leo went on, ignoring her remark and giving the paper a rustle as he read further down the columns: 'Ah yes, she's mentioned here. Let's see, doesn't really say much, just a list of the volunteers and the programmes they do. Moss is on on Tuesday evenings...I must tune in sometime. And Karen does Saturdays at ten a.m. Film reviews no less. I must say Moss is looking well - has a look of your father about him.'

Elaine snapped her face back to the feature. Karen Brady, the barrister's daughter...

'Heard it's great fun there,' Leo continued, mistaking her attention for interest. 'They do a fair few cheeky programmes... great training ground, of course...' But Elaine moved away, seething with the sense of betrayal she felt whenever people in her milieu succeeded or effected achievements without her intervention or influence, thereby denying her the credit. At the dining room table, she busied herself by wrapping up gifts and trying to allay a spate of angst-ridden speculations: Could Morris's girlfriend be Brady's daughter? The right age of course. But how would she have the time to volunteer, being a solicitor with such an eminent firm? And Morris looks...altered, she frowned, the impact of his happy dimpled grin shadowing her for rest of the evening.

CHAPTER 42

Donal was about to sit down to breakfast when he was alerted by sounds in the hall followed by the clunk of the front door being closed and, with a swift movement, took up his usual position by the tall window to peer intently through a tiny slit in the net curtains. He saw Maddie hesitate halfway to the gate to put up a green tartan umbrella against the drizzle then exit swiftly into the street. Off to work, he assumed, her white trousers protruding from a knee-length red coat - an apt colour for Christmas Eve, he thought, his thin lips twitching in amusement. He returned to his chair, poured himself another mug of tea, buttered a slice of toast, spread it with marmalade and bit into it hungrily, glancing with satisfaction at the other three slices lined up in the toast rack. For the third time that morning, he read the letter lying next to his plate. He had known for some time that Barry wanted to expand the business and now, there was the proof, Barry's confirmation of his appointment as the new manager of the firm, his eyes gleaming at the sight of the revised salary agreement, the digits filling him with possibilities. He would treat himself to a week in London, then Paris and plan for a holiday in Australia and see Ayers Rock and experience its colour for real. He could even afford to buy a place of his own, but he felt reluctant to take such a step just yet, maybe wait till house prices came down. He began to hum again absently as he mulled over other advantages of the promotion - he would be able to divide his time between the office and the outdoors, already planning to hire two extra men in early spring. And there were more signs of change, of optimism - yesterday morning he had checked the supermarket's notice board and noticed an ad for salsa classes starting in January, then found himself jotting down the number of the new dance studio in Ringsend on a receipt still residing in his wallet. The day before, he had won fifty euro on a Lotto scratch card and wondered, fleetingly, if there was such a thing as the

Christmas spirit that Barry enthused about so much. Of course, he has children, so he would say that, wouldn't he? Still...it rounded off the year nicely and made Christmas more tolerable now, he thought, topping up his mug and stirring in a little milk, imagining the consumerist outlets shutting down later on that day. He pitied people who felt obliged to make journeys to parental homes or those of family-in-law yet dreading them, their fate sealed long ago or the unsealing too daunting to even contemplate. He no longer allowed the traditional festival with its religious and commercial obligations to impinge on his life, gloating quietly over the fact that he was still free of such obligations, although he sometimes yearned for a new lover, but one that would not demand commitment or issue an ultimatum on one. He would keep his usual low, secular profile, he knew, treating the hyped seasonal days as an excuse for a pleasant hibernation, his cupboards replenished and his fridge well stocked with fillet steaks, smoked rashers, eggs, beer, his raspberries from the autumn crop nestling alongside a tub of ice cream and bag of spinach in the freezer compartment.

He gave a sudden, heavy sigh, realizing that there were consequences to mastering the art of giving people the slip, as he had done his entire family, his antecedents, written off into a history that contained the pursuit of misery, especially at Christmastime when his father – surly and glowering - had to drink at home, deprived of his local pub. Eamon, his elder brother, had absconded at nineteen, to England, then California, contact lost ever since although he had stored an envelope from him somewhere, his address inscribed on the back of it. In the privacy of his Dublin flat, Donal now relished the fact that he could cut his toast into narrow strips and apply a different variety of jam or marmalade or cheese to each piece without the beady eye of his mother upon him determined to find fault – 'Why can't ye cut it in half like a normal person,' she used to snap from her chair at the kitchen table, regarding him disparagingly, her arms folded against her wheezing smoker's chest. He remembered the long blue cardigan she wore and the stern line of a mouth that never stretched in a smile unless it was a downward one, the one accompanying her cheap mocking of the neighbours, her appetite for malicious gossip satisfied by the drip-feed of bad news and idle speculation from her copious female sources, compounded by the nursing of her stockpile of slights and wounds. To be normal, to be like everyone else, had been encouraged, even enforced, in that place and in this he knew he had failed. Just as Eamon had done when he had brought the wrong kind of paint and paintbrush into the house, committing an act so reviled that his father had gathered Eamon's canvasses and burned them at the end of the garden, watching them smoulder and leering at such destruction. Donal blinked the annual snapshot away from his mind's eye, although the memory of Eamon's disappearance that night had never left him, along with his chilling expression as he watched him pack his bags in the secrecy of the small hours, sneaking off before dawn to the awaiting car that took him to Dublin.

Refilling his mug, he acknowledged to himself that the house in Dawn View suited him in every way now, now that his tenancy was secure, Moss Mortimer's polite detachment a distinct bonus. And with Maddie he felt spared from obligation as they intuited one another's signals or lack of signals, their neighbourliness confined to civil greetings whenever necessary for there was no mutual giving, not even a greeting card. The night before, on his return from the pub, he had witnessed the absentee Karl make one of his reappearances by taxi, his cluster of luggage items abandoned at the bottom of the staircase, evidence of an engagement so pressing that he only had time to sprint up to his flat for a moment, perhaps turn on the heating, then sprint down again to the taxi still chugging outside the gate.

He heard the front door close again and saw, from his vantage point, the familiar figure of Moss in his long overcoat as he headed towards the gate, raising a hand in greeting to the postman who had just made a delivery. He went into the hall to investigate and discovered a festive paper gift bag outside his door. He then gathered up the post and sorted it at the table, casting a cynical eye over the miniature Christmas tree that Moss had put there over a week ago and festooned it with red and silver tinsel, its coloured fairy lights timed to come on at dusk. He took his solitary postal item and the gift bag into his domain and placed the bag on the table next to the bottle of whiskey that had accompanied Barry's promotion letter on the day they finished up for the mid-winter break. He then grudgingly examined the contents of the bag: a six pack of his favourite brand of beer and a box of Belgian chocolates, the tag attached to the handle reading Happy Xmas, Moss. He then snuck back to the hall, deemed the coast clear and peered into Maddie's bag and observed a similar assembly: a bottle of Australian red wine, an identical box of chocolates and a small item hidden by festive wrapping paper which he took out carefully, gave it a gentle shake then sniffed it. Perfume, he suspected, replacing it next to the chocolates then finally checked her tag which bore the same greeting as his. He contemplated tiptoeing up the stairs to see if there were gifts for Karl, but thought better of it. He felt confounded by Moss's puzzling tradition, the delivery of Christmas treats which varied only slightly from year to year, his brow furrowed as he tried to fathom the concept of such generosity, such thoughtfulness in a landlord; last year it was wine and a tin of chocolate biscuits, he remembered. Of course he can afford it, he thought grimly, what with him raking in the rent and he with a house worth a fortune. After breakfast, he read an art magazine for a while then went about his chores until one o'clock when he put on his dark green wax jacket, cap and scarf and set off to his favourite pub for a few festive pints and sandwiches, looking forward to a fillet steak dinner later on and a peaceful evening watching films.

CHAPTER 43

M oss returned to his flat around two o'clock, his Christmas day duty at the radio station over. He switched the kettle on, fished an envelope out of his pocket and put it on the kitchen table then returned to the vestibule to hang up his coat, unfurling a very long colourful striped scarf that Ruby had knitted. She had given it to him at Graham's party on the night of the winter solstice. 'Hey...a Doctor Who scarf!' he had exclaimed after ripping off the wrapping paper. 'I've always wanted one of these! Honest!' And he had kissed her lightly on the lips. A smile illumined his face at the memory of that party, for it had exceeded his expectations in that it was so urbane. The guests had assembled around the long oval table set for a feast, the huge Christmas tree in the bay window nearby entwined with tiny red lights, the presence of wine and beer a complementary backdrop to the frank talk, mirth and goodwill that he had often fantasised about and which delighted him, as if an outlandish wish had been granted. Graham and his wife Annabel had presided over the party like benevolent guardians of hospitality and generosity, Graham making witty speeches during the coffee when he paid tributes to the volunteers and the qualities that made the radio station such a success, the slender, brunette Annabel distributing cards, parcels and envelopes to them all, and which were opened with exclamations of appreciation and, in some cases, mock surprise.

He hung the scarf pensively on the coat stand – Ruby would be surrounded by people by now, a full house, he knew, remembering how her face had glowed at the prospect of being reunited by the legion of family members migrating to her home for Christmas. He felt grateful for her lack of interest in his own plans, that he ached to spend the traditional day alone, in a state of independence, away from the frailty of family enmeshment and dutiful togetherness. Another wish granted, he thought as he headed back to the kitchen where he prepared a hot whiskey with a slice of lemon and a fraction of honey – a medicinal one, he assured himself, to soothe a mild cough. He became aware of an intense stillness that had descended on the house, a quiet that also hovered about the streets of Sandymount, like the stealthy silence of snowflakes. It seemed as if the engine of life had been switched off for the day, a day that was formerly so sacred, now taking a twenty-four hour break until normal retail activities resumed, although he had enjoyed the carol service in St. John's Church the night before, his cynicism suspended as he sang the ancient hymns alongside so many strangers in their winter coats.

He sat at the table stirring his drink and admiring the cluster of cards which he had positioned on the kitchen dresser then remembered the envelope with its festive postage stamp that was left on the reception desk for him that morning. He had opened it ceremoniously in the control room, Lorraine's Goth eyes widening as he extracted a card with a traditional nativity scene, the star blazing overhead in a glittery sky. 'Wow - proof that someone is actually tuned in,' she had said as she examined the card wonderingly, her purple fingernails glinting, the simple message written flourishingly in blue ball point pen - To Moss, Best Wishes, Daniel - leaving them both otherwise speechless.

After finishing his whiskey, he placed the card on the dresser then decided to prepare his dinner, setting the table in the dining room for his meal of smoked salmon slices and potato salad garnished with lettuce leaves, accompanied by buttered brown soda bread. Admiring Sarah's painting, he enjoyed the meal in his revered candlelit solitude then took his coffee into the sitting room where the fire was already glowing, removed his boots, and sank gratefully into the sofa. There were no more appointments to fulfil although he had dutifully telephoned Clontarf that morning to convey his Christmas greetings, which, to his surprise, were accepted almost cheerfully, Louise saying 'See you tomorrow then,' with no discernable trace of umbrage in her voice, as if she had been rehearsing or trying out a different role.

Lazing by the fireside, he drew comfort from the presence of his tenants who had not fled the house, as if in solidarity with his own choice, although he spotted Maddie being collected by a man, her dark haired friend, around four o'clock when he was drawing the curtains on the dull, murky day, wondering if she would eventually leave to get married, like her predecessor. The good humoured Karl had knocked on his door around eight that morning to wish him a happy Christmas, giving him a bottle of Jagermeister then exiting the front door with a cheerful wave. Donal was keeping a similar low profile to himself, he figured, although he was intrigued by the unusual sound of him humming on Christmas Eve morning when he had left the bag outside his door, and now, the scent of frying steak and onions seeped appetisingly through the air.

He decided to finish wrapping gifts then settled down in the easy chair in the kitchen to watch The Shining, enjoying the thrilling tension while sipping hot tea from a bone china cup. Afterwards he went upstairs to check on Vincent's house, his indulgent surveillance feeling apt after such a film, shutting the door firmly behind him to ensure that his own spying shape would not be silhouetted in the window. The house was cloaked in absolute darkness, yet he sensed that Vincent was there, biding his time until the awkward day had washed over him. After a light supper in the sitting room, he listened to a cd of Gregorian chant for a while, then took to bed before midnight, filled with an obscure relief that the day was coming to an end, a day that had been subsumed into a hesitation of life, the suspension of usual activities. Wrapping himself comfortably in his duvet, he fell into slumber as the twenty-fifth of December slid quietly, unremarkably, off the calendar.

He came out of a comatose sleep in the pre-dawn hours, then slumped back into a twilight state trailed with dreams; he was waiting in the airport, but for what? For whom? - Valerie in a voluptuous snowy wedding dress, linking Kevin's arm, fragmented images that lingered after he regained consciousness. Yet the day began with an aura of optimism, even elation for he was to spend the latter half of it with Valerie, his usual Boxing Day visit to William 'Fangs' Foster – his former school friend and fellow Halloween vampire - postponed until the thirtieth. Instead of the usual lunchtime gathering with his wife Barbara and assorted family members and friends, William was hosting a special dinner to celebrate the retirement of his father Dominic. Moss relished another visit to the impressive house in Dun Laoghaire, a two storey over basement structure that oozed character. As he enjoyed a leisurely breakfast, amused by the slick radio ads for the sales, he felt certain that with Valerie at his side he would be impervious to his mother's gloom ridden household although he had come to terms with the revelation that the gloom emanated from Louise. Clare had somehow survived being tainted by her moods, by the deterioration in her disposition although he was unsure whether to attribute this to reserves of strength - so much was left unsaid, unquestioned, as far as he could ascertain. His elation was certain to infiltrate the atmosphere in the family home for he now felt almost incapable of repressing his good humour, the celebrant within at odds with its poker face. But the visit would be of a short duration, he reassured himself, a couple of hours at most, then they could take their leave and head off to Howth where he was invited as Valerie's guest to a little party in the home of Pat and Joan Byrne where Johann and Shane were to perform a medley of classical pieces.

Wearing Ruby's scarf, he went out for a brisk walk along the promenade, the air still, weighed down with dampness, the dull, heavy clouds turning his beloved vista of sky and sea to a solemn grey, the strand with its wading birds looking so forlorn that he turned back before reaching the tower, sensing rain on the way. Back home, he prepared for the day's visiting: he changed his clothes, put on a black shirt with narrow silver stripes and pulled on black jeans and the charcoal grey lambs wool jumper which Louise had presented to him last year, zipped up his buckle boots and finally put on Georgio's leather jacket. He then packed the car with gift bags and drove over to Seagull Gardens, arriving in time to witness a russet haired man usher Michelle out to a silver Mercedes blocking the front gate, a number of her travel bags gripped in his strong hands, a victorious twist to his mouth, her smile of anticipation mingling with her perfume as she greeted Moss with a cheery 'Happy Christmas and happy new year'.

'She's off to a hotel then on to London for new year,' explained Valerie welcoming him in and hugging him. 'Happy Christmas Moss! It's just ourselves. Elias is away in Copenhagen till the middle of January and Ming is staying with friends for a few days.'

The house seemed hollow, almost disruptive, in the wake of such absences and departures as he followed Valerie into the drawing room where he shook hands with Johann who was seated at the piano, finishing a practise, his handsome features containing a melancholy look, the residual ache or trace of an ache lingering from the end of the affair with Rachel.

'All set to face the northside?' he asked him kindly.

'Sure am,' replied Johann folding his sheet music away. 'I'm off for a shower now - excuse me.'

'So...how is he?' Moss asked Valerie when they were in the kitchen, Valerie busy laying a tea tray.

'Improving,' she said, scalding the tea pot. 'Poor Johann,' she sighed, throwing an extra tea bag in and filling it. 'He was devastated, you know. Broken hearted...Rachel was such a beauty. But: he has his music - he seems to have thrown himself into it.'

Moss nodded sympathetically, remembering the solace he had found in music in the wake of Aisling's absence so long ago. 'Thank God Elias was there that day,' he said fervently, 'Fair play to him.'

'Elias was fantastic with Johann - very protective of us both. Of course he loves this place. And his literati friends love it too.'

'*And* he saved you from being kicked out of your bijou apartment.'

'Yes, yes he did,' she agreed putting a milk jug on the tray. 'Otherwise I'd have had to move in with you,' she added, smiling broadly at his expression as she handed him the tray and led the way to the drawing room.

It was almost three o'clock. Outside a misty rain was falling but failed to dampen their spirits as they sipped tea by the unlit hearth, the cluster of glowing candles giving an impression of heat. Valerie gave him an account of her Christmas day, her Dutch friends visiting them in the afternoon, Moss admiring her knack of dressing for elegant comfort in layers of violet and black, her hair hanging loosely around her shoulders. Johann strode into the room looking transformed by his shower and a shave, resplendent in a white shirt, and jeans, shooting his cuffs for effect from the sleeves of a black corduroy jacket, his hair tied back neatly.

'Very distinguished,' said Valerie approvingly as Johann claimed a chair, Moss passing him a cup of tea. 'In fact, you both look rather distinguished for men with pony tails!'

'Why thank you!' grinned Moss. 'Well: it's time for prezzies,' he announced, relieved by Johann's smile as he delved into the bag.

At four o'clock they prepared to leave, Johann blowing out the candles and setting the alarm, Moss noting how occupied the building seemed behind the curtains with their chinks from the light of occasional lamps. He drove them to the northside, crossing the East Link Bridge and on to Griffith Avenue, telling them about his childhood Christmases when his father used to drive him up and down the wide tree-lined avenue to count the Christmas trees in the windows, rating them according to their display of fairy lights.

'Oh, look! There's a lovely one over there...in the bay window!' exclaimed Valerie and he slowed down so that they could admire a large tree with a generous coverage of red and white lights.

'Yep! That's a nine, I'd say,' said Moss. He dropped Johann off at Shane's house where he was invited to tea – '*Tot straks*!'

- then headed for Clontarf, to Lime Tree Road where he parked on the kerb outside the front gate.

'So…this is where you grew up,' remarked Valerie approvingly as they approached the mahogany door, Moss ringing the bell ceremoniously even though he still had his own key. Clare welcomed them in, looking elegant in a Chanel dress, divesting them of coats and scarves then ushering them into the sitting room. Moss was amused by the transformation in James from his usual placid self, by the novelty of seeing him spring to life for he had risen from his chair with unusual alacrity to welcome Valerie, shaking her hand then responding with a practised move to place the cheek kisses, an awkward move for Louise who hung back with her usual reticence, the ordeal of her fleeting, limp handshake over as James motioned Valerie to his chair by the fire. He then presented her with a glass of sherry, his manner chivalrous, his mouth expanding in a warm smile, for the group of two had imported a celebratory air that seemed to energise him as he poured himself a drink in response to the way Valerie said indulgently: 'And how about you James, are you having something?'

'Just a Coke for me thanks,' said Moss passing his sherry reluctantly to Clare. 'I'm chauffeur for the evening.'

James raised his glass: *'Prost! Prettige Kerstfeest!'*

'Cheers!' smiled Valerie. 'Happy Christmas everyone. And a happy new year.'

And so the afternoon progressed well, the amiable tone set, the exchange of gifts an opportunity to converse. Clare was taken by surprise when Valerie passed her a wrapped package, then one to Louise who accepted hers doubtfully, hesitating, as if considering giving it back, exclaiming in dismay 'But I've nothing for you; I hardly know you!'

'That's okay,' responded Valerie lightly. 'I enjoy it, it's just a little something, a little fun.'

Louise removed the paper and revealed a decorative transparent cosmetic bag containing bottles of bath oil and body lotion, a miniature bar of pink soap, a tiny pink teddy bear nestling alongside them.

'Oh that's gorgeous!' exclaimed Clare, knowing it was an item Louise would admire but never buy for herself. Perceiving his niece's awkwardness, James diverted their attention to the plate of turkey and salad sandwiches, taking over from Clare who seemed slightly distracted by the presence of so many people after a dearth of visitors, Kevin being the last such presence in the room. But she regained her composure after thanking Valerie for the illustrated book, a coffee table size, of English Wild Flowers and Roses, impressed with her robust appetite for there were no finicky refusals, no allergies to report, no obsessing about her weight. Valerie had just finished her third sandwich and was selecting a slice of Bakewell tart, issuing compliments as Kevin had done, '...There's nothing like home baking...' causing her to privately congratulate herself on that culinary skill, not regarded as obsolete after all. Clare was also amused by her brother's obvious enjoyment, pleased that she was capable of providing agreeable entertainment again and that it was not such a strain after all.

A sudden blank silence disrupted the flow of conversation when Valerie innocently asked Louise how she was enjoying Moss's radio programme and the way he sang 'I'm dreaming of a White Christmas' for a worthy cause the previous morning. 'Live on air!' she chuckled.

'I don't listen to pirate stations,' replied Louise stiffly after a slight hesitation.

Valerie merely smiled and, almost as if she was accustomed to such blank silences, the routine making of a faux pas or a fox's paw as Kevin would say, simply turned to James and asked him 'And what sort of music do you like James?'

But Moss, intent on accuracy, said 'It's not actually a pirate station, Louise.' He plucked a chocolate from the box on the table. 'It's community radio with a proper licence. Great fun altogether. In fact...'

Valerie's mobile phone gave a bleep: 'Oh...the alarm. Sorry! It's a reminder to collect Johann,' she said. 'My son,' she added in response to the questioning eyes, 'he's playing the piano tonight, in the home of friends of ours, in Howth. A Steinway grand.'

'*And* accompanied by Shane Turner on violin,' added Moss while Valerie composed a response. 'Well, it's back to Griffith Avenue so...'

Louise made an evasive move towards the tray, loading it up quickly then, calling her goodbyes from the sitting room door, retreated to the kitchen to avoid another round of handshakes or kisses as Moss and Valerie prepared to take their leave, Clare pressing a wrapped parcel into Valerie's hands at the front door. She had snuck up to her room earlier on, rummaged through her chest of drawers and found a scarf Elaine had given her the previous Christmas; silk, never worn, still folded within its tissue-clad box. She knew that it would suit Valerie's colouring, relieved that she had not given it away during the de-cluttering session and added a smaller box containing a bracelet that she had worn once.

'Thank you so much Clare, and for such a lovely time, really lovely,' said Valerie warmly, giving her a hug. 'I'll open it later on.'

As Louise assumed her domestic role, busying herself in the comfort zone of the kitchen, James and Clare relaxed in silence by the fireside, basking in the aftermath of a successful visit, James still inhaling Valerie's floral scent as they digested the knowledge that she was a mother, perhaps married or divorced. But neither spoke of such things, at least not for now. For a few hours their St. Stephen's day routine was altered beyond recognition, their lives re-activated, their faces emblazoned with the effect of visitors, the echo of farewells still lingering in the air, Claire pouring herself a another sherry, her cheeks glowing with the treasure trove of news to keep in reserve for Elaine, for the inevitable call that would come through within a matter of days.

Chapter 44

M oss stood by the sitting room window watching an unexpected snowfall, one so light that the flakes seemed to be floating, suspended in the air as if reluctant to land. He then closed the curtains on the final night of an eventful year for he decided not to go out, as if sated by such events, an extended lunch at the Library Club that afternoon a satisfactory social conclusion to the day. A couple of his radio station colleagues had issued open invitations to parties but these he resisted, settling instead for the ease of his fireside where he fell asleep on the sofa before the midnight hour. He awoke around two o'clock, having missed the resounding transition into the first day of January, an opened paperback novel sprawled beside him. He got up to peer through the windowpane again, hoping that the snow had stuck but the ground looked dark, damp, the flakes presumably melted on contact although he discerned a translucent sheen upon the roof of his car and an unexpected faint glimmer of light beyond an upstairs window in Vincent's house. After drawing the curtains, he returned to the hearth where the fire had died down and placed a couple of briquettes on top of the smouldering embers then set off to the kitchen to make his first pot of tea of the year, his routine recklessly broken. But he felt becalmed, unfazed as the expanse of time filled out before him, like a landscape to be negotiated at a pace wide open to review.

He spent a ruminative hour or so considering his present circumstances and toying with his future options. The radio station had turned out to be far more agreeable than anticipated, what with its share of risk-takers, of people who extended themselves beyond the conservative, conformist world he had inhabited for so long. At Eternity FM he felt unleashed into a place of vibrant affinity, sometimes of radiant delight, but he knew that much vigilance would be required by him to maintain such equilibrium. As he turned his thoughts to money, and the consequences of relying solely on his rental income and a few minor dividends and savings, he began to think about a return to work, to an employment destination, hankering after consistency, routine, a regular salary, although he could, if he exerted more discipline, live far more frugally now that he was well established in his sanctum. He also yearned – dare he admit it – to wearing a suit again, an updated one, and felt vaguely tempted to return to the world of banking although he immediately doubted the feasibility of this now that he had tasted his own time, had had his fill of doing his own thing as opposed to doing someone else's thing, as so many, puppet-like, seemed to do. He wondered if he was capable of sustaining traditional work hours ever again for he now possessed what Sam Hunter wistfully called the luxury of time as though time had become a commodity which he could not afford, was in fact priced out of the market. Of course if time were a commodity, Moss figured that he had been on quite a spree, had purchased a large portion of it by sacrificing a career in banking. No, he revised, he had not bought time, nor a luxury but had invested in a transformation, one that led to a way of life far more fulfilling than he had thought possible although it was, largely, an interior life, he knew. At Eternity FM he was spending - yes, spending! - much of his time, liberally, with the enlightened self-interest of the pragmatic volunteer, a smirk forming on his mouth as he realized how such pragmatism was at variance with the women, a group of four, he had observed one Saturday afternoon from behind the glass, in solidarity with Jason, as they recorded a fortnightly programme on equality and women's issues. He remembered Celine, the presenter, chiding Jason in a petulant tone for telling them to stop rustling their papers and thumping the table: 'Oh well, it's easy for you Jason; you're *paid* to do what you do. We're only volunteers, you know? You can't expect us to be like *professional* broadcasters,' her colleagues exchanging a condemning shared nod of agreement, their sense of humour, of spontaneity, decimated by the newly invented politically correct speech, bland and stilted, that they used, Celine omitting the mannerly '...and thanks to Jason on sound...' at the end of the programme.

Moss took the simple view: he had acquired a new skill, in fact a number of skills that could be put to use in a commercial station, even if it was to do an occasional voice-over or join a production team as others had gone on to do. He intended considering such a route, sometime in the year ahead, remembering the day in November when Graham had taken himself, Ruby and Martin on a radio tour, driving them around the city and its environs to visit a couple of commercial stations. Moss had sensed the excitement of newsrooms, of current affairs programmes with skilled presenters, producers, researchers and sound engineers. He realized that he needed far more experience to qualify for such places and felt it wise to continue with Chilltime and the occasional weather forecast, announcement or jingle for the time being.

As he sipped his tea, the fire flickering back to life, he was filled with a sense of glowing abundance, a private state which had evolved over the preceding months. He knew for certain that the successful elimination of a dark, invisible pressure - not just the familial but the grim force of institutionalised labour - had contributed to this developing lightness of heart, and this in turn had led to the liberty of absence, and the continuing mastery of it. A former bank colleague had called him a dark horse on learning of his mortgage redemption, he remembered, and realized that he had galloped, or perhaps cantered, unobserved through the grey, metallic noise of their lives, invisible to them now, but with a firm grip on the reins of his own life, the symbolic horse intent on reaching a cherished destination - not the sunset of romantic fiction, but an enduring place, or assortment of places, with a discreet lifestyle to nurture.

After yesterday's new year's eve lunch – it now seemed so long ago - he had inspected the Club's notice board, pleased at the number of activities, of concerts on offer through till March, the music room in regular use again by musicians and actors, for their rehearsals and performances. Then a notice had caught his eye, a pale yellow page bordered with gold and bearing the Club's logo. Printed in the centre, in bold type, were the words: *Assistant administrator required. Part-time. Knowledge of accounts essential.* He had written down the details on the back of an envelope for later consideration, the envelope now lying like a sign upon his kitchen dresser. He got up and made a swift, purposeful dart into the kitchen to take another look at it, plucked a pen from the mug of oddments on a shelf and drew a neat circle around 'Part-time'. It seemed ideal to him; he could apply his doctrine of enough principle by earning a modest salary, divide his time between the radio station and the Club, if, of course, he was considered suitable for the job. But a doubt crept over him, arising out of his keen intuitiveness to warn him, as he realized that working in the Club could spoil his love of it, alter its refuge-like status, and so, with much regret he scrunched the envelope up and disposed of it in the fire, placing it upon a glowing briquette where it seemed to melt into oblivion. He had never revealed his Club membership while at the bank to spare himself the tedium of hearing cheap shots about bookworms or uppity academics and writers, although he eventually mentioned it to Sam, passing it off as something peripheral to his life. But it was the jewel in his heart, a space that filled him with a joyous peacefulness whenever he set foot in the tiled entrance hall then treaded up the stairs to the reading room with its book-lined walls and green-shaded desk lamps, where sounds were limited to the rustle of papers, the thud of a book descending upon a polished wooden table, the creak of a chair, a muffled cough, an occasional but clamorous sneeze. The profound silence was also induced by the sheer lack of obligation to converse. It was room where he suspected women, or a particular kind of woman, would not feel at ease in, for they would need to fill the space with chat, confidences, confessional declarations in whispered tones, unless of course they were possessed of independent dispositions, the kind evidenced by members such as Amanda Stafford, her head bowed to her various tomes, utterly indifferent to those around her. And there was the occasional satisfactory sighting of Katarina Jansson engrossed in research, the light from the desk lamp illuminating her halo of frizzy blonde hair.

The echo of another conversation stole into his consciousness, one that had taken place in Nemesis in December when he called in to wish Susan a happy Christmas. To his surprise, she had offered him a job, saying if he felt like returning to the rat race to 'Come and work here!' and, after a brief discussion, said: 'Think about it Moss; I'll be in touch in the new year. No rush.' But would the same thing happen? he wondered now. Would he lose his love of reading, of the sight and texture of books, the evocative aroma of newly published ones, if he worked in their presence day in day out? But Susan had said it was office work, book-keeping and other administrations that took place in rooms above the shop somewhere, perhaps a room with a view of the attractive city street. Finishing his tea, he decided to go to bed. In the spare front bedroom, he looked at the outside world beyond the sash window, the isolated snow long gone, the light over at Vincent's still perceptible, the ink sky populated with its glistening, icy stars.

CHAPTER 45

Louise resumed her chores with renewed zeal now that the festive season was out of the way, a narrow shaft of sunlight infiltrating her bedroom where she was busy ironing her work blouses in their assorted shades of white and cream, her ache to return to the office the following morning enhanced by the absence of Dorothy. It was the third day of January, the resolution list she had written on new year's day positioned nearby on the dressing table filling her with determination to disprove Moss's claim that she was chasing an illusion, the memory turning her cheeks scarlet. On St. Stephen's day while she was busy with the tea trays, he had entered the kitchen to deposit a bottle of wine and a box of chocolates on the counter top, then snatched up a brochure that was lying there. 'Hmm... "A three bed red brick terrace in Marino,"' he had read. 'Perfect for you. So. Have you put in an offer? No, of course not,' and he had tossed it back on the counter dismissively, reminding her that she could still afford to buy what with her untouched savings and shares. 'Sell some of them,' he had urged her. 'Sell and be done with it! Buy your house!'

Easy for him to say, she fumed, still astounded by such an outburst, such an uncharacteristic show of authority. But the claiming of her place, that home of her own, would require other efforts, risks of which she dared not speak, her stomach clenching at the idea of telephoning a broker or the bank for information, then issuing instructions to move her money out of its static existence, her father's former area of expertise suddenly looming as unglamorous, frenzied work. As she obliterated creases from the sleeves of white cotton, deftly eradicating them with swift movements of the iron in the area around the cuffs, she was filled with foreboding at the upheaval involved in moving out, the packing that would have to be done, the furniture and decorative items to be procured and arranged for delivery to a new address. The enjoyment of their selection would be shadowed by the physical act of leaving the family home for another neighbourhood, for she craved the familiar, was constantly seeking out the landmarks of a known and unchanging landscape, skirmishing the worlds of others, worlds that were wide open to access. Now she was sullenly aware of a confinement, of a force that held her captive within while at the same time angling for an easy passage, yearning to be taken over, to have someone, somehow, transport her from her room, her life, to her new home, her new life, in one seamless, effortless transit.

As she put the blouses away in their usual position in the wardrobe, she felt frustration overwhelm her again, the changing world pressing in on her, a world with so many newcomers and survivors emerging happily, unscathed despite the risks taken. Even Robert had changed or been rescued by the force of change, or his response to such a force, the recent shock of his engagement cutting into her, her mouth immediately tightening. She had discounted him from marriage on account of an illness of the mind, the depression she had been so sure would haunt him, relapse him into a social outland where he would reside on a margin, recovery an implausible outcome, as if such illnesses should be dealt with by permanent disqualification. Their brief summer adventure had yielded the mysteriously altered Robert but his tightfistedness had put her off contacting him again, although she still kept watch for his car after her dwindling attendances at Mass on Saturday evenings, hoping for a chance meeting, but to no avail. On the day after Stephen's day, in the spirit of the season, she had telephoned him and was pleased by his response, and the issuing of an invitation: 'I'm having a few people over on the thirtieth,' he had said. 'Just a few drinks and a light supper.'

He had sounded kindly, almost sympathetic, telling her how fond he was of her, but things were working out for the best; he was sure she would be happy for him, Louise's eyes narrowing with the suspicion that he had had a lot to drink, or was back on medication. At the time she did not register his encouragement to 'Please, feel free to bring someone along', dismissing it as a casual politeness. Clare had insisted on driving her the short distance to the White's, with a promise to collect her at eleven, as a protection against the cold and the perceived dangers of the night streets, Louise feeling comfortable and dressed for warmth in a pair of black slacks, black court shoes, a blue silk blouse and the shapely, creamy cardigan that Anne Leonard had given to her when she visited them on Christmas Eve.

She had been welcomed into Robert's house by Maureen, a cousin on cloakroom duty who indicated the reception room, the bangles on her ample bare arms jingling. It was a room that Louise remembered as dark and unused but when she went in she was startled by its stylish redecoration and the sight of such a large gathering. As it dawned on her that this was a celebration of some sort, a glass of champagne was placed into her hand by Robert's father, his grey eyes twinkling: 'Happy new year Louise: good of you to come, very sweet of you indeed.' Robert caught her eye from across the crowded room and made his way over to introduce her to Evelyn, 'My fiancée,' Louise smirking at his characteristic wink as he moved off to make another introduction, leaving her in a haze of Evelyn's perfume and a flounce of her long, shiny red hair. Louise had suspected her of mercenary intentions only to discover at the dinner table later on that she had her own home in Glasnevin, a job she loved so much it sounded like a delightful pastime. She had noticed that Robert's eyes were transformed by some other quality, one that was not drug-induced although this she would not discount, utterly bewildered that he had emerged from depression to a future populated with a woman of barely thirty and whose even white teeth flashed in a confident smile, her strong physical form oozing sensual vitality and the assurance of healthy children to follow, Robert's parents' eyes following the pair about with sparkling tenderness.

Louise's ordeal of dining in such a populated setting had been diverted by the man sitting in the antique chair next to her. He introduced himself as John Peterson, and engaged her in amiable conversation, updating her on Robert's engagement and pointing out his wife Jill who was situated at the other end of the table next to Evelyn, and who beamed a smile back at them and raised her glass. Louise then began to sip the white wine, marking the moment when she regretted not telephoning Matthew, remembering how she had tucked the piece of paper with his number on it into the telephone directory at a random page. With the number out of sight, she had felt absolved of any obligation to contact him. He had called again, while she was watching the soap opera, just days before Christmas day. Clare had answered the persistent ringing, but dared not disturb her, asking him to ring back in half an hour. The phone had remained silent. Perhaps he has gone out, they said from time to time, the rest of the evening spent in a state of vigilance.

But John had proved interesting, an enthusiast of the property market, responding to her own detailed house hunt by suggesting that she consider buying his sister's house before it went on the market. 'Lovely townhouse,' he had told her, 'in a tiny enclave just off Griffith Avenue. Gina's moving to the country - not very far really - to Kildare: setting up a guesthouse with her partner.' And she had returned from the party with another piece of paper imprinted with a new telephone number and address, John assuring her that Gina would be delighted to show her round. 'No harm in having a look,' he had smiled at her charmingly. And she had looked, but covertly, on new year's eve afternoon, driving up to Paddock Court, her eyes scanning the small enclave of elegant terraced houses. After she had parked the car, she could see the multi coloured lights of a Christmas tree twinkling in Gina's front room, the driveway empty. She had spent half an hour in her car, barely moving a muscle, unable to find fault with the house, its design, its location, the convenience of the bus stop just around the corner.

Shutting the wardrobe doors firmly, she stowed the ironing board away and sat down at her dressing table and wrote neatly on her resolution list: Phone Matthew. She then opened her new diary and took out the loose page on which she had made a rough sketch of Gina's house from memory, the price John had quoted her 'Open to negotiation of course!' pencilled in beside it,

Gina's telephone number displayed conspicuously underneath. But little doubts began to creep into her mind until it felt crowded by them, and, when her mother's voice suddenly filled the air: 'Louise, lunch is ready!' she pushed the page promptly, randomly, into her diary and hurried off down the stairs.

CHAPTER 46

Moss stayed indoors during the first few days of the new year even though the weather was fine and dry, the morning air frosty and invigorating, the bright daytime sunlight dissipating the illusory greyness. At night time he stood at the bedroom window, drawn to the reassuring constellation of Orion and glittering Sirius emblazoned in the cold, impassive sky. January usually kindled a slight unease within him; he regarded it as a pitiless month with a doomsday dullness in the air despite the earlier sunrise, the increasing post-solstice light. A residual stillness had shrouded the house: Maddie was away on her well-earned skiing holiday and Donal had disclosed the fact that he was off to London for a week or so, their combined absences adding to the silence although Karl's hearty, infectious laugh occasionally penetrated the air.

Moss's cocoon of semi-hibernation coincided with Valerie's seclusion to work intensively on an urgent translation, their café meetings suspended for a couple of weeks. An email from Kevin informed him that Masami and Kim were looking forward to seeing him in the summer as they were coming to Ireland for two months and would be staying in Sandymount with John and Noeleen while he would remain in New York, drafting another book. I can't guarantee them a begrudger-free vacation, Moss had typed in his reply, but they're welcome to stay in the cottage anytime up to the end of July. Already it promised to be an eventful summer, for David was planning a visit to Dublin, according to his express delivery letter. Moss studied the photograph he had enclosed, an image of him smiling in that carefree way of his, sitting at a grand piano in a brightly lit lounge looking fit, durable, a healthy glow to his face framed by snow white hair. He was to accompany a number of his former students to Cambridge in the summer, in August, and would take a few days out to 'pop over' to Dublin to see them, perhaps treat them all to dinner in one of the new hotels. Now what will Clare make of that, he wondered, smirking, the old man returning after all these years, the smirk melting into a smile as he realised that she would be very pleased, and Louise too of course, that his visit would bring about a significant change in their lives. As he studied the photograph again, he felt a renewed affection for his father, for his risk taking, his optimism, for being so comfortable in his own skin, a quest he had initiated for himself and was, he felt now, making some progress in. He decided to keep his options open, perhaps travel back to Cambridge with him for a week or two, or even longer. His yearning to preserve the memory, sustained over twenty years, of those idyllic, youthful weeks there, ironically in the same month, was weakening. It's definitely time for a change, he thought decisively, placing the photo in a conspicuous spot on the dresser; time to take more risks, no matter how minor they are.

Yet he still kept a lower profile than usual, limiting his excursions to the local shops and the supermarket where he overheard two women greet each another - 'Now isn't that a grand stretch in the day?!', 'It is indeed, thank God!' as they wheeled their trolleys past him. He also deferred venturing into the city centre, lacking the incentive to investigate the sales or wait for the number 3 bus or make his way down to the *Dart* station in the wintry air. He had also taken a break from the radio station by recording a couple of his programmes in December and one of these had already been broadcast. Yet one morning he found himself taking the well treaded route over to the station, where, to his surprise, nothing had changed apart from the hollow absence of Jason.

'He's in bed with the flu,' explained Lorraine, waving him to the spare chair in the control room where he watched, somewhat raptly, a new trainee in the recording booth recite a couple of brief announcements in Russian. Moss felt gratified that his Pravda-flouting days were not in vain, the spectacle before him a sign, or one of a number of signs, of the coming of age of the island, and with it the exhilarating witnessing of such change, Lorraine's slender hands busy with the mixing desk until she was satisfied. 'That's great Konstantin; would you like to come on in here and I'll play them back to you, okay?'

Confirming his live broadcast for the following Tuesday, he made his farewells to Lorraine and Konstantin then set off to the canteen for a mug of tea. Ruby, who was rehearsing her lines with Paul and Eddie for the next episode of the play, gave him an unexpectedly feeble new year greeting, and after he had busied himself by sending a get well text to Jason, looked up and saw her in an amorous clinch with Paul, to his mild chagrin. 'Ach c'mon lads,' groaned Eddie impatiently. 'We haven't got all day,' and they disentangled reluctantly and resumed their rehearsal, exchanging lustful glances. The canteen suddenly seemed crowded especially when Graham then strode in, energising the room with his smile, wished them all a happy new year as he poured himself a mug of coffee then strolled out again. Moss finished his tea, shrugging inwardly, assuming that Ruby's new liaison had been established at one of the recent parties. Yet he was determined to continue their agreeable friendship, for he found her so much fun, her presence uplifting, glad that he had made no foolish moves, although this would not guarantee the cessation of his fantasies about her, he knew.

On his way home through the village he joined a short queue outside the bank's ATM, obligingly picking up the newspaper that the tall man in front of him had dropped as he was sifting through his wallet, then smiled as he recognised the familiar face of John O'Brien.

'Ah! Thanks, Moss. Cheers! And a happy new year to you.'

'And you John.' They shook hands firmly. 'So, how's life then?'

Life, he learned from John's enthusiastic account, couldn't be better, what with Kim and Masami's summer visit to look forward to, a trip to Italy with Noeleen in May, not to mention the new creative writing course he was presiding over in the Education Institute.

'Begins next week, if you're interested,' he told him as he fed his card into the slot then furtively tapped in his secret digits. 'Thursday evenings. Seven thirty. Nice place, the institute. Power of the pen!' he enthused, turning to face him with a challenging grin and fixing his intense blue eyes on him before putting away his cash.

'Nah...thanks John. I'll give it a miss for now,' replied Moss taking his turn at the machine. 'I'm a born reader,' he added simply, and they parted, with much well wishing. Once the seventh day of January had passed, Moss felt rejuvenated, as if some annoying weight had been unburdened. He removed the tree and festive decorations from the hall and stowed them away although he stopped for another read of the greeting cards before bundling them into a bottom desk drawer, for some of them contained information, notably the Mulcahys' annual decampment to Australia for a couple of months, leaving their slumbering land, livestock and guesthouse in the capable management of cousins. There was also a note to confirm an Easter booking for the cottage and so he transferred the card to his new diary then he set off to the city centre to reunite his senses with the beloved vista of streetscapes. After a customary stroll around the grounds of Trinity College, he headed for Bewley's Café on Westmoreland Street where he claimed a space on the long sofa under the majestic windows on the Fleet Street side. He returned a greeting from the occupant of the adjacent table - one of the regulars meticulous in a charcoal corduroy jacket, pale lemon shirt and dark tie, his black hair recently cut. He was tucking into a late breakfast of a full fry and, putting aside his cutlery, drew Moss's attention to the newspaper folded neatly beside his plate.

'Take a look at page five Moss,' he said in an ominous tone, pointing a spotless fingernail at a headline. 'Enjoy your coffee while it lasts. A sad day for the civilised world...a decidedly unfitting way to begin a new century,' and, with a defeated shrug, he took up his knife and fork and resumed his meal, slicing his bacon vigorously.

'Thanks very much,' said Moss. After pouring sugar on the froth on his coffee, he opened his own paper and read the recommended article, in morbid silence, his eyes seeing a death notice between the lines of printed words, the dismantling of what seemed an ancient tradition, for it was now a matter of months when the gracious rooms would be shut down to the public, the employees disbanded although they would not, he figured, be doomed to join dole queues as would have been the case during the recession. But some of them would, surely, miss the café long after their absorption into the new era of work opportunities and immigration. He would never again select a chocolate éclair from the display or be asked by the pretty girl if he wanted 'tea bags or leaves.' There was no mention of the closure of the Grafton Street café, and this he took as very good news, clinging to Stephen Devereux's conviction that it would remain open for business, that it would continue on as it was or be claimed by an entity rich enough, enterprising enough, to retain it as a vibrant café. Sipping his coffee and taking a bite from his muffin which he had crumbled in half, he resumed his concerns about his own future earnings, skipped the Letters page and turned his attention to the appointments section. It yielded an ad for an administrative assistant in UCD Belfield, in the admissions office, and in which he took a keen interest, suspending his reluctance to take on a full-time job. The discreet bleep of his mobile phone alerted him to a message - it was from Sarah, wondering if it they could visit him this evening around eight. Grand, c u then, he replied.

Distracted by the message and the pleasing prospect of his cousin's visit, he decided to lunch at the Library Club and spend the afternoon in the reading room composing his curriculum vitae. He finished his coffee, said goodbye to the regular whose name he could not remember, exited the café and set off to Reads in Nassau Street to browse the wide range of stationery paraphernalia and supplies. Feeling overcome with nostalgia for learning, for college life, he departed with a frugal A5 notebook and a new ballpoint pen then made a visit to Nemesis bookshop, the young woman with the red hair band telling him that Susan – 'Lucky thing!' - was in Rome with her mother and would be back the following day. So many people away, he thought after he left his regards for her. As he strolled off in the direction of

Merrion Square, two passing buses exhaled gusts of exhaust fumes that were carried away on the southerly breeze.

He had overlooked the Club's well organized and structured daytime life, as well as the punctuality of some of its members for he arrived just in time to secure a seat at the Long Table next to a number of academics who had downed aperitifs in the bar beforehand. Very sensible, he thought approvingly, promising himself to do the same next time. He hungrily consumed the meal of vegetable soup with buttered brown soda bread, succulent fish cakes garnished with an assortment of salad leaves and that aroused much praise, and for dessert, apple and peach tartlet topped with fresh cream. After a strong coffee, he set off to the reading room where he was astonished to see that most of the tables were occupied by others with similar, or more serious intentions, Stefan Katz raising a pale hand in greeting, mouthing 'Happy new year,' Moss saluting him back as he chose the smallest desk in the darkest corner of the L-shaped room. He switched on the lamp, tilting the green shade to avert the glare then removed his glasses, arranging them carefully behind the lamp's brass base. He felt slightly daunted by the blankness of the first lined page in his new notebook. After a few moments flicking his pen doubtfully between his fingers, he finally wrote the words Curriculum Vitae, and on the next page his name, address and other details, then put the pen aside, feeling rusty, out of practise as he tried to concentrate on providing a convincing account of his work history. Inspired by his knack of listing items on the weekly running order for Chilltime, he picked up his pen and began to make a list of the routine tasks he had performed in the bank, and was relieved to see the results, a map of experience and competence growing before his eyes.

Pausing to compose a cover letter, he heard the door swish open, emitting its usual signal creak and, putting on his glasses, craned his neck and saw Katarina Jansson enter the room clutching a bundle of files and books which she deposited noisily upon a table near Stefan. Feeling slightly disappointed by her new hairstyle, now a short, tight, masculine shape that squared

her profile and accentuated her broad shoulders, he returned
to his task, this time doodling in the margins absently. Around
a quarter to four there was a sudden but discreet exodus from
the room, reducing its numbers by more than half. It was time
for tea and toast in the bar, but Moss decided it was time to go
home. He boarded the number 7 bus on Merrion Square and
disembarked at the stop opposite the Merrion Centre where he
bought some supplies in the supermarket then strolled home via
Ailesbury Park with a bulging plastic bag dangling from each
hand, slowing down his pace to admire the Edwardian houses.
He waited patiently in the dusky air as the lights flashed red at
the level crossing at Sydney Parade *Dart* station, catching sight
of a motorist punch his steering wheel, his mouth shaping an
expletive at the sight of the red and white gates slice the air
as they came down to form the barricade. Moments later the
familiar green train glided by, the brightly lit carriages packed
with home-bound commuters. As soon as the gates began to
ascend, the revving cars accelerated, their drivers keen to catch
up on what was clearly lost time. Moss ambled across the tracks
and continued his walk along Park Avenue, on through the
village and home to Dawn View for the night, opening the door
of his flat to the welcome shaft of light from the dining room
lamp, timed to switch itself on in the mid-afternoon.

He unpacked his groceries, stocked the fridge, put an extra
bottle of white wine on the door shelf, lit the fire in the sitting
room, drew the curtains, switched on most of the lamps, then,
feeling deprived of his tea and toast in the Club, replicated the
treat for himself in the kitchen, consuming it in the company of
the television news which he watched absently. Mindful of his
visitors, he hastily cleaned the bathroom, put out clean towels,
tidied up the sitting room then collapsed into the sofa. He
tried to read the notes from his afternoon's efforts, but found
himself distracted by thoughts as they drifted over his day, a
day that culminated in a state of relishing his own space - his
exclusive, cherished space. Casting an affectionate glance at the
candlesticks on the mantelpiece, he got up to light them, then

admired their flames reflected in the mirror. He began to wonder if he could ever share his space with another, for a subtle shift in his euphoria of solitude and in the protection of that solitude had occurred, a chink of light penetrating his heart as he realised how he had overlooked love in the equation which he had laid out upon his sheets of paper to compose the blueprint for his yearlong liberty. He remembered how disappointed he had felt when Valerie could not come to Wexford in July; it would have been a different kind of holiday had she been there, he mused, even for a day or so. He still feared the destruction of their friendship by a clumsy sexual encounter, could not imagine undressing her in the state of lust he had done with lovers in the past. But he now aspired to marriage, or the married state, he realised, but felt that to transgress the invisible parameters of their relationship, he and Valerie would discover other, less desirable qualities that might lead to troubles, to discord and it was discord that he could not live with. And besides, he was convinced that she was still in love with Niels, perhaps always would be. He had met him once, a year after he was introduced to Valerie and Johann, when Valerie invited him to join them for a drink in Neary's, Moss intrigued at being included in what seemed like a family reunion as he sat in a chair next to Johann. Not averse to a little stereotyping, despite Kevin's humorous tutoring, he had imagined a much taller, more commanding sort of man, considering Niels's occupation. But sitting next to Valerie on the snug's green velour sofa by the fireplace was a middle aged, well groomed fellow in his fifties, chubby but strong looking with thinning, shiny light brown hair and jowly cheeks, the skin around his pale blue eyes etched with tiny wrinkles, his smile disarming. As Moss drank his beer more rapidly than usual, he noticed how Valerie's attention was fixed upon Niels as if memorising his image in preparation for another lengthy absence. By the end of the pleasant evening, interspersed with occasional exchanges in Dutch, it dawned on him then that Valerie's gaze was naked joy that quietly feasted on Niels who maintained a shrewd check on his expression, possibly the expression he wore at take off and landing, he figured, highly amused by this insight, one that sustained him for a long time, absolving him from the need to make any further effort to advance their friendship. But now such an insight no longer seemed amusing, in fact it loomed as an obstacle. Whenever Niels's name was ever mentioned he noticed how her expression instantly softened; Johann usually referred to him as Papa, and of course, thanks to Shane, he knew about the trips from Amsterdam to Paris to meet him. Moss realised that he had achieved the platonic friendship he aspired to, but still felt he should make further efforts, make some sort of gesture, feeling slightly doubtful about the Library Club after her response 'My father would love this place...' I'll invite her to the cottage, he decided suddenly, no longer fearing a refusal. After all, Masami and Kim had emailed him an enthusiastic response to his offer: Yes, they sure would love to stay in the cottage for a week in July - the dates already entered in his diary.

His thoughts were interrupted by the sudden buzzing of the doorbell. He snuck out to the hall, peered through the peephole and to his delight, recognized Sarah and Gerald who had arrived earlier than arranged. After affectionate greetings, he ushered them into the flat where they discarded their coats, hats and scarves exclaiming 'Fabulous place Moss!' as he hung the garments on the coat stand, then established themselves in the sitting room sofa, the pair looking completely at home in such a setting, as if they belonged there. Moss poured wine into crystal glasses for them, Sarah asking for a very light one - 'Miniscule please!' - Moss topping up her glass with soda water.

'Happy new year!' they chimed, raising their glasses ceremoniously.

Moss said he was treating them to a Chinese takeaway and passed them the menu which they studied with enthusiasm.

'So...you said you have some news then,' he said after he had phoned in the order for delivery.

'Well,' began Gerald 'you know that extra portion we ordered? Sarah's eating for two now.'

'Hey: congratulations!' exclaimed Moss. 'That's fantastic news!' his mouth stretched in a wide smile. He felt tempted to ask if it was the result of years of trying, but thought better of it, got up to give Sarah a hug and shook Gerald's hand firmly.

'Actually, we have more news,' said Sarah later on as she ate her pork chop suey hungrily, eyeing her painting on the dining room wall. 'It looks very well there Moss...anyway, we've been given an offer we can't refuse on the house and the gallery. We're going back to Cambridge. Dad's getting on, slowing down apparently and pining for company. So it won't be long before I'll be sitting on that very sofa,' she gave a smile, indicating the painting with her chopstick.

'With the infant at your breast,' grinned Gerald. 'Andrew's over the moon needless to say.'

'You will visit us Moss, won't you?' asked Sarah. 'There's plenty of room there, you know that.'

'Oh definitely,' he replied, rubbing his palms together. 'I'd love that. In fact I was thinking of going over in August, with Dad – you heard he's coming here? - provided the room is soundproofed from the squalls of offspring of course.'

'Oh Moss...that's *exactly* the sort of remark *my* Dad would make,' Sarah laughed. 'They're two of a kind, aren't they sweetheart?' she said to Gerald who was chuckling in agreement as Moss poured more wine into his glass.

'Well, they are twins my darling...But just think Moss:' he said, 'you'd be in your element in Cambridge, surrounded by colleges and libraries, punting on the Cam, getting pissed with me in one of the local pubs.'

'Not to mention the joys of babysitting our little sprog,' said Sarah, and they both laughed uproariously as Moss assumed his poker face, saying 'I *think* I'll leave that to granddad, if you don't mind. Or indeed great-uncle David...!'

They left around ten o'clock, their high-spirited farewells echoing in the street as they boarded the cab. Moss stood at the gate waving them off to Dalkey, watching the cab's tail lights receding slowly, then suddenly noticed a vaguely familiar figure moving along the other side of the street, an arm raised in a cheerful salute.

'Happy new year Moss,' said the man heartily.

'And the same to you,' he responded automatically with a polite wave back. Then he saw the darkly clothed figure enter Vincent's driveway and disappear into the gloomy depths leading to the side entrance.

'And many happy returns Vincent,' he whispered softly into the night.

CHAPTER 47

"Do not be afraid: do not be satisfied with mediocrity." Well, there you have it - the words of Pope Jean Paul the Second from his cd Abba Pater,' Moss informed his listeners as he faded the trak down, his finger poised for the next one while he thanked Daniel for sending in the cd and wishing him the very best for the new year 'from all of us here at Eternity FM.' After the programme he put the disc in an envelope for safekeeping, hoping that his mystery listener had tuned in to hear his request, for there were still no clues to his whereabouts. Back home in his kitchen, he sipped tea and munched on a slice of buttered toast, the curtains drawn against the blustery January night, and pondered the wisdom of the words he had quoted on air. It was relatively easy to obscure fear, was it not, to create a convincing veneer of confidence, of sophistication, by using a variety of defensive, protective tactics and distractions. But as for mediocrity - that was even harder to measure, he mused, or admit to. He suspected Louise as having settled for it, was even at home with it, but he doubted that she was satisfied. She had chosen her own path, as she was entitled to do, he reasoned, but it seemed to him an existence of half measures, of limitation, or self-limitation, her house hunt a charade. He wondered if she was better off leading an unexamined life, an unaware one, and blend in, go with the flow that people spoke of. But it was a flow that was often indirect, off course, or passive, subdued, its natural pace towards integrity and truth impeded by minds that had settled for mediocrity, or were 'governed by the canker of traditional envy and resentment of success in others' as Kevin had said in his November talk, putting out his usual challenge to those he assumed were accustomed to fudge, spin, a scapegoat or a stock of scapegoats, and the ultimate escape hatch: playing the victim and the martyr.

When he got up to put his mug and plate in the sink, he noticed the red button flickering on the phone and studied the screen listing of missed calls: two from private numbers. He listened to a message from Susan: 'If you're still interested in working in Nemesis, perhaps you would call in for a chat about it?' A chat, he thought as he pressed the disconnect button - very informal, a good omen. He replaced the phone on its charging stand, still mystified by Louise's repetitive phone calls which had resumed after a break since December, or was it late November? He knew it was Louise for the calls formed a pattern coinciding with her routine, around five spread out over a couple of hours in the evenings and the weekends, but never during the times when the soap opera was on. One time, when he had answered, reluctantly, she had said, in a tone of exaggerated surprise: 'Oh! *There* you are! You're never in are you?' adding 'Strange, really, for someone who doesn't have a job.' When he listened to the clatter of a clumsy hanging up of the receiver, after she had, perhaps, listened to his recorded voice and chickened out just after the beep, he had felt a pang of sorrow at the loneliness that this suggested. But such calls seemed harmless enough, he thought now, a passing phase of some sort, one that she would tire of eventually and he had no intention of querying. And so he put it out of his mind.

He rang Susan the next day and agreed to meet her in Nemesis the morning after, a Thursday, at eleven, Susan emphasising that the work was part-time only. Showered, shaved, his hair combed and tied back neatly with an elastic band, he dressed cautiously for the meeting. A suit seemed too formal but he decided to wear his black one all the same with a white shirt and violet silk Club tie, shooting his cuffs before the cheval mirror as he examined his appearance. He put his overcoat on, inserted a copy of his CV in the inside pocket then set off to the bus stop in good time. But to his dismay he saw the number 3 move away heavily from the stop to rejoin the city bound traffic, causing him to add an expletive to the cold breeze. Suddenly he spied an approaching taxi, hailed it and within seconds was absorbed gratefully into its warmth.

Susan greeted him cordially and escorted him to the rear of the shop, leaving the young woman to take over at the till, this time her hair secured with a black hair band. Their ascent up a dingy, narrow staircase was livened up by the pink jacket that Susan was wearing and her dexterous treading on high heeled boots with pointed toes. The offices were, as he had suspected, above the shop. Another firm, Susan explained, was located on the floor above and accessed by a separate entrance door. The main office looked vaguely dilapidated – it was furnished with two desks and filing cabinets, a computer screen glowing on one of the desks, a chaos of papers and books on the other, and, on the floor, a number of cardboard boxes. A greyish light filtered in through the tall Georgian window that overlooked the street below. Susan's office was situated next door, his brief glance taking in a smaller, slightly more organised space with books in neat stacks upon a shelf underneath the window ledge. After fetching a file from her desk, she then led him along the wide corridor to an opened door at the end. He found himself in a room which contrasted so dramatically with the offices that he had to raise his brows for it was so plain yet charming, with an aura of mellow elegance about it, opulence even. It was sparsely furnished by a mahogany table in the centre with a number of chairs around it, a large oriental rug underneath, his keen eyes taking in an oil painting of the shop front positioned above a white marble fireplace, the room illumined by a standard lamp with an ochre shade, the window flanked by olive green velvet curtains that reached the hardwood floor. Incongruously, there were no bookshelves. A masculine room, he decided, indulging in his habit of categorizing places by gender. A tall figure emerged from the ambient gloom to greet him and a smiling Liam King shook his hand, indicated a chair for him, then took his own place at the head of the table, his healthy face framed by sleek silver hair. Moss looked appraisingly at the pale linen jacket he wore and the black shirt with a cravat at his throat, the navy v neck wool jumper a sensible precaution against what Moss now realized was the distinct chilliness of the room, his eyes searching out a source of heating and finding the defunct empty grate and an ancient, probably ice cold radiator along the opposite wall. To his relief, Susan reappeared carrying a tray laden with white mugs and a matching tea pot. When she poured the tea, Moss had to suppress the urge to hold his hands over the steam to allay the cold in his fingers. There was, he felt, an almost comic quality about the interview so far, as if it were a relaxed family gathering, albeit a family operating on strict budgetary constraints, a formality now taking place as Liam perused his CV.

'Eternity FM', he remarked, raising his brows questioningly.

'It's a community radio station,' explained Moss, even though he had specified this on the page.

'Broadcasting on a supernatural frequency – *forever* - throughout the universe,' Susan intoned one of the station's regular jingles and proffered a plate of biscuits. 'You should tune in sometime Dad. Moss does a programme called Chilltime on Tuesday nights.'

'You're a DJ then?' Liam enquired.

'Ah no,' chuckled Moss, choosing a custard cream. 'Not the club scene for me. It's just relaxing music with spiritual overtones.'

'*Supernatural* overtones,' grinned Susan who then began to clarify the work which entailed basic accounting and administration tasks, for two days a week. He would be taking over from Patricia who had given in her notice. Susan would continue to work in the front of the shop; Liam would come in twice a week, sacrificing his golf. Declan, a cousin, would cover on Saturdays and holidays. Other names were alluded to ensuring ample backup for emergencies. Liam then told him that a temporary worker in for work experience in the summer – 'Seemed such a nice fellow...' - had swindled them out of a sum of money. Now they wanted someone they could trust, Moss feeling two pairs of hopeful eyes surveying him as he perused an item of correspondence that Liam had passed to him.

'Mm...ouch,' he murmured, noting a figure highlighted in phosphorescent yellow.

'Ouch indeed,' echoed Liam, nodding solemnly.

Moss accepted the job without hesitation, agreeing to start the second week of February and shook hands with them – 'See you in February then'.

He did not linger in town for he was eager to get home, discard his suit and ring Valerie to tell her the news and see if he could tempt her to abandon her translations and meet him in Bewley's Café later on that afternoon.

'Let's have a drink in Neary's, then a big fry up - in Grafton Street for a change,' he said. 'My treat.'

'I'd love to Moss. I definitely need a change of scene,' she laughed wearily. 'See you at five so.'

Moss poured himself a small scotch from the bottle James had given him for Christmas, then prepared a salad of sliced tomato, green peppers and lettuce leaves while a cottage pie was heating up in the oven. He had not lasted an entire year off, he realized, but he was close. He wondered if he should have sent on his application for the job in UCD, keep his options open, the wage offered by Susan being slightly disappointing, but figured that the college campus job would be far more suitable for a younger person, one that would fit the criteria of employers looking for 'dynamic' people who were able to work on their own initiative as part of a team. He suddenly realized how much he loved the location of Nemesis, knew that the hours suited him, that the work would absorb him but not rule him, that he would work well alongside Susan, already feeling like a member of their extended family rowing in to assist. There was a mischievous sense of humour behind Susan's benign smiles, but he did not underestimate her business acumen, their status as colleagues, not friends, a source of relief to him. He also knew that his love of books would not be diminished, in fact it would be enhanced in other ways, such as learning about the book trade despite its rumoured extinction by the internet. Within weeks he would be back in traditional employment, join the busy swarm as an obvious wage earner although the part time arrangement of his new job would eliminate him from making proclamations of working hard or being busy. 'Cheers' he said to himself and took a generous gulp of his scotch.

Around seven o'clock that evening, Louise stopped to peer through the window of Bewley's Café on Grafton Street, her appetite satisfied after her habitual burger and fries and a browse of the department stores where the sales were still in progress. To her astonishment she saw her brother make his way out through the café door and pause on the pavement to put on his fur hat then wrap a scarf snugly around his neck for protection against the bitterly cold breeze that funnelled its way along the street.

'Hi Moss,' she said loudly.

'Oh, hiya sis!' he greeted her with a smile as she materialised before him. 'Freezing isn't it? How are things? How's mum?'

'Okay,' she replied. 'You're looking very pleased with yourself. And where did you get that ridiculous scarf?' She gave a slightly scornful laugh.

'Christmas present. A friend knitted it for me. So, are you going in then?' he asked her.

'Are you leaving now?' she responded, her eyes filled with longing as she watched two men brush past them on their way in through the familiar doors and releasing another blast of the café's aromatic warmth.

'Well, yeah. Got a text from Jason – he's the sound engineer at the station. I'm off to do a recording,' he told her. 'It's for the weekly play tomorrow evening, they've changed the broadcast to Fridays. Anyway, they're short of a voice tonight - I've to play the part of a detective no less,' he grinned.

'Oh. Then you don't have time for a coffee now,' she said flatly.

'No, I've had my tea with Valerie.' He took a step forward. 'But she's still in there, on her own,' he added helpfully. 'In at the back by the windows. She's waiting for Johann, he won't be there 'til around eight.'

He stood there, poised for departure, in his long black overcoat, his fur hat and scarf rendering him impervious to the frigid air.

'Go on in,' he said, 'she'd be delighted to see you.'

Louise hesitated.

'No. I'll have to get home,' she said. 'It's getting late.'

'Suit yourself,' he said mildly.

And so they went their separate ways.